THE SNAKE MASTER
AND
THE OUTRAGEOUS PHILOSOPHER

HENDRIK J. TROSKIE

PARTRIDGE

To order additional copies of this book, contact
Toll Free +65 3165 7531 (Singapore)
Toll Free +60 3 3099 4412 (Malaysia)
orders.singapore@partridgepublishing.com

www.partridgepublishing.com/singapore

To Louise
The joy is in the writing.

CONTENTS

PROLOGUE

But I always liked side-paths, little dark back-alleys behind the main road, there one finds adventures and surprises, and precious metal in the dirt.

Fyodor Dostoyevsky

Come with me! We are going on an adventure. Adventures are messy. That is just how adventures are. The destination is uncertain and ambiguous, the route complex, and yes, sometimes it is volatile.

We will go into dark tunnels and discover dead ends. When we do, we will retrace our steps and see glimmers of light and hope. On the way, we will rediscover old wisdoms and we will discover new ideas. If we are lucky, we will leave the cave and go into the light. To do so, we must go back to places we have forgotten we have been before. We must go to places we have not been before, and hopefully, we will find treasure there and will never forget we have gone there. We must also go to places we thought we dare not go.

When we are done, we will be a lot smarter, wiser, and resilient against stupidity. I guarantee that. On the way, we will laugh a lot and cry a little. But that part is not guaranteed.

You do not have to do much. You go to your favourite reading spot, in front of a fireplace, if that is what you like. Take a drink or two. We are going to be a while. So be brave, gather your courage, and pack a sense of humour. Come on, let's not waste any more time. Come with me now.

PART ONE

DARK ALLEYS AND DEAD ENDS

Dialogues with John Allen, Robert, Megsum and Amanda,
Peter, Kristoff, Ricardo, Edwin, and Thomas.

MEETING JOHN ALLEN

On paper, you say exactly and completely what you feel. How easy it is to break things off on paper! You hate, you shout, you kill, you commit suicide; you carry things to the very end. And that's why it's false. But it's damned satisfying. In life, you're constantly denying yourself, and others are always contradicting you. On paper, I make time stand still and I impose my convictions on the whole world; they become the only reality.

Simone de Beauvoir

The eyes interrogate.

'So, Hendrik,' he says, 'how did you get yourself into this mess?' There is a familiarity in that question, like it is not the first time I heard it. It transports me back to my childhood, something my father asked on an all too regular a basis. The phrasing was different, and there was often despair in Father's voice, something like, 'Hendrik! What the fuck have you done now?'

I keep that thought in my mind as he turns to the last page of the letter. His name is John Allen, and I am in Allen and Overly's offices. Prestigious lawyers, I was told, and experts in libel defence. From the name, you can assume John is the Allen in Allen and Overly. Precisely why they assigned one of the partners to my case, I don't know. Perhaps it is based on the success of my novel. Perhaps they thought I am rich because of it. Also, the novel is why I am here. So perhaps it is because mine is potentially an intriguing legal case. For the sake of my meagre savings, I hope it is the latter.

John has just finished reading a letter. The letter is from another lawyer. I don't know, or rather did not know, about her until the letter arrived. A Jennifer Rawlings, I recall. The letter details a threat to go to court for a cease-and-desist order. So yes, this is a cease-and-desist letter. It comes before the order. The order comes if you don't cease and desist. It is like a final warning before being excluded from school. The letter also threatens me with a libel lawsuit. I am not entirely sure who the plaintiffs are. There are many apparently, but the letter isn't specific. If I were a business, you would probably call this a class-action lawsuit. That is why I am here with John Allen from Allen and Overly.

'I have no idea,' I say with feigned innocence.

John cuts straight through the innocence. 'Really, you think that this letter is a mistake, that you have done nothing to justify this action?'

It is my father all over again. The eyes are the same, dark brown and intensely intelligent. I don't get the fascination with blue eyes. They can only do two things—either they pierce you or they drown you in deep pools. Maybe three things. They can also be vacant. Blue eyes can be disconcertingly vacant.

You can never say that of brown eyes; brown eyes are never vacant. They can do everything else, from a warm sunrise to a spectacular sunset. Brown eyes can be curious. They can deceive, beam intelligence, say 'I love you', everything. Maybe green eyes can do one thing better; no other coloured eyes can say 'I love you' better than green eyes. But brown eyes can do everything else. They can also interrogate. That is what John's eyes are doing now. Fierce interrogation. Blue eyes, only three things.

I abandon the make-belief innocence. It never stood up to my father's interrogating gaze either.

I say sheepishly, 'I suppose I upset someone in the novel.'

John isn't satisfied with my answer. 'It says that in the letter, Hendrik.'

I start to defend myself more vigorously. 'Not sure why because the publisher included the usual disclaimer. You know the one. "All characters and events, even those based on real people, are entirely fictional, and any resemblance to people and events are purely coincidental, even when they are meaningful."'

'So you know them?' he asks.

I hate it when people use 'them' and 'they'. It is vague and ambiguous, so every opportunity I get, I drill down to specifics. I drill down to specifics. 'I know who?'

The eyes tell me not to muck about. 'The characters in your novel.'

The answer is obvious to me, so I answer with a question, 'How can I not? I sort of created them.'

I think I made my innocence stick that time. John decides to change tactics. 'You are going to have to tell me everything, Hendrik.'

That sounds like a lot of hard work. Time. Money, my money. So I try to get out of it. 'Everything? You cannot be serious. Where do I start?'

John's instruction is clear. 'At the beginning of course.'

Lawyers always want to serialise events, start at the beginning, work through the middle to the end. They want to establish a linear progression of events along a ticking timeline. I say so to John.

'Wrong,' he says, 'detectives build a timeline of events. Lawyers try to break it down.'

'Well, in that case, it is a series of dialogues,' I say, 'but I cannot tell them chronologically in the novel because that won't make sense logically. So I will start in the middle of the story somewhere, but in the beginning of the novel. I heard somewhere that good novels start in the middle. I think Lilly told me that.'

John wants details—names, identities—so he asks, 'Who is Lilly?'

'My wife,' I say, realising I must be more careful what I reveal to a prestigious lawyer. No more names outside the novel.

'Did she help write the novel or edit it?' he asks.

I protect her immediately. 'No, she is completely innocent.'

Why did I plead innocence on her behalf? It implies I am guilty. I see that judgement in John's eyes. Shit!

I try and divert his attention. 'Not even the Bible starts in the beginning. It might start by saying "In the beginning…", but that cannot be the beginning, not geologically and not even chronologically. Before that beginning, there must have been God. Then God happened on the beginning and said, "Oh, crap. This is the beginning, and there is nothing here." Then he started. He was in a bit of a hurry, so he finished in six days. That is why it is such a fucking mess.'

The eyes have a lot to say about the swearing and the blasphemy. John asks, 'Is that in the novel?'

'No,' I answer truthfully, 'I only mention it here because it is a safe place. Attorney-client privilege. You won't tell on me, will you, John?'

'I don't think I can protect you, Hendrik. I don't think attorney-client privilege stretches that far,' says John, and I sense a hint of humour.

'I don't think God is in the habit of taking people to court. He just sends his bloodthirsty warriors to take care of you. Anyway, I have just paraphrased the first few verses of the Bible, nothing wrong in doing that. Consider it just a clumsy translation. Religious cults do that all the time, but not in a clumsy way. They are more devious about it,' I say. John ignores the bait. He also appears to accept Lilly wasn't involved.

And just like that, John has the measure of my character. It is a skill you must have to be a prestigious lawyer: to get the measure of a character promptly. 'Start in the middle if you have to. But just start,' he says.

So I start. It is a bit like reading the novel, only I do not have the novel with me. Anyone who has written a novel will know that is not an issue. You read and reread and edit the story for what seems like a thousand times. That, of course, is no guarantee that you recall it perfectly.

* * *

So here we are. You and I, philosophers having coffee. It is emphatically true that all humans can and do philosophise. We talk about life, politics, and the how to be good. It is a preoccupation that goes back thousands of years, and it is our most important social pastime. It directs us to build our body of knowledge about the natural world and how we organise society. We are all intuitive philosophers. But good philosophising is more difficult than you think.

> It is hard to win an argument with a smart person, but its damn near impossible to win an argument with a stupid person.
>
> *Bill Murray*

Before you get all smug and think you are difficult to beat in an argument because you are one of the smart ones, consider this. Maybe you are difficult to beat in an argument because you are one of the stupid ones, but you are also too stupid to know that you are. We may all be intuitive philosophers, but intuition is not enough. That is because we are all also intuitively stupid.

Before you get all offended and throw your arms up in protest, the way I use stupid here is in the sense that I might say, 'I was stupid to try and take the shortcut at peak traffic times' or 'How stupid of me to forget my wallet'. I accept you might think I am devious rather than stupid for forgetting my wallet, especially if that leaves you with the bill. I am not doing that here. This is the kind of stupid that we are all guilty of at times. There are times when we are stupid and times when we are smart.

We are at our smartest when we can change our minds when the facts change or logic flows against our opinion. The danger we have is that we are inclined to travel from smart to stupid, not from stupid to smart. That might surprise you, but it is true. So we must guard against this direction of intellectual deterioration all the time.

The American philosopher Mortimer J. Adler called this being intellectually lazy. He went further and said that some people are habitually intellectually lazy. I have no reason to disagree with Adler, and some other philosophers also think that modern society and the age of the Internet has created generations of intellectual sloths.

Intellectual sloths are people who go to the Internet seeking knowledge. But not everything on the Internet is knowledge. To be discerning about what is knowledge and what is not demands of us to have an idea how to separate false from truth. Intellectual sloths are not able to distinguish between good theories and bad theories. They cannot quickly identify conspiracy theories.

I will touch on some of these in the book, but I am also concerned about those people who are intellectual sloths in that they learn fragments of complex theories and confidently stride into the world, proclaiming it is the only way to organise society, politics, or political coalitions. They even start to organise coalitions of people to promote their ill-conceived and incomplete ideals. Worse still are those who think they have an antidote to a good theory, that they can knock it down in a few sharp short sentences. We will meet one of those too.

These intellectual miscreants think that a loud, confident expression of their opinion alone is sufficient to persuade others to believe what they peddle, and sadly, they are right. People are too intellectually lazy and too stupid to thoroughly assess the rubbish these intellectual miscreants promote. That makes these modern-day ideologists the most dangerous ones for other people. Other people, good people, must learn to guard against the opinions of the miscreants. They must learn to protect themselves from their partial ideologies—no, not defend, rescue. Yes, they must rescue themselves.

Get busy with life's purpose, toss aside empty hopes,
get active in your own rescue—if you care for yourself
at all—and do it while you can.

Marcus Aurelius

Perhaps the most tragic of all is the intellectual sloth who learns about an old philosophical theory recycled into new language with catchy, new expressions and quotes and promptly claims they have discovered a novel way to fix the world's old problems.

Ideologist, theorists and conspiracy theorists, and their advocates and loyal followers are not able to justify their partial ideologies; neither do they fully comprehend their own opinions. Tragically, they never seek out criticisms. I should use the word *defend* rather than *justify*. Advocates of these poorly constructed and half-cannibalised theories defend their opinions. That is, they become defensive and try to justify *their* beliefs. They shout their opinions out louder. They insult and threaten anyone who might point out that their ideas are flawed. They claim they have a monopoly over the truth. They isolate themselves in little echo chambers where they put up barriers against counterarguments and criticisms.

Intellectual sloths do not have the courage to do it the correct way. The correct way is not to defend one's beliefs. The correct way is to justify through sound reasoning to someone else why they should believe what you believe. That will encourage you to make a persuasive argument through active reasoning for your belief. So hopefully, I will teach you how to rescue yourself from ideological confidence tricksters. When confronted by these snake oil ideology salesmen, you must, of course, be prepared and diligent and equip yourself to test their justifications.

Why do you have to learn to be able to justify your belief? I hear you ask. Like all of us, you have a natural ability for cognitive economy. That means to do as little thinking as possible. It is our default setting, the place we go to without effort. It is the intellectual equivalent of a preference for the comfort of a sofa over sweating it out in the gym.

I am sure that cognitive psychologists have a lot to say about this. I am referring, of course, to cognitive biases—the unavoidable mistakes we make in reasoning because we are hardwired to think in particular ways. There may have been an evolutionary advantage for this, but it no longer serves us. We make these mistakes when we are in a hurry or we have failed to make the necessary investment in thinking. Cognitive biases are unavoidable. That is why they are called biases. Know this about your mind. It is a significant neurological fact that our subconscious thinking is twenty-thousand times faster than our conscious thinking. That means our biases will rule our minds if we let them.

Psychologists have identified some 170 cognitive biases. When we look at those, we see that some vary only in the context but stand on the same cognitive mechanism. Please do not worry. This is not yet another boring book on cognitive biases, on how you can improve your thinking. I am not going to pick a fight with psychologists.

I am going to introduce you to some of Aristotle's thirteen fallacies, or what he called sophistical refutations. They bear an uncanny resemblance to many of the cognitive biases identified by modern-day psychologists. So not only did Aristotle identify these, he also gave us the cognitive tools to deal with them when we encounter them, either when we commit the fallacies ourselves or when other people commit the fallacies. I make the point of stressing *we*, which, of course, includes *you*. Do not be so naive as to think you are immune to your own biases.

But these are not the only ways in which we fall victim to our own cognitive laziness. Make no mistake. There are people out there who will take advantage of your cognitive biases—politicians, marketing and sales specialists, and social engineers. Yes, that is right. It has become a profession.

What we must learn is to recognise when our thinking is a victim of our own biases or when other people's thinking is making us victims of their biases. This is the hard part. This is the part of reasoning that requires investment and a commitment of time. This is what Daniel Dennett meant when he wrote that 'thinking is hard, urgh!' It is only through intellectual review accompanied by the diligent applications of thinking skills that we correct the mistakes that comes from intellectual laziness and cognitive biases.

There is a rich history in philosophical thinking that is not taught in Western schools, with the notable exception perhaps of France, where, if I am not mistaken, schoolchildren of a certain age learn analytic philosophy skills across the board.

In this book, I replay some of the philosophical dialogues that I have had over coffee or food with other philosophers since qualifying as a philosophical counsellor. Do not forget, I see everyone as a philosopher. I was lucky enough to have many opportunities to counsel with people on an informal basis, either in a group or one-to-one. At other times, I was invited to group meetups that talk about events reported in the papers in the last week. I was also lucky enough to be able to do this in a country with rich diversity where there lived many people from all over the world. Every time, this was done in a public setting, giving me the advantage that I now have a disclaimer against anyone who wants to impose a duty of confidentiality on me.

Nevertheless, I have obfuscated the identities of the persons somewhat so that they are not easily identified. Moreover, if you happen to read this book and you recognise the setting and the conversation, I urge you not to protest too much. Protesting will only serve to reveal your identity, in which case you will force me to deny it is you. Furthermore, if a third person recognises you in a dialogue, then simply deny it to protect your identity if you wish, and I will plead ignorance.

Many dialogues were prompted by political speeches or comments from their supporters. Nowhere else can you mine for a richer source of stupidity than when politicians speak. Or perhaps I should give them more credit. Perhaps they know full well what they are up to. Perhaps they know full well that they are poking at our cognitive biases and getting predictable responses. If they are, then they are using an ancient art, one put forward by Aristotle no less. They are deliberately exploiting prejudices. Nationalism and patriotism are prejudices too. We must learn how to defend ourselves against this: to immunise ourselves against this intellectual abuse. If we do not, then awful idiots get into positions of power and citizens pay the ultimate price for decades to come. I am sure the irony won't escape you when I say we can do that with advice from Aristotle.

You will notice a certain structure in the dialogues. I am a great admirer of Plato's Socrates, not just for the way he gently questioned people to provide a clear and agreeable answer to any specific question but also for the way in which he settled everyone down in preparation for the intellectual adventure. Socrates went to great pains to make sure everyone was properly introduced, painting their backgrounds, familial situations, places of origins, personality traits, and intellectual dispositions. No one was excluded, and clearly Socrates was not as concerned with diversity and inclusivity as much as we ought to be today. Most of the participants in his dialogues were from the near vicinity of Athens, so one can expect a harmonious group of people. Nevertheless, Socrates was concerned and respectful to individual differences and emphasised the need for respect, patience, and inclusivity. Only through diversity and inclusivity can we hope to build a common understanding of the world.

I am a little more economical in introducing only people who were active participants in the dialogue. I will take you directly there, intimately there. I am writing these dialogues up in the present tense, to give you a fly-on-the-wall view of what happens. I must do it this way so that you can experience the messiness of it all, the dead ends and retracing of steps as they happen, and the complete surprise when a dialogue veers off into a direction that I was absolutely not prepared for.

So with every dialogue, I will draw the context and, to some extent, the character of each of the participants. Whereas it may seem that we start the dialogues with a clearly defined question, that is not always the case. It must be a question. What is there to do if it is not a question? We must turn it into a question first before we can attempt a dialogue. To help express this, I replay to the best of my memory the tedious path we sometimes followed to get to the point where we can have a reasonable philosophical contemplation of the question.

If anyone can refute me, show me I am making a mistake or looking at things from a wrong perspective. I'll gladly change. It is the truth I am after and the truth has never hurt anyone.

Marcus Aurelius

I have just one more thing to say before we start. You will hopefully notice a couple of themes repeating in the dialogues. I have chosen these dialogues because they reveal a few intellectual practices. These intellectual practices are in fact ancient ones. And by ancient, I mean since early philosophical endeavours, even pre-Socratic.

The first one I would like you to keep in mind is one started by Plato. It will not surprise me if you know about the allegory of the cave—the allegory used by Plato to illustrate that the way we experience the world, reality, is incomplete. What makes it incomplete? Our prior knowledge. The stuff we learn as we grow up from family, community, and society, what some might call our culture, or our good old British common sense. If you are from another country then simply substitute the name of that country. It takes a considerable application of reason to learn about the world. To explore the edges of the cave. To see reality instead of the shadows created by our prior knowledge. Prior knowledge is all we have, nothing else.

For a while, philosophers became obsessed with reason and argued that our brains are effectively blank slates where knowledge is collected through our senses. This nonsense was called out by Kant. He proposed that we learn through transitivity. Essentially, that means we have an innate ability to learn.

That ability slowly expands our knowledge by building on our prior knowledge. I am not doing it justice, of course, but that is not the point of this story. Kant's proposal gave rise to the notion of interpretive repertoires and schemas. Think about interpretive repertoires as the tools we use to interpret new knowledge. That new knowledge expands, grows, and adds to our interpretive repertoires.

New interpretive tools help us absorb new information. We must also accept that we are limited by our current interpretive repertoires.

Kant's considerable work gave us social constructivism and a plethora of new academic disciplines, such as social studies, social psychology, and critical theories. It also drove a wedge between Anglo-American analytical philosophy and continental philosophy.

There is a point to make that continental philosophy explores what it is like to be human, an especially important exercise. Analytic philosophy focuses on our reasoning skills. Which is the most important? We should never have to choose. You will be relieved that that is the sum of this perspective.

There is one more perspective I want to prepare you for. It is also an ancient one, but I will quote a more recent philosopher here, not because I respect him; in fact, I do not. He is a 'so what' philosopher—a philosopher that states the obvious in such poetic language that it seduces one completely. He is also prone to leave his readers in complete despair. He is Friedrich Nietzsche, but I suspect you have guessed that already. Here is the quote:

> The individual has always had to struggle to keep from being overwhelmed by the tribe. If you try it, you will be lonely often, and sometimes frightened. But no price is high enough to pay for the privilege of owning yourself.

> Friedrich Nietzsche

Are you seduced by this quote, ready to go into battle with Nietzsche? It won't surprise me. Nietzsche dedicated an entire book, if not his life, on the perceived battle between the individual and the tribe. He doesn't really mean tribe though. He means culture. But the word *tribe* is easier to use in explanations, easier than *culture, subculture, corporate culture,* or *team culture*. There is also the notion that when we say culture we disconnect its values from the people, but when we use tribe we maintain the connection between people and their values. One word, *tribe*, can be used in place of all of them. That means you will have to do a little more work when you read the dialogues, but I am sure you won't mind.

Nietzsche saw culture as some sinister master that all individuals do battle with. A multi headed master. In this book, many of the dialogues are about this battle. Not with culture always but with culture at times. I will tell you up front that I disagree with this notion that culture is some sinister master to do battle with. I argue it is something we can tame and improve and that we must tame and improve it for the benefit of the future generations of people and also for our own benefit in the present.

At risk of being contentious I also see tribes as identities. Lately people have talked about personal identities, or social identities. Identities seem to be the internalisation of tribes. Tribes and cultures become identities when I talk about culture or tribe in an intimate way, as if it is me. So when reading the dialogues you may want to substitute tribe for identity if you wish.

I like this quote from Nietzsche not because of the obvious truth in his quote but because it offers these three ideas that are useful in providing perspective on our dialogues. That is the idea of the individual, the idea of the tribe, and the battle between them. We will see that it is often hard to separate the individual from the tribe. If you manage to do so, the individual becomes too simple, too clarified, too fixed a shape to be a realistic individual. You will soon find out I also write about the character. It is the same thing as individual. Why I do that will also become clear later.

The tribe is also problematic. We talk too easily about the tribe, too simplistically, just like we talk too easily and too simplistically about culture. Tribes are hidden and often secret amorphous structures. When we clarify the individual and the tribe to the point where they are both fixed shapes, we separate them. Both are poorer for that separation.

In any one person, there isn't a single tribe, just like there isn't a monolithic culture. See if you can identify the individual tribes in each of the dialogues. Do not worry if you cannot. I will cover them again in the conclusion.

There are also other dialogues that are supporting acts, dialogues that address some other stupid notions or ideas that undermine our ability to reason properly. I will not point them out as we go along. You will recognise them for their brevity and their getting to the point quickly. You may also identify tribes here. You will not be wrong.

* * *

John interrupts me. Correction, he thinks he interrupts me. 'You are not actually reciting the entire introduction to me, are you?'

'Yes, I must paint the context, don't I? I must give the reader some framework, some anchor to work from. I must tell them about the themes, the main topics, and the ideas.' What else could I say? I know it sounds a little obvious.

He is a bit more generous than I thought he would be. 'I suppose so, but there really is no need. And what about starting in the middle?'

I explain again. 'The dialogues start in the middle, not the novel. Once you have written a novel, the reader starts at the beginning.' To be honest, he has my sympathy. I get myself into a real muddle about this idea often enough.

He gives up, and I don't blame him. 'OK, continue.'

I shake my head, but not in an obvious way. I predict this is going to be a difficult long day. 'Well, I am done with the introduction now anyway. I just have one more thing to say.'

He nods.

I say, 'So if you are ready, let's begin with the first dialogue.'

The brown eyes flash annoyance. Did I mention they also do annoyance?

John says, 'Just get on with it. Time is money.' He says that to urge me on.

It urges me on. It is my money. I think that, too concerned about the money to say it out loud.

I continue.

BREAKFAST WITH ROBERT

If an opinion contrary to your own makes you angry, that is a sign that you are subconsciously aware of having no good reason for thinking as you do.

Bertrand Russell

We are meeting in a riverside pub on a Sunday morning. It is not a gourmet pub. Too Australian to call it gourmet. But the food is good for a pub, and the setting is fantastic. We have a table just by the promenade overlooking the marina. It is hot. Nothing unusual about that. It is always hot. Some ceiling-mounted fans provide relief. You should try and remember this. We come here often, and many of the dialogues take place here.

There are a few newcomers at the meetup this morning. That is not unusual either. The number of attendees has grown steadily since Raymond started the meetup. There are the usual round of introductions and greetings for more familiar faces. The atmosphere is convivial and friendly, even filled with anticipated curiosity.

We order coffee. Mine is a large Americano. It comes in a decent-sized mug and is also a decent coffee. I thought a coffee first before breakfast.

Introductions on my left continue, and I listen in, waiting for an opportune moment to make myself known.

'I'm Robert, from Cleveland, Ohio,' says Robert.

'Nice to meet you, Robert. Sudheer.' Brief but effective from Sudheer. He continues, 'From USA. Hey, things are a bit difficult there with the pandemic. Have you been back at all?'

I thought that was a bit rich from Sudheer. Coming from India, he can hardly claim they are doing better than the USA. I learned a little later that I am wrong, of course, not for the first time in my life, and on both accounts. Firstly, Sudheer is from Singapore, not India, and secondly, at that time, India was doing a lot better than the USA in dealing with the pandemic.

Robert nods his head, sips his coffee, and answers, 'Yes, I went back for a few weeks over Christmas to see my children.'

I calculate divorce.

Robert confirms my calculation. 'I am divorced, so they live with their mom.'

Sudheer asks with a statement, 'Must have been difficult with the quarantine restrictions.

'Not going to the USA. We don't care much over there.' Robert says, 'Coming back to Singapore and spending two weeks in a hotel room was a bloody nightmare.'

I see my chance and interject into the conversation. 'Well, America really screwed up with COVID, didn't they?' If you do not know this yet, you know it now. I am quite the provocateur.

It all kicks off just like that. Boom. Robert disagrees obviously.

Robert. 'We handled this virus better than any other country. This virus is no worse than the flu. The same number of people are dying. The whole world has fallen for this hoax.'

Me. 'How can you say that? More than half a million Americans have died—'

Robert. 'That is not true. Only around ten thousand died from COVID.'

Me. 'Oh, rubbish, the official number is more than half a million.'

Robert. 'That number is fake. Look at the CDC's numbers. It is on their website, only around ten thousand. That is less than those who die from the flu every year.'

Me. 'The CDC?' I do this for clarity.

Robert. 'The Centre for Decease Control'

Me. 'Don't they issue the official death toll? The figure of over five hundred thousand? Isn't that what the news agencies report? The news reports are all stating more than half a million. Only ten thousand? That cannot be true.'

Robert. 'You don't have the facts because you are not there.'

Notice the appeal to authority to strengthen his argument. Claiming the numbers are from the CDC. When I challenge this, he moves on to something else.

Me. 'I don't have to be there to have the facts. The facts travel easily all over the world. The facts don't go into quarantine. The facts state that America has done a crap job at controlling the epidemic.'

Robert. 'Where do you get your facts from? Hey, they are wrong. You have to go there to get the facts.'

Me. 'Well, CNN, Fox News, and a few other respected news channels have reported—'

Robert. 'Well, there you go. All lies and fake news. You don't have the correct facts. We have done the best job in the world.'

Me. 'How can you possibly claim that? If the USA has done the best job, then it is the best job in losing control of the virus, the best job in the number of people infected, and the best job in the number of sick, dying, and dead.'

Robert. 'You don't know what you are talking about. You don't have the facts because you are not there!'

Me. 'I get my facts from CNN and Fox and other reputable news channels. Where do you get yours from?'

Robert. 'Well, there you go, all fake news and misinformation. That explains a lot!'

You probably realise we are going around in circles and repeating ourselves. We are not going to agree with anything while we dispute facts and their sources. As is often the case in conventional arguments, it is 'my facts against yours', and when we cannot agree with the facts, then we will never settle the dispute. This conventional arguing or inductive arguing is in fact not philosophical at all. I will have to move this to a conceptual argument if we are to make any progress.

Me. 'Let's think about this differently. What is a virus, and how does it work?'

To my surprise, Robert follows me into the rabbit hole.

Robert. 'A virus is a microscopic living thing that infects animals and makes them sick to various degrees.'

Me. 'Close enough, although a virus is not a living thing, and viruses also infect plants. It is in fact active DNA, but not a complete cell like bacteria. That is neither here nor there. In essence, you have got it right. It makes animals sick to varying degrees, and in some cases, it is fatal.'

Robert. 'Hold on, why do they say viruses can survive outside of the body for up to seventy-two hours? How can it do that if it is not a living thing?'

Notice that whenever anyone uses 'they' in a sentence, you should be very suspicious. It is too vague and ambiguous a reference and prone to deceive.

Me. 'They are not virologists. If you listen carefully to virologists and epidemiologists, you will notice they use different phrasing, like a virus can remain active for up to seventy-two hours outside the body depending on the surface.'

Robert. 'Strange, I have never heard that. But let's go with it.'

This might be an example of Robert's interpretive repertoires. He interprets what is said based on his prior knowledge. But thankful that he has settled down somewhat and is engaging, I continue.

Me. 'Viruses infect animals by stimulating their cells or specific cells to reproduce new copies of the virus. Those copies are mutated in miniscule ways, evolution at work.'

Robert. 'What, are you saying that every time it infects a person, a new mutation is produced in that person?'

Me. 'Yes, and that mutation is in some miniscule way more or less effective than the one that created it.'

Robert. 'Why do viruses mutate every time they reproduce? I don't believe that.'

Me. 'For the same reason that all animal offspring are somewhat different from their parents. They are different because they have miniscule changes in their DNA.' Best to keep it simple, I think.

Robert. 'OK, but so what?'

Me. 'If we allow the virus to infect and spread unchecked, then its rate of mutation will increase exponentially, much faster than we can produce vaccines to control it. It becomes endemic. That is what happens with the flu virus.'

Robert. 'Why?'

Me. 'We can only produce a vaccine for viruses for which we have sufficient information. In other words, we use existing viruses, or information from existing viruses, to protect against future infections. If the virus evolves too much, the vaccines will not offer protection.'

Robert. 'So you are saying we must supress the spread of the virus in order to give ourselves a fighting chance to produce a vaccine to eradicate it.'

Me. 'Yes.'

Robert. 'Americans are free people, so they don't and won't comply with mandates to wear a mask. Americans like to make informed decisions.'

Do you see this unexpected change in direction from Robert? He tacitly accepts the conceptual point, but he is not prepared to concede the argument. He takes the argument into a different direction instead.

Me. 'Sure, don't we all want to make informed decisions? The CDC in the USA has informed you. You are informed to wear a mask and practise social distancing. You don't want to because you don't understand what it means to be informed.'

Robert. 'That is because we don't believe the CDC.'

Me. 'Why not?'

Do you see how Robert now dismisses the CDC but he appealed to them in his opening argument? When he quoted their statistics?

Robert. 'How do we know that they know what they are talking about? They keep changing their advice.'

Me. 'They are the experts. They have the education to prove that. They change their minds when the facts change. They will change their advice when the facts change. If you want to be informed, you go to a knowledgeable person to advise you.'

Robert. 'What Americans want is to be able to make informed decisions.' He repeats. He is getting really agitated again. I am glad that Raymond's substantial frame is between us.

I told you Raymond is the organiser of the meetup. He is Dutch and stands about six foot six tall. Both facts give him authority. You will learn I often rely on Raymond for my protection.

Me. 'The way you use *informed* is to suggest that you have become an expert in virology. That kind of *informed* can only be achieved by studying and putting the work in. You cannot claim that an illiterate redneck from a swamp in South Georgia is equipped to becoming that informed.'

Robert. 'So now you are calling me an illiterate redneck.' He is furious now. I am making myself increasingly smaller behind Raymond.

Me. 'I said in South Georgia.'

Robert. 'How do you know I am not from South Georgia?'

Me. 'You told us you are from Cleveland, Ohio, when you introduced yourself.'

Robert is furious. 'Who do you think you are, insulting every American like that!'

Me. 'How did I insult every American?'

Robert. 'You called us illiterate rednecks.'

Me. 'I called an illiterate redneck from South Georgia an illiterate redneck. I am quite sure even the redneck would agree with me.'

Robert. 'Americans are free people. All they want is to make informed decisions.'

Me. 'Many Americans hold on to the idea of individual freedom so hard that it makes them completely irrational when it comes to making informed decisions. You have been informed, but you think you are entitled to protect your individual freedom by claiming that you have not been informed enough. You think your right to individual freedom makes you smarter than the experts trying to inform you. In the meantime, you are outwitted by a simple virus.'

Robert. 'For God's sake.'

Sudheer comes to my rescue. 'Who are you? What do you do?' he asks me.

I welcome Sudheer's diversion but keep a wary eye on Robert. 'I am an author and philosophical practitioner,' I say.

Robert walks a few paces away from the table and swears under his breath.

The conversation around the table moves on to something different. I keep a wary eye on Robert. I am preparing myself for a quick getaway, which I think will be a futile attempt considering the age difference and the sheer physical size of the man.

I see the tribes now. Rednecks, Americans, and me, of course. I am from a different tribe, an out-group. Robert is from the in-group. The in-group can say redneck, but I cannot. If I say redneck, I insult everyone in the in-group. How subtle the composition fallacy? Do not worry. We will discuss it in more detail later.

Raymond says, 'Don't worry about him. He is stomping around now, looking for another smaller country to invade, preferably one with less firepower, where he can start a war, a war that he is certain he won't lose but with no guarantee he will win.'

I have an urge to recall a quote to Robert, but he has not yet returned to the table. It appears that most of the other occupants have some sympathy for Robert. So I recall the quote to everyone that is still interested in what I am saying. The quote is the one from Bertrand Russel where he says if an opinion contrary to your own makes you angry, that is a sign that you are subconsciously aware of having no good reason for thinking as you do.

Sudheer smiles, leaves to find Robert, finds Robert, has a conversation with Robert, and brings him back to the table. Robert leans over and extends me a reconciliatory handshake, a sentiment which is not matched by the vacant blue eyes. I am so relieved I forget all COVID-19 protocols and shake it vigorously.

* * *

I stop because it is the end of the dialogue. The eyes are fixed on me, wide open. I try and interpret what they signal. Disbelief, that is it. Total disbelief.

John speaks. His first comment is this, 'I don't care much for the way you write dialogue in the novel, Hendrik.'

I am completely blindsided. 'What do you mean?'

He explains, 'It's too quick. Too much like a legal transcript of a conversation for presentation in a court. You could have slowed things down.'

'Oh'—I stretch the *oh*—'you mean something like this?'

I ask Robert, 'Do you think the pandemic is a hoax?'

Just then, Robert's breakfast arrives. The waiter places it neatly in front of him, between the knife and fork. It is a full English breakfast—two English pork sausages, four rashers of bacon, two fried eggs sunny side up, two halves of grilled tomatoes, a small pile of sliced grilled mushrooms, and a hash brown—arranged clockwise on the plate. In the centre of the plate is a small tub with baked beans. It is not necessary to arrange the breakfast this way for it to be English, but that is the way they do it here.

Robert inspects his breakfast. Looking satisfied, he slowly rotates the plate so that the two English sausages are nearest to him. He takes up his knife and fork. Placing the knife flat on the first sausage to steady it, he pushes the fork into the other end, about an inch from the end. He hesitates and decides that that would be too big a sausage to put into his mouth in public. He withdraws the fork. A thin jet of warm, transparent pork fat squirts out of one of the holes vacated by the fork. It draws a straight, diagonal line on his otherwise pristine white shirt, right across his left nipple, which you can see clearly through the now transparent cotton. Robert doesn't notice. I don't mention it. Best for him to discover it later and for him to ponder the mystery of how it happened or who did that to him.

Robert inserts the fork about one-half inch from the end and cuts the sausage then swaps the fork into his right hand, standard practice for Americans. They can only handle two pieces of cutlery for short periods. He dips the section of sausage quickly into a small bowl of brown sauce that was placed to the right of his plate. He carefully places the section of brown sauce–coated pork sausage into his mouth and chews slowly. Clearly pleased with the result, he finally adjusts his priorities and takes the trouble to answer me.

'Like that?' I direct John to critique.

He laughs. 'Yes, something like that,' he critiques.

I am a little annoyed. 'I came here to consult a lawyer, not take advice from a literary critic.'

Big mistake. Maybe blue eyes can pierce, but brown eyes scorch. They instantly tell me to change my attitude. I change my attitude.

I now feel an urgent need to explain. 'In a setting like this, the conversations are often like machine-gun fire. If you hesitate for a second or two, someone else around the table will hijack the dialogue. So you must be quick. You make mistakes, and you must correct them quickly. I show that here in the way I wrote the dialogue.'

I forget to maintain my new attitude. 'I would like to have the authority of Socrates, where he has command of the room and asks the questions that slowly agree a shared understanding, but I don't. This is not a Shakespearean play either, where the dialogue progresses along a linear line, where the tragedy develops line by line to a dramatic ending. This is real life, and real life is not like a courtroom, where a judge controls the proceedings, you know, where prosecution or defence asks the questions and the witnesses answer, where the jury delivers its final verdict. These dialogues are not like that. These dialogues are very messy. They go everywhere.' As I say this, my new attitude slips.

'You will be glad then that I did not write it up the way Plato wrote up Socratic dialogues,' I say to John.

'What do you mean? he asks.

'No quotes, no tags. Let me show you,' I say.

So now you are calling me an illiterate redneck.

I said in South Georgia.

How do you know I am not from South Georgia?

You told us you are from Cleveland, Ohio, when you introduced yourself.

Who do you think you are, insulting every American like that!

How did I insult every American?

You called us illiterate rednecks.

'You know Hendrik, that would have been better, but you really do have to engage to follow the dialogue,' says John.

'I know. I must assume that Plato had a smarter audience than most writers can expect today. They have to write for the lazy.'

'Format and style dictated by academics, Hendrik, what else will they teach,' laughs John.

'Indeed, and every literary critic and editor would have fainted at the mere site of Plato's format,' I say, and I cannot hide my irritation.

The eyes remind me about my attitude. I reset to my new attitude.

'Hmm,' says John, then he changes the subject, 'real life, eh? So this dialogue really happened. I thought it was a novel?'

I am on the backfoot now, having to defend every angle. 'It is a novel, John, but where do I go for my inspiration? Where is the line between reality and fiction in the writer's mind? I go to my experience of real-world characters. Where else but the real world will I find my teacher?' I decide a diversion is required. 'Anyway, can you see the composition fallacy at work in Robert's response?'

John replays the conversation in his mind, even glances at his notes, but says nothing.

I help him out. 'I implied that a redneck from South Georgia is ill-equipped to deal with the problems of a pandemic.'

John looks up from his notes. 'Oh yes, I do recall you saying that.'

'And what did Robert say about that?' I ask.

John pauses. 'That you have insulted all Americans, calling them rednecks.'

'And—'

John interrupts and then completes the sentence for me. 'And Robert got really upset. Is that what you call a composition fallacy?' John is uncomfortable now. He is the one who normally gets to ask the questions.

Thankful that the diversion worked, I say, 'Absolutely correct. I may have insulted an individual person in South Georgia, but he extrapolates that as an insult to all Americans. He was offended himself, even though he is not a redneck from South Georgia. Robert went from a redneck to all Americans to himself.'

John takes a minute then says, 'You mean, he went from some to all?'

'Yes,' I say, pleased that it does not take more effort to explain. 'He would probably be happy to use the redneck pejorative himself against some of his fellow Americans, but when I used it, he thought it was an insult to all Americans.'

'You should have said more in the dialogue in the novel,' says John.

'I go into that in more detail in the following dialogues,' I say that with confidence because it is true, and I have now foreshadowed a discussion creating an expectation with John. 'Also, the themes and ideas have to build. If I do it in one dialogue, it will be a short story.'

'I thought you were brazening in that dialogue, Hendrik,' says John.

'What do you mean? How?' I ask, genuinely puzzled. This conversation is miles away from the legal one I expected.

'It seems to me that it was a difficult situation, that you felt threatened, but you maintained your confidence apparently,' says John to solve my puzzle.

I decide to ignore his attempt, and having tasted success with the diversion, I make my own attempt to move on, but then John says, 'I cannot help but feel it is incomplete, the dialogue. You leave things hanging.

'Well spotted, John,' I say. 'That is because I haven't done the reflection with you.'

'What reflection?' he asks.

'In the novel, I do a reflection of the dialogue. Think of it as a judge presenting his opinion on a case,' I say.

'Can you do it for me, please?' asks John politely.

'Sure. In the reflection, I start with a short summary of the breakfast with Robert and his misplaced illusion of the USA as the smartest nation in the world. What does that even mean? A nation cannot be smart. Only individual people can be smart. Robert lives under the illusion that the USA handled the pandemic better than any other nation. He is a member of a tribe that believes in American invincibility, but that sense of invincibility is their downfall. The tribe holds on to the idea that the individual is so supreme that they must be allowed to make informed decisions. The tribe with the internal contradiction. A tribe built on the premise that it is a tribe of free individuals.

'There are many occasions where he commits the composition fallacy, but we will learn about it some more as we proceed. Come back to this dialogue and see if you can identify those occasions.

'Robert confuses being a free individual with being smart. But those free individuals do not know what it means to make an informed decision. They confuse to be informed with being the informer. But making informed decisions means to listen to the informer, to get advice from an informed person, and to follow that advice. They cannot do this because they are blindsided by their irrational clinging to the free sovereign individual. We will discuss the sovereign individual in more detail later. They see that the individual reigns supreme, even over knowledgeable people. They are pitching a political right against a natural problem. The natural problem wins—'

'Yes, I do recall that now. But what about Robert losing his temper?' interrupts John.

I continue, 'Yes, John, he did. They all do in the first few dialogues. Well, almost all do. You will see. It reveals a kind of closed mind, a person trapped in Plato's cave. The facts were presented to him, but he only sees their shadows. The shadows make him angry. They make him angry because the shadows distort his shady illusions, the other shadows he thought to be crystal clear images.

'There is more of course. The dialogue started by us focusing on conventional facts, facts that we could never agree on, facts that are disputed. We will not reach a conclusion or agreement using a conventional argument where we do not trust the facts or their sources. More often than not, conventional arguments end in a dead end of disagreement. So I steered the conversation towards a conceptual argument—the concept of making informed decisions.

'The problem for Robert is that he misunderstood the concept of making informed decisions. The concept of informed decisions is not to become an epidemiologist or virologist but to listen to and to follow the advice given by an expert. Being informed is trusting a knowledgeable person to inform you, not for you to become a knowledgeable person.

'There is also the mythical amorphous being, the free individual, the sovereign individual. I don't do much about the sovereign individual in this dialogue. As I said, we will come to it later.

'So there is an important lesson in that we must distinguish between conventional and conceptual arguments. Or they are also called inductive or deductive reasoning. Philosophy is mostly about deductive reasoning, but even in normal conversation, we must be careful to separate the two forms of reasoning. We can use conventional facts to support conceptual arguments but must be incredibly careful when we do it the other way round. If we do, we are prone to develop conspiracy theories.'

I pause to let John know it is the end of the reflection.

'Ah, the reflection is good. It ties up the loose ends. There are a few lessons in the first dialogue. So it appears that the reflection of the dialogue reveals more detail about the lessons learned. Continue,' says john.

I continue. What else can I do? 'Yes, it does, John. The reflection does that. Isn't that what it is for?' I ask rhetorically. I get away with it.

John signals for me to wait while he makes a few notes. He looks up. The eyes signal concern. The pit of my stomach senses the signal. He nods for me to continue.

'The next dialogue is with two business managers, high-flyers in a bank. We are meeting at their offices. They are putting plans together to convince even higher flyers to invest in complying with a certain regulatory requirement.'

'What requirement?' asks John.

My mild annoyance returns. It is becoming a habit. 'Some risk management compliance.'

He persists. 'Be specific.'

I decline. 'There is no need to be specific. It is not in the novel, and it doesn't matter.'

The eyes pin me to my chair. That is another thing brown eyes can do.

John decides to let it go for now. 'We will see. Carry on.' And just like that, John has taken command of the proceedings again. What was I thinking!

MEETING WITH MEGSUM AND AMANDA

Perhaps the whole root of our trouble, the human trouble, is that we will sacrifice all the beauty of our lives, will imprison ourselves in totems, taboos, crosses, blood sacrifices, steeples, mosques, races, armies, flags, nations, in order to deny the fact of death, which is the only fact we have. It seems to me that one ought to rejoice in the fact of death—ought to decide, indeed, to earn one's death by confronting with passion the conundrum of life.

James Baldwin

I arrive a few minutes early and settle on the sofa in the coffee shop in reception. Fancy having a coffee shop with a sofa in the reception area of your office. I mean, most other businesses will expect you to go down the street to get a coffee or, worst still, pull one out of those automated coffee machines.

It is quite busy. People are being greeted and led into the office area, presumably into meeting rooms. Others are being let go. Having concluded their business and now being of little value to 'the business', the authoritative bankers that work here dismiss them with a polite 'Let me walk you out'. The visitors are discarded, having been stripped of whatever business value they were bringing into the office. That will be me in an hour if I am lucky.

If you are wondering about the business, it is the headquarters of a bank. It is a global bank, or is it multinational? There must be a difference, but I have never figured out what that difference is.

I am not here for a philosophical dialogue per se. Not formally anyway. But isn't a meeting just a form of philosophical dialogue? We may be asking questions within the constraints of 'the business' and demand answers within the same constraint, but it is all a form of philosophical dialogue.

I notify Megsum by text message that I have arrived. He responds that he will be down soon.

Megsum escapes the office area through the security barriers and walks up to the sofa where I am seated. He has brought Amanda along. They greet me with the kind of enthusiasm that tells me they need something. It is a good sign, but let's hope it is something that I have. Megsum signs me in at the security desk. I am issued with a card with limited access rights, access limited to the conference centre behind the coffee shop where there are also several meeting rooms and privacy booths that are open on all sides. The booths are private only because you can hear what is said, but you cannot identify who is saying it.

Megsum is one of those high achievers. He has just completed an MBA with a global much revered and well-known business school. I am deliberately not mentioning them by name. One of the big selling points of the business school is that you also become a member of an elite club: a network of ready-made business minds called an alumni association, but only after you graduated. Megsum is ambitious. Extremely ambitious.

He is accompanied by Amanda, like I said when I introduced them first. I did not know she was going to be here. She is Megsum's boss, and when she is in a meeting, all attention focuses on her. She has that kind of gravitas. Amanda is much more reserved than Megsum. She gives the impression that she is listening with great attention and curiosity to what everyone is saying. She is the one who makes the decisions. Not the final decision. She is not that high up in the hierarchy. Amanda gets to decide if she will take your proposition to the hierarchy. She is a crucial link towards any success you might wish for. Her verdict is final. Amanda has a remarkably successful track record in the financial industry, New York and Hong Kong, I seem to recall. It is on her LinkedIn profile, but she is also happy to tell you when you are first introduced. This is not our first time meeting, so I won't bother you with that part in what follows.

We settle in around the small circular table. The table is too small for everyone to place their laptops. I don't bother. To be honest, I never bother. There is truly little on my laptop that isn't also in my head. The meeting room is only slightly larger than the circular table. There is a computer screen mounted on the wall, but it is dark. When it lights up, it offers a digital portal to a distant meeting room equally equipped to provide access to the portal. Teleconferencing it is called. It eliminates the need for travel, but not entirely. That would also eliminate the need for first-class travel, something that will undermine the prestige of being a high-flyer. It feels crowded with three of us in here. There isn't enough room to throw ideas about. No room for thinking outside the box.

Greetings now out of the way, Megsum lays down the context. They have been buoyed by an instruction from a high-flyer higher up in 'the business' to assess how and why to proceed with a certain regulatory risk management requirement. Budget will be made available if the justification makes business sense, but Megsum and Amanda do not know how to make that business sense. They must work it out, present it to the hierarchy, and then get approval for the spending. That is why they asked me here to help them make the business sense.

Megsum orders coffees from the coffee shop, I assume. It arrives, and there is a short break while it gets distributed according to preferences. It is good coffee, made by a barista in a proper coffee shop in a reception area. *Banks are so rich,* I think to myself.

Megsum gets straight to the point now. 'The business has asked us to put together a case that justifies the cost for meeting the regulatory requirement for risk management. Can you help us with that?'

I feel a little pedantic today. I use it to state the obvious. 'It's a regulatory requirement, Megsum. That is the business case.'

It is not so obvious to him. He explains, 'No, no, we have to come up with ROI or case study or cost benefit analysis. How do we do that?'

If you do not know this already, ROI stands for return on investment. If you do, then I apologise for the delay. *High-flyers,* I think to myself. Megsum has the enthusiasm of a Labrador puppy when it comes to anything 'the business' wants.

Amanda thinks she has a better reason; it seems that way at first glance anyway. 'Actually, it is not regulatory, Hendrik. It is contractual.'

Well, that is a little ambiguous, so I push for more information. 'Oh, you mean a supplier or customer demands compliance with a certain framework?'

She provides more information. 'A supplier, or suppliers actually, up the value chain, and it is also regulatory. Some regulators now require us to meet the suppliers' standards.'

Don't you find it rude when people say 'up the value chain'? I do, and I cannot figure out why. Maybe there is an insult in there somewhere, like, 'Why don't you stick that up your value chain!'

I try not to let Amanda's response confuse me. The way I see it, the fundamentals have not changed. I point that out to them. 'So? Either way, that is the business case, isn't it?'

Megsum fixes his gaze on me. I can see he thinks I am ill-equipped to deal with the complexities of the demands of 'the business' of a global bank or multinational bank. I must try and figure that out soon. I stare back at him, friendlier I hope, but I think he is ill-equipped to deal with the complexities of simple questions.

The poor bastards. Do not worry. I do not say that out loud. I also do not say this out loud. *They are trapped, being held captive by an unseen force, a tribe too powerful for them to understand.*

My pedantic mood takes over. It is a risk, I know, but I let it. 'Help me to try and understand. The business has asked you to come up with a business case, ROI, or cost benefit analysis statement to secure the investment, right?'

Then something curious happens, something with Amanda's gravitas. She has become a lightweight, suddenly in an equal gravitas class with Megsum. She tries to be more helpful, or so she thinks. She adds another option, 'Or competitive advantage, we must find a good business reason to proceed with the investment.'

Good, now we have a foundation, a pillar to build on. A wobbly one, but one nonetheless. I start building. 'But it is clearly not that kind of question.'

Their minds are working overtime. Neurobiologists tell us that if the mind encounters something new and strange, it lights up like Times Square in New York at night. It's New Year's celebration in their minds.

Blank stares from both now. I recognise their world view is entirely shaped by 'the business', by that tribe that is holding them captive. A formless thing it is, without definition. They were taught all business decisions are made with certain methods. They are trapped in a sort of Plato's cave where the light only produces shadows of reality. The shadows are 'the business'.

In an attempt to swing gravity back in her favour, Amanda re-enforces the rules of 'the business'. 'We must make a case for doing this that the business will understand, Hendrik. You are the expert in this, so you must help us.'

There is a philosophical rabbit hole to explore in Amanda's statement—a whole world of careless use of language. What is 'the business', and how can it understand? Surely understanding something is a unique human capability. The business is not a human. Do you think she means management, flyers that fly higher than her and Megsum? But *management* presents the same problem; *management* is a tribe within a tribe. There must be people in that tribe, other people, and why don't we just say so? Why don't we just say, Eric. 'We must do this so Eric understands.' That will make the problem a lot easier to deal with.

I decide not to take them down that rabbit hole; there is another one waiting. I am just going to assume she means my company when she says, 'You must help us.' I am an expert at identifying bullshit. Not an expert at satisfying the needs of 'the business'. I have colleagues who are expert bullshitters who understand how to satisfy the needs of 'the business'.

I allow for a pregnant silence to enter the room. While the pregnant silence works through its full term, I think to myself again, *The moment you walk through the main doors and past the security barriers with your swipe cards, you become part of a system. A kind of tribal master invades your minds and controls your every thought. You become part of a kind of supermind, where you play a simple role in its mechanisms—mechanisms that are limiting interpretive repertoires.*

The pedantic me thinks it is time to have some more fun, to see if we can find the edges of their Plato's caves that may lead them to enlightenment. I feel the urge to take the individuals to battle against the tribe, to help them explore a new place of freedom. This I think in my head, of course, but this I say out loud, terminating the pregnant silence early. 'Why do you think there is a regulatory requirement for banks to comply with risk management?'

Silence. I try it somewhat differently. 'I mean, why does the government, the regulator, compel the bank to implement a risk management framework like this?'

Silence.

Then Amanda offers an answer. 'To protect the shareholders.' She finishes with confidence, an emphasis on *shareholders*. There is another tribe there. Do you see? This one is all-powerful, even more powerful than 'the business'.

I delve deeper. 'Why does the business not do this in their own right? Why do they have to be compelled to do it?'

Its Amanda who responds. 'If the regulator does not enforce the risk management framework, the business will not do it because it costs money, shareholders' money.' Megsum is normally the quick one, and I do not mean in an intelligent way. I mean in an eager way. The gravitas pendulum is swinging back in her favour.

'That explains why the business does not want to do it,' I say. 'It doesn't explain why the regulator wants the business to do it.'

Silence. God, this is like pulling teeth. The light outside the cave is too bright. They fear the clarity that may come from going there. Maybe even disabling them. Fear enters the room. This is too small a room to share with fear. I try to help. 'Do you think the regulator is concerned that if the business doesn't meet the requirements that the business might cause harm to the wider economy, the public, or your customers?'

It's Megsum. We have not lost him altogether. 'Yes, that is it.'

Time to go further out the cave. 'So the question, therefore, is not a business question. It is an ethical and moral question,' I say.

Megsum thinks he is back in control. The pendulum swings ever so slightly in his favour. 'The business' regains some of its power. 'Yes, of course, but that argument will not work for the business, Hendrik. The business is only concerned about making a profit for the shareholders.'

Marching them relentlessly towards the light, I ask, 'Why?'

There is silence, then Amanda responds first, 'Because the shareholders own the business, and the business is responsible for making a profit for the shareholders.' The pendulum swings back to her. Megsum has not yet learned how to throw his MBA around.

Let us build another pillar here. 'Are you saying that the business's only ethical responsibility is towards the shareholders because the shareholders own the business?' I ask.

Megsum gets in first this time. 'Yes.'

I told you he is fresh out of business school, so I decide to test his knowledge. 'Do you know who came up with this idea?'

'They teach you at business school.' It's Megsum. It is not a good answer, but he finally gets to use his degree. He grins from ear to ear. Despite that, I think the pendulum leans back to Amanda. It looks like gravitas is not affected by MBAs.

Notice this is another appeal to authority. We will look at it in more detail. People will often appeal to authority to win their case, but this appeal to authority is flawed. A business school teaches the ideas of people. It has no ideas of its own. It's a school.

I am a little disappointed that he does not recall who made the claim. I also decide there is little merit in showing off. Time to dismantle this pillar, so I ask, 'What if the shareholders don't own the business?'

Megsum is completely confounded by that question. Panic has set upon his face, and the light has gone out. 'But they do,' he pleads.

Megsum appeals to Amanda for help with his eyes. Amanda has gone suspiciously quiet. Fearful if she says something, she will be exposed. Happy for Megsum to field the heat. She gives up a little on the pendulum, and it moves in Megsum's favour.

So I correct years of business school education. 'Actually, Megsum, they don't, not legally, not philosophically, not in any way.'

Megsum goes for the obvious defence. 'What, that is not what I have learned in my MBA.' He appeals to the authority of the business school—the creator of 'the business'.

I continue to undermine the pillar. 'You mean, you just haven't been told. You have been told that the only responsibility you have is to the shareholders, so you assumed they own the business.'

Silence, so I press the point. 'You haven't told me who came up with the idea that shareholders own the business.' This is where I strip the business school of its authority. I reduce the authority to a person. It has a lot less authority when it is a person.

Megsum answers correctly, but in a question, insecure now. 'Isn't it Milton Friedman, the economist?'

'Yes, but not directly,' I say. 'He came up with the idea that management must make a profit for its shareholders and that it is their only ethical responsibility. It implies that shareholders own the business. But if they don't own the business, what then?'

Megsum mounts a fight back by avoiding answering the question. 'If the business has no ethical responsibility to the shareholders, then who do they have a responsibility to?'

Time for me to return the compliment, so I answer with a question, 'Who do you have a responsibility to, Megsum?'

Short answer from Megsum. 'The business.'

He answers the wrong question again, so I help him out. 'When you are not in this office, I mean.' I thought that was obvious. The pendulum settles in the middle. All the gravitas belongs to it now.

Amanda decides to get involved. 'It must be society, the wider community.'

But then Megsum loses his patience; he clearly finds it hard to leave his Plato's cave, to move towards the light, too comfortable with years of MBA training. The mood in the room turns aggressive. I can tell you again. Just like with fear, this is a really small room for an aggressive mood. It multiplies the aggression at least tenfold. 'We must make the case to the business as a purely business decision, not an ethical decision, Hendrik. That is not the way it works in business. There is no room for ethics in business.'

Amanda throws her weight in behind him. 'Yes, I feel we are wasting time, so can we get back to the problem at hand, or do you think we should ask someone else for help?' The pendulum swings strongly back towards Amanda.

She uses the threat of competition against me. That hurts, and I thought I was their trusted advisor. My pedanticism threatens to leave me.

But they are wrong if they think I give up that easily. I deceive them with a 'Sure', then a question, 'Tell me, though, will the business sell heroin to a five-year-old?'

It's Amanda. She drives hard. 'No, of course not.'

I respond, equally direct, 'Why not?'

Megsum is clearly on her side on this one. 'It is against the law, and it is morally wrong.' He has given up on the pendulum.

I've got them, so I push hard now. 'But hold on, I am sure we can make a good business case for it, and we can put in place a risk management framework to deal with the law.'

Amanda, boosted by Megsum's support, says, 'It is just wrong, Hendrik. The business will never do it.'

So I draw the parallel with risk compliance. 'But can you see that some business decisions are not made in the methods they teach you at business school? Some business decisions are ethical and moral decisions.'

I allow the silence to stretch. It becomes heavy. I have rattled their caves. They can see it, but they don't know what to make of it. Kant would have laughed at the limits of their interpretive repertoires or, as it is more and more commonly referred to, their world views. Come to think of it, there is no record of Kant ever laughing. There is also no humour in any of his writings.

The silence becomes impossible to bear. Whatever 'the business' is, it is too strong. They will not confront it by taking this discussion to 'the business'. I offer them an escape. 'The framework is designed to mitigate the risk to the business, the economy, and the society. So why don't we prepare a business case based on a return on risk mitigation?'

Normal gravitas resumes as Amanda takes up the escape. 'What do you mean risk mitigation?'

I explain further, 'We find a way to demonstrate quantitatively how much the risk to the business is for not complying, how it is reduced, and what the investment requirement will be.'

Megsum is on board as well. 'How do you demonstrate risk mitigation?'

I say, 'Don't worry. We have a framework for that.'

And just like that, we have created another illusion, another stupid and distorted business concept designed to placate 'the business', I think to myself. 'The business' has won.

* * *

'That's it?' asks John, sensing that I have come to the end of the dialogue. 'Why do I sense that it didn't work out for you?'

'You mean on the day or for my readers?' I must admit, I am a bit confused, but I only admit that to myself.

'On the day . . .,' John's voice trails off. The brown eyes look confused for just a second. *Now we are both confused,* I think to myself.

'Oh,' says John, sensing that I am confused too, 'I see. You want your readers to realise something, to learn some lesson.'

'Yes, principally that, but just so you know, we won that business, so in that way, it came through for us.' I thought I am helping to clear up the confusion, but I have walked into a trap.

'I thought it was a novel,' says John. The eyes are triumphant.

'It is,' I confirm unnecessarily, 'but I have to source my story from somewhere, and the only place I can go is my own life experience.'

I realise mine is a repeat of a now feeble response. I concede the point.

'But they didn't buy into your argument, in the "novel",' says John. And I feel we are going back and forth a bit. The air quotes are obvious in his tone; no need for the gesture.

'Well, it wasn't actually an argument,' I say. 'I was trying to demonstrate that there are certain domains for making different decisions. Scientific decisions are made using the tools of science. In business, it is the tools of business; in ethics, the tools of ethics; and so on.'

'Interesting,' says John and then reminds me, 'and a legal domain for libel cases. But you had to go into the business domain to persuade them.'

I am a little irritated now. I hope it doesn't show. 'Yes, but think about it. We could, in all seriousness, not decide in the business domain to address an ethical issue. That is why we have regulators. To force businesses to behave properly towards society and the community.'

'I see that now,' says John, equally irritated, 'but what should happen?'

'The problem lies with this thing called the business. What is it?' I ask.

John helps me out, gives me a compressed legal speak answer. 'Legally speaking, it is an incorporated entity with the objective to engage in a certain reasonably defined economic activity for a profit.'

I am not convinced, so I say, 'It sounds to me like you just made that up.'

Irritation in the brown eyes, pinning me to the chair.

'I did, but does it really matter?' admits John.

'It does,' say I, 'but I have written about that in another book.'

'Did you upset anybody in that one?' Sarcasm from John. I ignore it.

'No, because the bit that is in that book doesn't go there.'

John ponders his notes for a while. 'I sense no real problem in the dialogue, Hendrik, but I imagine if they read it in a novel, they might be upset. Are these meetings not held under implied confidentiality? Are they real people?'

'It is a novel, John. None of the characters are real. But yes, business meetings are normally held under implied or contractual non-disclosure. This one was contractual,' I say.

John replies, 'Then that could explain why we have a letter, Hendrik.'

A certain tension develops in the pit of my stomach. I decide to ignore his conclusion; denial I think it is called. 'The point I teach in the dialogue is that when faced with a question, we must consider what domain of thinking we are going to use to answer those questions.'

John says, 'Frankly, if you did not explain it to me, I would not have got it from the dialogue as you call it.'

I ask, 'Did you get anything else from that dialogue?'

'Yes,' says John, 'you make the business sound quite sinister.'

His voice suggested quotes around 'the business', like that.

I confirm his assessment. 'Good, that is because it is. It has a vague shape. Shall we go to the next one?'

John asks, 'Have we finished with this one?'

'There is the reflection. Shall I do that now?' I ask.

John nods.

'The dialogue is about a business meeting with Megsum and Amanda. They have been given a problem to solve, but the problem cannot be solved by conventional business practices and standards. It is an ethical and moral problem, yet they insist on finding a business decision-making methodology to apply—a business case template, return on investment, competitive advantage analysis, etc. Megsum and Amanda are hoping one of these will help to make the decision.

'I introduced the concept of examining the question and deciding what kind of question is being asked. Once you have determined the kind of question, you use appropriate methodologies or method to find that answer.'

'Yes,' says John, 'I do recall that. But there was more, wasn't there? Something about "the business".' John mocks me with the air quotes this time.

'Again, John, well remembered. Yes, you will see "the business" features prominently in several dialogues. It is a bizarre structure that holds so much power over individuals that they cannot open their minds. It is crazy to think that you will often hear managers say in meetings to think outside the box when the box is actually "the business". In Megsum and Amanda's case, they simply could not go outside the box. They simply refused to go outside the box. So in the end, I suggested something that will allow us to stay inside the box. But to do that, we had to deploy a distortion. We distorted the problem so we can use standard business formulae to satisfy "the business". I quote from Baldwin at the start of this dialogue—'

'I do remember that quote. I found it disturbing,' interrupts John to stop me from repeating it. 'Didn't he say something about being imprisoned, country, religion, God, and a few more?'

'He did, and I think we can add "the business" to that list. People like Megsum and Amanda, and more than I can count, are imprisoned by "the business", as if it were some reified super powerful thing. But it is just other people who lose their humanity the moment they clock into the framework.

'There is also the revealing of the problem of appealing to authority to strengthen an argument. This is particularly troublesome when the authority is an institution, particularly a revered institution. All ideas can be traced back to a person. Even the idea of the monotheistic God can be traced back to the Persian, Zarathustra, also known as Zoroaster. Apparently, he got fed up with the burden of praying to millions of Hindu gods and decided to economise; to consolidate all the gods into a single all-powerful God. The efficiency that the idea brought to the morning prayer routine was so immediately obvious that the idea spread rapidly throughout Persia into the Mediterranean and became the cornerstone of other religions. It also created a god with untenable internal contradictions. Once you trace an idea back to a person it rapidly loses its authority. Appealing to the authority of a person is one thing. Appealing to the authority of an amorphous thing is something altogether more sinister' I say. This time I pause so John doesn't have to interrupt me.

'Indeed. Continue,' says John.

This conversation with John is becoming just as messy as the dialogue with Megsum and Amanda. 'It is a story, John.' I feel the need to repeat. 'The themes develop over time. Also, I am quite sure not all the dialogues will translate into a case of libel. If you cannot see any in that dialogue, then perhaps there isn't any?'

'Well,' says John, 'you did make them look stupid, did make "the business" look stupid.' Once again, he mocks me with the air quotes. 'Let's just hope they or someone else in the business don't read your novel. And by the way, you did much better on the dialogue, Hendrik. I mean, in the way you wrote it. I thought you would like to know that.'

I am hurt by that. Not the comment on the dialogue, the other one about not reading my novel. I would like everyone to read my novel. 'I would give you credit for the advice, John, but then I wrote it a while ago. Can we move on now? Please?'

'Just one more thing,' he says. 'That room must have been really small because the characters lack animation.'

'I am sorry. What do you mean lack animation?' I ask.

'There is very little action. I find it hard to visualise them,' he adds.

'Oh, you mean they are like talking heads?' I say.

'Maybe.'

'So rather than tell you Megsum is confused, you want me to show you. Maybe say "Megsum scratches his arse" instead of "Megsum is confused",' I say.

John laughs. 'That will work, but maybe something less vivid.'

'OK, how about this? "Megsum frowns. His eyes focus on something a few inches away from his nose,"' I offer.

'Yes, something like that,' says John and laughs again.

I am irritated, or better still, I frown. My eyes capture John's. I lean forward, and in a voice that fails to hide my irritation, I say, 'I did that purposefully. I wanted the dialogue to stand out, to be the focus point. I am not sure how much unpacking the scene will contribute to the content of the dialogue. Perhaps I should give equal emphasis to showing and telling. I will make a note and try harder for my next novel.'

'That makes sense, to help the dialogue stand out,' he says.

The eyes are not so understanding, pinned. What is it about John's eyes and my father? What part of me is my father? Where does my father stop and where do I start?

COFFEE WITH PETER

Be discriminating about what images and ideas you permit into your mind. If you yourself don't choose what thoughts and images you expose yourself to, someone else will, and their motives may not be the highest.

Epictetus

Peter and I are having coffee at an outlet of one of those American chains headquartered in Seattle. Especially why they are successful is beyond me. The coffee is weak and all flavour scalded out by excessively hot water. You know the one I mean. We are talking like friends do, about this and that, nothing specific. Then Peter brings up something that should not surprise me because of who he is, but it does because it is such a flagrant mistake in reasoning. With Peter, I have learned you try not to teach him anything. He considers friendships as places of mutual respect and exchange, without conflict or an outward discussion of differences of opinion. That is, of course, opinions different from his.

I decide to recall a story to Peter, partly because I want to distract him from his emotional state and partly because I want to sneak in behind the emotions that protect the stupidity that he has brought into this conversation. What triggered this display of raw stupidity is the TV in the background. It is showing a repeat of Trump's now infamous speech to supporters where he promised he is going to build a wall on the Mexican border to keep out Mexicans.

Peter has previously expressed his support for Trump, and he expresses his support for Trump's wall now. 'The president is right, you know, about the wall and the Mexicans.' I must always check my own response when people use the title 'the president' when referring to Trump. Have you noticed how this happens whenever there is an arsehole for a president or an idiot for prime minister? I think their supporters try to emphasise the authority of the position to overcome the woeful shortcomings of the person.

'Peter, listen,' I say, 'let me tell you a story.'

Peter frowns in confusion. He is not sure at all why I want to tell him a story when he has clearly offered up a topic for discussion. He nevertheless agrees, and I get away with it for now. 'Sure.'

I continue, 'I had a job once. Actually, I worked for most of my life. Philosophical counselling came much later. Nevertheless, philosophy gave me an advantage over my colleagues, but not necessarily in my career. It is not always honest, smart people who make it to the top. There is something else happening there which I purposefully decided not to get involved in. So yes, I had a career as a business development manager—'

Peter interrupts, 'Isn't that just a salesman with a fancy title?'

I agree only because it is a diversion without merit. 'Yes, sure, but listen. I have written up a comprehensive proposal topped by an executive summary that I was particularly proud of. The exec summary drew from specific customer requirements and detailed briefly how we would add value by meeting and exceeding those requirements—'

Peter interrupts again, trying to look smart. I don't mind. It means the distraction is working. 'Which is exactly what you should do.'

Nevertheless, I welcome his support but more so his willingness to engage. 'As was practice in the company, I sent the final draft to several of my colleagues for review, including the new transferee from South Africa, a cocky, chest-out juvenile with all the confidence in the world. If you think I have an attitude going here, you are right. I want to be transparent about my dislike for the cocky juvenile South African.'

More engagement and support from Peter. 'I know the type, overconfident and underskilled. Dunning-Kruger, I think.'

It always surprises me how many people know about the Dunning-Kruger effect, but not as much as to how prolific the distortion is despite there being widespread knowledge of it. However, I am pleased that Peter is committing and engaging in the discussion. Even if that means avoiding his conversational tangents is threatening to become a full-time job.

'Yes,' I continue, 'Reg was transferred here to help me. However, there was a misunderstanding at work in his mind. I took it that he was transferred here to help by taking some of my workload off my hands. Reg seemed to think that he was going to help me get better at my job. The ignorant little shit.'

'Typical,' says Peter. 'His ambition outstrips his capability.' Getting Peter to focus on Reg's shittiness is pure genius.

I push on. 'The next day, I got his edited draft back. He had completely removed my exec summary and replaced it with an awful argument. Let me explain.' Peter lets me explain.

'Reg plagiarised a headline from a report by a competitor. It read something like this: "Asian businesses are bad at detecting and responding to cyberattacks". I can explain this technicality, but it is not necessary for the story. The headlines are full enough of reports of cyberattacks, so much so that it needs no explanation. The technical details are not relevant.' I realise I overworked the dismissal.

It appears that Peter did not notice. He agrees. 'Everybody knows about cyberattacks.'

I continue, 'Let us put to one side that Reg used a report from a competitor. The stupidity of that is already beyond belief. So I searched the report online and found that the competitor had surveyed a thousand businesses in Asia and only 30 per cent responded that they are confident in their ability to detect and respond to cyberattacks. The vendor who produced this report showed a grotesque disregard for a fallacy in writing the headline as they did, that "Asian businesses are bad at detecting and responding to cyberattacks". The failure in reasoning is the extrapolation from three hundred out of a thousand to "Asian businesses".

'The authors are suggesting that millions of businesses are bad at this and that the only connection between those businesses are that they are in Asia. If you think about it, there is no causal relationship or logical connection between a business being in Asia and it being bad at detecting and responding to cyberattacks. This is the composition fallacy at work, or also the some-and-all fallacy—'

Peter interrupts again, 'Wait, what do you mean the composition fallacy? I don't understand.'

Pleased that Peter is asking for an explanation, I take him up on his interruption. 'It means what is true for some is true for all. Let me give you an example. Johnny eats a lot of ice cream. Johnny is in the third grade. Therefore, the third grade eats a lot of ice cream. See? There is no way we can assume the third grade eats a lot of ice cream just because one of the pupils do.'

Peter agrees, 'Oh yeah, I get it now.'

I repeat the explanation in the context of the report. 'Some companies in Asia are bad, and some companies are good. Yet the declaration in the headline clearly implies all companies are bad. And because Reg replaced the exec summary for a proposal for an Asian bank, that headline implies the Asian bank is bad at detecting and responding to cyberattacks. But in fact, the Asian bank could be one of the companies in the 30 per cent. We don't know. That is the second faux pas in the exec summary, the assumption that the Asian bank is bad at detecting and responding to cyberattacks. This mistake is an example of the converse of the composition fallacy, the divisional fallacy. What is true for the whole is true for all its parts. Having made the first mistake, Reg is now making the second mistake.'

Peter needs more. 'Sorry, the divisional fallacy?'

Grateful for his continued engagement, I explain, 'Yes, let us use the same example as earlier, having made the mistake to assume the third grade eats a lot of ice cream. Carole is in the third grade.

Therefore, Carole eats a lot of ice cream. The truth might be that Carole hates ice cream.'

Peter gets this and judges immediately. 'That Reg sounds like a real idiot.'

I agree but try to soften the position in anticipation of where I am heading with this. 'Well, sure. He is a bit stupid, isn't he—'

Peter interrupts me, 'Hold on. Why are you telling me this story?'

Peter is one of those very right-leaning Americans loyal to Trump. I know you might be surprised that I know right-wing Americans loyal to Trump, or perhaps not. There are some seventy-six million of them, so the chances are good that we all know a right-wing American.

Remember at that instant, we were watching a repeat on TV of Trump's now infamous speech on Mexicans. You know the one. The one where he says, 'They send their murderers and rapists to America.'

But Peter is now fixated on Reg, perhaps because he sees something in my attitude towards Reg that sends warning signals. He doesn't wait for an explanation on why I am telling the story. His curiosity has already taken him somewhere else. 'So what happened to Reg?'

The change in direction is abrupt and catches me off guard. I answer him anyway. 'Oh, Reg is one of those lucky bastards who fail up. More confidence than substance. There was a right royal battle for control between Reg, Brent, and Kristoff, and Reg came out supreme. In the process, the three of them created a terrible, toxic work environment. They made everyone at the company miserable. Employee after employee resigned. Reg and Brent first worked Kristoff out of the system, then Reg came out on top of Brent.'

Peter states, 'And you, they worked you out of the system too?'

I reply, 'Perhaps, but the truth is a bit more complicated. I left a day or two after the incident with the exec summary. I had earlier, much earlier actually, a few years earlier in fact, banked a head-hunting approach, which I now called in.

'I came to the realisation that I am surrounded by a bunch of serotonin-driven juveniles, and I had better things to do with my time than to fix their parents' screw-ups. To borrow something from Kafka, it would have taken the effort of building the Egyptian pyramids to break through their thick skulls and bypass their juvenile overconfidence to temper their ambitions for power. Again, I had better things to do. Frankly, I would have preferred to clean the San Francisco Bay Bridge with a toothbrush.'

I was hoping to shut this topic down with my rant, but Peter is in full curiosity mode now, and I remain a bit on the back foot. He asks, 'My god, Hendrik, you are still pissed off by it. Are you keeping in touch with Brent and Kristoff?'

'Kristoff, yes. Brent, no,' I confirm.

But there is only more curiosity from Peter. 'Why not Brent?'

I answer honestly, 'Brent is not interesting enough. You can say everything about him in one hundred and sixty characters then swipe left.'

Peter looks confused. Clearly the reference to social media is unfamiliar to him. I am surprised by that unfamiliarity. I thought all Trump loyalists are on Twitter, but my estimation of Peter jumps up a few notches.

I say, 'Brent's ability to communicate is limited to Twitter, one hundred and sixty characters, and then wait for a response. Or Tinder, swiping left, or it might be swipe right. I don't use either. I didn't want to write about him because no one would be interested.'

I'm wrong about that. Peter is interested. 'I am interested,' he says.

I am annoyed. 'I'm annoyed, but sure.' I say because I want him to know.

Peter's face tells me being annoyed is not acceptable between friends.

'Brent is a naturally gifted person who unfortunately did not develop beyond discovering his penis and with an obsession for young Asian women with low self-esteem,' I say.

Peter is not amused. 'What! Are you trying to be sarcastic?'

I am defiant. 'Told you, of no interest to anyone. I never had a remotely interesting philosophical discussion with him. Even the business decisions he made was all about "I like that", "I don't like that", or swipe left, swipe right. He is not capable of anything remotely interesting.'

Peter won't give up. 'That's it?'

I insist, 'Yep, that is all I am going to say about him.'

Peter goes quiet. He is counting something on his fingers.

I see what he is doing. 'Oh my god, you are counting the characters in that sentence!'

He smiles and provides the tally. 'One hundred and sixty exactly,' he says.

For some inexplicable and completely irrational reason, I am pleased with myself. 'Uncanny. I feel you have confirmed my point.'

Peter realises he is not going to get anything sensible out of me. But that is because there is nothing sensible to say about Brent. He accepts my opinion and moves on.

'Young people hey,' says Peter, 'I don't get the hook-up game they play on social media. I cannot see how it can lead to happiness.'

'It doesn't. It leads to the end of decadence, or the happiness paradox: if you strive for happiness by doing things purely for the pleasure they bring, and not for the goal they help you achieve, they will lose their value, and when they lose their value, you will never reach the goal of happiness.'

'It is a shame that we have a generation, maybe two, who have not developed beyond social media limitations.'

It is not a question, but I agree with him. 'Imagine that the community spends ten, maybe twelve, years teaching children how to read and write. Then all they do with that skill is type sentences of less than one hundred and sixty characters. Also, they are limited to reading sentences of less than one hundred and sixty characters. I came across a piece written by Carl Sagan, you know, the scientist famous for producing *Cosmos*, the TV series.'

I wait for an acknowledgement. His facial expression gives it. 'I must remember to reference this in a book when I eventually get to write it. It goes something like this: "For 99 percent of the tenure of humans on earth, nobody could read or write. The great invention had not yet been made. Except for first-hand experience, almost everything we knew was passed on by word of mouth. As in the children's game 'Telephone', over tens and hundreds of generations, information would slowly be distorted and lost.

'"Books changed all that. Books, purchasable at low cost, permit us to interrogate the past with high accuracy; to tap the wisdom of our species; to understand the point of view of others, and not just those in power; to contemplate—with the best teachers—the insights, painfully extracted from Nature, of the greatest minds that ever were, drawn from the entire planet and from all our history. They allow people long dead to talk inside our heads. Books can accompany us everywhere. Books are patient where we are slow to understand, allow us to go over the hard parts as many times as we wish, and are never critical of our lapses. Books are key to understanding the world and participating in a democratic society" [Carl Sagan and Ann Druyan].'

'I am impressed that you can recite that. You may want to be briefer in a quote though,' says Peter.

'To less than a hundred and sixty characters you mean,' I say.

He laughs.

'There is no guarantee that it is an accurate recitation, Peter, but then how many people actually verify referenced material? Back to Brent, I am an optimist, but I fear that social media will see us slip back into an age where ancient and old knowledge gets distorted because people try to condense whole books into one-hundred-and-sixty-character sentences. You see that often when people cite quotes, thinking they can pick one short sentence to convey the contents of a whole book.'

'As you like to do?' asks Peter. The sarcasm is real. You would have thought sarcasm, like annoyance, has no place in friendships.

'What do you mean?' I ask.

'You are always quoting philosophers, Hendrik. I bet those quotes are mostly less than one hundred and sixty characters,' he teases me.

'Peter, I use well-placed quotes to emphasise important points or to draw attention to important points in dialogues I have with people, and these dialogues are substantially more than one hundred and sixty characters.' I make it clear that it is a reprimand.

Peter puts his hands up in a gesture of submission, but then he insists on knowing more about Reg. 'What do you mean by Reg failing up?'

I wring my hands. The delay is driving me mad. So I resist. 'Do we really have to go there? It is not relevant to the story.'

He insists we go there. 'I am curious to know about failing up.'

I offer a brief description, making sure it is more than one hundred and sixty characters of course. 'Failing up is common in business. Talented, committed people are overlooked for promotion, and confident arseholes get promoted despite consistent failures. It is extremely well documented, so I don't need to say more here.

'Two things counted in Reg's favour. He was the boss's favourite child or, rather, his pet project, and he had the arrogance of a thankfully rare type of white South African. What they lack for in sophistication, they make up in arrogance. It has something to do with a distorted, competitive culture. I had a brother who was one of those. He made life difficult growing up.

'These types of characters confuse their arrogance with confidence, but there is a fine line between arrogance and confidence. They seem to transgress that fine line in a reckless disregard for the consequences to other people, actually for the consequence to the wider business. They will go so far as to wreck the business if they can put one over their colleagues.

'When they present a business plan or business case and you poke at the obvious holes, they simply stare at you blankly, with vacant eyes, as if you were an alien creature or just plain stupid, unable to see their brilliance for what it is. They do that only because it gives them control.

'The reality is, you see it for what it is. Snake oil I think you Americans call it. The problem is, they have so much confidence and self-belief that you have no chance. They will proceed recklessly, making people's lives miserable. But what can you do? They are the ones who get promoted. They have the authority, the primacy over decision-making, and they control the hierarchy. All you can do is leave and find another more intelligent place to earn a living, until that gets screwed up by another confidently stupid.'

Peter says, 'You don't have to be a thankfully rare type of white South African to be that kind of arsehole. They are quite common in my country.' I am always surprised at the paradoxes in Peter's character. On the one hand, he is a Trump Republican with a strong America First national identity, and on the other hand, criticising some of his fellow Americans comes easily to him. With that, Peter accepts my not-so-brief explanation and now just appears curious about something else. 'So how did it work out in the long run?'

By now, my frustration must be transparent, but Peter seems to be completely oblivious to it. I have another go at closing the discussion. 'Well, Reg's boss eventually left by "mutual agreement". He acknowledged his failings to understand the difference in scaling a consultancy company versus a product company in a social media post. He presented it with pride as a valuable lesson gained to add to his repertoire of work experience. But he failed to express any regret for the people's careers and lives he screwed up in the process of learning the lesson. He failed to understand that employees give companies their most precious gift, the gift of their time, of which we all have a finite supply and can only give once.'

Peter frowns. He says nothing, but he is contemplating something. I have inadvertently given him something else to be curious about.

He says, 'I have never thought about it that way. Compensating people for time lost forever, I mean.'

I take a deep breath. This one is on me. I must stop opening rabbit holes. 'In general, employers don't either. They don't teach it in MBA programs. They teach that employees are cogs in a machine that can be replaced when they wear out. The old ones discarded, no longer of value to "the business". A consumable item, a resource, a product that can be scaled up. Something that can be managed as a supply chain item.

'Arseholes. It comes from a theory by Taylor, the application of science in "the business". Management schools were desperate to teach something when they were first established by universities. They grabbed at anything, so they grabbed Taylor because he claimed it was scientific, but it was far from science. Science in business is a completely bizarre idea if you consider the "the business" is not a "natural thing",' I say, and I do the air quotes around 'the business' and 'natural thing'.

'Workers are managed by human resource management like it is a supply chain. It is a grotesque failure of economists and economics education. The bizarre and tragic thing is that it is people doing it to other people. It is one person robbing another person of their most precious gift. Who are they to suggest that the time of a factory floor worker is less valuable to her than the time of a CEO is to him? If they are lucky, they have similar supplies of it. But if you listen to the person, the manager, doing this to employees, they blame that shapeless thing, "the business," which cannot afford to pay more. The business? Exactly what is that?'

I am worried now that Peter will go down that rabbit hole, but he surprises me yet again by choosing a different one. 'Sounds a bit Marxist to me, Hendrik.'

Peter has annoyed me now. This is classic diversion. Label something pejoratively to dismiss it.

'Oh, what rubbish,' I say.

Peter's face reminds me that annoyance has no place in a friendship. This time, I am simply going to push through and break that friendship rule.

'You don't like what I say, so you label it Marxist because that suggests it is anti-capitalist, from a political position left of where you draw comfort. Here is someone else who had something to say about this, and he lived long before Marx. "Let no one rob me of a single day who is not going to make me an adequate return for such a loss" [Seneca].

'People give their time but get measured for their skills and capabilities, or they get measured for the value they add to "the business",' I say. 'It is a ridiculous, inhumane, and deeply flawed economic model, and this business model is not naturally there. It is a human construction. There is no such thing as "the business". It doesn't exist. It is just other people. If you are going to hire people by the hour, compensate them adequately for their loss, because they can never replace that hour. In fact, they should put the words "Sorry for your loss. We hope this will make you feel better" on the payslip.'

'What do you mean the business doesn't exist? It is not a thing?' he asks. My gaze is fixed now. I slump in my chair. Bloody rabbit holes.

'The business is not a real thing, like a tree or a river. It is a mental construct, a shapeless, amorphous thing. Even when we incorporate the business, we give it a legal body. We create a legal person as opposed to a natural person. A piece of paper and a number on a list, to be managed by humans in compliance with its articles of incorporation.

'Whatever part of it—building, factory, or such—that comes into existence are constructed by humans. If you think about it, it is the most bizarre things humans do. They create an institution, construct an image of it in their minds, then reify it in buildings that symbolise its power. It's hilarious. But it is not as hilarious as then using science to examine it, to poke sharp measuring instruments at it, to ask questions like, What is this thing? Where did it come from? How does it work? You have got to have a laugh.'

Peter has a laugh. 'Gosh, you have a weird mind, Hendrik. You also have strong feelings about this. You should write a book.'

I take my win. 'I have. Can we get back to Reg? There is more to say about Reg. I am acutely aware of my own finite time and don't want to waste any, or any of your time for that matter.'

Peter ignores my dramatics and nods. I remind Peter that we talked about how Reg committed the composition fallacy but that we need to be a bit more sympathetic to Reg.

Peter looks a little disappointed that I am backing away from an all-out attack on Reg and his screwed-up personality. 'He is more than a bit stupid if you ask me,' says Peter.

I know if you took the trouble to read the intro, you will be familiar with some of what comes next. I am not going to apologise for that. Peter did not read the intro. I say to Peter, 'Oh, we can be a little more sympathetic to Reg. Psychologists have identified some one hundred and seventy cognitive biases, so when he goes to see his therapist, she will probably say to him, "It's not your fault, Reg", and then he will cry.

'A good number of those cognitive biases reflect the composition and divisional fallacies. They are called cognitive biases because they are unavoidable. We must learn intellectual techniques to recognise them and deal with them. That includes you and me and Reg of course. We are naturally inclined to make these mistakes in reasoning. Also, our language leads us astray, especially when we interpret statistics.'

Peter becomes a little defensive. 'Look, I can see how Reg was stupid, but not everybody is. I don't have that problem.'

I try and keep the focus on Reg for a while longer. 'Of course, Reg is an overconfident idiot, but remember the headline of the report he used? This was from a published paper. In other words, the authors wanted their customers and potential customers to read it.'

Peter has refocused. 'So you are saying they did it deliberately.'

I continue, 'Yes, and so did Reg. If you use a fallacy deliberately, it is considered a deception. You are trying to deceive your reader by making your arguments sound more convincing than it really is. In philosophy, that would call for the instant and total dismissal of all your argument. When I say instant, I mean at the point where the deception is identified. Other philosophers will not even bother reading the rest of the argument. They will, however, reprimand you in the kindest way possible.'

Peter looks pleased with himself for discovering that it is a deception to use a fallacy this way. 'I see,' he says.

I, in turn, am pleased that I don't have to explain it. 'The composition and divisional fallacies lead to all kinds of problems and, most disturbingly, prejudices like racism and gender discrimination.'

'What do you mean racism?' asks Peter.

I explain, 'You see one person of another race unlike yours do something that you judge to be unpleasant, and then you extrapolate that the entire race does that. If you then see someone else of that race, you assume they will do the unpleasant thing. But if you see somebody of your race do the same thing, then it is just that one person doing it.'

Peter is genuinely disturbed by this. 'That's awful. Who does that?'

Time to drive it home. 'You did, earlier.'

Peter looks at me in disbelief. The disbelief changes into anger. He protests, 'I am absolutely not a racist.'

I am not sure he left the door open, but I push anyway. 'Well, let's see. You earlier endorsed Trump for his racism, didn't you, on the Mexican thing.'

Peter sits upright and pushes his chest out now. He opens his hands and holds them up in mock disbelief. 'How is that racist?' His is more of a statement than a question.

I decide it is a question, and I answer it, 'Trump recounted a story about a Mexican immigrant who raped a white student, didn't he?'

'Yes,' says Peter, and then he insists, 'so the rape case is true.' In doing this, Peter offers an opportunity to go in a different direction—a direction where we dispute the facts about the rape case. I am not able to dispute the facts of the case as I have none, but I am determined to keep the dialogue conceptual and not conventional.

I avoid his offer to go down that rabbit hole, and instead I say, 'That may be so, but then Trump extrapolates from that that all Mexicans who come to the US are rapists and criminals.'

Silence.

I press the point. 'Didn't he?' I don't wait for an answer. 'Do you see how Trump has used the composition fallacy to strengthen his argument for building a wall?'

Peter backs down. 'I see that now, yes. Yes, but he also said, "Some Mexicans are good people."'

That is true, so I agree. 'Sure, but that is another bias at work called the anchor bias. Also, it reveals something about what else Trump is doing.'

Peter has recovered his curiosity. 'What do you mean by anchor bias?'

I offer an explanation. 'We tend to put more weight on the first fact we hear. The first fact expressed by Trump is that Mexicans are rapists and murderers. That sticks to the mind. Trump first deliberately and knowingly used the composition fallacy. He is deliberately deceiving the audience.'

Silence.

Time for the home run. 'Including you.'

Silence.

I try another home run. 'Trump then does a backtrack, saying that "some Mexicans are good people, I don't know". He does that so he can deny making the fallacious statement if challenged, but who is going to challenge him when he is on stage? The fact that he backtracks in an almost dismissive way does not undo the first fact he offered. You are being deceived, and you have completely failed to spot the fallacy. Shame on you, Peter.'

Silence.

He submits, 'Shit, that is embarrassing. Upon reflection, am I right in thinking Trump does this all the time? He does, doesn't he?' I think Peter does a double take because he sees the answer in my eyes.

Time to rescue Peter. 'He is a master of deception using the composition fallacy.'

Poor Peter. 'Fuck.'

I cannot recall Peter ever swearing, so is this a sea change moment for him?

Peter's gaze fixes on the table, head tilted slightly down. He is angry. 'I have been stupid. I feel violated, intellectually abused.' I am surprised at the dramatics from Peter. He is clearly upset and emotional. I have an obvious response, but it may not be appropriate considering Peter's mood.

Instead, I console him some more. 'It is not your fault Peter. You were defenceless against a master of deception because you were never taught about these fallacies.'

Peter looks up. He sees the opening I offered and takes me up on it. 'Is this a new thing, this composition fallacy or cognitive biases stuff?' He shifts around now, like an embattled teenager whose father just caught him smoking behind the garden shed.

But he now has my sympathy. 'No, I am afraid not. This is probably going to upset you more, Peter, but Aristotle first revealed this error in reasoning some two thousand five hundred years ago, along with the divisional fallacy and some eleven or so others. He called it *Sophistical Refutations*. Wikipedia has a reasonable explanation, but be careful as people are tampering with it all the time. Best to study the original.'

Seeking to blame someone else, Peter asks, 'Why are we not taught about this at school?'

I state the obvious, 'I don't know, but you can teach your children and everyone you know.'

> That some reasonings are really reasonings, but that others seem to be, but are not really reasonings, is obvious.
>
> *Aristotle*

Peter reaches for the last of his coffee and speaks, 'It is obvious to me now, and I am angry. If I think of the decisions I made whilst being deceived, it embarrasses me. But what is more worrying is, he has made idiots of all his supporters, all seventy-six million Republicans.'

'Oh, come on, Peter, they were already idiots. Trump knew that. He exploited their stupidity. He is not the only one. Populist politicians always look for ways to exploit prejudices.'

And just like that, I poke a stick at Peter's loyalty to Trump and his fellow Republicans, his tribe. All my hard work for nothing.

Peter says nothing. The look he gives me is a strong enough signal. He offers to refresh our coffees. I take it as a sign we will remain friends despite my considerable effort to destroy our friendship. I accept, and he wonders over to the barista.

While Peter is away, I have a moment to reflect on our conversation. Did I just miss an opportunity to rescue Peter from one of his tribes? Will he remain loyal to Trump? Will he remain a loyal Republican? Did I just enable some of his individuality? Don't you think it is a paradox that the political right in America claims a cornerstone of their beliefs is individual freedom when they display the opposite, kowtowing to a populist despot like Trump? Trump cries out that he is the only one who can deal with the enemies of their individual freedom, but he is its greatest threat. Time will tell.

How many of my own tribes did I reveal to Peter? He managed to control the conversation for a good while and took us down alleys and rabbit holes I probably did not want to go down. There is that thing I have about the confidently stupid white South Africans. I see now that I am wrong about that, that confidently stupid arseholes are everywhere. You don't have to be a white South African to be one. Brent is one for sure, and he is not white South African. I wonder what about my childhood makes me completely vulnerable to them. Was it really the people surrounding me? Have I lost at a battle of serotonin determined hierarchy? Or is it because my only defences are reason and reasonableness?

Of course, that must be it. My reason and reasonableness are permeable defences against assaults from the confidently stupid. Perhaps that is why it is easier for me to just move on elsewhere. But who loses the most? Me or them? We will never know.

Peter returns with two coffees and some Danishes. I am grateful for the Danishes. It makes the coffee palatable. But I am more grateful that our friendship appears to have survived our dialogue.

* * *

I look up to signal I am done. The eyes are telling me they are unimpressed.

Once again, John surprises me with his first question. 'I don't get much of a sense of the characters, Hendrik. I cannot build an image of them,' he says.

'Do you mean flat as opposed to rounded?' I ask.

'Perhaps. It depends on what you mean by flat.'

'Foster, I think it was. He made a distinction between two types of characters as they are developed by writers. Flat characters only make a brief appearance, and then they disappear. The more important a character is to the story, the more rounded they have to be,' I explain.

'So how would you go about moving from flat to rounded characters?' he asks. I find the subject fascinating, so I don't mind that John is curious about this.

'You develop a physical image of the characters, a physical description. For instance, I could have described Peter as a giant of a man, literally. He stands a good six foot ten tall, broad-shouldered, and build squarely. He moves slowly, not in a cumbersome way but in a deliberate and measured way, as if he were aware his body poses a danger to lesser people in a confined space. All but the outside world is confined space for giants. When he moves, people make way for him, so he has no problem getting to the front of the queue. I have seen people stand back and take photographs of him,' I say.

'That is quite vivid, Hendrik. Why did you not do that in the novel?' John asks.

'It would not have contributed at all to the dialogue, would it? I mean, would it have made the dialogue more interesting, would it have revealed anything about how Peter thinks, what he thinks, what tribes he belongs to? No,' I say. 'And Robert, I gave a vague description of him too, that he is physically much bigger than I am and also younger. I suppose I could have rounded out his description by saying he is one of those well-groomed Americans who moves confidently, who speaks confidently, a confidence that betrays common sense. It makes him appear athletic, but his body is carefully shaped under supervision in a gym. It makes him appear smart, but he just looks a lot smarter than he is.

'That is one of the things I can do to round out the characters, but what would that have done for the dialogues? Nothing. It would have made the characters more real. It will make them more real for Jennifer Rawlings,' I say.

'True, but you could also assemble characters by bringing in parts of different people,' he says.

'And why not add animal parts, part human part beast,' I say.

'No, that's been done Hendrik, ancient folklore,' says John joining in.

'That is good advice, John, a bit late but good advice,' I say.

'And Megsum and Amanda?'

'No, let's leave them flat. They make no further contribution. And Brent and Greg, they are flat characters in real life too,' I say.

John looks at his notes then asks, 'More quotes, Hendrik?'

After all that was said in that dialogue, that is where John goes? More literary critique?

'To emphasise the lesson, people like other people's quotes, especially from famous people. Also, I am expressing a frustration,' I offer, knowing that it is an incomplete answer.

He takes the bait. 'What frustration?'

'I am frustrated that these valuable lessons in reasoning and reasonableness have been around for thousands of years, but we don't teach our children.'

John agrees. 'Not all of them anyway.'

John's response is ambiguous. I cannot resist ambiguity. 'What do you mean? Not all the children or not all the lessons?' I do not wait for a reply. 'I am very frustrated about education in general. It looks like it is altogether wasted time. Pupils are not taught these lessons. Surely we must teach our children to reason properly. It must be more important to teach the composition and divisional fallacies than it is to teach them one plus one is two.'

John picks up on my earlier point. 'Well, exactly how much can they teach you at school? Only the fundamentals of subjects, basic skills like reading and writing. It is up to you to take it further. What do you think it means to educate someone?'

John's offer of a lesson is unexpected, but I am curious, so I take him up on the offer. 'To teach.'

He completes my half-formed answer, 'To teach how to educate yourself. It is up to you to take it further. Schools can only teach the basics. You must do the rest. Schools can teach you all the skills, but they cannot teach you curiosity. You have to do that bit yourself.'

The eyes look at me now. There is a mischievous anticipation about them. John asks, 'Are you not guilty of the composition fallacy, Hendrik?'

'What do you mean?' I ask, feigning concerned insecurity.

'You talked about how you are frustrated by education in general, but your frustration comes from not being taught how to recognise a limited number of fallacies. Not being taught a limited number of fallacies does not render all your education worthless,' he says. John smiles, which I can only describe as a smug smile. He is right of course, and I have no choice but to admit my guilt.

'You are absolutely right.' I thank him. 'Thanks, John.' I cannot help feeling a little sarcasm well up in me.

If John noticed, he decided to ignore it.

'The abuse of the composition fallacy is prolific. I think that part of the reason is that it is acceptable practice, even condoned in society,' I say.

'What do you mean condoned?' he asks.

'Take national sports teams for instance. Rugby. If the English rugby team beats the Welsh rugby team, then the whole of England celebrates, even those who don't normally bother watching the game. The whole of England goes and chants, "We beat the Welsh." I have even watched English rugby followers in Singapore go mad when this happens. That is the composition fallacy—people claiming credit for shit they haven't done. The only thing that ties them to the fifteen players on the pitch is a shared national identity. Nothing else.

'They spent the whole game in a pub somewhere getting pissed. They shouted abuse at the referee when he made a call against the English team. They pumped adrenaline at alarming rates. They got on to an emotional roller coaster for ninety minutes or however long a game of rugby takes. They did all of that without a snowball's hope in hell that it would change the outcome of the game. How irrational is that?

'You can say the same for every football club supporter or any other national team supporter. They claim credit for shit where they have made absolutely no contribution to the success of the team.'

I pause. John says nothing. I see that as an invite to go further.

'And when the Welsh beat the English at the game, then the opposite happens. The English hate people they don't even know, shout abuse at them. Bunch of sheep shaggers they call them. And lo and behold, if they find one in the street, they beat the crap out of him. That is the converse of the composition fallacy. It is the divisional fallacy at work. And all of this is considered perfectly acceptable. No. Wait. This behaviour is not just considered acceptable, the abuse of the composition fallacy is essential to sport, any sport. Without the composition fallacy, sports clubs and national teams will seize to exist. Without this irrational loyalty and support, they will have no income. No celebrity players to pay. No advertising revenue.'

I pause again. John still says nothing. The invite remains open.

'It is the foundation—'

'I don't think it is acceptable to beat someone up, and I don't think society or the law will think it acceptable either, Hendrik,' interrupts John.

I ignore John's objection and start again. 'It is the foundation of democratic systems. Fifty-one per cent of British voters voted to leave the EU. Much less than 50 per cent of eligible voters. Yet the headlines read: "Britain chooses to leave the EU." It is the composition fallacy at work, but it is acceptable because it is the law of democracy—the will of the people, tyranny of the majority, or the one that Isaiah Berlin warned us about after the Second World War, tyranny of populism.'

John has gone quiet again, no objection from him. Perhaps he is too wary now to interrupt again.

'I'll do the reflection now. In this dialogue, I recite the story of Reg to teach Peter about the composition fallacy and how he is both victim and perpetrator of it. I think the reflection is simple. We have already discussed it at length, but to summarise, the composition fallacy is the most abused cognitive bias in Western societies you can imagine. It is everywhere. It is even in our culture, sports club affiliations, nationalism, gender issues, race issues, and patriotism. The composition fallacy is tolerable and arguably has value, but it must be cautiously managed, or it will become a nasty, vulgar problem. The composition fallacy all too easily translates into tasteless prejudice, but when prejudices are deliberately exploited by politicians for personal political gain, then it takes on a nasty, sinister and dangerous vulgarity.

'The composition fallacy is the principal tool of populist politicians. I believe we discussed that at some length now. I do not need to repeat the detail that I go to in this reflection.

'You only need to look at the vulgar patriotism in English newspaper headlines. I saw a headline the other day that referred to Russians as Ruskies. The composition fallacy giving rise to pathetic vulgar patriotism transformed into racism.'

'Wasn't there more about Reg and'—John hesitates and looks at his notes—'Brent and Kristoff?' asks John.

'Yes, but that was just to show how dialogues can take unexpected detours. At times, there are new discoveries to be made. Other times, it turns into a dead end. With Peter, I don't think we made any new discoveries, so we eventually retraced our steps back to the composition fallacy.'

'Maybe not philosophically, Hendrik, but there were other revelations in there. How newer generations expect to get all their information in one hundred and sixty characters. How they try to live their lives on condensed summaries of great ideas,' says John, and he is right of course.

'Sure,' I say, 'newer generations have a mental capacity that maxes out at one hundred and sixty characters. That is why they try and live their lives by quotes, something you can conveniently fit into a tweet. But that was a distraction from the main purpose of the dialogue.

'It terrifies me when the tyranny of populism is abused by politicians like Donald and Bozo to satisfy their personal greed for power. When Bozo commands British naval gunboats to point cannons at a French fisherman, that is when I want to crawl into a hole, ashamed to be British. It is a composition fallacy followed by the divisional fallacy. Claiming shame for shit I haven't done just because I am British. And Bozo is not doing it because it is necessary to defend the modesty of Britain.

'There is absolutely no threat to the sovereignty or the security of Britain from a French fisherman discontent with arbitrary rules imposed by Britain. He is doing it because he is abusing populism to get more votes in the elections that coincidentally was on the same day. Bozo is using the composition fallacy to fuel anti-EU and anti-French sentiment. Just go and look at the popular press headlines on that and the next day. It is a sickening display of vulgar patriotism, a sickening display of national narcissism.

'They get a sniff of prejudice, and yes I include patriotism as a form of prejudice. Give them a sniff and they will tunnel through to prejudice to abuse it for political a power. It is a disgrace to human decency, reason and reasonability: a reprehensible abuse of weak minds for personal gain'.

My rant is over, so I look at John.

'Who are *they*?' asks John.

A warm red flush speeds up my neck and covers my face. Caught red-handed at my own pet hate. 'You are right, John. I committed the composition fallacy. I am embarrassed.'

He laughs. 'Don't worry, Hendrik. It is not your fault.'

I do not cry but reflect on how our language invites us to commit the intellectual crime.

'You seem a little left of centre politically,' says John.

'You have that idea only because you didn't hear me when Blair was PM,' I say.

'Just to be clear, Hendrik. The characters Peter, Brent, Kristoff, and Reg, they are not real people?' asks John.

'What can I say, John,' I say, 'there may very well be people like that, and they might even know me. So I expect someone might assume I wrote about them.'

'If they do, they could also decide you libelled them or that the novel is an intrusion of privacy,' says John. I see the concern in the eyes. The hint of tension in the pit of my stomach strengthens.

He changes the subject. 'Trump might not like it that you called him a despot, and he is certainly a prolific litigator. But if he sues you for calling him a despot, he will have to sue half the world. Still, I won't put it past him. He could see it as an opportunity to grow his base.'

'It will really help my novel sell, so I hope he does,' I say.

The vague humour provides some loosening of the grip.

There is something about the eyes that tell me they prefer it does not happen, for my sake. They also tell me there is nothing more to say on this dialogue. I have a lot more to say, but there is also a lot more to do on the novel.

MEETING LIZ

Consciousness is the brain's 'user illusion' of itself.' It feels real and important to us but it just isn't a very big deal. The brain doesn't have to understand how the brain works.

Daniel Dennett

Liz settles in next to me at the dinner table in the open-air restaurant. We are loosely affiliated friends who have developed out of meetups of Lilly's writers group. I am one of the lucky partners who gets invited. I am genuinely lucky; there is always great enjoyment to gain from these dinners. Writers are almost inevitably interesting people to talk to.

Being with a group of writers is like being thrown into a snake pit. They don't suffer fools gladly. It puts you in a state of high alert, and you must behave. No sudden movements, but it is no fun if you don't tease the snakes every now and again. There are no explicit rules to an invitation, but I have seen people uninvited when they become unpleasant and confrontational. That is when the snakes strike. It served as a warning.

This time, the restaurant was picked because it offers a good selection of vegetarian dishes. I am not vegetarian, not completely anyway, but more and more of our friends are, perhaps more and more people around the world are. And if I pay any attention to what Lilly and my doctor says I should be too.

You may consider this a tribe, but it is a tribe with an exceedingly weak hold on writers. Writers know all too well how difficult it is to give form to a character. Once you have done it, you don't want to hand it over to a tribe, ever.

We order drinks, and they arrive quickly. No one is in a hurry to order food. This is a leisurely affair that can take the whole evening.

'What have you been up to, Liz?' I ask. Getting to the point with Liz is easy. She is always up to something anyway, so it is a safe question to get the evening going. She fixes her ridiculously golden eyes on mine. That is their only distinguishing feature, or you may also describe them as quite small eyes for a woman.

'I met with my philosophy group to discuss whether artificial intelligence machines will develop consciousness,' she says.

'Oh, interesting. Did you reach a conclusion?' I ask.

'Not sure. There were lots of disagreements. What do you think?' She returns the compliment, not that it is a compliment of course. Asking a question is not necessarily a compliment. She asks a question.

I deliberately take a few seconds, having a sip of my wine. This is a perfect opportunity to tease the snake. 'I am not sure the question has any merit.'

Liz sits upright, but not in an abrupt way. She moves like a martial arts master, not yoga. Yoga is too submissive, too sleepy. More like a tai chi master—combative, precise, deliberate, and alert. Her thin lips have pressed even thinner. My response clearly takes her by surprise. I don't think she expected me to question the question. 'What! What do you mean?' She has turned her head, and her eyes are steadfastly focused on mine.

I shake my head in mock surprise at the challenge. 'Just that. It is a question without merit.' Her eyes track mine precisely.

'That is not enough. You can't just say the question has no merit. You owe me an explanation,' says Liz, asserting herself.

I decide to take the long way round to an explanation. There is wine on the table, and the snake is provoked, so why not? 'How would you know if a machine has developed consciousness?'

Liz looks momentarily confused. 'Well, that was the whole purpose of the discussion in the philosophy group, the Turing test. Do you know the Turing test?' She has turned slightly towards me. The challenge is now also in her body language.

'I know the Turing test, but look,' I say, 'I am not sure it will prove anything beyond the most familiar aspect of consciousness,'

'What do you mean by the most familiar?' She asks, her eyes relentlessly fixed on mine.

'I assume we all experience the familiarity of consciousness, to be awake, to respond to the environment. To react to pain. You may also call it sentience; to be a sentient creature,' I explain.

'That will also include animals.' she says in what seems like an objection.

'Yes, and perhaps machines, although I am sure ethical vegetarians will disagree with my inclusion of machines in sentient. That is what cybernetics is all about. Machines and animals regulated through information. That is what the Turing test measures,' I say.

'Are you saying that to be able to respond to a question is a sentient response?' She asks and tilts her head.

'I think I am, and here is why. You may want to look at John Searle who I think successfully claims that algorithmic linear processing can never be conscious. He writes about having a sealed box with a person inside that has no knowledge of mandarin. The box has two openings. People insert a paper with a mandarin symbol printed on one side. The person inside the box takes the paper from the slot and looks up the symbol in a table. Once he finds it, he picks the corresponding symbol from a pile of paper and insert the paper into the exit slot. The person outside thinks the sealed box passes the Turing Test. That it has consciousness, that it has interpreted a symbol and provided the correct answer. But the person inside the box has no idea of what is going on.'

'Wow,' says Liz, 'that really drives it home. Turing's test can be deceived altogether too easily.'

'There are certainly some philosophers that argue that machines can never be conscious,' I say.

'Why is that?'

'There are aspects of consciousness that are more perplexing, more difficult to get to grips with.' I answer.

'Like what?' She asks alert and tracking.

'I know I am conscious. I think therefore I am.' I thought I would throw in a bit of Cartesian humour even though I am sure that is not a test for consciousness either.

'So?' She does a little laugh. 'So do I. I know that you are conscious. Are you not stating the obvious here?' Her eyes never leave mine.

I expand just enough to lead the conversation. 'I am pleased you think I am conscious.' I pause for a few seconds. It is the kind of pause that signals there is a 'but'.

She anticipates it. 'But?'

I complete the sentence and quench her anticipation. 'But I am not sure at all that you are conscious. As far as I know, I am the only person in the world that is conscious.' I complete the sentence.

Liz turns her head and speaks, 'Oh, come on. Isn't that a bit narcissistic? Surely you must accept that other people are conscious too.'

'Solipsism I think it is called. But I am trying to illustrate a point. Of course, I accept that other people are conscious and have consciousness. But that is not good enough as a test,' I tell her. 'I, of course, have a theory that you and other people have a mind. What you are, your behaviour, and what you say are similar enough to what I am and how I behave and so convincing enough. It is reasonable to come to the conclusion that you have a mind and that you are conscious. But think for a minute. I have nothing to go by to confirm you are conscious. For all I know, you are an artificial intelligence robot with a squidgy body that have been programmed to simulate consciousness.'

She says nothing, but she moves her head from side to side, just a fraction. I realise it must be the reference to squidgy body, so I press on to distract her. 'That is not at all the same thing as having consciousness. To be able to confirm your consciousness, I must come up with a standard test for consciousness.'

Liz recovers enough to respond. 'That's funny, but I can assure you I have a mind and consciousness,' she says in her defence, 'and my body is not as squidgy as you might think.' Her eyes track again.

I continue, 'I am going to take your word for it because I cannot find enough reason to confirm or deny your consciousness. The only consciousness I am directly aware of is my own. It is a slippery thing. When I try and examine my consciousness, it looks like it is fixated on the question "What is consciousness?" And then it slips between trying to answer the question and getting stuck on the question. Even if I can come up with a standard test of what consciousness is, I can probably do no better than Descartes. I think therefore I am. Perhaps I can call on Jean-Paul Sartre to help. He claimed that "my thought is me: that's why I can't stop. I exist because I think . . . and I can't stop myself from thinking."'

She sits back a little but remain superbly alert. 'Isn't that a good enough test?'

I do not, so I say so, 'Well, no. Because how do I know that you are thinking or any other person thinks? How do I know that you are not simply programmed to come up with the perfect answer or response? Even if I ask you, you might respond by saying, "I think therefore I am." Of course, that is a response that is programmable. In fact, how do I know that I have not been programmed to respond that way?

'We have already agreed for you to pass the Turing test, to fool me that you are conscious, is no guarantee that you are. There is something more going on here. It is called intentionality and meaning,' I say.

'What do you mean by meaning? She asks.

'That words have meaning, life has meaning. Searle clearly demonstrated that logarithmic processing could come up with answers, but that the box, even the person in the box has no idea of the meaning of the symbols. Intentionality is also difficult; intentionality means that we have a certain attitude to things. The colour red for instance. You might have a certain attitude to the colour red that is different from mine. I have no idea what it is like to be you,' I say.

Liz laughs gently. The eyes never leave mine. 'Oh my god. You do not want to know what it is like to be me. You do not know what I get up to.' Liz winks.

'That is why I said I have no idea what it is like to be you. How do we test for meaning and intentionality in a machine? I still do not have a standard test for consciousness. And if I do not have a standard test for consciousness in other people what is the merit in trying to understand if an artificial intelligence machine is conscious. I have no idea what it is like to be you. And there is more. Having consciousness in the human sense also mean to be able to think about what we are thinking. To be aware that we are aware. That is what Descartes and Sartre wanted to tell us. That is how we know we are alive.'

'What do you mean to be aware that we are aware? She asks.

'The one that can think about what you are thinking about. The one that is in charge, the master of your mind,' I say.

'The master?'

'That is right, the one that says I will not think about this, or I will think about this. Or when an unwelcome thought, memory or emotion twitches it says, "Oh hello old friend, now fuck-off.",' I say.

She laughs, 'If only it was that easy'.

'I know. But there is always mindfulness; the superpower of the master. Also, one must get to know one's old friends before you tell them to fuck off. And sometimes one needs professional help, but even then, one must always strive to become the master.'

'The master,' says Liz to herself.

'The one that says there is no merit in this question,' I say.

'We should have had you at the meetup. You would have saved us a lot of time,' says Liz.

'Well, maybe,' I say, 'or hopefully, somebody can come up with a standard test for consciousness that is better than Turing's. It is a topic that receives considerable attention from philosophers. It is considered the hard question of philosophy: "What is consciousness?" Only when we can answer the hard question can we move to a question like "Is an artificial intelligence machine conscious?" Until then, the question "Is a machine conscious?" has little merit.

'Engineers are developing neuron-based silicon computers that are a lot more promising. These computers perform much the same way as human brains. The silicon neurons build connections through learning. Perhaps one day we will say they are conscious. That is a long way off though. So far, engineers have only managed to build machines with some two thousand silicon neurons. The human brain has an estimated nine billion with twenty thousand connections between each,' I say to Liz. She goes quiet. Her body turns away from mine, and the eyes stop tracking me. She sits back completely in her chair.

I totally misread her silence as encouragement to offer her some more wisdoms. 'Other philosophers like Dennett thinks that consciousness in machines is at least conceivable and that it is less of a mystery than some would make. You may also find he ridicules some of the more outlandish ideas that consciousness is epiphenomenal, that somehow it arises from our brains.

'Whatever we theorise, we will not move beyond our current understanding of consciousness until we can examine it in other people. We will need a lot more scientific advance before we can do that. By the time science can examine consciousness, the question might no longer be important.'

Liz has nothing more to say. The snake has gone back into the basket. It has lost interest. She starts a conversation with someone else.

I was probably hoping for more of an acknowledgement of my understanding of the subject. It is not forthcoming, and I am disappointed.

* * *

The eyes cannot be bothered to signal anything.

'I have never given much thought to this problem, Hendrik, But I am impressed,' says John. There is something disingenuous about that statement, some indifference in the voice. An insincere attempt to console me. 'I can see she disappointed you, but how much time do you think she spent discussing this with her fellow philosophers?'

I am somewhat confused by the line of questioning, not sure that it has anything to do with the letter. But I answer anyway. 'It was an all-day event.'

'And how long did the conversation with you take?' asks John.

'Perhaps twenty minutes, but probably less.'

'Then perhaps she felt that she wasted a day with them doing something she could have done in twenty minutes with you,' judges John.

'A day of philosophising is never a waste of time, John,' rebuke I.

The eyes tell me I'm out of order.

'Anyway,' I say, 'I think it has more to do with the way I handled the conversation. Liz wants to discover, not be lectured. I lectured, showed off. If I let her ask questions, then she would have discovered the answers herself. Perhaps then I would have held her attention for longer,' I say.

'I see,' says John, 'but how would you know?'

'I created the character, John, so I should know what is going on in her head,' I say, grinning smugly. 'Maybe I know someone like the character I created.'

John fixes his gaze on me for a while and then says, 'I am having difficulty establishing exactly where your characters end and where the real people begin, Hendrik. That is a problem for us both.'

'Who knows where that line is, John? Where would I go for my characters other than the shadows of the people I already know?' I am being a little high-minded, but I am fully aware of it.

John doesn't let me get away with it. 'The people behind this letter are real, Hendrik, not a figment of your imagination.' As he says that, he rattles the letter vigorously. The noise makes me sit up, alert to the threat. 'There is one exceptionally specific individual being accused here—you. That is how the law works. There are also specific individuals doing the accusing. We must find out who. I cannot defend you against a vague shape or form. The justice system does not do that.'

I decide to change the subject to rescue myself. 'In the reflection of the dialogue with Liz, we explore another case where people spend an extraordinary amount of intellectual capital discussing something for hours, but they never question the question. In this case, the question has little merit. There are no other glaring fallacies in Liz's approach. So I suppose there is little work to do in the reflection.

'There may also be a lesson in the dialogue for would-be philosophical counsellors. Do not lecture. Lecturing is showing off. No one likes a smart-arse. Having said all of that, I think philosophy groups are great for instilling into people the desire to think and the opportunity to exercise the thinking muscle. People who want to do this may also want to get the pocket guide on fallacies or indeed guides on how to have a Socratic dialogue. If you cannot find one of those, then ask a philosophical practitioner to lead the dialogue.'

John nods. I am not sure whether he means for me to continue or whether he agrees that no one likes a smart-arse.

John's indifference makes me feel completely inadequate as an ordinary philosopher, deflated even. A person unworthy of a conversation with a prestigious lawyer. Is this the dialogue I should have edited out? The darlings Lilly said I should kill off. Too late now. My only hope lies in a future dialogue that sparks his interest. Also I sense he is deeply frustrated by my willingness to dance around the characters.

I don't wait for instructions; I continue to the next dialogue.

DRINKS WITH KRISTOFF

There's nothing to mourn about death any more than there is to mourn about the growing of a flower. What is terrible is not death but the lives people live or don't live up until their death. They don't honor their own lives, they piss on their lives. They shit them away. Dumb fuckers. They concentrate too much on fucking, movies, money, family, fucking. Their minds are full of cotton. They swallow God without thinking, they swallow country without thinking. Soon they forget how to think, they let others think for them. Their brains are stuffed with cotton. They look ugly, they talk ugly, they walk ugly. Play them the great music of the centuries and they can't hear it. Most people's deaths are a sham. There's nothing left to die.

Charles Bukowski

We have settled down for an evening in a riverside pub. By we, I mean friends from years of working together, those rare colleagues who remain in contact despite your past differences, failed competitions, and awkward corporate hierarchies. The weather is the usual balmy thirty-two degrees despite it already being eight in the evening. This stretch of the riverbank is a popular drinking and dining spot for city workers.

It is in the shadows of gleamy office towers, a few hundred yards away. Those world-famous symbols of American disaster capitalism. The global financial institutions driven by greed that caused the 2008 financial crisis, rescued by ordinary workers only for the ordinary workers to be taxed and screwed again. *Why do people create an economic system like that? What kind of people create an economic system like that? The system is not naturally there. It is entirely a human construct. The theory came first then the system.* I contemplate all this quietly.

I dare not do any of this out loud. I am surrounded by the system's warriors. I don't bother to find an answer either. I know the answer already, but knowing the answer does not make it any more rational. People have moved on, the rescue done and dusted, and the system back to its old filthy habits.

The riverbank is protected from the city developers. It is the old Singapore. Shop houses have been converted into bars and restaurants. The narrow streets place it in sharp contrast with the twenty-first-century tower blocks run by a certain tribe. That tribe being the business. Like Megsum and Amanda, remember? The individual characters migrate from their homes and hotels in the mornings to join the rest of the tribe in the tower blocks. In the evenings, the individual characters migrate here to escape that tribe only to meet up with a different tribe. The different tribe in the old Singapore seduces the individual character into a false escape. But the escape is temporary and into a bottle. All too soon, the individual character is liquefied by the very thing it uses to escape the tribe. Late at night, some caring person pours the liquefied character into a taxi which takes them home, but not before the liquefied character has spilled the beans about what is going on in the city tribe to the servant tribe. The next day, the process repeats. First, there is the migration, then the escape, then the liquification, then the spilling of beans, and finally, the pouring. I wonder what Bukowski will say about this.

The old Singapore looks up at the new Singapore who looks down at it, like a servant looking up at the master and the master looking down at the servant. In a tragic paradox, the old Singapore is protected from the new Singapore but is placed into servitude. Protected for now, but a servant to the city tribe nevertheless. Inconveniently the servant knows everything that is wrong in the master's house.

I see Kristoff approaching from the direction of the city. He reminds me of a retired middleweight boxer in his mid forties. He has that sinewy strength, the remnants of a fitness from years of intense training. His movement is all in his footwork. Quick steps, but shockingly efficient. Kristoff was never a boxer, a fact that is belied by his face. He looks like he could have been. Small alert eyes, but the constant weaving, ducking, and diving of his head can be quite distracting, even though it is very subtle. You learn soon enough not to keep eye contact for too long. It makes you quite dizzy. If you are not taken down by the dizziness, then you get drowned in the bluish blackness of the deep-set eyes.

He greets us with his usual abundant affection. It is genuine affection. He hugs the women gently. Lilly gets an extra gentle hug. With Lilly he lingers longer. Longer than the others.

The men, less so. A bear hug I think they call it. Stiff upper body and a safe distance at the groin level. A hard tap on the back with open palms. Quick, perfunctory, and hopefully no one notices the affection. It is a peculiar thing about him. He carries his heart on his sleeve when it comes to friendships.

Make no mistake though. Kristoff fits perfectly into the tribe of the corporate world a few hundred meters away. He totally buys into Adam Smith's self-interest theory of the free market. Kristoff, though, has taken the principle of working in his self-interest to the next level, no, to the highest level possible. The ruthless level. He will stop at nothing to win, even destroy the efforts of his colleagues if that is what it takes, all in the notion that everyone works in their self-interest. Kristoff is constantly on the lookout for number 1.

We settle down with drinks, and the conversations start up. Kristoff and I talk about the COVID-19 pandemic. What do you expect? We are in the middle of the pandemic; you cannot avoid talking about it.

After a while, it occurs to me that Kristoff believes in the conspiracy that China somehow deliberately released the virus. I am shocked, of course, but I shouldn't be surprised.

> Be discriminating about what images and ideas you permit into your mind. If you yourself don't choose what thoughts and images you expose yourself to, someone else will, and their motives may not be the highest.

> *Epictetus*

I challenge Kristoff, 'You cannot be serious. You believe that China deliberately released the virus? Why would they do that?'

Kristoff does not hesitate. He has the answer ready. 'Simple reason, they want to overtake the USA as the biggest economy in the world.'

I refine my question. 'That is not what I am asking. It takes one person to release a virus. You are accusing the whole of China, almost one and a half billion people, of doing it. That cannot be right.'

'It happened in China. China. That is why it is China's fault.' Kristoff repeats China just like that, as if repeating it will make it more true.

'Sorry, Kristoff. You cannot blame all of China's population for the mistake or deliberate act of one person. That appears a bit racist to me. It is also a grotesque failure of reasoning.'

Kristoff ignores my objection. It is a missed opportunity to show him the composition fallacy. But that is the way it goes sometimes.

'The virus started in Wuhan. The Chinese also has a lab there researching viruses. You can put two and two together.'

'What do you mean the Chinese has a lab there? Do you mean all of China? All the Chinese?' I ask. But predictably, he does not pick up on the composition fallacy. I decide to test his theory instead. 'But that could just be a coincidence,' I say.

'Coincidence my arse. The virus is first seen in the same city where they research viruses. That is more meaningful than a simple coincidence,' explains Kristoff.

Do you see the abuse of 'they' in what Kristoff says? By going vague, he insinuates there is someone or some many people involved in a sinister plot.

'The problem is that you are providing the meaning between the two facts, Kristoff. I am worried about that meaning. It seems like an irrational suspicion of all Chinese people. It also seems to me that it will be incredibly stupid for someone in the lab to deliberately release a virus on their own doorstep,' I challenge.

'Synchronicity, Hendrik. Have you ever heard of synchronicity? That some events have meaningful coincidences?' Kristoff challenges back. I am a bit frustrated at the detour, but that is how it goes with Kristoff.

'Carl Yung,' I say.

'Who?' asks Kristoff.

'Carl Yung is the arsehole who came up with the idea of synchronicity,' I say.

'So what!' is all that Kristoff has. Oh, and a noticeable ducking to the left, more pronounced than the constant weaving of the head. But then he adds, 'What is wrong with synchronicity?'

'Yung was trying to explain how people form meanings between two completely unconnected events. You are interpreting synchronicity as an actual connection between two unconnected events or facts. Yung's idea of synchronicity is abused a lot, mostly as proofs of alternative facts and conspiracy theories. If you provide the meaning between two unconnected events, then those events are only connected in your head. In other words, it is bullshit.

'The problem with synchronicity is that you provide the meaning. That means you are looking for evidence to support your theory, not build a theory from the evidence you see. The coincidence is not evidence at all,' I say. Kristoff says nothing. He seems to have moved back out of reach. He clearly has no appetite to argue with me on that point. I move forward.

'Let's get back to the economic reasons for releasing the virus. China's economy will overtake the USA anyway. There is nothing the

USA can do about it, short of blockading China. And if the USA does that, then what happened to the great American ideal of free and fair competition? If this is going to happen anyway and if China was going to release the virus, why infect their own people?' I ask.

My question irritates Kristoff. He has clearly not thought through his theory well enough. He quickly makes an adjustment and stands his ground. 'This way, they will do it sooner, and they infect their own people so that they can hide the fact they leaked the virus. Simple really, a typical Chinese deception.'

There is a rapid combination of new facts in there. I pretend being taken aback but move forward again and deliver my own rapid combination of facts. 'Really, Kristoff, almost one and a half billion Chinese conspiring as one? And gosh, don't you think that is a risky thing to do? And how do you know it will spread to the rest of the world?'

Kristoff makes up more new detail on the fly now. You must admire his agility to come up with bullshit just like that, another rapid-fire combination. 'Well, they tried to hide the fact the virus was spreading in Wuhan City. You know that. They silenced the doctor who blogged about it, denied its existence. They were making sure that it infects visiting foreigners first before they acted. Why do you think they could build those hospitals in record time? Answer that question.' Kristoff's defence turns into a late challenge.

I have forgotten to tell you something else about Kristoff. He has this uncanny ability to shift his attitude in a mercurial instant. From the warm, heartfelt affection to outright aggression in the blink of an eye. I imagine it serves him well in the tribe. It must be beneficial to some serotonin-driven hierarchy.

I try to match his combination with a probing question. 'Another meaningful coincidence, Kristoff. It is not evidence at all. But let me understand this. The Chinese releases a virus into their own population with the hope that it will spread to visiting foreigners to take into the wider world and hopefully the USA, all for achieving global economic superiority over the USA, which they are destined to become anyway?'

'That's right,' blocks Kristoff.

I reiterate a point, 'Isn't the Chinese economy destined to overtake the US economy anyway?'

Kristoff is ready with an answer. 'Yes, but this way, they will achieve it much quicker.'

You must have noticed that we are circulating around the same problem now. Typical when you deal with conspiracy theorists. They recycle already discussed points. I back down a little to see if I can get Kristoff to make a mercurial shift back to a reasonable state of mind. 'Wow, it seems to me that they are taking a huge risk by infecting their own people first to try and achieve something that the Chinese economy will do anyway.'

The mercury wobbles in the same place. Kristoff digs his heals in. 'That's right.'

I nudge him a little harder. 'I am not sure you understand.'

Big mistake on my side. Kristoff now leans forward; he stares down at the table, straight into his half-empty beer. His right foot is drumming the floor, and he looks like he wants to get up and punch me right there and then.

I back off a little again. 'I am sorry, Kristoff, but it doesn't make sense that China would effectively damage its own economy to also damage all economies around the world so it comes out on top. This is particularly true if you think how dependent China is on global trade.'

Kristoff fights back with a new fact. 'Just look at the Chinese economy, Hendrik. It is the only major economy that has grown at all during the pandemic.'

'Don't you think that has more to do with the way the Chinese government responded to the pandemic?' I ask. 'A complete and severe lockdown for some six to eight weeks to get the spread of the virus under control and then a gradual controlled opening up.' I summarise in a combination of my own.

'Exactly, that just proves the point, Hendrik,' says Kristoff. I thought he was going to bang his fist on the table to emphasise the point, but he must have changed his mind. 'They were prepared to respond to the virus because they planned its release.'

I counter by recycling a previous objection, 'It sounds to me like a really big risk to release the virus on China's own population.'

Kristoff comes back strongly. 'The Chinese government doesn't care a fig about its own people, Hendrik. They will happily sacrifice a few thousand for world domination. History shows that governments will happily sacrifice their own citizens to achieve their ends. Why would the Chinese be different?'

I do not have a comeback on that one. Tragically, it is true that most governments don't care a fig about sacrificing their own people. They will let the bodies pile high and people die by the thousands. I concede the point and move on to another objection.

'But they could not have known how many people in China would be infected. It could have swept through the whole nation. Also, they could not have known who would be infected. It could have killed off the leadership. In other words, they could not have known that a complete lockdown would have been so effective compared to what happened in Western countries,' I deliver another combination of my own.

Kristoff goes from the sublime to the ridiculous. 'Of course, they could. They practised it before with SARS and other viruses. They also created the virus, so they knew exactly what it is capable off. The whole world knows how to deal with a virus outbreak.'

I am ready for this one. 'If the whole world knows how to deal with a virus outbreak, then why did the West get it so wrong? Surely the West would have known that a complete lockdown is the only way to suppress the virus, lessons learned from the Spanish flu and SARS and MARS, lessons learned from the bubonic plague some eight hundred years ago. The village of Eyam in Yorkshire proved it. No one can and no prime minister can claim they are dealing with an entirely new problem.'

My counter has had no effect on Kristoff. He says, 'Precisely, Hendrik. It just shows that China prepared in advance for releasing the virus.'

What! I did that in my head of course. The temperature was already too high around the table.

I repeat to make sure I understand, 'So what you are saying is that COVID-19 is some kind of biological war so that China can become the dominant economy in the world.'

This appears to please Kristoff. 'Exactly. That is exactly what I am saying.'

It doesn't please me, and I say so. 'It doesn't make sense to me. If China prepared in advance for the virus, they could have done it out of prudence. If they had done it with the view of gaining global dominance, they would have had to know in advance that the Western world will respond dismally to the outbreak in ignorance of lessons learned from previous pandemics.'

Kristoff changes tactic. 'I cannot believe you, Hendrik. You are defending the Chinese Communist Party? You are taking sides with them rather than the free world!'

I become a little defensive about Kristoff's whataboutism. 'You are going too far, Kristoff. Defending the Chinese government's handling of the pandemic is not the same thing and does not transfer to a defence of how they treat the Uighurs or what they are doing in Hong Kong. This is about the conspiracy theory that the Chinese government deliberately spread the virus to become the dominant global economy. There is no moral equivalence. What you are doing is just vulgar whataboutism. So let's stick to this one issue. We can agree on the other issues later.'

Kristoff sees an apparent weakness and aims for it. 'All of which means you cannot trust the Chinese. So why would you trust them not to have released the virus? Hey! Hey! Answer that!'

I have another attempt at instilling some calm in the conversation. 'Which is what I am trying to do. I want to understand your theory first. It appears that the Chinese preparation to deal with the virus comes from lessons learned and not because of some devious plan to start a biological war. If you start a biological war, you also prepare an antidote for the pathogen. That is the general idea anyway. Which means that the Chinese would have had to develop a vaccine beforehand and would have had to vaccinate their entire population before releasing the virus. Also, it would have been a simpler, less risky business to release the virus into some Western city rather than hope it travels there by itself.'

Kristoff does not concede a point that easily. He explores a previous weakness. 'How do we know that the Chinese success is down to lockdown? Hey!'

Kristoff is doing some rapid footwork under the table. He is again staring into his half beer. The aggression is palpable now. It fills the air.

He tries a wild hook. 'Well, you cannot prove my theory wrong, just like you cannot prove God doesn't exist.'

> Sometimes people don't want to hear the truth because
> they don't want their illusions destroyed.
>
> *Friedrich Nietzsche*

For a second, I feel like conceding the match. Instead, I deliver a direct rebuke, 'If you think I am trying to prove your theory wrong, then you are mistaken. I am trying to help you prove it is true, and so far, we are not getting there. It is your theory, so you must prove it true, just like if you believe in the existence of God. It is up to you to prove it. It is not my job to prove your theory false. To prove something false, one must first assume it is true. I am not going to do that. So I am just pointing at the failures of your theory. You are failing to convince me.'

Kristoff answers abruptly, 'Piss off.' He moves to retreat into his corner, signalling that the dialogue is over.

I try to placate him. 'Look, Kristoff, the only thing we have proven so far as to make your theory work is, it has become incredibly complex. Is there a simpler theory for the virus? Yes, viruses jump species all the time. That is the most likely explanation for this one. That it jumped species too. It is a much simpler explanation than some conspiracy theory that involves a whole country of almost one and a half billion people, not to speak of the other countries that dealt with the virus in the same effective way.'

Kristoff says, 'Just piss off!' He retreats completely into his corner, goes on to a pronounced sulk, and I think it is better to move on to a conversation with someone else.

> If an opinion contrary to your own makes you angry, that is a sign that you are subconsciously aware of having no good reason for thinking as you do.
>
> *Bertrand Russell*

No other conversation is available. So I try and soften the blow to Kristoff. 'Look, there is a possibility that you are right. But a possibility is not the same thing as a probability. A possibility is no proof that somehow the virus has escaped the research institution. For there to be proof, there must be physical evidence that goes beyond meaningful coincidence. And if it did happen, then that physical evidence will exist.

'I expect all known viruses are DNA sequenced. And typically, that DNA sequencing is shared between research institutions. It is inconceivable that there won't be a DNA record within a research institute that does research using DNA. Therefore, one can safely assume that those DNA records exist for all viruses in the lab before the outbreak. If a match is found, then you will have a reasonable claim to the theory that the virus escaped the lab. But that does not provide any substance for your claim that there is a conspiracy. If you don't have any physical evidence for the conspiracy, then it will be pure speculation. If you want to prove the conspiracy, then your job will be to find evidence of that conspiracy by the Chinese government.'

Kristoff will not come out of his corner. He says, 'Why will you not just piss off and leave me alone?'

The threat is clear; I leave him alone.

* * *

'What do you mean by American disaster capitalism?' asks John, sensing correctly that I am at the end of the dialogue.

It never seizes to amaze me how people are wired. How did John go there after all the things I discussed in the dialogue? 'It means deregulated capitalism, the kind of capitalism that right-leaning Americans promote. It is quite bizarre. Corporations are legal persons much like natural persons. You know this.' John nods. 'But in disaster capitalism, the legal person enjoys more freedom than a natural person. That means in business, everything goes. The legal person can do things the natural person cannot do. Sell harmful products like cigarettes, opioid-based painkillers, unsafe cars and aircraft, and dangerous buildings. Legal persons can even treat natural persons with utter contempt. Tragically, it is natural persons who provide the character of the legal person. Therefore, it is natural persons with bad characters doing it to other natural persons.'

'What do you mean by that?' John asks.

I am genuinely confused, so I seek clarity. 'By treating natural persons with utter contempt?' I ask.

John nods.

I explain, 'Just look at some of the harmful employment practices, inhumane long hours, or zero-hour contracts. Furthermore, think of poverty-level compensation packages. And there is more. Think of child labour, servitude, and even enslavement. Without legislation to stop these, the legal person can do what it wants. "The business" can do what it wants.'

'You seem to have a habit of doing air quotes every time you mention "the business", Hendrik,' says John and does the air quotes around 'the business'.

I see irony in that, but I say, 'It's a bad habit.'

'It would be interesting if you expanded on that in the dialogue, Hendrik,' says John.

'It is in my other book, John,' I say.

'You have chosen an extremely sensitive subject for this dialogue, Hendrik. You may have been a bit too adventurous. There is still a lot of doubt on the origin of the virus. I can imagine that you will make a lot of enemies in the West or in China or maybe even both,' says John.

'Strange. On the one side, I am accused of defending China with a government that allegedly does unspeakable things to its citizens. I suppose that they would like to silence me, not perpetuate a story they would rather not want to have to deny. On the other side, I have kept an open mind about the ongoing investigation. My issue is with the composition fallacy—blaming all of China for the accident, mistake, or deliberate action of a few,' I say.

'And you make the West and notably the USA look stupid,' adds John.

'I refuse to take credit for that, John. Western governments by and large screwed up because they were more interested in not interfering with the individual freedom of their citizens, were not willing to take the economic hit from doing the right thing—lock down hard at the very beginning of the outbreak. They assume that individual freedom guarantees individual accountability. That is a serious flaw in the principle of individual freedom.

'This will all become apparent when they do their lessons learned exercises to placate the families who have lost loved ones. Lessons learned? For Christ's sake, did they not learn lessons from MARS and SARS and the bubonic plague and the Spanish flu? And I can go on and on. Utter stupidity. No, I will not take credit for making them look stupid, and it is not the West or the USA.

'It is Donald and Bozo and whoever oversees the EU countries. Stupid populist leadership who would rather see the bodies pile high by their thousands than act on the lessons learned over hundreds of years. And lessons learned this time? Forget it. Just forget it. The next pandemic will have the same impact on the West because it is more inclined to forget lessons and make the same mistakes repeatedly. They are already trying to shift responsibility to the World Health Organisation,' say I in my defence.

'Why do you think there will be no lessons learned?' asks John.

'Because everything is about politics. Everything, and it is even worse in the USA. Most Western politicians are not capable of doing unpopular things even when they are the right things to do. Western democracies work on the principle that what is true is what most people think,' I answer.

'Rant over?' asks John. What can I do but nod? I nod.

'Except I should point out that some Western leaders learned from the past or at least looked at the past lessons when the pandemic hit and did the right thing. New Zealand and Australia, and arguably, Singapore,' I say.

'Are you sure Singapore can be classified as a Western country?' asks John.

'Why not? Are you suggesting Western countries are only for white Caucasians?'

'No, of course not,' remonstrates John.

'Singapore has adopted a government and a democracy that is widely based on the British system of parliamentary government. I would suggest that qualifies them as a Western government,' I say, forcing the point home.

The fight has gone out of John, I think. He turns to his legal pad and makes a few notes. 'If you are right, you have just produced a counter in that not all Western governments fall fowl of the populist ideals, Hendrik,' he says.

'True enough, but I did correct my earlier claim by laying the blame at the feet of the populist leadership. I must thank you for pointing it out. I am guilty of abusing the anchor bias,' I say.

John smiles and rolls his hand in a new command for me to continue.

'There is still the reflection to do, John,' I say.

BREAKFAST WITH RICARDO

All opinions are not equal. Some are a very great deal more robust, sophisticated, and well supported in logic and argument than others.

Douglas Adams

Its early in the morning, and we have met up for breakfast at a coffee shop a block away from the river. It is one of those great independent coffee shops that have a comfy seating area where there are often people working away on laptops, having coffee with a friend, or they might prefer to spend a few hours quietly reading a book. They don't mind in the coffee shop. They are quite happy if you hang around and make the place look busy. The other half of the coffee shop is set aside for dining. It offers an all-day breakfast selection, presumably to cater for night owls where the timing of your breakfast is determined by what you got up to the night before. It also offers a decent lunch menu for ordinary philosophers.

The coffee is good, Italian, I think. It is prepared by a barista and served in a European-sized coffee cup. I would say that is the only flaw. You need a steady supply to complete a decent dialogue. I receive my coffee and remove myself and the coffee from the cafe. I take them to the designated area outside to smoke. I admit that I loved smoking, but like all sensible ordinary philosophers, you eventually accept the fact that the joy is not matched by the price you pay. The price you pay is an early death. There is more joy in living longer. Nevertheless, the combination of coffee and cigarettes is still one of the best.

When I finish both the coffee and the cigarette, I return to the cafe. Ricardo is leaning forward towards Lilly. He is clearly trying to make some point with force, a point that doesn't carry enough weight on its own, so he throws the weight of his body behind it. Ricardo is also the owner of the cafe.

Ricardo appeals to me for help. 'Hendrik, this is my cafe, and I am entitled to my opinion, am I not?'

I have no idea how the discussion progressed to this point or what the dispute is about, but it appears to have come to an impasse, an impasse Ricardo wants to break by claiming his right to an opinion and, moreover, his right to an opinion in his own cafe.

'Of course, you are, Ricardo,' I say. Ricardo beams triumphantly with self-satisfaction. Prematurely. 'But let's be clear. You are entitled to your own opinion anywhere and in your own cafe. But being entitled to an opinion does not guarantee the quality of your opinion.'

Ricardo's expression changes instantly. His eyes have become a little fixed in their sockets. He uses his body to rescue himself and sits back in his chair. He looks more comfortable this way. There is more room for his substantial girth. I am grateful to see he also sees the humour in my response. 'What?' He laughs. It is all he can muster.

'I am sure Lilly is not challenging your right to an opinion or your right to express it, particularly your right to express it in your own cafe, not that there is anything that says you don't have that right everywhere else. If anything, she is probably questioning the quality of your opinion,' I explain to him and pause.

No response. Ricardo bites down on his teeth. It makes his square jaw more pronounced. His black hair is perfectly combed. He has only a sprinkling of grey on his day-old sideburn stubble. It helps to deny his age and yet makes him distinguished. In a strange way, the combination of square jaw and dusting of grey makes him look more regal. I am beginning to worry that my explanation was discombobulated. Ricardo's eyes remain fixed in their sockets, but not in a way that suggests he is confused. More like he is mystified by what just happened.

I try to expand on my point, 'You cannot assert the quality of your opinion by claiming you have a right to one. You cannot assert the quality of your opinion by claiming ownership of the location of where you express your opinion.'

More silence.

No response from Ricardo. Lilly takes a little pleasure in his discomfort. She has an uncanny smile on her face. She is a beautiful woman, especially when she feels uncanny. That is what I think.

I press on, 'Anyway, Lilly has an equal right to an opinion, also in your cafe. Her opinion is probably that there is something about the quality of your opinion that calls out for a challenging. She is simply expressing her opinion, and if you have a right to do so, then so does she.'

More silence from Ricardo. Then he shakes his head slowly. 'Fucking cunt,' he says.

I smile to defuse any resentment he might feel. 'The quality of your opinion is determined by the quality and the effort of reasoning behind it, Ricardo.' I am driving the point home now. 'Lilly is challenging the quality of the reasoning behind your opinion. It is a good thing. If the quality of your opinion is supported by considered reasoning, you should be able to defend it based on its merit.'

Ricardo makes one more attempt. 'My right to an opinion is guaranteed by the constitution,' he asserts.

'Absolutely, the constitution guarantees your right to an opinion, but the constitution does not guarantee the quality of your opinion.'

He closes the conversation with a second forceful 'Fucking cunt.' I notice he says it with a smile, but I cannot help the rising indignation.

I am rescued at that moment when my refreshed coffee is served, and I escape outside to the designated smoking area for another cigarette. I am joined by Lilly. 'He doesn't mean it that way, Hendrik,' she says. 'The way he used it is what boys do these days. It is an expression of admiration.' She looks directly at me. Her eyes tell me that her understanding is real.

What did I expect? Did I really expect to confront unfairness, stupidity, and ignorance and not get injured, not carry away some marks to indicate that I have been in an intellectual battle? That would be naive.

* * *

'He didn't really say—' John interrupts himself. 'You didn't write—' And again. 'Of course, you did.' And then. 'Unbelievable.' And again. 'Unbelievable.'

Profanities are frowned upon in this office. If there is any doubt, look at the eyes. I say nothing. What can I say? What is done is done.

'You know that it is just an expression people use, don't you?' says John.

'Which one?' I ask, confused. I did not expect him to defend Ricardo.

'The one about having a right to an opinion,' he clarifies.

'Oh, I thought you meant the swearing,' I say, and I feel a little stupid for guessing wrong. It says something about my character, about a hidden guilt for having written it down in the first place, a twitch in response to a poking. 'Yes, I know, but it leads to a conversation down a dead end,' I say.

'What do you mean dead end?' asks John.

'It closes down the actual point of contention without resolving the tension. It is an escape,' I respond, 'and it is normally used by the person whose opinion is of poor quality.'

'What do you mean tension?' asks John.

'Tension? Have you not felt the tension when there is disagreement or when your opinion is poorly informed?' I ask to elucidate.

'Of course, yes, I do,' says John. He gives up defending Ricardo.

But now I have more to say. 'You are right to say the use of that expression is common. It is used by pornographers to defend their right to publish pornography. And no one can defend the quality of expression of pornography, can they? Not as an art form or any liberal idea,' I say.

John nods his agreement.

I press on, 'It is always used to defend poor opinions. What is that TV presenter's name? The one who lambasted Meghan. Piers somebody?' I say, knowing full well what his surname is.

John confirms his full name.

'He used that expression to defend his attack on Meghan on live television. The one he got sacked for—'

John corrects me, 'Left by mutual agreement.'

Lawyers! I think to myself. In my head, there was also a profanity ahead of that word. '*Got fired, sacked*, those are just cowardly weasel words for the arsehole getting fired,' I say out loud.

'Now, now!' says the eyes.

But I press on, 'Look, he is an awful bastard. I cannot, for the love of me, understand how that kind of presenting came into television. Arsehole presenters with poor manners and even poorer mental faculties become celebrities. It says something about the state of affairs in the country, doesn't it? All because they have a right to an opinion. And we accept that right as a valid defence for an impoverished mind.' I have finished. I let the eyes know.

John makes a note and says, 'No tribes, no references to character either in that dialogue, Hendrik.'

I suppose I should appreciate that John is helping me tie up loose ends in the novel or close off glaring mistakes and omissions. 'This dialogue is a supporting act, John. If I wanted, I could have written about the tribe of people who has an opinion that their right to an opinion is all they need to express whatever they want. To speak "their" truths. Do you want to think how prolific that tribe is? How it permeates society and particularly politics? Politicians will use their right to an opinion to say anything they want, to claim the most bizarre things are true. I could have written about that, I suppose, but don't you think it presses the definition of *tribe* too far? I would think a tribe shares more than just a common expression.'

'What do you mean shares more?'

'I mean that the tribe is more organised, even informally organised. It most probably has a label or is labelled by people outside the tribe. You must have come across labels like liberal lefties or right-wing rogers, or have I just made that up?' I say.

John abruptly closes the discussion. 'We will probably have to come back to this one. Let's move on for now.'

'Shall I do the reflection first?' I ask.

'Sure,' says John.

'In the dialogue with Ricardo, I deal with the rather stupid defence where people claim their right to an opinion when their opinion is challenged. It is used often, also by some people who should know better. Having a right to an opinion does not guarantee the quality of that opinion. Also, the right to free speech does not guarantee the quality of your free speech. The quality of an opinion is what matters. The quality of an opinion is determined by the quality of reasoning behind it. When an opinion is challenged, people do not challenge your right to an opinion. They question the quality of that opinion.

'In respect of the principle of free speech, you should extend as much freedom as possible for people to express their opinion, but do not hesitate to robustly and forcefully challenge poor-quality opinions. In doing so, you will express your right to an opinion. That is how the principle of free speech works. And do not hesitate to call people out who claim their right to an opinion as defence for stupidity, unfairness, and ideology,' I say and hesitate.

'That was a bit short, Hendrik, a bit perfunctory,' says John.

'But sufficient, I hope. We talked about that some more, you and I, so I think the reflection on this one is justifiably brief.' I pause.

'For us, yes. But what about the novel? Would that have been enough in the novel?' he asks.

'There may be more in the novel, but it is a supporting dialogue. I want to keep it brief, to the point.'

John nods.

COFFEE WITH KRISTOFF

A writer that says there are no truths, or all truths are 'merely relative', is asking you not to believe him. So don't.

Roger Scruton

Kristoff and I are having coffee. I know you might find this unusual, but both of us are taking a break from alcohol. The joy alcohol brings is no longer worth the regret and the hangover the next day. We have also both given up smoking. This is the first time in a while since we last met, and I am secretly hoping that Kristoff won't repeat his mercurial shift. I am secretly hoping that it has something to do with excessive alcohol consumption. I am also secretly hoping that it works for me too, that I can somehow avoid sending Kristoff into a mercurial transformation. Kristoff shimmies into the coffee shop and joins me at the barista queue. He greets me with a bear hug. All is well.

The coffee shop is one of those Italian franchises. This may surprise a lot of people, particularly if you think coffee shop franchises have all sprung out of America. Also, if you get to visit Italy, which you must do at least once in your life, you will find that the barista is also the owner of the coffee shop, even when it is a franchise. Not only that, but Italians also invented the espresso coffee machine at the heart of all decent coffee shops. They also invented the profession, the barista. Coffee drinking is more than a tradition in Italy; it is also a ritual. The ritual is organised round a complex set of rules. So if you think you are going to walk in and get American-style non-descript 'Have a nice day' service, you are going to be surprised. Just like you might be surprised to hear that coffee shops are not an American invention.

The coffee is good, but the cup sizes are European, so you need two cups of coffee for a decent dialogue. I gave you my view on this before. European cup sizes offer an advantage though. It offers an opportunity for a strategic break if either the dialogue gets tied up in a knot or the dialogue causes someone's emotions to get tied up in a knot. We order. Mine is a tall double-shot Americano, which sounds bigger than it is but is even stronger than it sounds. Do not be confused by tall. The coffee fits neatly into that European-sized cup. We collect our coffees and retire to a table for two in a corner of the shop.

For some peculiar reason, our dialogue shifts to the current president of the USA, Donald Trump. If you recall the first dialogue with Kristoff, you will not be surprised about this shift for two reasons. Firstly, Donald Trump has a filthy habit of sneaking into a lot of dialogues around the world and quite annoyingly so. Secondly, Kristoff is a not-so-secret admirer of Trump. I asked him why once, and he said Trump is a decision maker. That's it. Yes, I know.

He said that is what the USA needs, what the world needs—someone who makes decisions. If you see it written down like that, you realise just how stupid a reason it is. At the time, I challenged Kristoff, saying that a president should be judged on the quality of his decisions, not whether he has an aptitude to make them. It resulted in an instant mercurial shift. I can only hope he has forgotten about it. He has. I have high hopes for sobriety.

I don't know whether I told you before, but I must point out that Kristoff is not American or in any way affiliated with the USA. Our dialogue shifts to a comment made by a Trump spokesperson. I forget now who that was, thank goodness. Isn't it great how our memory can serve us by being imperfect? She defended a decision by Trump, claiming it is based on 'alternative facts'. I point out to Kristoff that she has been soundly and quite rightly ridiculed for that.

'Well, Hendrik,' Kristoff responds, 'the truth is relative, you know.'

Now let me be clear. If there is one thing that gets an ordinary philosopher going, then it is this claim that the truth is relative. You may accuse me of a mercurial shift when it comes to this claim, and you have good justification for doing so. I will put my hands up, I swear. It gets me beyond going. It is the sort of statement that makes me sit upright, spill my coffee, and I make my best effort to mimic my father's most severe angry look. Let me show you how I deal with this claim; the truth is relative. If it seems juvenile to you then you are probably right. It is a juvenile problem that has to be dealt with in a juvenile way.

'Let's write that down,' I say to Kristoff. I write *the truth is relative* on a napkin in my best handwriting, but despite my effort, it is still difficult to read. It is just about legible enough for our dialogue. I let Kristoff read it. He shrugs.

'Is that statement true or false?' I ask.

'What do you mean is that statement true or false?' asks Kristoff in return.

'It is a statement of fact like any other. Therefore, is it true or false?' I repeat.

Kristoff ponders this for a while, then he states emphatically, 'True.' Just the one word.

I write *true* next to and slightly underneath the statement. I also write his name next to the *true*. 'The word *relative* has two potential interpretations,' I say as I double-underline the word *relative* on the napkin. I do that for dramatic affect. 'The first might be that it is a relative true, like 50 per cent or 80 per cent. Agreed?' Kristoff nods agreement. 'The second one is that it is relative to the viewpoint of the person speaking it. Which one do you mean?'

Kristoff glances at me then looks away quickly. His face has distorted into confusion. We take a break and have some coffee. 'Relative to the person, the observer,' Kristoff eventually confirms. His voice does a terrible job at hiding his uncertainty. I suspect he knows we are heading for the rabbit hole.

'Good, that means if you read the statement, you will declare it is true. True?' I ask.

'True,' he answers.

'But if I read the statement, I will declare it is false,' I say. As I say that, I write *false* below the *true* and my name next to it.

'Wrong,' he says. 'The statement is true.' Kristoff emphasises the word *true*.

'But relative to me, the statement is false,' I repeat.

'But you are wrong,' insists Kristoff.

'Prove me wrong,' I challenge.

You should know by now that this is Kristoff's favourite defence. I am doing my absolute best to hide my pleasure at having trapped him with it, taken him into the rabbit hole. All that remains is to see how far we can go.

'It is true for me, Hendrik. It is my truth,' says Kristoff. It is a feeble attempt and not much different from claiming that it is an alternative fact.

> In an ever-changing, incomprehensible world the masses had reached the point where they would, at the same time, believe everything & nothing, think that everything was possible and that nothing was true.
>
> *Hannah Arendt*

'Kristoff, be serious for a minute. You cannot claim that something is universal and relative at the same time. Neither can you claim that something is partial or complete at the same time,' I say. I try and capture Kristoff's eyes, but it is impossible to hold on to them for the subtle bobbing and weaving of his head. I let go.

'It is always a subject, like you and me, that reasons for the truth, Hendrik. Therefore, the truth must be subjective,' says Kristoff. I have another go at maintaining eye contact. It leaves me dizzy, and I must let go.

'You are equivocating two different meanings of the same word. In one sense, you use subjective to mean subject, the person, and in the other sense, you use it to mean subjective as in emotional reasoning. That is a mistake, a fallacy, and a well-documented one,' I counter.

I hear nothing from Kristoff. Below the table, his feet has started some intricate footwork. I counter some more, 'A subject, like you and me, can reason objectively for a universal truth. The fact that we are mere subjects doing the objective reasoning takes nothing away from the objectivity. The quality of our objective reasoning is all that matters.'

I am a little bit worried about the mouthful sentence. Still nothing from Kristoff. His footwork becomes visible in more pronounced headwork.

I continue to counter, 'If you think about it, you are trying to convince me objectively that there is one universal truth, that the truth is subjective. You claim this is the only universal truth. That is an untenable contradiction.'

'Well, that is just your opinion, isn't it?' says Kristoff. I predict we are going to see a mercurial shift imminently. Then he says this, 'the embodied self begats the truth. The embodied self beholds the truth. The truth is to the embodied self.'

'Jesus Kristoff, what happened now!' I say, 'have you turned into a medieval monk?'

'That is the way you philosophers speak, isn't it? I am putting it into a language you will understand,' says Kristoff.

'Only if you are a medieval English philosopher, or a pretentious git. And it doesn't make your argument any more convincing. It is still the same nonsense,' I say.

'Like I said. It is just your opinion Hendrik.'

'I do have opinions, I admit. I believe they are well-reasoned opinions most of the time. I am also happy to re-evaluate my reasoning, and I change my mind if the facts change or the logic flows against my opinion,' I say, 'but the word *truth* has a certain meaning, and we cannot change the meaning of the word.'

Kristoff appeals to an authority. 'You are trying to argue with Gandhi, Hendrik. He said the truth is relative.'

I am familiar with the Gandhi quote. It often appears on those posters people put up in their offices or on their bedroom walls. It goes something like this:

> Nobody in the world possesses absolute truths. That is God's attribute alone. Relative truth is all we know. Therefore, we can only follow the truth as we see it. Such a pursuit of truth can lead anyone astray.
>
> Gandhi

It is not clear by which pursuit of truth you will find yourself led astray, the search for absolute truth or the search for relative truth. If you look hard enough, you will find quotes where Gandhi contradicts this view. I think he also said that truth is by nature self-evident, that as soon as you remove the cobwebs of ignorance that surround it, it shines clear. But never mind. Kristoff is clearly selective in his appeal to authority. To Kristoff, I say, 'Gandhi also drank his own urine.'

Kristoff's posture takes on more confidence; the footwork and headwork become more controlled, as if they were signalling a win. He is mistaken of course. Unbeknownst to him, we are going deeper into the rabbit hole. 'Hah, you cannot argue with Gandhi, Hendrik!'

We make eye contact, but his head bobs and weaves and shakes mine off.

'Why not?' I ask. 'If Gandhi declares the truth is relative, then whatever he says is relative to him. It doesn't change my position at all. It doesn't change my position if the whole world believes Gandhi is right. Something isn't true because someone believes it is true. If the truth is relative, then it is my truth that Gandhi is wrong. He is, after all, only a mammal like me, with tits and an arsehole,' I say.

'Now you are just being disrespectful. What a way to go to try and defeat an argument, Hendrik.' Kristoff is on the edge of that mercurial shift. We are now deep into the rabbit hole.

I go for the inevitable dead-end tunnel. 'Gandhi, and everyone who believes him, is trying to modify the meaning of the word *truth*. It seems to me that you are using the word *truth* like you should use the word *belief*. "These are my beliefs."' I draw the quotes in the air. 'You cannot modify the meaning or attempt to modify the meaning of a word to make your arguments stick,' I say. I have Kristoff backing into a corner.

He escapes by trying a different angle. 'Scientists will tell you that they cannot find the truth in their research, Hendrik.' Kristoff is pitching me against a whole community of scientific thinkers.

'Scientists are not after the truth, Kristoff. Scientists are after proofs. They are seeking to develop theories that they can prove wrong. That is not the same thing as seeking the truth,' I declare.

'Of course, what scientists achieve is something we can confidently call objective reasoning in search of the truth. In contrast, people who try and modify the meaning of the word *truth* to be relative are probably lying to you,' I say. 'As for Gandhi, I don't care how many followers and admirers he has. The quality of an opinion or the truth is not determined by the number of people who believe it.'

'That is what truth means to me, Hendrik, that I decide what is true and what is not true for me. Those are my truths,' says Kristoff. Every time Kristoff says 'me', he thumps his chest with his fist, like he is trying to claim the 'me' for himself. The mercury has started to wobble dangerously now.

'Please don't say that, Kristoff,' I plead.

'Say what? Those are my truths,' he says again, and it looks like he is sensing my discomfort, that he has me in a corner.

'You cannot say 'my truths', Kristoff. You do not have a monopoly on truths,' I plead with more detail.

'And why not?' Kristoff asks defiantly, irrationally sensing that he is winning.

'Because then nobody can believe you, Kristoff. You have devalued truth to nothing, less than nothing. We may as well discard the word. And isn't that precisely what you don't want when you tell people things? Surely you don't want people to say, "Those are your truths, so I don't have to believe you." Truths are universal, Kristoff. There is no such thing as 'my truths'. Never has been. There are only universal truths. If it is not universally true, then it is not a truth,' I say, and I escape the corner.

'Rubbish!' exclaims Kristoff. 'My name is Kristoff. That is *my* truth.' He does the fist-on-the-chest thing to emphasise *my*.

'That is a universal truth, Kristoff. Everyone everywhere in the world accepts that it is true that your name is Kristoff,' I say.

'Well, I have God in my life. That is my truth,' he says, trying a different belief.

'That is not a universal truth, Kristoff. A lot of people will say to you that it is not true for them that God exists. You will have to prove God exists for everyone before that will become a truth. So far, you and every other evangelical has failed. In fact, your so-called God has a lot of competition for that position. That is not a truth. It is just a belief,' I say. 'No one has a monopoly on what is and what is not true. The truth belongs to everybody and is and must be universal.'

'That is not what truth means to me. To me, truth means it is true for me,' declares Kristoff in a death throe of assertiveness.

'Well, I suppose I should be relieved. It means I don't have to believe you, so I choose not to,' I say.

'But my truths are truths Hendrik. You cannot deny me my truths.' Insists Kristoff.

'What are you like, Kristoff, like seven? Humpty Dumpty in Alice in Wonderland? You cannot modify the meaning of a word to suit you. The meaning of a word does not belong to you,' I say.

First learn the meaning of what you say and then speak.

Epictetus

And just like that, I have gone too far. Kristoff gets up and leaves, the mercurial shift in full physical flow.

'So that happened again,' I say quietly. The new loneliness threatens to overwhelm me. I decide to have that second cup of coffee anyway. There is something about coffeeshops having become our communal living rooms. There you will find other people quietly getting on with life, but you are not obliged to talk to them. Pubs in the UK serve the same purpose, but the coffee is not that good.

> If you really want to piss people off, you can do two
> things: Attain some happiness or tell the truth.
>
> *Tennessee Williams*

* * *

John makes a note. I am not sure he knows the dialogue is over. The eyes tell me otherwise when they look up. They know, and it is not good.

John explains why, 'You seem to have a habit in the novel of insulting people, a lot of people.'

I act innocent. 'What do you mean?'

Acting innocent did not work the first time. Acting innocent does not work now. Acting innocent never works. I know because the eyes tell me. I will never learn that lesson.

'You have just demeaned a venerated person, Hendrik. That is what I mean,' says John.

'I wouldn't say Kristoff is a venerated person,' I mock.

John leaves no room for humour. 'You know very well I mean Gandhi, Hendrik.' The eyes are stern.

'Oh, come on, John, surely everyone that venerates Gandhi must know that he had tits and an arsehole. They all do. The pope, the queen, every president of every company and country. They are mammals like you and me. At what possible point in their social elevation do they lose their tits and arseholes?' I say with mock exasperation.

The head shakes slowly left to right, but the eyes stay fixed on me. 'Shameless,' says John.

I drive it home. 'So does Trump. Every single one of them has tits and an arsehole.'

Home is not a good place to go with this. The eyes tell me that.

'Please tell me you didn't write that in your novel,' says John.

'And what if I have? I have no hesitation pointing out the truth. And pointing out is all that I do. The truth is there, we just need to dust it off to remove the misinformation, misunderstanding and illusions that cover it up. The truth is what it is. Do you really think Trump will claim I am lying about him having tits and an arsehole?' say I.

'And what precisely do you mean by that, Hendrik?' asks John. I get the feeling it is more of a challenge than a curiosity.

It is my turn to act exasperated. 'Oh, come on, John. Did I not just recall the dialogue with Kristoff?'

John says, 'That is not what I meant, Hendrik. I am very much in agreement when it comes to the truth. I make a living from it—'

'Or from hiding it,' I finish the sentence for him.

The eyes tell me to regret I said that. I regret I said that.

'I meant to ask why you take pleasure in upsetting people with the truth,' he finishes his own sentence.

'The truth makes me happy, John. It should make all of us happy,' I say, hoping that we can move on. 'Shall I do the reflection?'

'Kristoff and I discussed something innocuous when he claims that the truth is relative. It is an abhorrent defence of an opinion that is clearly false or invalid. I dismantle the idea that the truth is relative, but as with all things Kristoff, he has a mercurial shift in mood, so I am left to have a second coffee on my own. I feel sorry for myself, but one must realise that it is hard for some people to change their minds when the facts change or when the logic flows against their opinion. It reminds me of one of my opening quotes, "If you think it is hard to

argue with a smart person, then try and argue with a stupid person."
I am paraphrasing of course.'

'That's it?' asks John.

'Yes.'

'It is a bit perfunctory, again,' says John.

'Yes, not much else to reflect on, unless you want to revisit the concept of truth. I thought we had done that, and now we agree,' I say.

'No, please. There is no need,' says John impatiently. 'Do we meet him again?'

'No, I retired him from intellectual sparring after this. He served his purpose, and it was an unfair fight, don't you think?' I say. If John looked at me, he would have noticed the smile.

Instead, he asks that we move on to the next dialogue.

DINNER WITH PETER

We must be careful not to believe things simply because we want them to be true. No one can fool you as easily as you can fool yourself.

Richard Feynman

Peter has invited me to dinner. Apparently, he has some exciting news to share. He has offered to pay and has chosen the restaurant on the seventieth floor of a Swiss hotel in Singapore. So I expect his news is more than mediocre exciting. I have been here before. The restaurant and bar next door offer stunning views of the city and beyond. Near beyond lies the Singapore Straits, heavy with shipping traffic vital to the economies of the East and the Middle East and the East and Europe. Further beyond the shipping lane with global importance lies the Indonesian islands of Batam and Bintan. Those are not the only islands you can see. There are many more, too many to mention.

When you look out over the Singapore Straits, it is hard to understand how on this side there is an impressive, thriving community of people with a vibrant economy reflected in the spectacular buildings that fill the skyline. On the other side, life appears to have taken a more leisurely economic strategy. This leisurely economic strategy to life is a lot more apparent when you visit those islands. They have taken more care in building beautiful holiday resorts than building the roads to get you there. The holiday resorts are for people from this side of the straits who want to escape the spectacular buildings that fill the skyline. Two tribes separated by a stretch of water but also separated by different economic desires and outcomes.

Peter and I meet in the bar and spend a good half an hour chatting about life in general and admiring the golden sunset reflecting off the spectacular glass tower blocks. We are all too soon invited to take up our table in the restaurant. The waiter insists on carrying what remains of our cocktails to the table. This place is proper posh.

As Peter stands up, he towers over everybody and everything. He follows carefully behind the waiter who leads the way to our table. If you did not know better, you would have thought it is like a child leading an adult. Peter needs to do things carefully because he needs to be considerate of his surroundings. I want to make sure you understand he is not obese, definitely not obese. The only way to describe his size is that of an upscaled person, a true giant. He has the added problem of living in a world designed for smaller people. Peter finds himself permanently in a confined space.

We enter the dining area, and the vista opens up to the east. We can see more islands, more ships. It is without any doubt an extraordinary place for an ordinary philosopher to be. It must be something special that brings us here. We are seated at a table for two. Peter takes the seat that gives him access to the view. I have access to Peter's face. As a consolation to the occupant of this seat, the restaurant has installed a mirror on the opposite wall. I can see a reflection of the view punctuated by the back of Peter's head.

Peter and I study the menu and order. The restaurant follows the Western tradition in serving individual plates. First, you select your starter, then main course, and then dessert. The food is also delivered in that order with plenty of rest between courses to drink more expensive wine and enjoy the company. But I am getting ahead of myself. We order. The wine is served first. The waiter offers the wine bottle up for Peter to inspect. Peter inspects the label and nods. Presumably, the label matches the order. The waiter then carefully pulls the cork and offers the cork to Peter to inspect. Peter nods his approval. The wine is poured, but only after Peter tastes and approves. It is good wine. I mean exceptionally good wine. The sort of wine that blows your mind; it is that good. You did not think wine can be that good. It is from somewhere in France, and it has one of those fancy French aristocratic names which an ordinary philosopher will never remember. It also comes with an extraordinary price tag. So there is no point in trying to remember the name.

Before we continue, I am compelled to remind you that Peter has a wonderful wandering mind. You will hopefully remember that from our first dialogue. I am reminding you just in case we go wandering again tonight. You have been forewarned.

'So, Peter,' I say, 'what is this news that brings us here?' I thought it is time to get to the point behind this celebration.

'You know about the mystic matrix, don't you?' asks Peter.

I must have answered with my facial expression. My face must have said, 'What are you talking about?' I tell you that because Peter laughs and then clarifies for me.

'That is what we call it in the office. But you know the one I mean.' Peter uses the right name. 'It is done by that business and technology research consultancy. They assess companies for their services and products and then present the results in a square. The square is divided into four equal smaller squares. Your product or service is assessed, and the assessment is plotted into one of the squares. Depending on which square the dot of your product or services lands dictates how you are categorised,' Peter lays that out and then pauses, waits for me to acknowledge recognition.

I do recognise what he is talking about now. To confirm this, I say, 'I do, and isn't there a competitor that has something similar? Except they have quarter circles in the square. I think they call it a wave.'

'Yes!' Peter cries out as if he had achieved something mystical himself.

'So why the excitement, Peter?' I ask.

'Well, guess what?' Peter asks.

'What?' I say just to play the game. His excitement is intoxicating, and I feel we have returned to being seven.

'No, you must guess,' he insists. Yep, we are seven again.

So I guess. 'Some company you know has made it to the mystic matrix.'

'Not some company, Hendrik. My company!' says Peter, bursting with pride.

I am going to let you into a secret. I do not get this. Peter does not own this company. He works for it. He is an employee on a contract. He can have his butt kicked out of there tomorrow or leave tomorrow or, at best, stay until he has worked out his notice period. He could benefit from the greatest invention ever, gardening leave. Why does he have this loyalty? Why does he have this pride? What will Bukowski say about this? Perhaps something like, 'Peter swallowed the company, and now the company is feeding off his insides. It is making him ugly. Dumb fucker.' It is a puzzle worth figuring out, don't you think? This unfathomable loyalty to an amorphous thing, 'the business'.

'What for?' I ask to try and figure out the puzzle.

'For our phalanges,' he says. I have replaced the name of their mighty mystic product with phalanges. The actual product name is irrelevant. Phalanges, of course, is what we call the bones in the fingers. I can assure you no one has fingers sufficiently mystical enough to be in the matrix.

'But that is not one of the products you manage or develop, is it?' I ask.

Peter looks significantly deflated now. I have just pissed on his battery, short-circuited his enthusiasm. He tries to recover.

'But it is one of our products, Hendrik. So it works for the whole company. It is good for me too,' he says, no, he pleads.

Now if you paid attention to the previous dialogues, you would have noticed something here. There is an instance where Peter is committing the composition fallacy. He is claiming credit for shit he did not do. It is not his product, but he has offered to pay for my dinner to celebrate as if it is his success. The second one is the divisional fallacy. He thinks the company's achievement is also his achievement. This problem is so common it is extraordinary. One part of a business does well, then workers in the other part of the business shouts out about it.

I know that some people will object to this assessment and some people have. They say everybody does it, so there is nothing wrong with doing it. Their main objection is a comparison with a team, let us say a soccer team, where one player scores the goal but the whole team celebrates. That is different, however, from when an employee in Australia claims 'We are experts in this' when, in fact, another employee in the UK actually crafted and published the book on the *this*. Here is an employee claiming credit for shit he has not done because he is claiming credit for shit the company hasn't done and cannot do. The company is an amorphous thing, a tribe. The tribe cannot do anything. Only individual characters can do things. I have seen that happen. I thought to point that out to you, but I do not want to go there with Peter. There is something else happening here that is of much more interest.

I take it up with Peter. 'Peter, tell me about the other companies in the matrix.'

Peter's spirit lifts. 'All prestigious companies, Hendrik. The elite of the elite,' he declares.

What is this other than a deliberately fabricated prejudice? A prejudice against those businesses and products not plotted on the mystic matrix. What is the opposite of prejudice? It is fairness, but can you really call elitism fairness? I think not. Would it be legitimate to say that this is a form of prejudice for the elite, and prejudice against the ordinary, but a completely fabricated prejudice brought on by a judgement of the few against the many. Is Peter tunnelling through to that prejudice? All this I do in my head.

Peter continues. 'My leadership is particularly happy about this. They have given us all a budget to celebrate.'

'Fantastic,' I say, and I mean it. I am benefiting from the celebration after all.

'Yes, but don't get me started on leadership. Man, the rubbish that people suggest you do when you are a leader,' says Peter and promptly continues with a story. I told you he has a wandering mind. Off we go.

'I saw something on LinkedIn the other day. Some self-proclaimed leader posted a picture holding his three-month-old daughter up to the camera and a statement about how he is teaching her to be an open and transparent leader, that leaders are humans too and having a family is OK as a leader.'

'I bet you had something to say about that,' I say.

'Hah, I did. I said it looks like a *Lion King* moment,' he boasts.

'And? What did he say?' I ask.

'Nothing. He deleted his post, the little prick,' boasts Peter as if he had achieved a small win against a grotesque irrationality.

'I must admit that the whole thing about leadership perplexes me. Have you noticed that there are many contrary theories of leadership? Things like the servant leader, management theory, participative theory, relationship theory, and the worst of the lot, the great man theory. And what about Machiavelli? The only thing I get from this is that it is a load of arbitrary bollocks. Leadership is about claiming a spot on the hierarchy of decision-making,' I rant, but my rant is not enough to return us to the original question.

'Indeed, they are blind to the paradox that people are free to make their own decisions, except when one claims to be the leader. Then the leader takes primacy over decision-making,' adds Peter. He often surprises me like this. He surprises me because he clearly knows what is happening, but he is also impotent at doing something about it, happy to work within the tribe, 'the business'. Perhaps that explains his relative career success. He knows how to game the system.

'I see the notion of leadership is about claiming a monopoly over creativity and talent,' I add.

'Yes. They are now training our HR department to do leadership selection and then leadership development. How crazy is that? If they have selected you because of your leadership skills why do they need to develop you?' He says.

'And don't talk about sales training. The one thing I found about sales training courses is that you should always do them twice. The second time you will see how they used the sales methods they teach to get you to buy the sales training. I suppose that demonstrates that it works,' I say.

'Sounds like you have done a few in your life Hendrik.' Mocks Peter.

'I have, but they stopped inviting me. Something about me being too critical or negative. I merely pointed out the deception and flaws,' I say.

'Why am I not surprised,' says Peter.

That seems to shut down this particular wander from Peter, and he goes quiet.

'Back to my question, why are the companies on the matrix the elite of the elite?' I ask.

'Because they are in the mystic matrix!' says Peter. I sense he thinks I am a dumb shit.

'So you are saying your company has now joined this rare and exclusive club,' I say.

I must pause here because our starters have arrived, and we are both admiring the food the other one ordered. Well, I am admiring Peter's starter. I am not sure he would swap. Peter helps himself to some of the warm freshly baked bread in the little basket. He splits the bun open with his flesh-covered phalanges and applies a thick layer of butter to the middle of the opened bun. The butter melts almost immediately. It is driving me crazy, but I refrain. It is one of those self-control must-not-do things that my doctor reminds me off every time I see him. I tuck into my caprese salad, whilst Peter knifes through his foie gras. He is clearly in a celebratory mood, and I am glad that I have not dampened his spirit too much.

'Yes, Hendrik,' he says. I forgot that I have asked something. Upon reflection, I probably made a statement, and he interpreted it as a question. Or perhaps there was enough ambiguity in the way that I said it that makes it quite right to interpret it as a question.

'Have you ever come across the idea of circular reverence, Peter?' I ask. I am going to come clean and say that Lilly introduced me to this problem first.

'To what?' asks Peter, which is probably what I did when Lilly mentioned it first.

'Circular reverence is when the revered reveres the one giving the reverence,' I say, which now, when I write it down like this, does not make any sense at all.

It did not make any sense to Peter either. 'What?'

'OK, wait. The other companies in the mystic matrix are all considered elite, revered companies,' I say, trying to slow things down.

'I just said that,' says Peter. It is true; he just said that.

'And the companies that are revered this way reveres the mystic matrix,' I say.

So now Peter looks at me as if I am a douchebag, as if I were playing some kind of word gymnastics. So I try a different route.

'You are immensely proud because your company is listed in the mystic matrix,' I say to confirm.

'Of course, Hendrik,' he confirms again. I could swear he rolled his eyes a little. Also, that could be because he put a large chunk of warm buttery bread in his mouth to push the foie gras down. He followed up with a significant gulp of the expensive French red wine.

'So you revere the mystic matrix,' I say.

Peter looks at me now. He has finished whatever he was doing in his mouth. I take a small respectful sip of the expensive and increasingly rare French red wine.

'Are you saying that my company is revered because it is plotted somewhere in the mystic matrix?' he asks. I am a little worried that he is looking annoyed now. Luckily, we have already ordered.

'Yes,' I say. 'Is that not what this celebration is all about?' I ask.

Reminding Peter that we are celebrating is an accidental stroke of genius. He immediately looks happy and nods.

'You also said that this is an elite club, the best of the best, I mean the companies that are all listed here,' I say.

Peter nods. His generous nature returns, and he reaches for the wine bottle to top up both wine glasses but gets interrupted by the waiter who steps in and resumes what he clearly considers to be his role in the proceedings. I am a little jealous now that I have been respecting the wine too much. It takes around half an inch to restore my wine to the level acceptable in a decent restaurant. Peter has near emptied his glass, so it takes more like two inches.

'So would you say the group of elite companies revere the mystic matrix?' I say that as a statement and do not expect an answer. I do not get one. At that precise moment, our main courses arrive, and we go through the ritual of checking out each other's order. Once again, I suffer from food envy. Peter's fillet steak looks suitable to be plotted on the mystic matrix. The roasted chicken leg I ordered, not so much.

'Yes, but so what?' asks Peter. I guess it was more of a challenge, and he considers my probing a waste of time and not worth discussing.

'Well, the problem with circular reverence is that no one dares challenge the methods by which one gets on the list,' I say. 'Do you know how they select companies for the list?'

'Apparently, they have a panel of experts who apply certain criteria,' he says. 'It is described in the report that accompanies the list.'

'It is indeed, and I had a look at it once,' I say, 'not for tonight. I didn't know.' I add clumsily, 'On a previous occasion.'

'Bet you were upset that your company wasn't on the list,' he says.

'I was,' I confess. 'We were excluded from a bidding process. They are quite secretive about those criteria, are they not?' I say.

'What do you mean?' he asks.

'Well, there is some statement about it being a trade secret, isn't there?' I say.

'So they are entitled to their intellectual property, are they not?' defends Peter.

'Indeed, but we can still look at the actual mystic matrix, can we not?' I ask. We are finishing up our main course now, and the empty plates are cleared away by the impossibly attentive waiter. Peter suggests to him to wait a while before bringing the desserts and orders another bottle of the wine.

'Have you got it here?' I ask.

'The mystic matrix? On my laptop, yes,' says Peter. Without me prompting, he opens his laptop up, clicks around, turns the laptop so we can both see the screen, and there it is—four neat squares in one larger square. He had circled the name of his company at the bottom left. The aim is to get to the top right-hand corner. Then your company is the elite of the elite. There are only about ten companies plotted on the matrix. I suspect that is the limit. If you fall out the bottom, you are replaced by another more elite business. They must limit the number; otherwise, it will dilute the eliteness of the revered.

'Very impressive, Peter,' I say, and he beams. 'Are you familiar with graphs where they plot correlations?'

'Uhm, oh yes,' says Peter. 'That is when the correlations are plotted on a square like this one, but they are considered statistically significant when they follow a diagonal line from bottom left to top right,' Peter explains quite adequately, I thought.

'What happens if you draw the correlation line in the mystic matrix?' I ask.

Peter draws an imaginary diagonal line on the laptop screen. 'Look at that!' he says. 'All the companies except for two follow the diagonal, almost exactly, including ours.' He glows at his own achievement.

'And what does that tell you?' I ask.

'That there is a statistical significance between the two measurements they use for plotting the companies,' he says, and I am impressed. I am also pleased that I do not have to explain.

'And what are the measurements?' I ask.

'The one across the horizontal axis is "completeness of strategy", and the one on the vertical axis is "ability to execute strategy",' he reads from the graph. I give him time to absorb. Peter absorbs. 'That means they are measuring the same thing, doesn't it?' he cries out, also pleased with this discovery.

'Looks like that,' I say.

'But that is meaningless,' says Peter.

'Looks like it is,' I confirm again.

'But wait. What about these two companies. This one. It has a very low score for strategy but an excellent score for ability to execute,' he says, but I leave him to reach a conclusion. 'What kind of company would have a crappy strategy but a magnificent ability to execute that crappy strategy?' is his conclusion.

I do not have time to intervene. Peter has moved to the other outlier now.

'And this one has an excellent strategy but a crappy ability to execute. What the fuck are they measuring?' he asks.

I told you before it is rare for Peter to swear. I assume the question is for me, so I attempt an answer. 'It looks like they are measuring a company's strategy, but what are they measuring it against?'

'Exactly,' says Peter, "and whose strategy? A company cannot have a strategy, can it?' Again, I am not sure that was a question for me, so this time, I leave him to ponder it. He does.

'It looks like their so-called experts claim to know the best strategy for the industry or product,' says Peter. 'That is a bit audacious, isn't it?'

I feel no urge to respond.

'They call it the market's strategy. How can a market have a strategy? A market is a place where sellers and buyers come together to trade. It is a place, virtual or physical, not a person. It cannot have a strategy. That means either their experts have perfect strategy of where the market is going or they glean the strategy from those that trade in the market. If that is true, then at least one company should have a complete perfect strategy, a strategy that scores a ten on the mystic matrix. It appears they think they do,' he says. I say nothing. I think Peter's examination is pretty good, but there is one alternative missing.

Then he gets there. 'Wait, do you think they assume the market's perfect strategy is the combined strategy of all the traders?' he asks.

'That is a reasonable conclusion,' I say.

'Which again means they have access to the market's perfect strategy. They must measure other companies against their idea of the perfect strategy,' adds Peter.

I allow him space to continue with his own assessment.

'And if they think they have a monopoly over the perfect strategy, why don't they just sell that strategy?' he concludes. I have no reason to disagree with him, so I do not.

Instead, I guess this is a question for me, so I answer, 'It is the leadership problem, isn't it? Is that what they call companies in the top right-hand square? They claim leadership and therefore claim a monopoly over the strategy.'

Peter looks at me now, then he says slowly, 'Well, it opens up markets for my company, Hendrik. Do you know how many times we have been excluded from opportunities because we were not on this list? Hey, do you know? Hundreds, I tell you.' He is exaggerating, of course, but he has a point.

'I know, Peter, that is why I took a closer look at the mystic matrix before. It even has deception in its real name, doesn't it?' I say.

Peter laughs just as our desserts arrive.

'I think buyers should pay more attention to the advice from their lawyers,' I say.

'What advice? Whose lawyers?' asks Peter.

'The mystic matrix's lawyers. Something about not using the information as advice to purchase products or services, that it is basically just opinion,' I say. 'Don't you think it is disturbing the crap that floats around in "the business"?' I realise too late that my metaphor perfectly matches Peter's chocolate volcano dessert. Thankfully, he doesn't notice.

We finish up, and the bill arrives. 'Shall we split the bill?' suggests Peter. Apparently, he changed his mind about this being a celebration. I suppose that will teach me.

'No, let's go Dutch,' I say, grateful that the healthier choices on the menu are also the cheapest. 'I have had only one and a half glasses of wine,' I add just to rub it in.

As we leave, I notice the TV in the reception is showing some celebrity talk show, and I think, *Celebrities celebrating celebrities.* Another form of circular reverence. It reminds me of this poem by the great Bukowski, which I think ends like this:

> The famous gather to
> applaud their
> seeming
> greatness
> as
> the fools are
> fooled
> again
> humanity
> you sick
> motherfucker.

Charles Bukowski

I thank Peter. It may surprise you as he did not keep his promise to pay for dinner. But these days I am grateful for any company. And despite our differences Peter always shows a certain resilience when it comes to our friendship. That our friendship is more important to him than our differences.

* * *

John looks concerned, deeply concerned. I ask why.

'You seem to have rubbished a much-respected company in that dialogue, Hendrik,' he says.

'You mean a "revered" company,' I mock.

'Be serious, Hendrik,' rebukes John. The eyes do what is necessary to castigate me.

'I am,' I protest. 'I have obfuscated the names completely.'

'You may have tried,' says John then cautions me, 'but not enough. The magic matrix you talk about is an extremely well-known brand. I am a lawyer, and even I am aware of it. We use it in our procurement department.'

'I never used the word *magic*, John. You did!' I am still protesting.

He ignores my protest. 'This company is really wealthy. This is also one of their most important products or brands, Hendrik. They can throw money and lawyers at you no end.'

My mind wants to go to an image of someone tossing lawyers, like it is a competition in the Scottish Highlands. Instead, tension grips the pit of my stomach. John is right. We are referring to the same company. I am still worrying when John says, 'And the wave. They too will be upset by this.'

As if I did not have enough to worry about. 'Oh, you know them too,' I say.

'Yes, Hendrik, everyone does,' says John.

'Well, in that case, my only defence would be that I am right, won't it?' I ask.

'Right about what?' asks John. There is an urgency in his voice that sends alarm signals through me.

'About the matrix being rubbish or the wave being rubbish,' I say in my defence.

'If you are right, Hendrik. But that is not a given,' says John.

'Well, they will have to prove I am talking about their products, won't they? And all they have is what I wrote. If they prove that what I wrote is wrong, then clearly my defence will be that it is not their product,' I say.

'That is if they don't employ an investigator to find Peter and to prove a connection between Peter and you,' says John.

'I created the character, John. That is the connection,' I say.

John is not amused.

'If they can find a Peter with a connection to me, then that Peter will have to either deny the connection or deny that he contributed to the assessment,' I say. The worry is beginning to leave me, but judging by John's expression, I should be more careful.

'It won't be as difficult as you think, Hendrik. There are only around ten companies on the matrix, and they don't change that often,' says John.

I am defiant now. 'Well, I will be happy to see them in court. Can you imagine what will happen? They will have to publicly defend their product. They will have to argue with me in open court. They will have to be transparent about their methodology. That will expose their IP. I am sure they would rather just say it is not them, deny any similarity, or claim it is pure coincidence. And I bet their future graphs will show a lot less statistically significant correlation.'

John seems to visibly relax. 'Let's hope so, Hendrik.' Then he glances worryingly at the letter from Jennifer Rawlings.

I don't wait for permission from John. 'The reflection? Peter and I meet to celebrate his company achieving the venerated distinction of being listed by the venerated. I help Peter to reveal the problem. The problem is that we are blinded by the accolades and the veneration so much so that we do not question the venerator. In his case, we see that there are serious concerns over how these accolades are bestowed. I also question the power of the tribe, "the business", over Peter, the irrational loyalty he feels towards it, a compliment "the business" will not return if push comes to shove. In the end, the celebration is deflated, and I pay for my own dinner.'

'So here is an example of a dialogue where you showed your gentle side, Hendrik. So you can do it. But you opened yourself up to legal jeopardy with that attack on the consulting firm,' says John, except he mentions the name of the firm; I didn't. I tell him. He shrugs.

I just move to the next dialogue.

BRUNCH WITH EDWIN

The creation story is ridiculous garbage and has given us a completely false picture of our origin and the origin of the cosmos. If you want a good mythical story it would be the life of Socrates.

Christopher Hitchens

You have guessed correctly. This is our regular Sunday brunch meetup. Fewer people have come today. The monsoon rains have washed away the motivation of the less courageous. It has been raining for a few days now. There is barely any respite from the rain; it is near constant. It is also colder, much colder than usual. It is so much colder that the fans mounted high up on the walls have been turned off. Someone has mentioned that it is only twenty-five Celsius today. I think they call it air-conditioning weather in Singapore.

There are six of us, and to my surprise, there is one newcomer. His name is Edwin. He is a recent arrival and has joined the expat community in Singapore. He also came across the online notice for this meeting, so he has braved the weather to join us.

Edwin tells us he is from Eastern Europe, the liberated side, not the side still in the grips of Putin. Apparently, it is a lot colder there in winter, so he is enjoying the weather. 'The wetness of it all can be dealt with an umbrella,' he says.

I am not so sure. Umbrellas do not protect you from the tropical rebound. The raindrops are so big that they seem to bounce a meter or two when they hit the pavement. The umbrella might keep you dry from water falling from the sky, but you get soaked rapidly from the rebound. Judging by Edwin's clothes, he wasn't as successful as he wants to make us believe. If he were dry enough, you could have mistaken him for a Jehovah's Witness, the way he dresses and his demeanour, but the rain has washed some of that away. If he were a good Jehovah's Witness, you would have thought his faith would have kept him dry.

My strategy is to follow the covered walking routes that link all the buildings. That way, you only have to sprint through the rain at road crossings. There are even some air-conditioned tunnels that connect buildings in the CBD.

'So what are the topics being discussed here?' asks Edwin.

'Anything you want. It is up to what interests you,' says Raymond. I told you before that Raymond is the organiser of the event, remember? In the dialogue with Robert.

Conversation has started up with the rest of the group. Then Edwin comes up with this: 'If evolution is real, why is it selective for some apes to evolve and almost an equal majority to remain apes? Why is there no communication channel between the evolved and still evolving apes? What is the expected time to see the next evolution for the race *Homo sapiens*? Or the still evolving apes? What is the benefit to changing the facial features during evolution? How can the still evolving population be a perfect fit for the environment, with plenty of room to breed and abundant food, while evolved [superior race] is still fighting for air and food? Why does the evolved race have no natural food in nature? Why is the evolved race weaker than the predecessor in strength, gram by gram of body weight? Just too many anomalies in the theory of evolution!'

I kid you not. That is exactly how he blurted it out. The response around the table is total bewildered silence. Raymond is the first one to pick himself up from the floor. He speaks, 'Say what?' I told you Raymond is Dutch. They take pride in being open-minded. They also take pride in saying exactly what they think.

Edwin starts to repeat the question, 'If evolution is real, why is it selective for some apes to evolve and almost an equal—'

Raymond interrupts him, 'Wait. Wait. What do you mean with why is it selective for some apes to evolve—'

It is my turn to interrupt. 'Raymond, I think the real question is in the last sentence.'

'What was in the last sentence?' asks Raymond. Everyone else starts to gather themselves from the floor now, but their bewilderment lingers.

'There are just too many anomalies in the theory of evolution,' states Edwin.

'Oh,' says Raymond. It is all he can say.

'It is not the question though,' says Edwin. 'It is the conclusion.'

'It doesn't sound like a conclusion to me, Edwin, more like you are trying to imply that the theory of evolution is flawed,' I say.

'That's right. To make the theory of evolution work, you must answer the anomalies,' he says.

'You did not ask it as a question, Edwin,' say I, 'but it is the question I am asking you.'

'No, I ask other questions,' protests Edwin.

'You make them sound like questions,' I say, 'but they were really not questions, were they?'

'What do you mean? They were questions,' insists Edwin, glancing at his phone. It is then that I realise he prepared in advance and was reading from his phone.

'Why don't you repeat your sentences? But one sentence at a time, please,' I ask.

'Sure.' Edwin picks up his phone and repeats the first sentence. 'If evolution is real, why is it selective for some apes to evolve and almost an equal majority to remain apes?'

'Your statement is a bit confusing, but the confusion does not hide the fact that you have made a glaringly obvious mistake,' I say.

'What mistake? There is no mistake. That is exactly how I wrote it down,' says Edwin. By now, you should realise that Edwin is not out looking for a decent exchange of ideas. He came here with an ulterior motive, an ulterior motive that includes a lot of confrontation.

'Yes, there is,' I insist. 'Do you want me to spell it out for you?'

'There is no mistake. There are different rates of evolution and also different directions of evolution. Some evolve, and some stay apes,' says Edwin.

'OK, I see now. There is more than one mistake in your understanding of evolution,' I say as kindly as I can.

'What? You explain to me,' he demands.

'The first one is that you assume all species of apes developed in the same environment,' I explain to him.

'Well, they did. They evolved on the world,' he says.

'No, they obviously did not. The world is not a universally uniform environment. The environment changes across different regions of the world. The environment changes over time throughout the existence of the world. The environment also includes other natural living things. They are part of the environment, and as they change, they change the environment. There was the Ice Age. With Ice Age, some natural barriers to migration disappeared. Some apes took advantage and migrated to different regions with different environments. Continental shifts meant that certain environments were isolated that way. The differences in apes can easily be explained by a fundamental mechanism in the theory of evolution.'

I acknowledge that I should take Edwin through the composition and divisional fallacies, but do you think he is ready for that level of sophistication? I do not. I also think there is something else going on with Edwin, some form of intellectual corruption that will disable any ability to think properly.

'I don't accept that,' insists Edwin. 'What is the second mistake?'

And just like that, he proves my point about the intellectual corruption. I am somewhat impressed that he remembers that I said there is more than one mistake. 'You suggested that some apes remained apes and some evolved to something different.'

'Yes, humans are different,' he says confidently.

'Humans are apes too,' I disagree equally confidently.

'Yes, but a different race,' he says.

'Races and species are not the same thing. You make that mistake a lot,' I say.

'Nonsense. I will not accept I have evolved from an ape,' he says.

'You must if you want your objection to evolution to stick,' I say, but it is immediately apparent that pointing out the contradiction will be an intellectual step too far for him. The intellectual corruption has done too much damage for me to fix it in a Sunday brunch meetup.

'You have not dealt with my anomaly,' he insists again, 'and what about the others?'

No one tries to take him up on his invitation. It appears that I have been given the floor, and I am relieved. It is hard enough to keep up with Edwin and not also deal with everyone else's attempt to see him right.

'So I know you have stated your last sentence as a question, but judging by what you have just said, it is in fact your anomalies you don't expect anybody to prove wrong. But you are really using your anomalies in support of your statement to reject the theory of evolution,' I say.

'You must reject. Look at all the anomalies I have identified. And there is more,' says Edwin.

I expect him to give us more, so I pause. I am mistaken though and somewhat relieved. He offers nothing for now, so I say, 'The problem, Edwin, is not that there is a problem with the theory of evolution. The problem is, you are completely and wilfully ignorant about the theory of evolution.'

'You call me ignorant? You insult me because I am right!' shouts Edwin. I am sure you are as surprised as everyone else that a newcomer would come to a meeting like this and launch such a brazen attack on complete strangers.

'I said you are ignorant about the theory of evolution, Edwin. That is not the same thing as calling you ignorant. You are being ignorant about a specific thing. That is not an insult,' I say softly, hoping that he will calm down and listen to reason.

'What about my questions are wrong? I bet you cannot answer them. You are ignorant about my questions,' says Edwin.

'I admit, your questions do not make much sense to me. They are completely incompatible with the theory of evolution,' I say.

'So now you say I know nothing about the theory of evolution?' spits Edwin.

'I am not saying it now. I have been saying It ever since the first time when you brought it up,' I say.

Edwin leans forward. A red shade has crept up from his neck and is beginning to cover his face. He fixes his gaze on me. There is no doubt that he thought he could come to this meeting, ask a provocative question, and recycle an old argument.

'Edwin, please,' I plead, 'you must do more to understand the theory of evolution. Please read the book. It is a lot more accessible than you think. And if you have trouble, then there are books that simplify it considerably. But please show some respect to Darwin and to all of us here. You cannot come here and treat us with such disdain.'

'How can you say that? You treat me with disrespect because you won't answer my questions!' shouts Edwin.

'Are you a religious man, Edwin?' I ask.

'I am a Christian. And we don't believe in evolution. Do you believe in evolution?' he asks.

And just like that, he confirms his tribe, the source of his intellectual corruption—Evangelical Christians who think they have discovered flaws in a theory that has withstood scientific scrutiny for 250 years. The more scientists discover and understand evolutionary biology, the more this theory is endorsed. Such ignorance. Talking about swallowing the tribe. I hear Bukowski again, 'They swallow religion. Dumb fuckers.'

'I don't believe in evolution. I believe the theory of evolution,' I answer.

Edwin misses the subtlety of the point I make completely. He confirms that I am not religious. 'So you are an atheist.' I do not think that was the question, but why argue about something that is true? 'Atheists cannot answer my questions. You cannot answer my questions,' declares Edwin.

'Your questions are not answerable because they are completely ignorant of the details of evolution,' I repeat.

'So why don't you teach me then?' challenges Edwin. He challenges not because he wants to learn but because he relishes this stupid game.

'No, Edwin, I am not going to teach you. You have formed a conclusion about the theory of evolution without bothering to understand it. That is outright disrespectful. You have probably huddled around with other religious fanatics who thought you could come up with reasons to reject evolution, not because you are smart but because it destroys a fundamental tenet of your belief system— the illusion of creationism,' I say.

'First, I am ignorant. Now I am religious freak,' he says. And for a second, my spirit lifts; I thought we finally agree on a few things. 'You insult me because you know the problem with the theory of evolution is that it is just a theory. There are no proofs of the theory,' he says.

'Great, now you have said something we can work on,' I say.

'What do you mean?' asks Edwin.

'You said the theory of evolution is just a theory, did you not?' I ask.

'Yes, it says so in the title of the book,' answers Edwin. I don't know about you, but I am impressed he knows there is a book with the same title. Frankly, before this, I was wondering how he manages to dress himself. Of course, I am assuming he dresses himself. Judging by what I have seen so far, odds are, he has a lot of help.

'There are also two meanings to the word *theory*. Did you know that?' I ask.

'What do you mean two meanings? It is one word,' says Edwin, undaunted and fearless.

'Two meanings,' I repeat. 'The first meaning is that a *theory* is a hypothesis. A hypothesis must meet the strict standards of scientific enquiry. It must also be falsifiable,' I say and wait.

Edwin simply shrugs, so I press on, 'The second meaning of a *theory* is the same as to speculate.'

'So what!' says Edwin. 'That does not change anything.'

'It changes everything. You are guilty of an equivocation,' I say.

'A what? Now you insult me more' is all he can come up with. I fear this is going to be a tedious and drawn-out affair, and I regret that I went down this rabbit hole.

'When you say the theory of evolution is just a theory, you are using two different meanings of theory in the same sentence,' I try to explain.

'I am what?' asks Edwin. Just to be clear, it is not a polite question or repeat request. Edwin spits it out.

I try anyway. 'The first time you use it, you use it the way Darwin did, as a hypothesis. The second time you use it is as in speculation.'

'You are talking Greek to me. I don't understand,' says Edwin. There is no signal that he is going to change his mind. There is also no signal that there is a mind to change. I have run out of my reserve of philosophical generosity.

'You are basically saying that a hypothesis of evolution is a speculation. But you cannot be further from the truth. A hypothesis is designed to be proven. It is precise and not speculative at all,' I say.

'You don't make any sense at all. You speak nonsense,' declares Edwin.

'Which explains why you cannot understand something as clear, precise, and beautifully argued as Darwin's theory of evolution,' I say, but I let my frustration get the better of me. 'You have been dumbed down by your freaky religious friends to believe creationism. You construct what you think is a counterargument to evolution, but you have not even bothered to try and understand what you are trying to counter. If you and your religious fanatics are anything to go by, then God created shit for brains on the sixth day.'

'I don't have shit for brains!' shouts Edwin.

'I would agree with you, but then we both would have shit for brains,' I say, annoyed now and trying to shut him up.

'What—' begins Edwin, but Raymond interrupts.

'Let's move on to another topic, shall we? But let's get some food first,' he says.

Edwin makes another attempt to protest, but Raymond stands up. Edwin looks at his substantial frame and changes his mind. You should not be surprised that Raymond has that effect on disagreeable people.

The waiter arrives with menus, and we focus on ordering food. Hopefully, we can do something more useful when we start up again.

'There is nothing here I want to eat,' says Edwin. With that said he gets up and puts his COVID mask on so that it covers his mouth, but not his nose. He turns and leaves without another word.

'I hope he puts his underwear on better than his mask,' says Lilly.

We all laugh, partly out of relief that Edwin has left but mostly because of the image Lilly invoked.

What was the quote from Christopher Hitchens, the other one? 'There can be no progress without head-on confrontation.'

* * *

John has his head in his hands. He rubs his eyes. I can see he is smiling behind his hands. He looks up, supresses a laugh, and says, 'Oh god, I am trying to get that image out of my head, Hendrik. That was hilarious from Liz, wasn't it?'

'Yes, it was,' I say.

'It appears that everyone would agree that you have had a brazen dialogue with this Edwin, Hendrik. Why do you think you lost it like that?' John asks.

'I am just an ordinary philosopher, John. I am a human being like everyone else. Edwin came looking for trouble. I think he does that. He has developed this list of so-called anomalies, and he goes from meetup to meetup to cause trouble,' I say.

'That much is clear, Hendrik. But surely you can handle people like that by now,' says John. There is a look in his eyes that says I should take the fatherly advice.

'I'd like to think I am always nice, but just sometimes I meet somebody who is just so belligerent I cannot help myself,' I say sheepishly.

'Couldn't you just say nothing at the meetup, let the others handle him?' he asks.

'And let stupid do what stupid does? I cannot do that, John. Stupid provokes me. Stupid pokes at one part of me and the whole me twitches. Stupid drives me mad. I cannot leave stupid alone,' I plead. 'It reminds me of an instruction from Christopher Hitchens, "Never be a spectator of unfairness and stupidity. The grave will supply plenty of time for silence."'

'Well, no harm done in the novel, Hendrik, except you may have called religious people freaks,' says John.

'Oh, I am not worried by that. Christopher Hitchens made a living out of challenging religious freaks,' I say.

'Oh, really, I thought I would remember something like that,' ponders John.

'Do you honestly want to tell me you don't know Christopher Hitchens?' I ask.

'Only vaguely. Didn't he pass away recently?' he asks.

'Yes, but from cancer, not some religious intervention, a tremendous loss to reason and reasonableness,' I say.

'Unless the cancer was it,' says John.

I sense though that he is teasing me, but I don't appreciate the context.

'Don't tell me you are a religious fanatic, John,' I say.

'Oh god, you are impossible. That is a shameless distortion of what I just said,' says John.

'Well, never mind, eh. Religious fanatics are unlikely to take me to court. They probably have another avenue for revenge,' I say.

'Let's hope it is as ineffective as you think, Hendrik.' John smiles.

'Anyway,' I say. 'This dialogue was with a real person, not named Edwin, of course.'

'I gathered that Hendrik. It would be near impossible to creatively write an incoherent conversation like that,' says John.

I smile and take that as permission to move on to the reflection.

'Edwin is on a mission. The mission is to provoke a discussion on the validity of Darwin's theory. Edwin is an example of a particular kind of idiot who thinks he can knock down a well-considered and intelligently constructed theory with a few sharp short sentences. What he reveals through his so-called anomalies, though, is his own inadequacies and intellectual laziness. He never bothered to study Darwin's theory, and that was clear in his so-called anomalies.

'I challenged of course. What else is an ordinary philosopher to do? Edwin poked a sharp stick at a small part of me, and the whole thing twitched uncontrollably. I admit I lost it and that I helped drive the spiral that took the dialogue out of control. I hope I made the point clear to the readers of the novel. The point is to study what you disagree with before you dismiss it as nonsense.'

'Nothing about tribes, amorphous structures?' asks John.

'No, I focus on that one lesson: do your homework before you open your mouth,' I say.

'I beg your pardon?' says John.

'I meant the lesson, not you,' I say, my heart racing because of the misunderstanding.

'Indeed, if only you did that,' says John with a big grin on his face. I feel his mood is beginning to turn. 'This is the second time we come across the equivocation fallacy. There is something about this problem that is recognisable,' says John.

'There is an ancient wisdom here, John. It is called arguing at cross purposes. I am sure you know it,' I say.

'Yes! That's it!' exclaims John. The eyes are triumphant again.

I smile and say, 'Often when people argue, they assume they agree with some things, but the source of their disagreement lies with that assumption: the things they think they agree on. So the advice is always making sure you agree with the things you think you agree on.'

'That is a bit tricky. Can you give a simple example?' asks John.

'Sure, Lilly and I disagree on the prevailing weather in Georgia. We settle that disagreement when we realise that she is talking about Georgia in Eastern Europe and I am talking about Georgia where the rednecks live,' I say.

'Yes, that is a good one, and a good lesson too,' says John.

'In a proper dialectic, a dialogue that follows Socratic processes, we will work through every significant word of the question to get a shared agreement in place for each word. Often that is enough to resolve a dispute,' I add.

John has fixed his gaze on me. I could swear a noticed a hint of respect. The eyes appear to echo that hint. Just a hint though. The eyes are hard to please.

I assume we are done and move on to the next dialogue.

DRINKS WITH THOMAS

Rule your mind or it will rule you.

Horace

We are gathered in a pub in Sydney. It is the company's year-end celebration. We have spent the morning being reminded by our leaders of every one of our successes, in fact gloating about those successes. Some of us get a special mention. Those who don't are facing a performance improvement plan. They spend the afternoon worried about getting fired. The others spend the afternoon getting fired up and motivated to do even better next year. Both types of fires are treated with copious amounts of alcohol. For the tribe, for 'the business' of course.

The pub is in one of those Victorian buildings. It is on three floors. Inside, it reminds you unambiguously that it used to be a house. The rooms are that size. Somehow, the workings of the pub have been horseshoed into the available space. We were lucky enough to find a few vacant chairs and a table on the balcony on the first floor. Lucky because those of us who want to smoke were allowed to smoke there. It is approaching December, and the weather is already hot, but this time of night, it is quite pleasant outside. We promptly made sure that those chairs were no longer vacant. In fact, we claimed them until the pub closed or, to be honest, until we got thrown out. A tradition apparently. One which the pub's landlord is ready to forgive the next day and allow us back in to do it again. Oh, the silly games we play.

Thomas has come on to the balcony. He doesn't smoke, but as always, smokers offer the most effervescent conversation. Smokers live in the moment. Smokers have a delightful reckless disregard for the future.

Thomas is one of those tall athletic-looking Australians who does no actual sport at all. He is like that by accident of birth rather than hard work on the sports field or in a gym. You know the type.

Mitt greets him, 'Hey, Thomas, how are you, mate?' It is the standard greeting in Australia. Good old mateship. I feel that it means something, that it genuinely expresses a term of endearment Australian men feel for each other. Perhaps it has something to do with being a frontier country.

Thomas returns the favour. 'Good, mate, you?'

Tim is more forthright. 'Hey, mate.'

Thomas returns that favour too. 'Mate.'

It leaves no space for me to say anything.

Tim and Mitt. You cannot make it up even if you are a writer. And they are neither twins nor complimentary opposites of each other, if you were thinking that. If you were a writer, you would probably have used Tim, Mitt, and Tom. But that would have made it even more bizarre, and it would have sounded like you are writing a book for kindergarten toddlers.

'What's on your mind these days?' asks Tim. His body language says he is aiming the question at Thomas.

Thomas answers then asks, 'I am pissed off with taxes. Did you know that Australia has one of the highest tax rates in the world?' Thomas was one of the ones singled out this morning, a high achiever.

'I did not know that, but you also have free healthcare, don't you?' I answer, thinking the question was directed at me, that somehow Thomas wanted to bring me into the mateship. Good old Australian mateship.

I guessed correctly. The question was for me, so he answers mine, 'Sure, but that is just so they can manipulate us in believing they are concerned for us.'

'Wait! What do you mean by *they*?' I ask, my favourite question when the word *they* is used. I will discuss this more in a later dialogue. Just keep in mind that this is one of my triggers.

Thomas expresses some real anxiety, 'The state, they are conspiring against us, mate.'

I probe a little more. 'The state is just an institution, mate. It cannot think. Who does the thinking?' See how quickly I picked up on the mateship?

Thomas looks directly at me now. I am not afraid; I see an image of a startled non-venomous snake, not a six-foot-six athlete. Somehow, he seems even taller, more alert, like he realises he is being challenged, and he is getting ready to flee. 'People' is as far as he is prepared to go to offer an alternative.

'People?' I ask.

'Yeah, people, mate. They are controlling us, mate,' he says. Thomas turns to pick up his drink and looks at Tim and Mitt for a new topic, hoping that he has done enough to close this one down.

Tim and Mitt are enjoying the intellectual scrap too much to offer him a rescue, and I do not give up that easily. Thomas is an easy target if a somewhat unfair fight intellectually, not physically of course. That will be the other way round.

'The people who work there are just other people like you and me,' I say.

> Where men build on false grounds, the more they build,
> the greater is the ruin.
>
> *Thomas Hobbes*

Thomas refuses to concede his position. 'Yeah, but the state, particularly the deep state, is manipulating us, controlling our lives.'

It is time for us to go down the rabbit hole. I repeat, 'The state, or the deep state, is just other people, mate. That means you must identify them and their motivation. Who are these people who are conspiring against you?'

Thomas is in a battle with an illusionary tribe. An illusionary tribe has no characters. Real tribes are a conspiracy of characters. I am hoping we can separate the characters from the tribe. If there are no characters, there can be no conspiracy.

One-word answer from Thomas: 'Politicians.' He tries a different label for the same illusionary tribe.

'No,' I say, 'that is not good enough. Politicians, the state, the deep state are meaningless when you are talking about manipulations and conspiracies. You are just offering different names for the same thing. Name the people whom you accuse of this conspiracy.'

He tries another vague answer, even if it sounds more specific, 'The people in Canberra, the people in parliament.'

I probe him to see if he can go more specific. 'You mean, the politicians in parliament?'

Thomas looks around again for a rescue. None is available. Tim and Mitt are leaning back in their chairs and grinning like idiots. They are enjoying Thomas's awkward squirming around. 'Yes, all the politicians,' he says, trying yet another label for the same thing.

I probe some more, 'Are you suggesting all the politicians are conspiring against you, Thomas?'

'No. Just some,' he concedes. Even though this is some progress, I let it go.

'I meant you, Thomas, personally. Why do they take a special interest in you?' I ask.

'Not just me, mate, all of us,' he claims, attempting to drag us into his conspiracy.

'Then we all have an interest in knowing who they are, and you must be able to name them. Who are they?' I drive forward.

Thomas is in a little bit of panic now. He redirects, 'Yeah, but I don't like being manipulated.'

'But who's manipulating you? You must name them, Thomas,' I say.

'They say that the politicians are manipulating us,' he says.

And just like that, Thomas introduces a second illusionary tribe, 'they'. Now we have two illusionary tribes, the one that is conspiring against him and the one that thinks the other one is conspiring against him.

'But who specifically is manipulating you? If they are conspiring against you, then you must be able to identify them,' I say.

'That's the point. They are an organisation, a cabal of some kind, conspiring to control us and manipulate us,' he says.

> It is easier to fool people than to convince them they are being fooled.
>
> *Mark Twain*

My impatience is growing now. We are circulating around the same point and making no progress at all. I try a different more direct approach. 'So you have created this amorphous thing, and now you are spending precious time and energy fighting it.'

Thomas looks bewildered. 'What do you mean amorphous—' He struggles to get his mouth around the word. It is difficult when you hear it the first time.

I thought I'd help him out bye spelling it out. 'Amorphous, A-M-O-R-P-H-O-U-S.'

He tries again, 'Amorph—'

I write it down for him. That helps.

'What is an amorphous thing?' he asks, getting the pronunciation right.

'A shapeless, formless thing. A thing without definition. In your case, some sinister thing dead set on controlling your life,' I explain.

'Now he is just fucking with my mind,' Thomas says to Tim and Mitt. They laugh and shake their heads.

'I am not fucking with your mind, Thomas. Your mind is fucking with you. I am trying to rescue you from it,' I say. I feel I must match the standard of language for the sake of mateship. 'And the saddest thing is that you are spending your most precious asset, your time, fighting and arguing in your head with a shapeless illusion you have created all by yourself. You are burning intelligence on a wasteful purpose,' I say.

Thomas fixes his gaze on me. 'What do you mean burning intelligence?' he asks.

'You are spending time thinking about an illusion, an illusion that you think is real. Thinking does not come cheap. It is not for free. It burns time, intelligent time. Finite time. Think what you can do with the intelligent time if you apply it on something that is real,' I say.

'Like what?' he asks.

'Like going back to school or adult learning centres or whatever they might be called here and learn something new—literature, philosophy, anything. If you don't want to do that, read a classic novel. Read Dostoyevsky. Spend a few hours a week doing that rather than burning intelligence on this rubbish.'

I sense Thomas needs more time to process his new words and ideas. I am intrigued that introducing him to the notions of amorphous things and burning intelligence has somehow allowed him to escape the tribes.

I try to close the topic. 'If you listen to me and allow me to explain, you will realise that we create these mental structures and illusions ourselves. They don't exist anywhere except in your head. Amorphous masters of your mind that you create yourself.

'You don't even have a clear definition of the characters, the individual people in your cabal. It is that vague. Cabals cannot think. It requires living people to think. Living people have bodies, and bodies have names. To conspire is to have a body and a name. Without those, I have no choice but to dismiss your conspiracy as an urban myth. In fact, it is probably a far-right myth.

'So don't tell me I am fucking with your mind. It is fucking with you. Your mind is complicit in an intellectual atrocity to give a non-existent amorphous thing authority over your and for it to decide how and what you think. I am trying to help you take back control of your mind. Thomas, this is the best life you will ever live. You do not get to do it again. This is it. Do not waste your time making up formless amorphous crap you tell yourself is out to get you. So don't you be a warrior for this illusionary tribe, Thomas.'

> We can never know what to want, because, living only one life, we can neither compare it with our previous lives nor perfect it in our lives to come. There is no means of testing which decision is better, because there is no basis for comparison. We live everything as it comes, without warning, like an actor going on cold. And what can life be worth if the first rehearsal for life is life itself.
>
> *Milan Kundera*

Thomas blinks, but other than that, he maintains eye contact with me, as if he were looking out for sudden movements, ready to flee. Then he turns and looks out over the balcony.

Thomas stares into empty space, as if the enormity of his wasted time is sinking in. He repeats his accusation that I am fucking with his mind, but it is a feeble gesture. Behind me, Tim and Mitt have collapsed with laughter. Mitt says, 'I just love it when Hendrik does his philosophising.'

* * *

The eyes question the need for all the profanity. I am compelled to make my excuses. So I say, 'Don't look at me like that! The language is common in pubs and locker rooms. Dirty old pubs in Sydney are no exception. Australians are no exception. Even school playing fields. Yes, that is right. I am not using any language that you will not hear a thirteen-year-old use.'

John says nothing about the profanities. Instead, he says, no, he despairs, 'Unspeakable, Hendrik, unspeakable. My god, what you did to that poor Thomas. You humiliated him in front of his colleagues.

Shameless. Have you ever considered that there is a nicer, more respectful, and more dignified way to go about it?'

There he is. John has turned into my father. I feel a bit stupid now for drawing attention to the profanities. First, the literary advice, then the moral advice. Where is the legal advice?

'What are you suggesting? That I am a bit harsh?' I say, offering no immediate excuses.

John looks directly at me now. 'Not harsh, Hendrik, more like vicious. That was as close to a savage verbal attack as one can get, without getting physical.'

Anger swells up in me. 'How can I possibly insult him? He is being stupid! And this way, I really drive the message home. Sometimes that is the only way to rescue people from their illusions. Sometimes it is the only way to get through the psychological barriers.'

'Nonetheless, Hendrik', says John, 'I can see how you upset people. You seem to have an uncanny ability to do it.'

'People have an uncanny ability to be stupid, John,' I say. 'I am just stripping the pretence and revealing it. People get upset because I use logic that destroys their illusion. Do I need to repeat the quotes from Kant and Russel?'

John holds his hands up to stop me. 'No, please don't. Tell me again. Why the quotes? I find they really disrupt the flow of the dialogue.'

'The quotes?' I ask rhetorically. It is my turn to hold up my hands briefly. 'I use quotes in two ways in the novel. When I use it in the dialogue, I draw specific attention to it for the person I am having the dialogue with. Mostly, though, my quotes are for the readers. They are placed strategically to draw attention to a point I want to make about the dialogue. The point is that much of what we believe and much of what we debate in society today has been believed and debated for millennia. I am using the quotes to show readers that we have been here, done this, and it is astonishing that we are circling back and repeating many of the old stupidities. It is a tragedy that we do not teach children the basic elements of philosophical practice—how to analyse an idea, how to test it for validity and soundness, how to discard the ones that do not stand up to scrutiny—instead of hiding behind the right to have an opinion, no matter how crappy that opinion is.'

'Are you not just appealing to authority Hendrik?' Asks John. It is a valid question.

'Not really, I reference the original author to give recognition where it is due. It follows a long-standing tradition in philosophy. I do not use it as an appeal to authority, to strengthen my argument,' I say

John ignores my answer. 'Do you live your life by other people's quotes, Hendrik?'

I cannot believe that he would say something like that immediately after I gave my reasons for the quotes. I am too tired to go to battle. I simply say, 'No, only this one: "Stop living your life by other people's quotes." I do not know who said it first.'

'If you didn't swear as much, you could have suggested your novel to children, Hendrik,' proposes John. I am perplexed by the moral challenges. It is not at all what I expected from a meeting with a prestigious lawyer.

'I'd rather teach parents now. They can teach their children. Then they can screw up their children in their own preferred way, depending on their parenting style,' I say.

John goes quiet. In the meantime, the eyes tell me they do not buy my excuse for the profanities, but they won't punish me for it.

I have an urge to fill the silence. I am too slow. John interrupts my urge, 'It is an interesting view, Hendrik, or should I say opinion. The thing about amorphous mental constructions. Am I right in thinking that you were heading this way with all the dialogues, that somehow there is an amorphous structure at work in each of the dialogues?'

I am struggling to keep up with the change from moral critique to literary critique, but I am also relieved that the discussion can move on. 'Amorphous structures, tribes, cultures, subcultures, yes, indeed. "The business" is one that's featured in almost everyone. The business has a corporate culture. Its leadership sets about a process of social engineering, to install pride, loyalty, unconditional love in all its employees, but it never returns that loyalty. The system of *employment at will* takes care of reverse loyalty.

'If you think about it, amorphous structures are at work in all our daily lives. We create them and develop policies, practices, and standards for them. Bind them in legal terms. Create a person, a legal person to be precise, so that we incorporate them, embody them. We reify them by constructing buildings to house them. We even create professional consulting firms to teach the amorphous structures the business management frameworks. Whole industries spring up around it.

'At least a business, like many other institutions, serves society, or that was its intent. Ever since that first-class idiot Milton Friedman, business is all about serving shareholders. In the first half of this novel, I am trying to create awareness of the amorphous structure—'

'Milton Friedman won the Nobel Prize, Hendrik,' John interrupts. 'You cannot possibly call him a first-class idiot.'

'Of course not. Apologies to Friedman,' I say, 'an example of the composition fallacy, committed by an ordinary philosopher nonetheless. I should have said first-class idiotic idea.'

John smiles with self-satisfaction. 'Apology accepted. On behalf of Friedman.'

Having dealt with the diversion, I finish my explanation about amorphous structures, 'We cannot live with them. We cannot live without them. We create them, but we do not question their existence. They create us, but we do not want to admit it. The most bizarre thing is, we create them out of nothing, then we try and use Aristotle's first principles of science to examine them. How bloody bizarre is that—'

'So Thomas was right,' he says.

'No, Thomas was creating amorphous structures entirely by himself, and that is a problem for him. Most shared formal amorphous mental structures really serve society well. Think of families, communities, schools, democratic systems, ethics and morals, and other institutions. It is the ones that Thomas is working on that is problematic, that can be sinister and life-destroying, like religion.' I put the bait out.

John doesn't take it. 'The ones listed in the quote from Bukowski,' he confirms.

I nod.

John asks, 'Well, do you think your readers would have picked up on that?'

'A piece of advice that aspiring writers receive early on in their writing career is to choose your audience and write for them. I prefer to ignore that advice. I write what I want and leave it to an audience who wants a smart writer to find me. They will get what I want to say from the introduction and will look for it throughout the novel,' I say with a writer's high-minded smugness. To confirm the point, I finish with 'You did.'

'Unnecessary,' says the eyes. Did I mention brown eyes can do unnecessary?

John points out the critical flaw in my strategy. 'You write for smart people, but you try and teach stupid ones,' he says but does not smile. I don't offer any resistance. I have none.

John starts to make more notes on his legal pad. As he does so, it occurs to me that he is showing empathy for Thomas. If I am not mistaken, he did so for most of the characters. Isn't that exactly what writers want? That his readers empathise with the characters, the protagonists that he creates. Does a writer really create a character, or do they resource those from people they know?

Are the characters in fact amorphous things? Is a person in part an amorphous thing? They must be. We are seduced by the body, but the body is not the person. The person is what psychologists try to poke scientific instruments at. And look at the mess created by psychologists when they attempt to reify an amorphous thing that does not exist in the real world.

Think of the enormous harm that was done when the practice of sexual deviance was first defined. The coining of the word *heterosexual* came first: the sexual deviance of an obsessive preference for the opposite sex. Then came *homosexuality*: the sexual deviance of an obsessive preference for the same sex. It implies that the only acceptable preference would be an obsessive preference for both sexes, but that cannot be an obsession. That tribe, the state, picked up on this and decided for the sake of promoting old-fashioned family values, heterosexuality is the only acceptable obsessive preference. Homosexuality and bisexuality became a problem, a problem that they thought could be fixed by criminalising it or religious fanatics thought could be resolved through conversion therapies.

Psychologists come up with all kinds of psychometric tests to determine your personality type, your mental deviations. Your mental deviations from what? From what they think is a standard? What is that standard, the psychologist? How bizarre. The only thing that is real is the body. That is the thing we punish. That is the thing we kill. What was that quote from Russel? Oh yes, this:

> You may kill an artist or a thinker, but you cannot acquire his art or his thought. You may put a man to death because he loves his fellow-men, but you will not by so doing acquire the love which made his happiness.
>
> *Bertrand Russell*

If John has empathy for Thomas, then he has empathy for an amorphous thing, an amorphous thing I created. And what is Jennifer Rawlings trying to do? She is trying to do the same thing I did with Thomas, to prove that the amorphous things we created must have real bodies. Otherwise, they are just illusions.

She knows where they are and that somehow I have injured those bodies. But injuring bodies is not libel; that is a different kind of crime. She is claiming I have injured the amorphous things that live inside those bodies. She needs the bodies; I do not. Without the bodies, she has no case. With the bodies, I am in trouble.

'Are you doing the reflection, or have you already done that? It feels quite complete,' says John.

'No, I do summarise. Thomas is an example of the dark alleys and dead ends that we sometimes encounter in a dialogue. This is the difficult part with dialogues where my "opponents" are so close-minded they'd rather get angry than get wise. They are also the most likely to commit fallacies and errors in reasoning. I also work on revealing more about the amorphous structures that we create, how these amorphous structures rule our lives, consume our intellectual energy and precious time. We have enough trouble with the ones we need, no need to create ones we don't. And new ones that we give authority to dictate what we think.'

'I was about to give up on you there, Hendrik. Another brazen encounter,' says John absent-mindedly.

'You must see by now, and I am sure you have experienced this too, that sometimes you need to deliberately poke at the parts of a human to see what other parts twitch. The other parts that twitch will reveal their world views. I dislike the term *world view*. It is a dumbing down of Kant's transcendentalism and interpretive repertoires. Those other parts that twitch reveal tunnels in a cave that might lead to dead ends or might lead to the light. You must provoke them into a twitch to know where they lead. Those twitches may just offer a way out of Plato's cave,' I say.

'Still, you could try a gentler approach. You have demonstrated that you can do it,' says John still absent-mindedly. I don't see a need to respond, so I don't. John doesn't expect a response.

I am bracing myself for the 'Is Thomas real? Is he just a character?' debate, but John doesn't go there. I have no energy for it.

PART TWO

GLIMMERS OF LIGHT AND HOPE

Dialogues with John Allen, Rosemary, Liz,
Martin Victoria, and Jeremy

LUNCH WITH JOHN ALLEN

J ohn has left his office, and I am left on my own, without supervision. He didn't leave unceremoniously. He announced it with 'We should break for lunch' and 'Wait here'.

I take the opportunity to explore. It is a large rectangular corner office. 'Of course, it is a corner office,' I mutter to myself. I wonder over to the other end where an imposing rosewood desk, polished to the extreme, is placed so that its regular occupant has his back to the floor-to-ceiling window at the far end of the office. I am not sure whether the desk is designed to give authority to the occupant or the occupant must have that authority already to occupy the desk.

Either way, this is not the kind of desk where one toils all day long. It is the kind of desk where the occupant calls in subordinates and seats them in the two low-back leather chairs on the other side. Club chairs, I think. Comfortable enough but only enough for a short stay. Moreover, the imposing desk and the high-back maroon leather chair on the other side will make anyone seated in the club chairs uncomfortable by design. The only possible other function of this desk is to sign contracts, new lucrative deals to defend the honour of some sleazy politician who likes to 'grab them by the pussy'.

I am not sure why I thought that. John doesn't strike me as the kind of lawyer who would tolerate that kind of sleaze in his office.

I try the chair behind the desk. Within an instant, the chair begins to impose its dislike for me. I cannot find any comfort in the way it supports me, no matter how I position my body. This clearly is no place for an ordinary philosopher. An ordinary philosopher does not have the authority required to occupy this chair. 'I wonder if philosophers can benefit from learning to occupy desks like this, from sitting comfortably in chairs like this,' I mutter to myself. 'Probably not,' I mutter on. 'Philosophers like to reach consensus understandings, not intimidate people into submission.'

The chair has tolerated me for as long as it can. I get up quickly and walk over to the window that stretches the full length of the office. It overlooks a riverside walk, a promenade I think it is called. People are out and about. They seem to hurry along in a completely relaxed fashion like only people in a big city can do. No one pays any attention to the people around them unless it is to avoid knocking their lunch and coffee from their hands. 'How worry-free they seem,' I mutter on. 'I bet they don't have a letter from a Jennifer Rawlings in the hands of a John Allen, partner at Allen and Overly.'

I turn around. The long wall opposite the window is in fact a large glass-fronted bookcase. Inside are leather-bound copies of case books, court reports, and other legal reference books. Great care has been taken to ensure the leather bindings match, and the books are placed in chronological order. There is nothing of interest to an ordinary philosopher in those books. There may be something of interest to a clerk or intern or junior lawyer who looks for something the defence council can use to dismiss or win a particular point in a court. All they need to do is find an old ruling so the defence can point out to the judge he has not done his homework, and since another judge has already ruled, he doesn't have to break his pretty little head over this point.

I glance at the other end of the office. The far end where we were seated and will be seated when John returns. You might call it a snug, but only if you are naive enough to think snug things are discussed there. For the first time, I notice that the wing-backed chair that John occupied is ever so slightly more imposing than the one allocated to me. More decorated, a darker maroon, and a marginal but noticeably higher back. I decide not to try the same little stunt to sit in it. I gained nothing but discomfort from my earlier excursion behind the rosewood desk.

On the wall behind the chair arrangement, the snug, there is a photograph of a handsome man in cap and robe. It is John, of course, and it appears to be him receiving his degree. 'Cambridge University,' it says. 'First class honours,' it says, 'Master of Law [LLM].' It says all those things. I spent a little time trying to figure out how master of law shortens to LLM but then decide the question has no merit. It is one of those amorphous things that burns intelligence for no good reason. What strikes me are the eyes in the photo. Uncanny how they remind me of my father. Intense, intelligent brown eyes that miss nothing. Did I mention that brown eyes miss nothing?

I have looked at them for too long. They tell me to sit down. I turn back towards my allocated chair. The idea of sleazy politicians comes back and haunts me for a second. I imagine them putting their fat, slimy arses in my allocated chair. I back away, but just then, John returns. 'We disinfect this office every day after work, Hendrik. Thought you would like to know that.'

My god, is he reading my mind? 'I do like to know that,' I say, and I imagine I look a little surprised. Perhaps that is what compelled John to expand on the explanation.

'Ever since the pandemic hit,' John continues, 'seems like a sensible thing to do.'

'Only once a day?' I enquire, not sure why.

'I only do one consultation a day, Hendrik.'

My mind races to my ever-diminishing savings account. I hear father's voice again, in my head of course, *Hendrik, what the fuck have you done now?*

I ask for directions to the washroom; it has been a long morning, and we have shared a few cups of coffee already. Did I mention the coffee? A person, a young man, refreshed our coffees on a periodic and well-timed basis. Seemed to appear from nowhere, said nothing, and left the room like a ghost, vanished just like that.

Refreshments has been laid out during my absence. The young man, if it was him, has vanished already. The food has been divided into two tidy arrangements—a bowl of crisps, an impossible-looking sandwich made from rye bread, filled with thinly sliced beef pastrami, about an inch thick, and topped with pickles. Additionally, there is a small bowl of fruit and a fresh pot of coffee. I inspect the sandwich. It looks like it is enough to send an ordinary philosopher into a coma, but apparently, this is only just enough to fuel a prestigious lawyer for an afternoon's interrogation.

We eat in silence. The sandwich is deceptive. It appears bigger than it is and is delicious, goes down a treat. In fact, I am compelled to finish the crisps and the bowl of fruit. Whilst eating, my mind wanders to amorphous things, to tribes.

Have you heard people say, 'I am searching for my tribe'? Does that mean they wandered too far from their tribe, adopted too many unwelcome values and habits, or rejected too many values that are necessary for the cohesion of the tribe and got ejected?

Does that mean the tribe sent them away to get educated, and when they returned, they found the tribe had become foreign to them, or the tribe thinks they have become foreign to the tribe?

Does that mean they have migrated to a new country, a new tribe, and they now find themselves torn between two tribes, fitting equally uncomfortably in both? When they are a patriot to one, they are a traitor to the other?

Does that mean their tribe collapsed in an apocalyptic event and they find themselves lost without it?

Does that mean they have escaped one and it is no longer theirs?

Does that mean they have won Nietzsche's battle for him? And now they are looking for a new battle?

And what about storytelling? We are in the middle of this story, so is this where I should have begun the novel? Or is this the beginning place of a new novel? If I followed the advice to start in the middle, would I start with a description of this room? But how can you give a description of this room if you know nothing about the occupant? Or would the room have told you enough about the occupant, and would you have been better prepared for his arrival? But what would you have? An amorphous thing, incomplete and somewhat shapeless. Whatever shape you create will be defined by the room. Surely the room will provide an incomplete character, an illusionary, amorphous thing.

What if you start at the end? Isn't there a novel that starts like this? 'Carl is dead. This is the story about how he died.' If I wanted to start at the end, then what would be the first line? 'Hendrik lost the court case. This story is about how that happened.' Something grips the pit of my stomach.

John rescues me from my mental muddle and from the grip on the pit of my stomach.

'Shall we continue?'

I thank him for lunch a second too late, a second after I realise it will probably be on my bill. 'Sure.'

He takes the lead. 'It seems to me that your dialogues have reached rock bottom, Hendrik. I hope things get better from now on.'

'Well, I am not the one to judge the rocky bottoms of the dialogues, John. I will leave that to the readers. The readers bring their own interpretative repertoires to the reading, their own worldviews, their own prior knowledge, their own twitching. They are complicit in their responses. They decide. That, by sheer coincidence, is the topic of my next dialogue,' I say, but the eyes tell me he needs more hope. I give it to them. 'I am told that every good story has an arc. It travels between two contrasting views, from an existing place of comfort that is dismantled through an uncomfortable encounter, to a new position, a new normal. You are right to anticipate we have reached rock bottom or at least are heading in that direction. At some point, the dialogues will turn the corner. They become more dignified, more respectful, and more curious too. That is the way I collected and organised the dialogues. I cannot guarantee that you will see it that way. The reason behind the arc in my novel is that the reader will contrast stupidity with smart and see a better way to examine ideas. I hope that the reader will recognise amorphous tribal structures, will become courageous enough to poke a sharp logic stick at them, to make them twitch to test the alertness of their warriors. That is our only hope if we are to make life better for all humans.'

John takes what little hope is on offer. The eyes tell me to continue.

COFFEE WITH ROSEMARY

Any person capable of angering you becomes your master.

Epictetus

Rosemary and I are meeting in a coffee shop outlet that is part of a chain. According to the notice behind the barista, the brand originated in Southern California. The coffee is good, exceptionally good, and a regular is sufficiently large for a long dialogue. We are here because Rosemary asked to see me. We have a mutual friend whom I must thank someday, and I hope Rosemary will do the same when she reports back to her with a review. Rosemary was described as an imposing person, one I would recognise as soon as she walked through the door. I recognised her as soon as she walked through the door.

We do introductions first, then we order coffee, wait for the coffee, collect the coffee, and finally, settle down in those comfy chairs which have become standard furniture in coffee shops since they featured in a sitcom. The high back chairs face each other and provides some privacy. However, I think the privacy offered by the chairs will be ineffective against Rosemary's booming voice.

'So what question do you want us to contemplate, Rosemary?' I ask. In a setting like this, it is always easier to drill down to the question quickly. There is an implied prior agreement that I can do it, that I will just ask for it.

Rosemary shifts around trying to find a comfortable place in the chair that seems to elude her. 'OK, I have been a teacher all my life, and I am now keen to change careers.' Her answer throws my implied process completely out of the window. That is clearly not a question.

'OK, do you want to give context first?' I say to encourage her to continue.

'Yes, please. I have decided I have had enough of teaching. I have done it for nearly twenty-five years. I have sent enough children up to higher grades to eventually find work in an Amazon warehouse several times over.' She smiles. I enjoy the sense of humour but secretly hope that at least some of her students will graduate with higher aspirations. I calculate she must have developed that voice trying to keep the attention of third-grade pupils.

'Nothing wrong with that. But why is that a problem that brings you here?' I ask.

'Well, the decision is not as simple as that,' she says.

'Still, it is not exactly a philosophical problem or even a question,' I say, trying not to be impatient. There is too much coffee in my mug to be impatient. I try to move things forward. 'What career do you want to change to?'

'I have been training to be a life coach, joined a professional organisation, got certified and everything. Secretly.' She almost whispers the last word.

There is something about the whispered word that draws attention. I decide to probe the whispered word. 'Do I sense you haven't told everybody about your plans, your husband?' I ask.

'Oh no, he knows.' Rosemary's answer pleases her.

'I don't understand, Rosemary. If your husband knows and supports you, what could be the problem? It is purely an economic decision, isn't it?' I suggest.

'What do you mean economic decision?' she asks.

'I mean, you have discussed with your husband that the new career will carry economic risk, that it provides the same income or maybe not, the same financial guarantees or maybe not, the same financial security or maybe not. You get my drift? Those are not philosophical questions. So unless you are concerned about whether you are going to continue to contribute positively to society or not or there is some other trouble on the horizon, then how do you think I can help?' I say. I am really worried now that I am not going to be able to finish my coffee. I wrap it up. 'If your husband agrees and supports you, then what could possibly be the problem?'

She folds her ample arms over her even more ample breasts. Quite how she manages to do that, I am not sure. She comes back passionately from a direction I did not expect. 'Why do you think I need my husband's approval?' she asks.

There is a simple answer to that question, so I give it to her, 'Oh, I don't think you need his approval, but it would be wise to get his agreement. I assume you have been married for a while and your finances are intertwined. As such, you cannot reasonably make an economic decision without his participation.' I did not think I was going to give marital advice, but there you go.

'Oh, I see, of course, I agree. That is not the problem though. I told you I have his full support.' Which she did tell me, that is.

'So what is the conundrum then, Rosemary?' Time to motivate her to get to the question now. Enough of the context.

'I am worried about what they will say,' she says.

And there is the problem. The most dangerous word in the English language. Seemingly innocent, hiding in plain sight. *They*. I have told you about this word before with Thomas. This time, we are going to look at the problem it causes in a bit more depth.

> It never ceases to amaze me: we all love ourselves more than other people, but care more about their opinion than our own.
>
> *Marcus Aurelius*

The word *they* is at the heart of one of the most common fallacies in everyday speech, the composition fallacy. It lets us slip from precision to ambiguity in one word. We slip from one to more individuals or one individual to a group of people with undefined boundaries: vague, sinister, amorphous. Let me just add that if you have chosen *they* as your gender pronoun I am absolutely not suggesting that you are sinister.

Allow me to explain. Joe's parents are dead. They have died. In my mind, I am applying the same precision. You, on the other hand, receive the information with a risk of lost precision. The two sentences must be kept together, must be spoken as one. If they separate, then it injects ambiguity into the second sentence. You repeat, 'They have died.' And now the *they* have become vague and the *they* demands explanation. But it is an explanation that is rarely asked for. We just continue living with the ambiguity and this use of *they* can become sinister.

In Rosemary's case, she is living a situation that she finds troublesome enough to seek help for because of that ambiguity. She is obviously in her mind referring to some clearly specific people or perhaps just one person. However, I am hearing a vague and ambiguous reference to some people, a tribe, a conspiracy of characters that must have some power over her.

'What do you mean by *they*?' I ask.

She frowns, turns her head down, and fixes her gaze on the table. She appears to be surprised that I would even ask the question. 'They?' she repeats then hesitates, as if I had opened a door to somewhere she didn't want to go. 'People,' she says. She tries a diversion, taking the ambiguity with her.

'They, people, who are they?' I insist.

'His family. They are going to have something to say about this when they find out,' she explains.

'So let me be clear, his family will say something, his whole family,' I try to undo the ambiguity. I try to give the shapeless, amorphous thing some shape. It gets its shape from the characters that is its substance.

Once you clarify the characters, you will eliminate some of them. The one that is left over will be the troublemaker. Then you have just one amorphous thing to deal with, still somewhat shapeless, still intricate, but just one character and no longer a conspiracy of characters, no longer an illusionary tribe.

Rosemary says nothing. She shifts around uncomfortably, busy with a private battle. The dark eyes focus on something outside the window. I seek more clarity, more definition, more shape. 'All of them or some of them? Surely your husband is not one of them? I cannot imagine it is the whole family. Are they sending a representative?' I ask.

'No!' she says emphatically. 'Of course not, not everyone, his sister mainly. Actually, it is just his sister. She can be a real bitch.' Rosemary's imagination focuses her attention on the sister. Her face tells me she means what she says.

I am quite sure Sigmund Freud will have something to say about Rosemary's avoidance tactics by referring to her sister-in-law as 'they'. Psychologists might call the condition vagueness as ignorance. But then they must give it a name so they can develop an expensive treatment that lasts for months. In Rosemary's case, it reveals itself in the composition fallacy. There is more work to do, but she offers to do it without my prompting.

'She really likes to push my button, and I lose it completely. She makes me so angry,' says Rosemary. She shuffles her ample bottom to the front edge of her seat in preparation of demonstrating something. I can see from the changing expression on her face that it is true but also that she is deeply troubled by it.

Like I said, Rosemary has done some work. She says it happens 'at times'. I suggest that she gives an example. She does.

'Last year was my turn to host Christmas dinner at my house. She goes on and on about my husband, his job, our relationship, and how we are bringing up our kids. I try my best not to respond, but I lose it and turn over the entire dinner table on everyone, well, everyone on the other side, including my in-laws and her and her husband.' With that, she grabs the coffee table and pretend to flip it over. She is so convincing that I push it down to save our coffees.

At that moment, I thought a change of career will be best for the children in her care at school, but maybe not life coaching.

'She is an evil woman who always wants to demean me and embarrass me in front of her parents.' Her attitude settles down to something more defensive as she shuffles her ample bottom back in the chair and folds her arms again.

But I am not done. 'Are there any times when the two of you get along?'

She turns her head and look at me sideways. 'What do you mean?' she asks. She is trying to avoid giving an answer. She might begin to realise her strong position on this is built on shaky ground. We have reduced 'they' or 'people' to one person. Then Rosemary reduced it from all the time to some of the times. Now we have to go from all situations to some situations.

It takes Rosemary a while to come up with an answer. I suspect the hesitation has more to do with a reluctance to admit that sometimes the sister-in-law is not a bitch than it has to do with a search of her memory for good times. I also think by now she must realise that the truth is her best strategy.

I encourage her, 'You have asked to see me, Rosemary. If our time together will be helpful in any way, then you need to be transparent and truthful.'

'We do get along just fine at times,' she admits.

'I want you to think about something. Your sister-in-law needs help to send you over the top. You are providing that help. Think about these words from an old philosopher: "If someone succeeds in provoking you, realize that your mind is complicit in the provocation [Epictetus]."'

For some peculiar reason, perhaps not unexpectedly, this triggers an angry response. First, she leans forward, places her hands on her knees, and turns her elbows out. She appears larger than she is, a pose that is completely unnecessary in consideration of her imposing frame.

'Oh, it is all my fault, isn't it? You are saying that if a young girl gets raped, then she is complicit in the rape? Is that what you are saying?' Her voice, tone, and words draw the attention of the two young women at the table next door.

This kind of 'whataboutism' is an awful counter to a point, a form of redirection that is prolific in politics. It is quite frankly a despicable tactic. I think political coaches call it one of the ways to put a dead cat on the table. You use this ploy when you lose an argument.

I match the volume of her voice and her tone. After all, we now have an audience, and that audience need to know my response to this awful accusation. 'Stop this. Shame on you, Rosemary. How can you possibly suggest that there is a similarity between you losing your temper and a young girl getting raped? How can you possibly suggest there is a moral equivalence between those two things? Explain that to me!'

Rosemary fixes her gaze on me but says nothing, so I continue with my rebuke, 'What happens to women when they get raped is terrible, and I am not suggesting at all that they are complicit, but if you want to discuss whether they are complicit in it or not, then we can do that separately and at a different time. But right now, I want you to admit that your mind is complicit when you lose your temper with your sister-in-law.'

She leans back and folds her arms again. She whispers an apology. Keeping my voice at the same level as before, I ask her to repeat.

'I am sorry, that was wrong of me,' she says loud enough to reach the audience, but not loud enough to kill their curiosity. I glance at them in a way to suggest case closed and kill the curiosity. They start their own conversation up again.

We take a few minutes to drink coffee to allow the temperature to come down to a tolerable level.

'Rosemary,' I prompt her, 'you have to admit that your response to your sister-in-law's provocation is evidence of your mind being complicit in the whole event. You two are co-constructing this.'

'I am beginning to see that, but it is difficult,' she says.

'Think about it this way. There are specific circumstances where you have primed the rocket, get it launch ready, and turn on the green launch ready light. Your sister-in-law sees the green light and pushes the launch button, sending the Falcon Heavy into space,' I say, injecting a little humour into the discussion.

She smiles, and I am relieved that the mood has changed. She says, 'So what you are saying is that I prepare everything in advance, so all she has to do is push the launch button.' With that, she pushes an imaginary button in front of her.

I am genuinely pleased that we can talk about this around the analogy. It is like discussing cheese on a cheese board. No one has a vested interest in the cheese. I nudge her. 'Just think of the time you spend prepping that rocket.'

'What do you mean prepping?' she asks.

I answer, 'It takes weeks to prepare a rocket for launch. You are doing the same thing. You are anticipating a launch, and you are already prepping the Falcon Heavy. You are at least subconsciously aware of it. That is why we are here having this discussion.'

Rosemary stares out of the window for a while. I hope she is thinking about prepping that rocket. Then she states the obvious, 'If I don't prep the rocket, then the green launch light will never go on. Then it doesn't matter if she pushes the button,' Rosemary says this almost absent-mindedly, simultaneously pushing the imaginary button repeatedly. She is saying this to herself, so no need for me to respond. 'Strange feelings I am having, Hendrik, like relief. I was getting ready to argue why this happens, that it is all her fault, that there is something wrong with that woman that I can fix.'

'But now I see it. It is a game we play. It matters not how the game starts. It matters not that there is something wrong with her. Even if I can, it is not my place to fix her. If I stop playing, stop prepping the rocket, it will never launch,' she says, still to herself, despite mentioning my name. She leans back into the chair, her arms relaxed by her side and her hands on her knees.

We sit silently drinking coffee for a few more minutes. I can see that Rosemary is making significant adjustments, so the quiet time is well spent.

'You know what,' she says, 'that is exactly what happens. I have been prepping that rocket for weeks in anticipation of her pushing the button. But if I think of dismantling the rocket, then I feel complete relief, not just relief, empowered. I can think clearly about it. I am not going to try and change her. I will change me. I have the power and the authority to do that.'

We drink more coffee. Rosemary's dark eyes look softer now, less fearsome.

> Even people who love you, will not necessarily agree with
> your ideas, understand you, or share your enthusiasms.
> Grow up! Who cares what other people think about you!
>
> *Epictetus*

'Good for you, Rosemary. If you do that who will be the master of your mind?' I ask.

'What do you mean master of my mind?' She asks.

'If your mind is complicit in the offence and it send you skywards, can you claim that you are the master of your mind, or is it this thing you co-constructed with your sister-in-law? I explain.

'Of course, I see what you mean now. I must become the master of my mind,' she says.

'Yes, you must and be nice to yourself. It might take a few goes for it to become permanent,' I say.

'I know that, Hendrik. I teach children, remember?' She smiles.

* * *

'And . . . ?' asks John.

'And what?' ask I.

'That's all? No insults, no edgy jokes? She does not report back in the novel whether she was successful or not?' he hints.

'Nope, never see her again,' I hint back.

'Oh, she is a real person then, is she not?' he interrogates.

'Who knows, John, who knows,' I avoid.

Perhaps the lunch break has restored some of our sense of humour, and I realise now I missed this game in the dialogue with Thomas—this game where we try to give a physical body to an amorphous character.

'But we do not know if it worked for her, do we?' More interrogation, but should I take pleasure that John is now curious about one of my characters?

'Does that matter?' I turn the tables on the interrogation.

'It does for the reader,' he deflects.

'I expect the reader to bring something to the table. What do you think happened next?' I have the advantage, so I ask the questions with the emphasis on *you*.

'You leave it up to the reader to decide the ending?' He tries to reverse the new order.

'No, the ending is in the lesson in reasoning, not the long-term consequences to Rosemary's life. Your own creative mind can do the filling in if it is important to you,' I dismiss.

The eyes accept the dismissal, and we move on.

John makes a few notes, looks up, and asks, 'You hint that she may or may not be a real person, Hendrik. If she is a real person, do you think she will be able to identify herself in the dialogue?'

'If she is a real person, she will have to have ample bosoms with a habit of turning over dinner tables on her guests, notably her bitchy sister-in-law. I imagine there are, no, hope there are many ample-breasted women with a propensity to turn the dinner table over on their bitchy sisters-in-law. And oh yes, they have to be third-grade teachers too,' I say with just a hint of sarcasm.

The eyes tell me there is too much sarcasm.

John is a little more curious and joins in, 'And presumably they are all called Rosemary.'

'That will be a hell of a coincidence, won't it?' I say.

'Not if it is also a Rosemary that knows you. Don't you see it, Hendrik? Your dialogue with Rosemary could be humiliating for her if it gets into the public domain,' says John.

'There is nothing I can do if people would like to identify themselves with one of the characters in my novel, John,' I say defensively.

'There is also the challenge on the whataboutism. Don't you think you were just a little bold with that approach?' asks John. The way that he does this makes me wonder if he can tell the difference between the character and the real person. I have nothing; all I can do is shrug.

'But what if you have given enough of a description and detail to give away Rosemary's identity, Hendrik?' John speculates, but I thought he asks, so I answer.

'There is a disclaimer in the front of the novel, John,' I remind him.

'There is a letter on this table that suggests that is not enough, Hendrik,' he says.

There is a hint of tension in the pit of my stomach. I have no other defences. I say nothing.

John allows the tension to grow. The tension grows. I am disabled by the tension. It grips the pit of my stomach. So I do nothing. John is the first one to give.

'Do the reflection now, please,' he says.

'The dialogue with Rosemary is again about the composition fallacy, but this time, it goes down to the dispositional versus situational bias. The conversation with her revealed how certain events can be misconstrued as personality traits, that people might act in certain ways based on the context or situation rather than suffering from a character flaw: always being a bitch as she put it. Looming in the shadows is the amorphous structure, the co-construction of certain patterns of behaviour between people. All it does is for one person to disable the behaviour, and the amorphous structure dies away. There was also the lesson on whataboutism.'

John has gone back to his notes on this dialogue. There is clearly something about it that worries him. He says nothing and nods for me to continue.

'The next dialogue—'

John interrupts me, 'Wasn't there something else, something more to do with the whataboutism? That one's mind is complicit when another person offends you?'

I am impressed. I say so. John accepts the outside approval, but he gives no explanation on why it triggers his curiosity. None whatsoever. Instead, he gives me permission to move on to the next dialogue. We move on to the next dialogue.

DINNER WITH LIZ, I

The last century has produced an abundance of ideologies that pretend to be keys to history but are actually nothing but desperate efforts to escape responsibility.

Hannah Arendt

The informal group of friends meet at a different restaurant tonight. You will remember this group when I tell you it sprung out of meetups of Lilly's writer friends. We are eating somewhere new tonight so that we can try a different menu. This is a Spanish tapas restaurant at the end of a cul-de-sac, right in the middle of a residential area. It is hard to get to by car. It is easy to get to from all the condominiums around it. A ready-made captive market of several thousand apartments. Not surprising then that it is packed to the brim.

There is the usual round of polite greetings, the 'How are you?' and the 'Nice to see you' greetings.

'You're looking good,' says Liz.

I mistakenly assumed she is talking to me, so I respond with 'Oh, thanks, Liz. It must be the light in here.' But she wasn't talking to me. She was talking to Mary, and Mary now looks a little upset.

We settle down. There is an apparent seating protocol at work—partners and couples split. Each member desperate for fresh company, I suppose. Liz finds the only chair available is the one opposite me, so she curls up in the seat, meticulous, measured movement.

For the sake of polite conversation, I say to her, 'So what did you get up to this weekend?'

She takes it as a real question and answers, 'You know me. I went to a meeting of the Philosophy of Life group.'

'Was it good?' I push on with the polite conversation.

She takes me up on it. 'We discussed libertarianism.'

I encourage her. 'Oh, interesting. What is meant by libertarianism?' Now let me be clear. Any ordinary philosopher worth his or her salt will know just about everything there is to know about libertarianism. But I have learned a lesson with Liz. You don't lecture Liz.

She sums it up for me, 'It means that individuals in society take full responsibility for their lives and the consequences of their decisions, and we therefore do not need governments.'

I do not agree with her summary, but the best thing to do is to try and clear up her understanding through dialogue, so I ask, 'What, no government at all?'

She raises herself in her chair; her golden eyes seek mine out and starts to track. 'Only a police force to protect the rights of the individual and a military force to protect the border of the country.'

I want to know more about the citizens of this country, so I ask her to explain.

She does. 'People in this country are considered rational human beings with certain rights.'

I need more, so I prompt for more. Liz obliges. 'So a person is a rational being. They can reason for themselves and make decisions. Presumably, that means they make decisions about what brings them happiness.'

I could have introduced the Kantian principles here—that a person must be respected as a free rational being and therefore should have the autonomy to decide what makes them happy, free from interference. Such a person must be allowed to live autonomously. A person must never be used as a means to an end but always also as an end in themselves and all that stuff. Alternatively, I could have discussed the ideas of utilitarianism framed by Bentham and Mill. Or maybe go as far back as Aristotle and what distinguishes humans from other animals. It is a keystone concept in philosophy, an axiom, a self-evident truth. Upon this concept, we rest all arguments for systems of justice, for capitalism, and yes, for Marxism. It seems also libertarianism.

Remember, I have tried lecturing with Liz before, or perhaps if I am honest, I was just showing off. Lecturing doesn't work. Showing off most certainly does not work. She seems to be dead set on reinventing the entire world with her mates in the Philosophy of Life group.

She pauses, and I cannot resist but add a bit more, 'And if a person can make decisions about what brings them happiness, I assume they must be allowed certain freedoms to make those decisions, to act autonomously.'

'Yes,' she says, keeping her head high, 'free from interference by other people and a state.'

Building this idea up further, I propose, 'I assume they are also entitled to keep the fruits of their labour.'

Liz nods her head ever so slightly; never does she stop tracking. She adds, 'Yes, that is how they gain property rights over things, like land and money. And if any of the proceeds from the fruits of their labour is acquired by the state, it must be limited to protect the citizen from interference or coercion from the other citizens of the state.'

I hesitate. Good decision. Liz has more. 'Any form of taxation for other state activities is pure enslavement.'

I feel I should tell her that is what Nozick argues for in *Anarchy, State, and Utopia*. But that will be a conversation killer. Best thing to do is to take her by the hand and lead her down the rabbit hole.

'What else can the state tax for, any other funding?' I ask.

'Nothing' is the emphatic answer, her head dead still.

I dig a little deeper. 'What about infrastructure building, education, and healthcare?'

'Nope,' she insists, a slight swivel left and right. 'That is all a matter of arrangement between the free rational people driven by free market economic forces. Adam Smith.' She appeals to authority. 'Do you know Adam Smith?'

'I do,' I say, 'but I am more interested in understanding this individual person you talk about.'

She invites me to go ahead. 'Go on then.'

I lay it out to her, 'It sounds to me like you are talking about someone who has supreme decision-making power over what happens in their lives, what they do to their bodies, and what they do to the property they accumulate. Individuals are the supreme decision-making authority over themselves and their lives and carry full responsibility for the consequences.' I realise it is a bit clumsy, but it is the best I can do without preparation.

'Yes,' she says, 'human rationality is the gift. We must respect it and use it fully.'

'No argument there,' I say. 'Would you agree we can call this person a sovereign individual?'

'I like that.' Liz beams. 'Sovereignty and supreme decision-making authority. I like both ideas.'

'Great,' I say. I thought it best not to tell her it is the same thing and not two separate ideas. 'So we have a nation state where everyone is considered sovereign individuals. Also, the state taxes the minimum necessary to fund a police force and a military force. All other things are a matter of negotiated agreement between sovereign individuals.'

'That is a good summary, Hendrik.' Liz congratulates me smugly, pleased at what she has achieved. She leans back a little but maintains height.

Time to go deeper into the rabbit hole. 'So tell me, who serves in the police force or army? Actually, let's focus just on the police force, shall we?'

Liz sits up, alert. Her eyes continue to track mine. I suspect the Philosophy of Life group has not considered this question. I allow her time to think.

'Police officers?' She presents her answer as a question. It either means it is obvious and a stupid question or she is not sure she understood the question. I reckon she is perplexed by the question. I suspect she wanted me to go down the route of arguing for more state services and how that brings value. The trade-off is that a bigger state is accompanied by more enslavement and denies individual sovereignty.

This is one of those instances where people talk about a 'thing'—in this case, the police force—as it if it were clearly defined and understood. But it is not. It is an amorphous thing defined by its characters. To understand it, we must first understand the characters. That is where the rabbit hole is leading us. For libertarians, 'the police' barely needs to be explained. It is used in this argument for libertarianism in a way that does not invite challenge. That is precisely why I challenge.

I help Liz out. 'You mean other sovereign individuals?'

'Yes!' she exclaims, still getting used to the new terminology, and she clearly likes it. She sits back a little, but the eyes still track mine.

I should mention to her that the idea of the sovereign individual goes back centuries. That in fact the term has come into use in the eighteenth century. It follows from Locke's declaration of natural rights, which, upon inspection, sounds a lot like the necessary conditions for a sovereign individual. Locke tried to wrestle individual sovereignty away from the then only sovereign in the state, the king. That is why the king is also called the sovereign and the citizens are also called subjects. It was the first step towards a break from feudalism, where everything belongs to the king and everyone else can use it only through serving the Crown. At His Majesty's pleasure of course.

I press on down the rabbit hole. 'OK, so the police officers, other sovereign individuals are charged with enforcing what?'

Liz hesitates then answers, 'They ensure that the rights of the sovereign individual are not circumvented or denied by other people.'

'Fair enough,' I say, 'but other people are also other sovereign individuals.'

'That is correct,' says Liz. Liz is American, but she has picked up on a Singaporean habit. I like the way Singaporeans stick to the correct way of confirming something as opposed to the English habit of saying 'That is right.' You try that with a Singaporean taxi driver and see how it confuses them.

Taxi driver. 'Go left here?'

Passenger. 'That is right.'

Taxi driver. 'No, that is left. You want me to go right?'

Deeper into the rabbit hole we go. 'So tell me. When police officers intervene in a dispute between two sovereign individuals, do they exercise their rights as sovereign individuals?'

'I am sorry,' says Liz. 'I don't understand.'

I restate in simpler terms for her, 'Let's say the police officers are called to a dispute over property between two sovereign individuals.'

Liz nods.

'How do the police officers decide right from wrong, guilty or innocent?'

Liz is taking her good time to think about this, sitting dead still again, so I help her out. 'Keep in mind that the police officers are sovereign individuals and therefore have every right to exercise their rational faculty to settle the dispute, in a way that makes them happy.'

She nods. Her eyes momentarily leave mine but then returns to tracking.

'So we have a situation here where one sovereign individual is rationally making a decision, but the consequence of that decision is for the two sovereign individuals in the dispute to tolerate.'

Liz is clearly struggling with this paradox. I let her stew on it for a while as the food arrives. The waiter gets it all wrong. The meatballs in tomato sauce is placed at the far end of the table, and so is the spicy grilled prawns, the calamari, cheese platter, cured meats, and the bread. On this side is the patatas brava, Spanish omelette, olives, and a few other clearly vegetarian dishes. Now I don't mind vegetarian food, but Liz is clearly distressed by seeing her favourite foods placed out of her reach, that it has been placed within easy reach of some other hungry sovereign individuals. She alerts the waiter, who, sensing the dire urgency of the matter, hurriedly corrects the placement of the various dishes. For a while, I get relief from the tracking.

We help ourselves to reasonable portions of the various options at hand, eat for a while, and wash some of it down with a delicious Spanish Rioja.

I nudge Liz. 'Do you see the problem with one sovereign individual deciding something with consequences for other sovereign individuals?'

'Yes' is all she says.

'Do you see now that the idea of the sovereign individual is becoming increasingly opaque?' I ask.

'What do you mean opaque?' she asks. She looks up; her eyes seek mine out.

'Not as crystal clear an idea,' I answer.

'Yes, it is a problem,' Liz confirms and gives up on the tracking.

'What if a sovereign individual leaves the territory of the state to visit another, do they carry their sovereign individual rights with them?'

'Oh, dear,' she says, 'you are right. This idea is not as clear cut as it seemed in the Philosophy of Life meeting.'

Liz, to me, is an example of an open mind—a mind that is free to change if the facts change or the logic flows against her opinion. This is what Plato meant to leave the cave and go into the light.

She asks, 'Do you think there is a way to solve the problem of the police officer and the sovereign individual?'

I pretend to think for a while. It gives me a chance to savour some more of that wine. We order another bottle. Then I offer her this, 'How about this. Perhaps there is a way, but it is not going to reduce the opacity of the sovereign individual I am afraid. To prevent a situation where one sovereign individual has supremacy over the decision of another sovereign individual, all sovereign individuals agree to a set of rules, laws if you want. In any given situation, the police officers simply shrug and declares, "Hello, hello, hello. What is going on here then? You have broken the law, mate."'

'Hmm.' Liz thinks. She sits back and looks around like she has lost interest in the subject. I am a little disappointed she didn't respond to my imitation of a British police officer. She presses on, 'But does that not impair the sovereign individuality of the police officer or the other sovereign individuals?'

I suspect correctly that the question was rhetorical. She ponders it for a while and then says, 'I suppose it is fair if the law treats everybody equally. That is to say, everyone's sovereign individuality is impaired equally.'

'That will work, but we have not cleared the opacity of the sovereign individual. I fear for the idea. It is slipping through the fingers of the mind.' She is not impressed with my metaphor, and again, I feel a little disappointed. It is going to be a night without humour.

'I suppose it is a compromise. Can you see any other problems with it?' she asks.

'Let me think.' I pretend again to think whilst I am helping myself to some more food, being careful not to exceed the perceived limits of my fair share. There is no point in rushing the dialogue. The evening is young.

'Do you think we should be concerned about how the laws are agreed?' I ask her.

'Oh yes,' she says. She sits up again. Her eyes tracking. 'For the sake of fairness, it has to be done in a democratic system of some kind. Do you think?'

'Good one,' I say, 'but does that mean we need more institutions than just the police and the military?'

Liz has the answer seemingly at the ready. 'Oh yes, it looks like we also need a legislature, perhaps also a more complex judiciary system. We cannot let police officers be detective, prosecutor, judge, and jury, can we? We need some system that enforces the equal application of the law and one that creates the law in a way that every sovereign individual can agree.'

Can you see what is happening here? Liz started off by stripping the sovereign individual of all its tribes. Well, all except the police and the army. But now she must add them back in. By tribes, I mean institutions, the institutions we need for the proper functioning of the state, the tribe.

'So the state is going to be, by necessity, a lot more complex, bigger, with more institutions, and therefore more expensive. More taxes. It also means that there is now another sovereign individual, the state, except this time, it is a somewhat formless thing rather than a clearly defined person, a sovereign individual. Also, there will be more enslavement?' I expand, finishing with a question.

Liz adds, 'Unless the country is a monarchy of some sorts.' Smug with pointing out my obvious omission, Liz continues. 'Oh, dear,' she says, 'utopian libertarianism is in trouble, isn't it?'

'It looks that way. But let's not give up on it altogether. Do you see something familiar in the "system", the formation of the state?' I ask.

'It looks positively like a normal state, like the kind of states we already have or most countries already have. The different institutions, I mean—Military, police, the judicial system, legislature, electoral system, and so on,' She confirms. 'Looks like we will always construct these things, or at least whenever we seek to cooperate or collaborate.'

'Indeed, so it looks like the system or human society will always self-correct to something like we have in place in most countries, if we make allowances for variations, of course,' I say, and to throw a spanner in the works. 'Or it appears essential when we "create" that other thing called a "country" and lay claim to a territory.' I do the air quotes to indicate that these ideas are not as clear cut as we assume, but Liz ignores me.

'I suppose you will also have to have some form of political checks and balances, maybe an upper chamber and a lower chamber, or senate and house of representatives, if you are American,' she ponders out loud.

'And don't forget the tax collector,' I add.

Liz laughs out loud. 'Who can forget the tax collector, Hendrik.' It is more of a statement than a question. 'But it looks like there are other things that might not be necessary for the state to do, like healthcare and education, and oh yes, labour and welfare.'

'Agreed, but is that not a matter of political negotiation?' I ask.

'I would say so. It does not seem a necessary function of the government, so it should be left to sovereign individuals to negotiate.' Liz is about to return to what is left of her food, signalling that she has had enough of this dialogue for one night.

I try and keep the dialogue alive. 'I don't think it is that simple. I think it is a matter of what the sovereign individual is. Right now, it looks like an opaque idea. The concept of a sovereign individual is lacking in clarity and definition, and it looks like it fades the more we look at it. We cannot leave it like that. It is incomplete.'

'I fear you are right. We need to understand it better to be able to draw a line around healthcare, education, and other socialist ideas,' she confirms, but she also signals that the dialogue is over. She sits back and looks down at her now near empty plates. Her eyes have stopped tracking.

'Perhaps next time,' I suggest.

'Perhaps,' she says. Then she adds, 'At least this time, you didn't make me look stupid, Hendrik.'

I suspect this is a reference to my lecturing her last time.

'Oh, please, Liz,' I say, 'I don't deserve any credit for that. You do a fine job all by yourself.'

* * *

John does what I can only describe as a suppressed chuckle. The humour is reflected in the eyes. He realises that is the end of the dialogue. 'You did so well, Hendrik, and then you screwed it all up right at the end.' For a second, I could not tell the difference between him and my father. 'And she let you get away with that?' he asks.

'She is a character I created, John. I get away with everything.' I smile.

It does not wash with John, not any more. 'I bet she is real, Hendrik, and she might be one of the many behind this letter.' John taps on the letter, which is now lying face down on the coffee table. The eyes flash a reminder that there is still trouble in my world, a reminder of the tension in the pit of my stomach.

'I am sure there is a compliment in that statement somewhere, John,' I say in my defence.

'Only if she has an enormous sense of humour, Hendrik,' he says. 'I must admit that if it is indeed how you wrote that dialogue, then it is altogether more dignified, respectful, and helpful, even though the two protagonists didn't resolve the issues.'

With that, I am not sure John accepts that Liz is entirely of my imagination. I press on with the philosophical discussion regardless. 'Perhaps I should inform you, John. Philosophers rarely close a discussion on a topic under total agreement. There are always niggling differences that just will not go away. Liz and my discussion only scratched the surface of libertarianism, and it seems that some problems are covered by a thin veneer, a pretence that it works as an ideology.'

'Perhaps that is why you cannot satisfy my desire to put to bed whether these characters are real people or they are entirely fictional,' John says. I read it as an accusation, not simply a statement of fact.

'Who knows, John, who knows.' It is not a question.

'The people behind this letter knows,' says John.

'Then they know more than I do, John,' I say.

The eyes fix on me. 'You have forgotten the reflection, Hendrik,' he says.

It is, of course, not true. I am waiting for the right time to do it. 'Having learned my lesson with Liz, I take a different approach when she starts to talk about libertarianism. I help her discover the incompleteness of this amorphous structure, this ideology, and that the way she describes libertarianism will not work. I help her reveal the intolerable contradiction, that the sovereign individual needs a police force, which dilutes the sovereign individual's rights.

'We also see that having just a police force is insufficient, that the system also needs lawmakers, a democratic system for electing them, a system of justice, and more. So to complete the ideology, we move more and more towards the system of government already in place in most countries. It leaves us with serious questions about what the sovereign individual is. There are important lessons about testing the completeness of a theory and to reveal contradictions. Contradictions will always destroy a conceptual argument.

'There is a hint that Liz is the master of her mind. She is curious, prepared to debate and to try an understand a concept. Unlike the first time we debated she was fully engaged to the end. But it is interesting that she participated as long as she was the master of her own thoughts, as long as she was allowed to explore her curiosity and not to be told what to think.'

'Thanks,' says John. 'Shall we move on?'

DINNER WITH MARTIN

I t's getting late in the evening. Martin produces another bottle of red wine just as I thought we will wrap up proceedings for the night. My resistance is futile, so I accept a top-up of my glass. Everyone else does. It makes me feel better that they do.

Martin has that kind of personality—generous to a fault, assertive, 'like a boss' some would say. What you can never say is that an evening in his company is boring. Neither is the view from the apartment. It is halfway up a tower block. I forget the exact floor. The apartment itself is one of those surprising architectural design achievements that I have not seen anywhere else in the world. The apartment is for ordinary people. Ordinary families I should say. Three or four bedrooms, large open plan living and dining areas. It is on three floors. That is right, like a regular townhouse but halfway up a tower block. The view is spectacular. Out towards the west. If you arrive early for sundowners, you can watch the sunset whilst you enjoy their generosity. I am not sure people still say sundowners; perhaps it is cocktails now.

They make an odd couple, Martin and Julia. Julia is tall, elegant, and attractive. Martin, not so much. Julia is charming and quietly spoken. Martin, not so much. Julia likes to exercise. Martin, not so much. But despite that, you will like Martin. He has a certain directness of speech. He does not beat about the bush, but he is also keen to provoke a response from you. Well, most of the time. He sometimes needs a little nudge to remind him. I don't want to leave you with the impression that Martin is a slob. He is not. I think he is one of those lucky people who seems to maintain his physique without putting any effort into it. In fact, he makes an effort not to maintain his physique and still manages to do it.

More food appears almost simultaneously. Martin has something to say, some challenge to be placed on the table, that is clear. When he puts a question forward, it is done with such conviction it is almost like he dares you not to engage. But how can I resist?

Martin presents the challenge. Even the way he phrases it sends a clear message. 'Prisoners should not have the vote. What do you think?'

It is a clear message because the first sentence sounds more like a conclusion. Then he dares you to challenge the conclusion.

I disagree with the conclusion, and I'm up for the challenge, so I ask, 'Why not?'

'They have given up their rights to vote when they committed the crime. You cannot be a full member of society and break its rules,' he proclaims.

I decide that the best approach would be to counter the challenge directly.

'Well, I definitely disagree with that. Voting—'

My challenge is met full on. 'How can you possibly disagree? They broke the law, so they lose the vote!'

I try again. 'Well, I disagree because—'

Martin must feel he has the advantage. He claims the high ground. 'Oh, this is going to be good. Some goody two shoes argument about rehabilitation.'

'And why would that not be a good enough reason?' I ask.

Martin spells it out, 'It's not going to work. Prisoners broke the law. Punishment or rehabilitation. They break the rules of society, so they lose their rights. They lose the vote when convicted of a crime.'

'I wasn't going to counter that way anyway, Martin, so can we just let it go? But you are going to have to give me a chance to explain my views,' I say, attempting to push past his belligerent stance.

Martin gives me some leeway. 'I bet this is some human rights argument.'

I try again and wrestle some control away from him. 'Listen, Martin, give me a chance to explain my position. Otherwise, we will spend the night listening to a monologue from you.'

Martin's injured expression says it all. He smirks and takes a large sip of wine.

'Let me ask you a question. Where do you sit on abortion rights?' I ask.

Martin puts his glass down quickly. A little spill out, so he wipes the spillage with the palm of his hand. He is annoyed at the apparent attempt to divert. 'What has that got to do with it?'

I reassure him that I will remain on topic and that it is relevant. 'It is just a thought experiment which will hopefully illustrate a wider issue. Where do you sit on abortion?'

'It is a difficult issue, but I do believe a woman has a right to choose,' he answers.

I push him to make a definitive statement. 'So you are pro-choice? Even if you find the topic difficult.'

'I am pro-choice, yes,' Martin confirms. 'If that means I am pro a woman's right to choose abortion, then yes.' He makes it absolute, I think.

The thought experiment will work equally well with someone who is pro-life, with a few modifications of course. Having laid the groundwork to avoid a further diversion, I proceed, 'OK, so let's consider a country where abortion is a criminal offence. A medical doctor or practitioner that performs abortions can go to prison for ten years when found guilty. There are many countries around the world where this is true, even in parts of the UK. It is not a far-fetched idea.' I wait for him to acknowledge so far.

'Sure,' he acknowledges.

I press on, 'I think we should also assume that doctors who break the law has, like you, the best interest of the women in mind.'

'Agreed,' he says, 'we shall assume they are pro-choice.'

Appreciative that we are making headway, I press on, 'Now let's consider a situation where fifty doctors are committed to prison for performing illegal abortions. However, the sentiment in the country is split, roughly fifty-fifty, for and against. Thanks to some vigorous lobbying, the ruling political party agrees to a referendum on the issue.

'The result of the referendum is so close that it forces a recount. The recount comes out with a difference of twenty votes in favour of keeping the criminal laws on abortions. Thanks to your policy of no voting rights to prisoners, the fifty doctors could not vote. Therefore, the law stays and the doctors remain in prison. They had no say over their own tragic life circumstance.'

Martin thinks. That is clear. He takes another large sip of his wine. I do the same. The silence is his to fill. He fills our glasses instead.

After a while, I press him for an answer, 'Do you think that is a fair system?'

There are a few more minutes of silence, which I allow to linger. It is not an uncomfortable silence. We both drink more wine. Martin refills our glasses. We drink more wine.

Finally, he concedes, but not all the way. 'I am going to have to think about it.'

Well, I could not have hoped that Martin will change from such a vigorously held position to mine in an instant.

I let him off the hook. 'Of course, but keep in mind that societies' laws are not universally accepted by all its members. And denying the full privileges of membership, including voting rights, to some citizens will inevitably create grossly unfair consequences for some.'

I do not expect you to see the hidden composition fallacy, but if you think about the view Martin has of the law, then what I just told him might lift it out for you.

Still no complete concession from him. 'It seems that way, but I have to think about it.'

Of course, Martin is trying to think of a way to defeat my argument. I give him room to think. My glass of wine is almost empty. Martin has returned with another bottle. I did not notice that he left to fetch it. I protest unconvincingly and without conviction when he tops me up again.

So I thought I'd drive the point home with another example.

'The thought experiment I gave is to illustrate a more sinister problem,' I say.

Martin breaks out of his mental quandary and asks, 'What do you mean sinister?'

'One where a law like that can be abused to supress voting rights,' I explain.

'You mean to stop some people from exercising their legitimate voting rights for political reasons?' Martin asks, but clearly, he is somewhat alarmed that it would even be a possibility.

'Indeed,' I say.

He protests, 'But surely there will be an outcry against that.'

I confirm, 'Indeed, there is. But the tyranny of the majority prevails and, in this case, a majority that is maintained only because of a voting suppression law.'

Martin is confounded. 'I am confounded. That does not happen. Give me an example.'

So I do. 'The USA has many examples of voter suppression based specifically on voter rights being withdrawn following a criminal conviction. In closely fought elections that could have a dramatic effect on the outcome of the elections.'

'Like when?' he asks for more detail.

I provide more detail. 'In the 2000 presidential election in the USA. It came down to the swing state of Florida.'

Martin remembers. 'Oh, is that Bush and Gore?'

I confirm, 'Yes.'

He disagrees, 'That had nothing to do with voting rights of convicted criminals. It was about punch card chads.'

I help him out. 'Not entirely. Prior to the election, the state legislators had a private contractor remove one hundred and seventy-three thousand voters from the electoral role because they were either felons or suspected felons. They were also mostly African Americans and likely to have voted for Gore.'

'Would that have changed the outcome of the election?' asks Martin.

'Almost certainly. Bush won by about five hundred and seventy votes if my memory serves me right,' I confirm.

Martin remains uncompromising. 'Well, I can buy into the thought experiment, but not this one. They were convicted felons after all. The fact that the outcome was probably changed is neither here nor there.'

'They were not all convicted felons. Many people were removed because they were suspected felons with no conviction whatsoever,' I clarify.

'So was the law changed?' he asks.

'No,' I answer, thinking he means if it was removed. 'In fact, it was changed, but not in a way you might think. Convicted felons must now also prove that they have repaid their debt to society before being allowed back on the voting role. Keep in mind that also means anybody being convicted of bad debt such as missing rent payments.'

'Are you telling me people cannot vote because they are behind in rent payments?' Martin asks.

'Or they forgot to pay a parking fine on time,' I add.

You know that Martin doesn't concede that easily, so you won't be surprised when he says, 'I have to think about it. It looks like there is something about this that needs my further consideration.'

I give him more food for thought, 'Can you see how breaking the rules of society can be used against a fundamental right? There is a lot more to say about this, Martin. After the abolition of slavery and particularly the civil war in the USA, laws like these were used to suppress voting rights of African Americans across the South. Freed slaves were loitering about in their newfound freedom. Loitering was declared against the law and became a criminal offence. Being convicted of a criminal offence meant no voting rights. Not being able to vote meant not being able to change the law. But also being imprisoned meant prisoners were used on farms as prison labourers, slavery of another form. So it's the abuse of any law that supresses voting rights that becomes a major issue of injustice. That is why it is considered a human right—the right to vote irrespective of your criminal record.'

Martin edges a little closer to a concession. 'It sounds almost impossible to believe.'

'History is a different country, but many people in the USA claim the Jim Crow era laws are still affecting African Americans to this date. I am not an expert on Jim Crow and do not want to be, but don't you think that denying voting rights have terrible consequences for individual people and the system of justice?'

Martin mutters a mouthful. 'I am going to have to think about it' is what I hear. He reaches for the bottle and tops us up again. I promise myself this is the last one. I also know I will probably break the promise.

* * *

John looks at me. I think he is assessing the dialogue for libel.

'Is Martin a real person?' he says, and we start the dance. Proverbially speaking, of course.

'No, a figment of my imagination. But I had a stonking headache the next day,' I tease.

'If the headache is real, then Martin must be real,' says John, closing the trap behind him.

Realising that I am heading for trouble, I suggest, 'There is nothing in that discussion that should be a problem if, say, Martin is a real person.'

'I cannot see anything. You didn't insult him as far as I can see. Does he remember the dialogue?' John asks.

'The character, no. He doesn't feature again in the novel,' I say smugly.

'You know what I meant. The real Martin,' insists John.

'He never brought it up again,' I say that in full knowledge that I as much as admit that Martin is real.

'So you still meet up with this "character" of yours?' asks John, making air quotes around *character*.

'He is a good friend, and we have had other dialogues,' I admit.

'He is a good friend,' John repeats, 'so presumably will not sue you for libel or intrusion of privacy.' I thought it was a statement, not a question. It was a question.

'Will not sue you?' repeats John.

'I hope not'. Is all I can offer. I move to the reflection without asking.

'In the reflection I discuss how we talked about the problem of denying voting rights to prisoners or convicted criminals. This is a topic that was in the national discourse in the UK when it was still in the EU. The UK was castigated by the European Court of Human Rights for denying voting rights to prisoners and convicted criminals. If my memory serves me right, it was a topic that headlined the news leading up to the referendum.

'That idiot Cameron defended stripping prisoners from their right to vote against a judgement from the European Court of Human Rights. I think he said it would make him sick to the stomach to give prisoners the right to vote. He is despicable and incoherently stupid, isn't he? His stupidity makes me sick to the stomach. It is a completely arbitrary punishment piled on without due process.

'People in favour of denying voting rights base their belief on an idea that all laws are just and fair and apply equally to everyone. But this ideal is an illusion. It is an illusion brought about by the composition fallacy. Some laws, perhaps most laws, and their complemented punishment are arguably clearly just and fair. But all laws are not in fact universally just and fair. Much work must be done to weed out laws that are not, laws against certain sexual preferences or gender types are two examples.

'There are also some cultural or religious practises that are unjust that in fact should have laws forbidding those practices. So once I got Martin to inspect laws to find some that he would think is unjust, I showed him how that would prevent those convicted for crimes under those laws from changing them. That, in fact, such laws are open to political abuse as is the case in the USA.

'In the USA, the abuse of voter suppression is specifically racist, aimed at excluding minorities from the democratic process. There is a glimmer of light and hope in Martin's response. He appears to accept that he must change his opinion, but he won't do it openly.

'There are important lessons here about the composition fallacy and how it can hide in plain sight. Like the dialogue with Liz, we have a tendency to simplify certain things to their collective nouns. We forget that within that collective noun, there are many parts that are not the same as the hole. It leads to awful decisions.'

John interrupts, 'I found that quite an eye opener, as someone practicing law, Hendrik.' A rare win for me, a little outside approval, which I wasn't really looking for.

I continue, 'Martin appears to accept that the logic flows against his opinion, or the that the facts don't stack up in his favour. In some way he is the master of his own mind but know this. Our believes are not simply based on logically reached conclusion. They are also emotional, and sometimes very emotional. We see that in Kristoff, remember. To be a true master of one's mind one must be able to overrule that emotional response. Martin has some way to go to do that.'

I get the nod to continue.

DINNER WITH LIZ, II

The fact that an opinion has been widely held is no evidence whatever that it is not utterly absurd; indeed in view of the silliness of the majority of mankind, a widespread belief is more likely to be foolish than sensible.

Bertrand Russell

L iz settles down across the table from us. We have just left a theatre production of *Singing in the Rain* and thought of having a last drink and conversation before heading home. The bar is skilfully placed opposite the main Central Business District. The gleamy office towers rise majestically on the other side of the Marina. It is called the Marina here, but it is in fact a man-made lake. In what can only be described as an incredible feat of engineering, the Singaporeans added considerable real estate by reclaiming land from the sea. I am not sure why people say reclaiming. Do they mean the sea has claimed the land at some point, some kind of Crimean annexation? And now it has been claimed back by the land lobbers hungry for more land for their own use? In reclaiming the land from the sea, the city managed to also close off the old harbour bay by building a barrage across the newly formed river mouth. That in turn created a substantial freshwater lake. It is that lake that is called the Marina.

The conversation meanders somewhat and settles on US politics. I had nothing to do with that just in case you are suspicious. Trump and Biden have just won the primaries. So rather than bore you with what is now history, lets focus on the point in hand, the inevitable conservative versus liberal argument. The peculiar thing about this conversation is that it follows on from the last dialogue with Liz. What makes it peculiar is that I thought it would, but it didn't. It is almost like we are starting again, but from a different angle. Perhaps because this time, Liz had a larger audience, and she felt it appropriate to invite the others into the conversation. Or perhaps she simply forgot.

Liz declares, 'I will never vote Democrat. Neither will my parents.'

'Oh, so why is that?' ask I.

'We believe in the sovereign individual,' she proclaims, and there it is. She has adopted the name for it from our earlier dialogue, but she gives no credit.

Ray asks, 'I am not sure I understand what you mean by sovereign individual. What is that?'

I should perhaps give a proper introduction to Ray, but he is useful only to the extent that he asks questions I would consider obvious.

Liz lays it out for him, 'That every person is a sovereign individual, the supreme decision maker in their lives and fully capable, and therefore fully responsible for their own decisions and the consequences thereof.' A bit of a mouthful, I thought, but close enough.

'And you think Democrats don't believe that?' asks Ray.

'No, of course they don't. They want to tax people to pay for welfare for other people. That is a form of enslavement,' answers Liz.

Ray surprises me here. 'So you are what one might call a Nozickian or libertarian, personal freedom and small government and all that stuff.'

Liz declares confidently, 'I am libertarian. Have you read Ayn Rand's books?'

Our earlier dialogue has had little impact on Liz's enthusiasm for the notion of the sovereign individual; that much is apparent.

Ray answers, 'I am aware of it, but I have not read it.'

'You must read it,' insists Liz.

I must come clean here. As much as I love reading, I rile against being told what to read. And Rand's book is a tome.

I intervene on Ray's behalf. If I don't, the conversation might come to a standstill. The evening is too young for that. I say, 'I don't think that would be necessary, not whilst we have you around, Liz. Are you saying that Republicans are more likely to be libertarian than Democrats?'

I know that Ayn Rand's writing has been largely ignored by academics except for Nozick. He never referenced her but admitted later in life that he was inspired by her. He expressed more admiration for her outside of his academic career. Perhaps that is because her writings were largely fiction, not academic. Nozick is famous; in fact, he won several prestigious prizes for his book *Anarchy, State, and Utopia*. He wrote this in response to Rawls's *A Theory of Justice*. If life is too short to read Ayn Rand, then I suggest you read Nozick. I am only suggesting, not insisting. For all I care, you could read a collection of J. M. Coetzee novels, as long as you read.

She completely ignores me. Liz is still answering Ray's question. 'Yes, but why won't you read her books?'

'Because we can study Nozick's *Anarchy, State, and Utopia*, it won't consume as much time as Rand's tome, and it is worth it only from the point of view that it illustrates how to win prizes but come up with rubbish theories,' says Ray. I must admit, I am looking at Ray with fresh admiration. Always thought him a rather dull writer. I cannot judge of course; I have not read any of his books.

'A lot of people who read Rand will disagree with you. In fact, her book is still a bestseller years after it was first published,' she declares, and I am compelled to repeat Bertrand Russell here.

But I am not given any opportunity to recall it.

'The quality of the argument is not determined by the number of people who believe it. The quality is determined by the quality of reasoning behind it,' responds Ray. I am mightily impressed, and I am sure old Bertie would have been too.

Liz sits upright and tracks Ray's eyes now. She questions him, 'Are you suggesting Rand is wrong? That her reasoning is flawed? Are you saying libertarianism is flawed as an ideology?'

The dialogue is turning quite hot. There is no need for me to add fuel to the fire. I am tempted, but I leave them to carry on with it.

'Yes, absolutely,' says Ray. 'I don't buy it at all.'

Liz strikes back, 'Surely you must see that taxing one person for the benefit of another is a form of enslavement!'

'Absolutely,' says Ray.

'I am confused,' says Liz and sways a little.

Ray feels he is winning. 'Unless it is justified' is his simple solution to the quandary he caused.

But Liz is fast furious and fearsome now. 'What do you mean by justified?' she says. 'How can you possibly justify enslaving a person?' The apparent deadly strike, the knock-down strike. She is tracking Ray's vacant blue eyes with the golden ones, unblinking.

'How can you possibly justify allowing discrimination against a poor person because of their accident of birth, their disability, or lack of access to education? That is a form of enslavement too, particularly if their poverty disposition is exploited by the more fortunate!' It is a statement from Ray; he means it as a question though.

But Liz is a fighter. Liz strikes again, 'So you are saying that I should be enslaved because of my accident of birth, that I am lucky to be healthy, capable, and educated, that I should be enslaved?'

Good one, Liz, although she has revealed the good fortune of her birth and that this disposition makes her prone to be enslaved. I say that to myself. No point in becoming an involved spectator. Just be a spectator. I remind myself.

'What's happened to building a better society, to work towards the greater happiness of the greatest number?' fires Ray.

Liz is not deterred. 'What happened to you should never use a person as a means to an end, always also as an end in themselves.'

By this time, I am so impressed I am ready to faint. Instead, I take a large gulp of my red wine and top up my glass. Things are getting too much to bear without help. We are outside in the open air, and I light up. Lilly smiles, leans into me, and does the same. I am completely gobsmacked. The two of them pitching deontological and teleological ethical theories against each other. Imagine an ordinary philosopher left speechless. That's me right now.

'Isn't it using people also as an end in themselves asking them to help create a better society?' fires Ray again. I am losing focus now, although that might be the large gulp of wine. Never did I imagine a dialogue of such elevated sophistication coming from ordinary people.

Liz has an answer. 'There is no such thing as society,' she declares.

Ray gives up. He throws his hands up dramatically. 'Oh, Margaret Thatcher all over again. If you believe that, you will believe anything. You will be nothing without society.'

Liz abandons tracking Ray's eyes and tracks his waving hands instead. 'Society has never done anything for me' is Liz's final words on the matter.

Then Ray says something that profoundly affects Liz's mood, 'You know about Gold Star families, Liz?' She nods. 'Think about a Gold Star family who had two children.'

She nods again.

'One child has fallen in service in Afghanistan. You are grateful for the sacrifice made by that child and that family,' says Ray.

Liz's eyes track Ray again, unblinking.

Ray continues, 'So you think it is OK for one child of that family to take responsibility for your well-being, security, and freedom, even to pay the ultimate price?' he asks.

She does not respond. She correctly anticipates there is more to come, and a response from her is superfluous.

'But you are not prepared to help take responsibility for their other child's needs for healthcare and education, even though the sacrifice you have to make is only a miniscule increase in your taxes. That's all,' he says.

There is silence. Liz stops tracking Ray and sinks back into her chair. After a few moments, she says, 'You bastard, that was below the belt.'

Ray knows there is no need to say anything more.

They are both exhausted from the encounter and retire to concentrate on their drinks. I am grateful from having been saved from certain fainting. I have much to say but feel it is better to leave that for another day.

There is a deadly pause in the proceedings. I have a few minutes to quietly reflect. Hannah Arendt's quote comes back to me. Remember, from the first dinner with Liz. Arendt said something about proposing ideologies for the purpose of escaping responsibility. It seems to me that Ray is claiming that we have a responsibility towards our fellow citizens, a responsibility to contribute to the health and well-being of everyone. This would include contributing to the education of everyone. Liz, on the other hand, is trying to escape that responsibility. In the process, she is denying the existence of society, of the other individuals. To escape her responsibility, she is creating a new tribe, a tribe that is designed to kill off Ray's tribe. But if she reflects on our discussion of the other night, she will realise she is just creating Ray's tribe afresh. Liz rescues me from the deadly pause.

She slowly turns to me and says, 'I am smarter than I look you know.'

I have no reason to disagree with her, so I nod. 'Which of course is a lot better than looking smarter than you are.'

* * *

John looks up, surprised at the abrupt ending to the dialogue. Is he trying to supress a giggle at the joke? That would be astonishing. I imagine there is not much room for comedy in a prestigious lawyer's office.

He glances back at his notes and realises that I made a minuscule contribution to the dialogue and therefore probably did not put myself in legal jeopardy in the process. He says as much.

'You forget I created those characters, John, and I wrote what they said,' I say.

The eyes tell me they are rather exhausted by this little interlude, the 'Is he real or is he imagined?' game that we play.

John looks at his notes again. He confirms for himself that there is probably nothing to be concerned about. He repeats his assessment.

'Perhaps I should have mentioned that Margaret Thatcher was a mammal with tits and an arsehole,' I say. 'I bet that would have helped to upset some people.' The eyes flash exasperation, and I realise that is another thing that brown eyes can do.

'And upset half of Britain again, every Tory voter in the country?' He smirks.

'Don't be silly, John,' I say. 'Tories are so thick-skinned nothing upsets them. Not even when they get caught with their hands in the till. I think they secretly take pride in their sleaze and corruption. I imagine Bozo having a laugh at the raw, vulgar greed that he is an exemplary exponent of.'

My attack on the Tory government does not go down well. John makes no attempt to defend the party, but the eyes tell me enough is enough. They leave me with no uncertainty about that.

'You are a labour supporter then.' It sounds more like he leaves me with the option to interpret what he said as a declaration or a question. I choose question, so I answer.

'I am not particularly aligned. I vote for the candidate who demonstrates character and integrity. If that tells you I voted for labour, then you are judging Bozo correctly for what he is. Think about that. You are confirming something we both know, and by doing so, I should ask why you voted for him.' I didn't mean the accusation, and I immediately regret making it.

John makes no effort to confirm or deny the accusation. He doesn't have to. He is in the bigger, more imposing chair.

'I cannot believe that you insulted Liz again. Women who read this might think you are showing disrespect,' says John, changing the subject and fishing for legal jeopardy.

'I am going to insist there is a compliment in that joke, and it works just as well with men as it does with women,' I say. 'Notwithstanding that, it would be a mistake to go from Liz to all women.'

'The composition fallacy,' John says, being smarter than he looks, which would be a considerable achievement if it is true.

'Indeed,' confirm I.

John smiles with self-satisfaction, and I take it as permission to move to the reflection.

'In this dialogue, Liz engages in a debate with Roy. I am an observer, but I am nevertheless impressed with the sophistication of their discussion. What I am not impressed about is the partial retreat from what Liz and I discussed previously. The topic is again the sovereign individual and the state. Democrat versus Republican.

'The dialogue demonstrates the failure of conventional wisdom to move the debate forward. It gets down to a value judgement based on ethics and morals. What is the right thing to do? Should one have empathy for one's fellow citizens, or should they be left to fend for themselves? Should one take responsibility for the well-being of the less fortunate, or should they be left to suffer? Is suffering the greatest teacher or not? The debate circles around who is the slave, the privileged, or the poor. It ends in acrimony. Liz seems defeated by the burden of guilt bestowed on her by Ray. But the burden of guilt is easily relieved by a steadfast belief in individual sovereignty. If there is a place for guilt, it can be solved by philanthropy. There are flashes of light and hope here, but they fade away. The inevitable dead end provided by conventional wisdom.

'I am not going to reflect much on Liz being the master of her mind. We will see that develop further over some more dialogues with her.'

John says nothing. He is looking back at his notes, and I think he expected more from the reflection. He says, 'That one seems rather thin to me, Hendrik, like it hasn't achieved that much. I get more from the reflection than from the actual dialogue.'

'Isn't that what a summary is supposed to do, tie up the loose ends?' I ask.

'Possibly, but wouldn't it be best to do it in the dialogue?' he asks.

'The dialogue was between Ray and Liz. I didn't want to interfere with it. If I built all the wisdom into the dialogue, don't you think it will become too artificial, too fictional, too focused on my voice? Don't you think it will strip the characters of any secrets, give them too much definition so they are no longer real?' I ask.

John looks at me as if he knows where this is heading. He won't go there.

BRUNCH WITH VICTORIA

The progress from an absolute to a limited monarchy, from a limited monarchy to a democracy, is progress towards a true respect for the individual.

Henry David Thoreau

It is shortly after the death of Prince Phillip. We are meeting for a regular Sunday brunch networking morning in the Australian pub on the riverbank. You know this pub well enough by now, and I have little other detail to add, except for this perhaps. The granola and yogurt breakfast is deceptive. It is not the healthy choice you might think, but it provides enough calories to keep an ordinary philosopher going for a complete dialogue plus a few hours more. It also provides a great balance to the strong large coffee I told you about. There is nothing unusual about the weather, so I won't bother mentioning it, except, of course, I have now.

There are a good number of people, and sitting directly opposite me is a young woman originally from Japan. She tells us she lived in Hong Kong for a while before moving to Singapore. It is her first visit to the group.

The conversations settle down after basic introductions. We order coffee. Mine is a large Americano. I told you before. The coffee is good here. I suspect it is from the Dimbulah Mountains in Australia. It has that distinctive Dimbulah taste, and it is good and strong.

Victoria opens the conversation about the passing of Phillip. People are respectful and justifiably so. Phillip served with dignity.

'Isn't it funny how we talk about Phillip as if he were serving when in fact he was the next best thing to a king?' I ask, putting the question on the table.

'Ha,' says Victoria, 'yes, that is funny. What do you think of him?'

Victoria will surprise you. She is tall and model slim. Japanese, but much taller than you expect. I have read somewhere that current generations of Japanese people are just about as tall as their European counterparts. Except for the Dutch, of course, they are taller than everybody else. She is groomed to perfection and displays a friendly disposition.

'I would agree with what most people say, those who say we should recognise his good service and not the ones that are reminders of his many gaffs, and there were many. I suppose it is not unusual to remember only the virtues of the dead person.'

Victoria expresses her forgiveness, 'Indeed, everyone makes mistakes.'

'Exactly, that is why pencils have erasers', I say, injecting a bit of humour before the conversation takes on a funeral mood.

Victoria laughs. 'Is that true? Is that really why pencils have erasers?' I felt there is no need to answer, and Victoria realises the silliness of her response. No one else laughs.

'I am not a great supporter of the Crown though,' I say to steer the conversation into a different direction.

'Oh, why not?' Victoria asks, taking the bait.

I go straight to the point. 'I think it is an awful institution.'

Victoria probes more, and down the rabbit hole we go. 'Why? It seems to be bringing a lot of value to the UK.'

'Oh, undoubtedly, but that makes it even more distasteful as an institution,' I say.

Victoria is following me into the rabbit hole now. 'Why?'

Time to expose my reasoning. I answer, 'Well, imagine the citizens of a country create an institution or maintain an institution that holds captive a family for generations, actually in perpetuity.'

Victoria nods for me to say more.

I continue, 'If you are born into that family, you have a predesigned role in life. A servant of the people yet you are also revered and entitled. The entitlement is your reward.'

Victoria agrees and says, 'They cannot complain about that.'

'Certainly,' I confirm. 'But they lose their individuality. They cannot be normal people or live normal lives. They are scrutinised by the press, every detail, what they get up to in their showers, bedrooms and how they behave at parties. Their lives are under constant threat, so they have permanent security. Imagine creating an institution where a human being is held captive like that. No freedom, no privacy, no individuality. Unlike all the other citizens in the country, members of that family have no rights of freedom, from the day they are born to the day they are dead. It sounds pretty awful to me.'

I quietly think how things have turned around. In feudal times, it was the royal family that held the sovereignty. Everyone else served. Now individuals are considered sovereign, and the royal family serves. How bizarre that the roles of the characters have changed. How bizarre that the tribes have swapped around. The tribe that used to serve is now the tribe with the authority. The tribe that had the authority is now the tribe that serves.

Victoria nods. 'You are right. I never thought about it that way.'

I press the point home. 'Imagine the press follows your every move, from the day you are born, where you spend your holidays, how you mother dresses you, what your mother wears today. Is she bonking one of her bodyguards? Is father being faithful? They even take pictures of your mother's boobs using long-range lenses from several kilometres. Imagine seeing your tits or your mother's tits splashed on newspaper front pages everywhere.'

Victoria covers her breasts. 'Really, they did that?'

'Yes,' I confirm. 'And it is not your choice. You were born into captivity. If you dare to leave, then you will be ridiculed by the press, rejected by an entire nation of people. People will hate you forever, hate your wife and children, cut you off from every resource you might have had.'

Victoria looks visibly shocked. 'Oh my god, that sounds like an awful thing to do to another person.'

'It is an awful thing to do to a person,' I agree with her. 'And they have no choice. It is their birthright, a so-called privilege.'

Victoria attempts to shift blame. 'But surely the problem is the press and journalism.'

I won't let her. 'The press and journalists are doing what the citizens want and are prepared to pay good money for. Citizens buy the papers to see pictures of the royals sucking toes, hanging their boobs out, meeting up with their lovers. The kind of thing that if ordinary people do it, no one would blink an eye. It is the same citizens who maintain the institution, the monarchy, the Crown. They keep it for its source of bizarre entertainment.'

Victoria refocuses her blame. 'Oh, so it is the citizens who are to blame.'

I am glad she sees it that way, so I say, 'Yes, the subjects of the Crown. The people who should serve the queen or king now are being served by the king or queen. We, the citizens of Great Britain and the UK, are holding a family captive for our selfish benefit. They provide us with gossip, global recognition, tourism, and economic value. We are using them as a means to our end.'

Victoria fixes her eyes on me now. I am surprised at how big they are, brown eyes, like dark chocolate. I am sure she is privately reflecting on Japan's monarchy. 'I have never seen it from that perspective. What an absolutely awful thing to do to a family.'

'And if they dare try and escape from the institutions, to be free individuals, the very same thing every citizen cries out for, then we punish them. It is extraordinary that otherwise really nice people can turn into what amounts to a severe form of abuser,' I say to nail the dialogue down.

Victoria helps to nail it down. 'How awful. What a terrible thing to do to a person, a whole family.'

> Something as curious as the monarchy won't survive unless you take account of people's attitude. After all, if they don't want it, they won't have it.
>
> *Prince Charles*

Thankfully, the coffee arrives, and we break away from that dialogue, both eager to find something more uplifting to talk about and preferably with another person. I have mistakenly ordered the granola and Greek yogurt. It takes me almost an hour to eat through the grains. Today everyone gets a rest from me.

* * *

John realises that we have come to the end of the dialogue, but he says nothing. He appears lost in his own thoughts. I am beginning to wonder if he lost interest in the dialogue somewhere in the middle, if readers of the novel will do the same. Where did I go wrong? And how do I fix it? That is what I am thinking about now.

John breaks the silence, 'You are going to piss off a lot of people with that dialogue, Hendrik. In fact, it seems you have an uncanny ability to piss people off. So far, you have insulted Australians, Americans, British, and South Africans.'

I am surprised at John's word choice. Perhaps I got it wrong. Prestigious lawyers are not necessarily stuck-up prestigious lawyers. Or perhaps I am the one guilty of lowering the tone in the office. I don't say that out loud. If John is right, I have already pissed off enough people. More might come when we do the rest of the dialogues.

'Maybe I have pissed off some people. If people get pissed off because I show they are stupid to support or embrace certain amorphous forms, then they are welcome,' I say defiantly.

The eyes signal enough of pissed off. It's OK for John to use it, not for me.

John needs more time to reflect on the dialogue. I don't think there is a threat in there. I could not possibly have upset Victoria. I think he agrees, but I am wrong.

'There are a lot of people in Britain who supports the monarchy, Hendrik, not only supports them but are fiercely loyal. If you think they are going to be happy about what you are saying, you are wrong,' said John.

'Do you think I don't know that?' I ask rhetorically. John knows it is rhetorical because he gives me space to answer myself. 'Did I not quote Berlin earlier, that when you are offended by a challenge to your opinion, that is when you should investigate your opinion?'

'You did. Hopefully, your readers will remember that,' John says with an attempt to close the conversation.

'Well, let me repeat a quote by someone else who had something to say about this,' I say.

The eyes say, 'If you must!'

> If you really want to piss people off, you can do two things: Attain some happiness or tell the truth.
>
> *Tennessee Williams*

'I get my happiness from looking for and finding the truth and speaking it,' I say to John. 'I do not get it from trying to please all the people by hiding the truth from them.'

'And then you have to come to people like me to help you hide the truth, Hendrik. That is what make lawyers happy,' quips John.

It might be meant as a joke, but the honesty nevertheless shocks me. 'Shall we go to the next one?' I ask, thinking that I have control of the proceedings.

John ignores me and makes a few detailed notes on his legal pad. While he is doing that, I wonder why lawyers have their own type of pad.

'The reflection?' I ask, hinting that he has forgotten.

He has. 'Yes, of course.'

'This dialogue with Victoria will be a difficult topic for royalists, I expect. In my experience, talking about this invokes severe emotional responses. I helped Victoria to switch perspectives, to think about the royals as generations of the same family being held captive by a particularly cruel institution and will be for generations to come. They, as well as royalists, are seduced by the glamour and the perceived privilege. But the reality of the Crown or monarchy is vastly different.

'The institution, the Crown, is an amorphous structure that is reified in pomp and ceremony, in palaces and castles, in traditions and protocols. But for all the seeming privilege it offers the family, it also hides awful consequences, not only hides but prefers to supress and deny the horrendous consequences it has for some. It is sustained by tribal instinct, one which Charles recognises. That turns every member of the royal family into a slave to the institutions. A slave to culture dogma.

'I think it is certainly an institution that is out of place in a modern society, contravenes the human rights act. It goes against philosophical principles of how to treat other people. It fills me with horror every time that I think I might be part responsible for holding generations of a family captive this way, for my pleasure, for my economic benefit. There is no humanitarian justification to continue with this institution.'

'I expect you will get a significant backlash on that one, Hendrik. A lot of people are emotionally dedicated and loyal to the royal family,' says John.

'I expect you are right, but I suspect that is largely to do with Elizabeth and her dedication to dignified servitude. That will inevitably change one day, and I am hopeful that British people will banish this awful institution to the history books.'

'Well, you didn't express your personal opinion that strongly in the novel, so probably nothing to worry about, but some people might burn your novel,' says John and nods for me to continue. What was that quote from Bertie, the one about killing the artist?

DINNER WITH LIZ, III

One has either to take people as they are, or leave them as they are. One cannot change them, one can merely disturb their balance. A human being, after all, is not made up of single pieces, from which a single piece can be taken out and replaced by something else. Rather he is a whole, and if you pull one end, the other, whether you like it or not, begins to twitch.

Franz Kafka

The restaurant we are meeting at tonight is directly on the riverside. I told you about this part of the city before, with Kristoff, remember? It is a few hundred yards from the Central Business District, a protected remnant of the old Singapore. The main part of the restaurant is housed in a proper building, but the area where we are seated is on a platform right on the river's edge. The main thoroughfare is pedestrians only, which is lucky because it separates the platform from the main building.

The river's edge is a steep bank of carefully placed stonework. The stonework forms what looks like a staircase leading down to the water. Being a staircase, it also offers a self-help escape for anyone who happens to fall in. It may seem bizarre, but several people have found themselves in the drink after the drink, so to speak. Having a staircase leading out of the river therefore looks like an efficient solution to a regular problem. Sadly, it doesn't always work.

The riverbank stretches half a mile in either direction. Restaurants and bars along the edge all benefit from a little platform on the edge. Not one of the restaurants appears to have an adequate barrier between the platform edge and the riverbank, hence the convenient staircase out of the water, I presume. A simple loosely strung rope is considered sufficient. It is up to the patrons to stay safe. *Libertarians would love this,* I think to myself as we settle.

Liz is not here yet, but again, the only available chair is the one right opposite me. It occurs to me that it happens every time now, and I wonder if our friends consider the seat opposite me the hot seat, to be avoided at all costs. Enter at your peril. Only for the brave and the stupid. Stupid arrives and pleads with her golden eyes for someone to make space for her. No one does. She sits down in front of me.

I try my best to be friendly, to avoid confrontation or any discussion that might turn confrontational. I seem to be successful as we chat about the weather, involve ourselves with other conversations around the table, and order drinks. The food can wait. This is an Italian restaurant, and although some starters are suitable for the Asian tradition of sharing food, the main courses are designed for individual people, the sovereign individual you might say. Funny how that is much like the dialogues Liz and I have. The unavoidable conflict between the collective and the individual. The character trying to escape the tribe. As an ordinary philosopher, I am content with either. Whilst I am contemplating this age-old quandary, the drinks we ordered is served, followed by the obligatory and pleasant exchanges of best wishes and good health.

There are a few minutes' reprieve as the discussion turns to menu choices, the taking and the sharing of dietary advice from each other and asserting our sovereign individuality by the ordering of our own preferences. There is an inevitability in this process. The inevitability of suffering from food envy when others have ordered the less than sensible options and you stare down at the green salad on your plate. The waiter leaves with our orders.

Liz surprises me by going straight to the end of our last dialogue. I mean, the one she and I had, not the one with Ray. I was a mere observer then, a spectator to a respectable spectacle.

'Remember we talked about the sovereign individual?' Liz asks. So much for avoiding confrontation. I suppose the hot seat does that to a person and that is why it should be avoided.

'Remind me please. Where did we get to?' I ask.

'We talked about how opaque the idea gets when we try and organise society, the state. How it is inevitable that we build a system much like the ones that are already in place. I think we disagree on how far the state should go. I say it should not extend beyond protecting the sovereign individual. You say it should also provide healthcare and education,' she explains.

It is a great summary, but I cannot recall making the case for healthcare and education. I thought that we agreed to take a deeper look at the sovereign individual. I say so.

'Yes, but you left the door open, didn't you?' she says, adjusting her original claim.

'Perhaps, but I recall it somewhat differently. That's neither here nor there though. I thought we should contemplate the libertarian theory in more detail. For starters, there is the claim that a person is a sovereign individual. What is our basis for that claim?' I ask. I think that I am being clever. That I am proposing it as a matter of collective effort by the two of us, not a matter for dispute between the two of us.

It works. Liz joins me by coming into the rabbit hole. 'What do you mean the basis for the sovereign individual?'

I have seen Liz put forward a reasonably knowledgeable philosophical case when talking to Ray the other night, so I up the game. 'Any theory that concludes we are sovereign individuals must rest on an axiom, or axioms,' I say.

'What is an axiom?' she asks. Her shoulders pull up slightly, like it does when one feels a little tense.

'The self-evident truth from which the argument builds to claim sovereign individual rights,' I explain.

'Why can I just not claim my rights as a sovereign individual, as a human being? It is like making a declaration,' she asks, or at least I think she asks. She turns to face me square on, more upright. Her golden eyes search mine out, finds them, tracks.

So I answer, 'If you argue like that, you are inviting a dispute or disagreement. If you build your argument on an axiom, a self-evident truth, or a keystone, then we both agree with a starting point.'

'OK, I get it,' she says. 'I think we can both agree that a person is a reasonable being capable of deciding their own happiness. Such a person must be the principal decision maker in their lives or the supreme decision maker.'

'I agree. That, in fact, is the keystone in almost all reasoning about personhood,' I say.

'Thanks,' Liz says. She sinks back into her chair a little. The eyes continue to track.

'Now if you claim that, then everyone can claim it,' I say, building on the keystone.

'Yes,' Liz says, coming deeper into the rabbit hole.

'And by everyone, I mean everyone else in the world,' I say to invite her to really commit.

'Yes, of course,' Liz says, committing herself completely. We can no longer see the entrance to the rabbit hole.

'So what is the role of the state here?' I ask.

'To protect my rights as a sovereign individual,' she explains.

'Why does the sovereign individual have these rights?' I ask.

Liz frowns; her eyes turn to one side, to look into empty space. 'I thought we just agreed that. Because of the keystone, the fact that they can reason about their own happiness.'

This is a bit like walking behind two fat people on a narrow pathway. No room to pass and being held up by two fat people who have had God knows what for lunch at the local pub. They think they can walk it off, but they have eaten enough to make a dietitian sick.

'You are claiming certain rights as a sovereign individual, right?' I ask.

'Yes, I am,' she says, confident with the answer.

'Why do you feel you need to claim those rights?' I ask.

Her eyes stop tracking and looks to one side for a brief moment then tracks again. 'Because I am a sovereign individual, Hendrik, please keep up.' The joke fails. We are still behind the fat people.

'Liz,' I say, 'you are claiming the sovereign individual rights from other people, which means you don't have them naturally as a sovereign individual. You are negotiating with other sovereign individuals. These rights are a matter of mutual agreement,' I explain.

'So?' she asks. She sits back, leans into the back of her chair, and rolls her eyes.

'You are asking permission to be a sovereign individual?' I ask.

Liz's eyes do a quick search for mine, finds them and tracks. I hope she is thinking rather than trying to control her temper. I thought a little distraction is in order. 'Was there a libertarian party in the USA last presidential election?' I ask.

'Yes, that's right. Didn't get many votes,' she says.

'Jo somebody was the presidential candidate,' I say, knowing full well it was Jo Jorgensen.

'Jo Jorgensen,' she confirms.

'Don't you think it is contrary to the principles of the sovereign individual to ask for permission to govern the party and for other sovereign individuals to give permission to be governed?' I ask.

'Oh yes, that seems odd.'

'And if you think that is odd, then what about Jorgensen wanting to claim the position of primary decision maker amongst primary decision makers? Don't you think that primary decision makers are by consequence equally primary?' I ask.

'What do you mean by equally primary?' asks Liz and she has a point.

'I mean that primary is number one, that primary equals primary equals primary. If you are not primary then you are secondary or tertiary and so the regression goes,' I explain.

'Oh my god. Of course! It is a paradox, a paradox that creates a hierarchy,' she says. We slip past the fat people.

'It is an untenable contradiction,' I say.

By now, I hope you have recognised the tribe here. Libertarians, in their desperate battle against the tribe for the privilege of owning themselves as Nietzsche claimed, create another tribe. A political party with the promise of a vigorous collaboration to claim that freedom. This new political party goes to voters and asks for permission to rule. Libertarians, in their pursuit of personal freedom, submit that freedom to another amorphous structure. This new tribe promises to give them their illusionary personal freedom only to claim ownership over the individual characters. And so the cycle repeats.

We drink in silence for a while. Then she says, 'But that still does not justify taxing people for public schools and hospitals.'

You may think that her dialogue with Ray would have softened her stance on this, that she would have accepted the principle of reciprocity and take on some responsibility for the well-being of her fellow citizens, just as some of them are prepared to take responsibility for protecting her sovereign rights as an individual. That is the weakness of value-based arguments. Not everyone places the same value on the same thing.

'Absolutely right,' I say to encourage her. 'I know we said we will come back to your claim that you are a sovereign individual, but you require a state to protect this right and therefore grant this right. Do you see the tension here?' I ask.

'What do you mean by tension?' Liz asks.

'Your claim to sovereign individuality has to be protected by the state. The state is other people, other sovereign individuals,' I say to lead her down the rabbit hole.

'I don't understand why that is a problem. Why should there be tension?' she asks.

'Really, you don't see it as a problem that you need permission from another sovereign individual to be a sovereign individual, that it is a matter of negotiation with other sovereign individuals? Surely if you are a sovereign individual, you won't need anybody's permission to be one,' I say.

'I thought I have accepted that,' Liz says, looking a little bewildered.

'If you are not a sovereign individual based on your keystone argument, one that we can reason for or against, then to ask for permission from other sovereign individuals undermine the keystone argument, doesn't it?' I ask in a way to make it sound uncertain. But to drive the point home, I add, 'You limit the state to providing protection for the rights of the sovereign individual, but the idea of the sovereign individual appears to be built on shaky ground.'

'Yes, the police to protect the rights in the country and the military to protect the border. The state can do nothing else,' she insists.

'So now you have also slipped the country back into the picture, the bit of global real estate where the sovereign individuals live. It raises serious questions about how the country comes about, who determines the border, and why it should be recognised by other countries. Additionally, it raises questions if other countries should recognise the rights of the sovereign individual from a different country. If it does so, does that deteriorate the borders of the country? Do you feel the idea of the sovereign individual becoming a bit opaque and that it slips from the fingers of the mind, so to speak? In fact, the sharper the amorphous state becomes, the more defined, the opaquer the sovereign individual becomes.' I realise too late that I am lecturing.

I propose a different direction, 'But we have some more fundamental questions about the police and the military first.'

She takes the bait. 'I have to think about it some more, but what is the issue with the police and the military?'

'Who works in the police force?' I ask, going over familiar ground.

She knows this and says as much. 'People who agree to work there of course. They get paid a salary to be police officers.

Liz shifts around in her chair. Her eyes fish around for another conversation. None is available. 'Yes, other sovereign individuals.'

Somewhere, somehow, the slow, fat people slipped past us. Now we are behind again, and the footpath has narrowed.

'I know we have been here before, Liz,' I concede to her. 'I just want to understand something, so I am making sure we agree on the things we think we agree. These sovereign individuals are presumably going to have to intervene in a dispute between other sovereign individuals, a dispute where one claims the other has infringed on their sovereign individual rights, let's say the rights of ownership.'

Liz has settled in her chair again, but now she leans forward impatiently. It might have something to do with the repetitive use of sovereign individual. But how else could I put it?

I press on, 'We discussed the question, I know. Do the police officers apply their own sovereign individual rights, their own reason in determining the guilty or no guilty verdict?'

Liz humours me, 'No, of course not. They have to enforce the law.' I sense this is my last chance.

I continue to replay our previous dialogue, 'So they are not allowed to exercise their sovereign individual rights but must apply a set of rules, the law.'

'Yes, but again, what is the problem with this?' she says, looking around again for an escape.

'We agreed that police officers give up their rights to sovereignty when they enter the police force. Since they do it voluntary and can leave at any time, they can regain that sovereignty. However, there are periods when they are on duty when they don't act as sovereign individuals.'

Silence. She is no longer bothering to answer.

'If I am right, then it seems the system requires that some people abandon their sovereignty so other people can enjoy theirs,' I say, 'even if it is voluntary.'

More silence from Liz.

'It seems to me that there are quite a few logical tensions here that need to be resolved. The first is, what is the basis for the individual's claim of sovereignty? Secondly, why do some people have to sacrifice this sovereignty for the sake of others? Thirdly, does this sovereignty survive national borders? And finally, if this sovereignty is a matter of agreement between other individuals, how do we resolve the issue of asking permission from others to be sovereign?'

'It looks like we are right back at where we started, Hendrik,' Liz says in a direct attempt to close the dialogue down.

'Indeed, perhaps we should revisit the keystone argument, the axiom. Perhaps we agreed to that all too easily,' I say.

Liz looks to her left, catches the eye of someone, and just like that, finds another conversation. She escapes the rabbit hole. 'I am going to talk to someone else now.'

Liz picks up her glass, refills it with wine, and gets up to stand at the other end of the table. Franz Kafka comes to mind.

I have lost my last chance. I have pulled too much. The twitching becomes unbearable. The hot seat is empty. No other stupid around to replace Liz.

* * *

John looks at me. There is no sympathy in the eyes.

'That seems like a brutal encounter, Hendrik,' he says with a satisfactory smile. It is clear to him that I lost. 'You really laboured those points too much, didn't you?' he finishes with the question.

'These dialogues don't always play out like a conversation in a TV show or a novel, John. They are more likely to be messy. Novelists don't like to write messy dialogues. Critics don't let them get away with it. Words are too precious. Clarity and precision are too precious,' I say.

John takes a moment to think about what I said. 'Despite what you might think, court hearings are often messy too, Hendrik. It is only in TV shows where the hero lawyer asks the killer question that reveals the guilt of the person in the dock. That is not what is on my mind, Hendrik. What I am concerned about is that you talk about this much like it was a real dialogue with a real person.'

I have nothing. I feel we have been over this point too many times now.

'No quips about Liz being a character, not a real person. No attempt to defend yourself, Hendrik,' he challenges me.

I still have nothing, still feel we have been over this. I am beginning to think John sympathises with Liz. Isn't that what writers try to do? To generate a certain empathy for the characters with the reader. In the process, the amorphous shape of the character gains more clarity, becomes more real. I think Lilly would say that.

'You were really bruised by that encounter, Hendrik. No joke with her at the end,' he says, building the case that Liz is a real person. You cannot put much past a prestigious lawyer, I think. I don't admit.

'I am trying to make my characters appear as real as possible,' I say. 'If I had another clear and precise dialogue with Liz, it would have been artificial. You seem to have bought into the dialogue, John.'

'The claimants in this letter bought into it too, Hendrik. That is a real problem for you, for us,' he says, tapping on the letter lying write side down on the table, as if hiding the content somehow makes it less threatening. It doesn't make it less threatening. Reminding me of the letter makes it grip the pit of my stomach.

'Anyway,' I say, 'it seemed inappropriate to joke with Liz. I think her sense of humour went for a walk halfway through the discussion.'

'And again, you cast doubt on the reality of the people in your novel, Hendrik. God knows we can never put you on the stand,' John says, exasperated.

'John, you should never ask a philosopher to be your defence lawyer,' I say.

'Why not?' asks John.

'He will say to the jury, members of the jury, "My client is absolutely innocent, but let us entertain the thought that he is guilty for just a minute,"' I say.

John laughs. I see it as a signal to continue. I take the signal and continue, but I was mistaken.

'I thought your analogy of the fat people slowing you down was really cruel, Hendrik. And I did not care for the imagery of the dietitian either,' says John.

'Thanks, John, I will consider editing that out in the next edition,' I say, hoping to close the discussion.

'Oh, so there is going to be a second edition?' asks John.

'There always is for two reasons. It corrects mistakes in the first edition, and it makes the first edition more valuable as a collectors' item,' I explain.

'So the edition insulting fat people will become more valuable,' concludes John.

'Ironic, isn't it, John?' I do what I can to supress a laugh.

> Men are so simple and so much inclined to obey immediate needs that a deceiver will never lack victims for his deceptions.
>
> *Niccolò Machiavelli*

'Will you do the reflection now, please,' John suggests.

'This particular dialogue became quite brutal and argumentative. But we covered some good ground. Principally, we were in dialogue to put some more shape, definitive border around the amorphous idea of what a sovereign individual is. The dialogue introduced the philosophical tradition of anchoring a theory in axioms, keystone assumptions on which the theory is built.

'Liz and I uncovered a profoundly serious problem with the notion of the sovereign individual. Here, I showed just how important it is in any theory to look for and uncover your assumptions. In this case, there is an assumption that the "police" is a clearly defined shape, that we can talk about it in the singular form. In the process, we dehumanise the people who work there. We have stripped them from their sovereign individuality. When we restore that individuality, we undermine the shapes of the amorphous things.

'Either we undermine the shape of the sovereign individual or we undermine the shape of the police. This is an untenable dilemma that invites further inspection of our assumption of the keystone ideas or the axioms of the sovereign individual. In the process of doing this, we go back to re-examine the things we think we agree on, the self-evident truths to see if there is a mistake there somewhere. There is a glimmer of light and hope in the realisation that one of our keystones are not resting on a solid foundation.'

'Yes, you are right about that being brutal,' says John, but no enthusiasm in his voice for further discussion.

'Sometimes people respond emotionally when an idea they hold on to with complete confidence is challenged, when their illusions are shattered. I suspect that is what happened there. Also, I am a bit grumpy at times,' say I.

'You don't say!' says John. But I did say.

I pause as I have finished the reflection, but John's sense of humour has joined Liz's somewhere. Feeling abandoned, I escape to the next dialogue.

DINNER WITH JEREMY

The free soul is rare, but you know it when you see it—
basically because you feel good, very good, when you
are near or with them.

Charles Bukowski

It is the middle of the COVID-19 pandemic. Living in Singapore at the time gives a whole different perspective on my homeland and perhaps most countries who claim to follow Western liberal ideals. I am having dinner with colleagues. We are eating at what you might call a gourmet pub. Not the one where we meet for Sunday brunch. This is a different one. It has a large outdoor seating area that is conveniently covered. The convenience it provides is to protect the patrons from the frequent early evening tropical rainstorms. That convenience is in full protecting mode as we sit down. Rolling thunder can be heard in the near distance, and the rain is coming down like a curtain. This type of rain is a familiar sight in the tropics.

We have already ordered. Or should I say some people have ordered. The Western concept that we order together and eat together doesn't count for much here. People arrive separately, order separately, and drink separately and eat when their food arrives. Everyone gets a personalised bill at the end of the evening. Precisely how the waiter keeps tab of who consumed what is still beyond this ordinary philosopher. That is probably because ordinary philosophers tend to focus on one problem at a time.

The problem on my mind is the paradox at play in the eating habits. In Asian countries, we expect eating to be a communal affair. In the West, it should be a sovereign individual affair, but it's not. In the West, we expect to synchronise our eating starting with appetisers, through the main course, and finishing with dessert. But what is being demonstrated here tonight is that Asians can take sovereign individuality even further. There is no synchronisation whatsoever.

The topic of personal freedom is raised, and it is raised centred on a CNN television news report. I forget now who raised it. Apparently, the reporter is asking Trump supporters going to a political rally why they refuse to wear masks. One Trump supporter's response ignited a discussion in the group.

The CNN correspondent asks a supporter why he is not wearing a mask. The supporter responds, 'I am a free man, and I will not wear a mask because the government tells me I must.' The level of aggression and intensity used in expressing that opinion, re-enforced by some seriously aggressive body language, compels the poor reporter to take a step back. Or perhaps he was simply concerned about getting caught under the misty spray from the supporter's mouth as he shouts out his opinion. Isn't it strange that conservatives think the quality of their opinion increases the louder they express it? I should have rolled that into the dialogue with Ricardo. I think too late.

Jeremy says, 'I don't get it. It just doesn't make sense that people refuse to wear a mask.'

I completely understand where Jeremy is coming from. In Singapore, we went from partial lockdown to full lockdown within six weeks of the hint of a pandemic, for six weeks. Wearing a mask became standard attire when we started coming out of full lockdown or indeed going shopping during lockdown. Of course, there were grumblings and questioning, but nobody seemed to really object to wearing a mask. Much has already been said about the compliance and obedience of Eastern citizens compared to Western citizens. But there is more going on here; it has a lot more to do with the very thing that Western citizens hold on to with such frightening, fierce force:

their right to freedom. In the East, it has a lot to do with the Confucius principle of respect and concern for family and community, a principle that over time became deeply embedded in most Asian cultures.

I say to Jeremy, 'For people like that, there is more going on than accepting the advice of scientists to wear a mask. You can explain until you are blue in the face that wearing a mask saves lives, might even save their life.'

'What do you mean?' asks Jeremy.

'The problem is that they hold on to the notion of personal freedom so fiercely that they are in fact not free,' I explain.

'Sorry, I don't get that,' says Jeremy.

'Personal freedom means a lot of things. In the one sense, it means that you are not held physically captive by someone else, that you are not held in a form of servitude or enslavement and forced to or coerced to work for someone else. That is the meaning of personal freedom in the obvious sense.'

Jeremy responds, 'Sure, I get that, but being told to wear a mask for your own and other people's safety does not do anything like enslavement or coercion.'

I agree, 'No, it doesn't. But personal freedom also means not to be held captive by an idea. You cannot call a person free when they are captivated by an idea in the sense that they are members of a cult, for instance.'

Jeremy tilts his head and frowns. 'Are you saying they are enslaved by a cult?'

This is not what I meant, but it will help to tunnel through to what I am trying to say. 'In a way, yes, people in cults are also held captive by an idea, a belief. In a similar way, these so-called self-proclaimed free people are also held captive by an idea. The idea is that they have an inalienable right or, heaven forbid, a God-given right to personal freedom. And nothing and no one can intrude on that right. If you think about the absurdity in claiming that freedom is a God-given right but people serve a religion, then the paradox becomes clear.'

You might have realised that the apparent parallel with tribes is obvious by now. Whereas cults are obvious tribes in Nietzsche's take on culture, the one about personal freedom is not. It is a hidden tribe, hiding in plain sight. You may call it a Western value embraced politically, but what are cultures other than the habitual habits of people, the hidden amorphous structures that shape our daily lives. If you want to join Nietzsche in his battle against the tribe, how are you going to deal with this one? The tribe insists you own yourself. But how can you own yourself and be a member of a tribe? How can you claim personal freedom but submit your loyalty to Trump? Personal freedom is the core of the tribe's existence. In that, there is a paradox, an untenable contradiction.

Jeremy rephrases, 'So you are saying they are being held captive by an idea, that idea is that they are free persons and being told to wear a mask intrudes on that freedom.'

I am impressed, so I say, 'Absolutely, but how can they claim to be free persons when they are being held captive by an idea?'

'No, they can't. Obviously,' agrees Jeremy. 'It raises questions about what is meant by a free person.'

'Indeed,' I say. 'If we look back, we see that being held physically captive is to be denied freedom as a consequence of the actions of other people. If we look back in the history of human thought, particularly Western philosophy, we see that personal freedom and self-ownership has been contemplated many times. Some philosophers like Locke and Rousseau argued that we are born free, that we have certain natural rights. This has been contested successfully, I think, by other philosophers who argue these are political rights. In fact, if you look at these rights, they are typically either ignored or enforced in the constitutional laws of a country. Also, these freedoms don't always travel internationally. You might enjoy certain rights in your own country, but you cannot claim those rights when you travel to another. So in a simple way, that demonstrates that they are political rights.'

Jeremy picks up on the point at hand. 'But wearing a mask is not a political issue.' Isn't he a delight? A pristine example of a smart person.

I agree with him. 'No, it is not. It is a scientific response to a natural problem. All decisions about wearing a mask should be made on scientific advice. The science does not intrude on political rights, but these people are confused about the difference. Not only are they confused by the difference between scientific decisions and political rights, but they are also being held mentally captive by an idea that happens to be a political right.'

'I see that,' says Jeremy, 'and bizarrely they are held captive by an idea that they are free persons, but they are clearly not free persons at all.'

'Precisely,' I say. 'Free persons will change their minds when the facts change or when the logic flows against their opinion. I must give credit to John Maynard Keynes. His actual words were, "When the facts change, I change my mind. What do you do, sir?"' I say to Jeremy.

'I like that,' says Jeremy. 'They claim to be free persons, but they are in fact not free because they cannot change their minds when the facts change on something that is absolutely not a challenge to their political right to be free persons.'

I say to Jeremy, 'We can take some wisdom from an ancient philosopher. "No man is free who is not master of himself" [Epictetus].'

'Good one,' says Jeremy. 'To be a truly free person, you should be a master of your own thoughts. In this case, you be smart enough to understand the difference between science thinking and political rights thinking.'

We pause for a minute or two whilst ordering more drinks. Then Jeremy adds, 'They are incredibly stupid, you know, Trump supporters. They believe anything he says. I can see now how they hold on to illusions so hard that they will put their own and other people's lives in jeopardy.'

I was still contemplating a response when Jeremy adds, 'You can potty train a toddler quicker than the time it takes to teach a Trump supporter how to wear a mask.'

* * *

John looks up. 'And just like that, you insulted seventy-six million Americans,' he says.

'I didn't,' I say. 'Jeremy did.'

John throws his head back in exasperation and looks up at the ceiling. 'Oh, for God's sake, Hendrik. You created the character. You are the author, and you are responsible for what Jeremy said. Therefore, you insulted half of the USA.'

'I am sure they won't know, John. They are probably used to being called idiots. Even Trump calls them idiots, or perhaps not. That might have been one of those memes that he disputes. But he knows full well what he is doing. Anyway, how can I be wrong? There are seventy-eight million other Americans who will agree with me,' I say.

'The quality of your opinion is not improved by the number of people who believe it, Hendrik,' says John.

The eyes take great joy in using my own lesson against me.

I have come to a realisation. It seems to me that since lunch, John has become less concerned that I am insulting individual characters but more concerned that I am insulting the tribes they belong to. Should I be worried about that? The tension in the pit of my stomach returns.

I don't share my thoughts. John appears to be contemplating something, so I take a moment to rest my mind.

'The reflection?' says John impatiently.

'Jeremy and I talked about the idea of a free person. That it is one thing to claim you are free physically—not enslaved or coerced, not in servitude of some kind—but it is another thing altogether when you are held captive by an idea or ideas, that those ideas prevent you from making the right choices. If you are in government or are leading a country, then your decisions can be particularly harmful, even catastrophic.

'American rednecks are not alone in this. The average British person has an irrational attachment to the same ideal. A scepticism of government, which makes strong leaders wobble. Leaders like Bozo with a spongy, cheesy brain has no chance. He flip-flops in decision and policymaking more often than a Russian Olympic gymnast in a floor exercise final.

'There are clear and defined differences in decision frameworks. You do not use one to make decisions that are inappropriate. We saw that in the dialogue with Megsum and Amanda. There is no room in that amorphous master called "the business" for ethical decisions. In the dialogue with James, he thought he was asking a philosophical question, but it is really a biological question.

'When you reframe the question and ask it appropriately, it is a lot less mythical. It might still be difficult, but step 1, what framework do we use for answering this question? How many apples are there in the basket? is an economic question, not a philosophical question. Yes, yes, I can hear the jokes too. Be serious. In Jeremy's dialogue, we address two thinking problems: being held captive by an idea and answering a question in the right framework—'

'For my sake, remind me what good looks like. When is someone not held captive by an idea?' interrupts John. Well, he didn't really interrupt because I was just winding that summary up.

'When the facts change or the logic flows against your opinion, you change your opinion. It is a pathway to more enlightenment. What beliefs do you have that stand in the way of your pathway? What parts of you twitch unexpectedly when another part is probed? You are the master of your mind when you see the twitching, recognise it for what it is and greet it with a friendly "Oh, hello old friend, now fuck-off".' I say.

'Yes, that is a good one to remember,' says John. Then he nods for us to continue, well, for me to continue.

DINNER WITH LIZ, IV

We seldom realize that our most private thoughts and
emotions are not actually our own. For we think in terms
of languages and images which we did not invent, but
which were given to us by our society.

Alan Watts

We arrive late. Not late in the sense that people were
waiting for us. Late in the sense that we are the last to
arrive. Everyone has taken up their seats but have not
yet ordered cocktails. Two seats remain vacant. Lilly takes the one
across from Ray. They always get along, so I am not surprised. The
other seat is across from Liz. Another factor in Lilly's decision, I think.
It occurs to me that Liz has turned the tables. Liz had taken control of
the hot seat, the one for the brave and the stupid. Stupid has arrived
and takes the seat.

The table discusses drinks, agrees on drinks, and places orders
with the waiter. The waiter is instructed to return later for us to decide
on food. He leaves to fetch the drinks. While we wait, there is a round
of polite catch-up. No surprises worth sharing there. It is the familiar
protocol. At least this time, I don't embarrass myself by embarrassing
someone else with my awkward sense of humour. Drinks arrive and
general well-wishes resume. As the table settles down, Liz fixes her
golden eyes on me. There is an unusual twinkle in her eye, a hint of
excitement.

'I was hoping we could talk tonight,' she says. 'I have been sharing our dialogues with the Philosophy of Life group. It has really livened the discussions and debates. Not everyone agrees, but they find it difficult to argue with me.' Liz smiles with a level of self-confidence I have not seen before. No hint of gratitude towards me though. I do not expect outside approval, and I seem never to receive any. I think it comes with being an ordinary philosopher. People try to impress you. You cannot impress them, so they never acknowledge you. I tell you this but also want you to know that I am always a little disappointed. I think it has something to do with being a middle child too. People might pay attention to you, but you are never allowed to know. *Oh, hello old friend, now fuck off.*

'Oh, that's good to hear, Liz,' I say, and I mean it. 'You have come up with some great ideas, and you can discuss them well,' I add, and I mean it.

'Thanks, Hendrik.' Liz smiles. 'I was hoping we can continue where we left off.'

'Remind me, please?' I say, playing up to her self-congratulatory disposition.

'We arrived at the conclusion that the more we crystalise the state, the more opaque the sovereign individual becomes.' Her explanation is good and concise. I like it. 'Yes, we also talked about the police force and the sovereign individuals that serve there,' she says.

I am a bit wary now. If my memory serves me correctly, this is where the dialogue broke down. I try a different tact.

'Agreed,' I say, 'other sovereign individuals.'

She nods.

'To enter into the police force is an expression of their sovereignty if they agree without there being any form of coercion, would you agree? I ask.

She tilts her head, but the eyes continue to track.

'And they can express their sovereignty at any time by leaving the service, provided they meet their contractual obligations,' I say.

'What do you mean contractual obligations?' she asks.

'They will have to hand in the tools of the trade—weapons, badges, uniforms, etc.—and they will have to work their notice period,' I answer. 'So at no point do they lose their sovereignty,' I say to fix the point down.

'Would you say that is the same for Britain when it entered into the EU?' she asks. I am impressed. She is not from Britain, but she has taken a keen interest. It was a tenet of the Brexit argument that Britain will take back its sovereignty.

'That is correct. It was an expression of British sovereignty to enter into the EU and an expression of its sovereignty to leave. At no point did Britain lose its sovereignty,' I say.

'And when one gets married or accept a job or buy something, all of that is an expression of one's sovereignty,' she adds.

'Very good, Liz.'

'So arguably, Britain lost out in leaving the EU. It never lost its sovereignty, so it had nothing to take back, but to trade with the EU, it must still follow EU rules. After Brexit, it no longer has any rights to influence those rules. It also lost all free movement rights for its citizens. When it comes to its sovereignty, nothing changed,' she continues.

Any concern I might have about the diversion is adequately compensated for by her grasp of the stupidity of Brexit. She takes a moment, has a sip of her wine, then says, 'Back to the sovereign individual.'

'Oh yes, I do remember. Did we not say perhaps we should revisit the sovereign individual?' I lead her, unnecessary from me.

'Yes. Can I go first?' says Liz. She does not wait for my permission. 'We are born free. We are naturally free persons, and that is precisely why we are sovereign individuals. Being born free means we have natural rights.'

If you paid attention to our previous dialogue, you might be as surprised as I am that she makes this claim. I am quite sure that we agreed there is no such thing as natural rights, only political rights. I have no appetite to go over previous terrain, so I play along.

'I am not sure what you mean by humans are born free,' I offer her. 'Are you suggesting that some animals are born captive?'

The direction of this question surprises Liz. Whatever she prepared for the dialogue tonight has gone out the window. 'What are you saying, Hendrik?'

'I am saying there must be an opposite to being born free, don't you think? Like captive. We are either born free or born captive.'

'Wow, interesting angle, Hendrik. Let me think.'

We pause while she thinks. We drink while she thinks. I refill our glasses while she thinks. In anticipation, I order more wine while she thinks. If you are worried about where tonight is heading, you have good reason to be so.

Liz speaks, 'You know what, perhaps *captive* is not the right word. Perhaps *dependent* would be better. We should consider whether we are born free or born dependent. What do you think?'

'I like dependent, Liz. To say we are born into captivity sounds like we are born to horrible parents or into sinister communities. Being born dependent sounds a lot more acceptable,' I say, 'but the opposite of dependent is independent.'

'Of course, it is, Hendrik!' Liz exclaims. 'But you cannot call yourself free unless you are independent. The two things must go together.' Then she caught me on the back foot. 'I cannot imagine a one-hour-old baby crying "I'm born free" and then reaching out for a nipple though.'

I am absolutely not sure what to make of the analogy. She continues, 'Unless you are a boy, then you never stop reaching out for the nipple.'

I try my best to ignore her analogy. There is something going on in her life that she needs to share, but preferably not with me. Is she getting nipple action? Is that what it means? I ponder. It is not usual for an ordinary philosopher to talk about nipples. I glance over at Lilly. She appears to be deeply involved in a discussion with Ray. I can barely make it out, but it has something to do with storytelling arcs, about distributing the imagery throughout the novel as opposed to offering it all in the beginning or the middle or as an afterthought.

I am relieved but still feeling irrationally guilty that I am discussing nipples with another woman. I try and redirect the discussion. 'I think you have made your point, Liz. It is difficult to see how we are born independent.' Perhaps I have misunderstood the source of Liz's newfound confidence. Perhaps it has something to do with her nipples.

'Are you saying we are not born free?' asks Liz. I am a little surprised. I thought drawing the contrary with dependent would have made that clear. I was wrong.

'Well, I can also ask how free,' I try. 'And I mean this in a literal sense, not philosophical sense. Let's think of it as to be born into the "state of nature".'

'Oh, I see,' says Liz. 'Yes, I think that is true.'

'Well, you are not alone. Some classic British and French philosophers will agree with you.'

Liz looks extremely pleased with herself. 'Really, who?'

I tell her who, 'Hobbes, Locke, and Rousseau, but before you get too excited, Hobbes warned against putting too much into this idea.'

'Why, what did he say?' asks Liz. She appears to be ready to relinquish control of the hot seat.

'I can't quote his exact words, but it goes something like this: "Born into the state of nature means life for man is solitary, poor, nasty, brutish and short,"' I say and leave it to her to absorb.

'So what does that mean for being born free?' she asks.

'It means we are born naked, wet, and hungry. If we do not fix these problems immediately, we die. To fix these problems, we bond with our mother first. If we are lucky, we also bond with our father and wider family, the people supporting and protecting our parents while they go through that trauma,' I say.

'Not as independent as I would have hoped,' says Liz quietly. 'What implications does it have for the idea of being born free?'

'It means one of two things. Firstly, that we can insist on the claim that we are born free but being born free is an altogether dangerous and precarious event that leaves us extremely vulnerable. It leaves us where no man respects the right of other men. Or secondly, it means that we are born dependent, and we remain dependent until we deserve to call ourselves free,' I explain.

'So what now?' she asks, giving me control of the hot seat.

Let's go down the rabbit hole, I think quietly to myself. To Liz, I say, 'Well, let us dwell on this idea of being born dependent. Maybe there is something there.'

She nods, so I continue, 'The reality of man's situation when he is born is quite precarious. He comes into the world wet, cold, hungry, and lonely. He must fix those problems immediately, or he will perish.'

'You have already said that,' says Liz. 'But we cannot really shape our philosophy around man's state as a baby now, can we?'

'Absolutely right, we can't,' I agree. 'Few philosophers bother.'

Liz rises high, her eyes fixed their gaze on me again, and she tracks. 'So why are we bothering with it?'

'Because I want us to contemplate the contrast between the fully dependent baby and the fully functional adult—the adult we consider as a sovereign individual,' I say.

'But why is that important?' Liz is getting a bit edgy now. Luckily for us, the waiter arrives and takes our order for food. I top up our wine, and we sip whilst the table settles down and seeks out the loose ends of almost forgotten conversations. Luckily, nobody steals our dialogue. I am convinced now that everyone has too much dread for the hot seat to dare.

'Why is it important?' I repeat to grab the loose end of our conversation. 'Because how do we get from fully dependent baby to fully functional sovereign individual?' I ask.

'Isn't it a natural thing, like with most animals,' offers Liz.

'Quite possibly, at least some of it is. I am sure evolutionary psychologists will seek to explain the benefits to the survival of the species for some form of independence,' I say. Before she can interject,

I continue, 'But no species other than humans will talk about it, discuss it, write about it, plan for it, execute the plan, and then claim their sovereign individuality from others, or demand certain rights because of it. So the question persists, how do we get from fully dependent baby to fully functional sovereign individual?'

Liz's head is perfectly still, the eyes tracking. I cannot believe that she is struggling to see the answer. I drink some more wine and top our glasses up again. I inspect the bottle, and I envisage a long night and a difficult morning.

Liz returns with a decent response. 'We are nurtured and intellectually developed by our parents,' she says.

'Just our parents?' I ask.

'I was homeschooled, so just my parents,' she says. 'I cannot speak for other children, although I think the same is possible for them, so it is irrelevant that they went to a school.'

'And what did your parents teach you?' I ask.

Liz shakes her head as if to indicate it is a stupid question with an obvious answer. She never stops tracking. 'To read, to write, maths, biology, science, literature, you know, probably a standard curriculum for the time.' Liz is a little restrained. She is entering familiar terrain. It is the rabbit hole.

'I mean, who set the curriculum?' I ask.

'The school board, of course, the department of education,' she answers.

'So the state,' I say.

Liz sinks back in her chair, but she tracks, says nothing.

'Why do you think the state sets the curriculum?' I ask.

Liz raises her hands slightly in a small gesture of defeat.

'Is it because it develops sovereign individuals who can collaborate?' I ask.

She repeats the gesture. I feel she is giving up, that perhaps I am moving too quickly to the conclusion. I try a different tunnel.

'Would you say there is a body of knowledge available to teach, a body of knowledge that brings together thousands of years of human endeavour into the intellectual arts?' I propose.

'What do you mean body of knowledge?' she asks.

'The wisdom of our species, but I think someone else have put it better than I can. Do you know Carl Sagan?' I ask.

'Only that he had a TV series, didn't he? Can't remember what it was called.'

'Well, that TV series gave me a glimmer of hope, an escape from a dreary right-wing conservative religious education which I dismissed privately but was too afraid to do publicly. Until *Cosmos*, that is. Here is a quote from Sagan: "Books changed all that [the fragile impermanence of knowledge]. Books, purchasable at low cost, permit us to interrogate the past with high accuracy; to tap the wisdom of our species; to understand the point of view of others, and not just those in power; to contemplate—with the best teachers—the insights, painfully extracted from Nature, of the greatest minds that ever were, drawn from the entire planet and from all our history. They allow people long dead to talk inside our heads. Books can accompany us everywhere. Books are patient where we are slow to understand, allow us to go over the hard parts as many times as we wish, and are never critical of our lapses. Books are key to understanding the world and participating in a democratic society."'

'Yes, of course. Without the body of knowledge, we all go back to paradise and start again, don't we?' she asks.

'Indeed, solitary, poor, nasty, brutish, and short lives,' I say.

'So what?' she says. 'We do not need the state for that. My parents didn't need the state. They homeschooled us then put us through university and paid for it all.'

I am pleasantly surprised that Liz has come to this realisation, that we are heading for this point where we argue whether the state should provide education. 'But who owns the body of knowledge, the language you speak, the maths you use, the science, the biology, the arts? The ancient wisdoms of our species? Who owns that, Liz?' I ask.

'No one,' she says quickly, too quickly.

'What about the rights to property that you are ready to defend in the name of the sovereign individual? Doesn't that extend to intellectual property too? What about all the people who contribute to that body of knowledge and the fruits of their labour? Do you think they should make it available for free? If so, is that not a form of enslavement?

Our food arrives and offers a rather welcome break in the proceedings. I take a break to the smoking area a few meters away but return promptly. Did I mention to you that we are in a Mexican restaurant? We are in a Mexican restaurant, so there is a mix of shared plates and individual plates. Things get quickly shuffled around to satisfy the orders as they were placed. It is Liz's turn to top up the wine. She does so and waves at the waiter for a replacement.

'What about the last sentence in Sagan's quote, that it is this knowledge that makes it possible for us to participate in a democratic society?' I ask.

'I can see how knowledge helps us, but is it strictly necessary?' she asks.

'For a successful democracy, yes, it is. But I am keen to get to something else. What do we assume about the individual in a democratic society?' I ask.

'We assume a certain level of individual sovereignty?' Liz says. Her voice rises at the end, which make it sound like she wants my confirmation. The food forces her to break off persistent tracking. Tracking is now punctuated by quick glances to her plates to select the next bite.

'Indeed,' I say. 'Knowledge, capability, and education are essential to be a sovereign individual.'

I have a thought, something Lilly said to me one day when we were on this topic. 'If not the state, who then will rescue those poor children from negligent parents? Negligent either because they survived negligent parents by some miracle or those whose parents were so focused on rescuing themselves on an hourly basis that they had no time to teach their children, only time to force them into labour as infants?' I ask Liz.

'I don't like to say this right now, but I think you have made your point, Hendrik,' says Liz. 'But to what extent do we provide publicly funded education?' she asks.

'The richer the nation, the more the funding. Simple, really,' I say. 'There is also no reason why rich European countries, the USA, and other similarly wealthy countries cannot fund the education perhaps to undergraduate degrees at least.'

'That seems to me to go too far. I am not sure I am willing to pay for another person's undergraduate degree course,' she says.

'Not willing to pay or not willing to share responsibility,' I say, reminding her of the closing statement from Ray.

Liz fixes her gaze on me and sighs in resignation to the low blow.

'It is ultimately a matter of political negotiation,' I say, 'but don't you think we have uncovered yet another problem?'

Despair washes over Liz's face. She is ready to give up, but the night is young, the food is on the table, and a fresh bottle of wine has just arrived.

Liz eats for a while before she answers. 'Sorry, I was drifting. Another problem, like what?'

'It seems to me that the sovereign individual is in fact created by the community of people. We are not naturally sovereign individuals, unless we want to be poor—'

Liz stops me by showing her open hand, the way a policeman would. 'Yes, yes, I get it, and I agree we become sovereign individuals by transitioning from fully dependent babies to fully functional adults,' she says impatiently.

'If you as a sovereign individual refuses to fund education for the next generation, then you are effectively killing off the thing that created you.' I say, but somehow, I think this is superfluous.

It is superfluous. 'I know. I have already agreed.'

'And what about healthcare? Do you think a person can be a fully functioning sovereign individual if he is sick, hungry, riddled with disease, and wandering a desert?' I ask.

But Liz is in no mood to pursue the dialogue any further. 'I said I agree, Hendrik. I probably will agree to healthcare as well,' she says.

It is my turn to top up the wine.

Liz finds a way to accept the new paradigm in her thoughts. She collects herself together and comes back with a completely unexpected question.

'You know how we discussed how the institutions of the state all seem necessary for the state to function?' she says or asks. I am not sure, so I just nod.

'Is there a risk that the state as it is designed will simply continue to grow unchecked?' she asks.

'That is a really good question,' I compliment her. 'What do you think are driving forces for this unchecked growth or the overreach of the state?'

'Oh, let's see,' says Liz, and she takes a minute to think and drinks from her wine glass while she does that. 'It seems to me that as soon as the state has taken control of rogue behaviour, unscrupulous people will find a way to undermine the rights of other sovereign individuals that does not break the law, or at least test the law to see how far they can go.'

The more corrupt the state the more numerous the laws.

Tacitus

'But when these actions of the unscrupulous seem unjust to the community, they enact new laws that control that behaviour. But unscrupulous people simply find new ways to test the law. So new laws are required. A vicious hidden feedback loop.'

'Very good point, Liz. So if we want to keep governments small, we all have to behave like good citizens,' I say.

Liz smiles with self-congratulation. 'Indeed, see, I am not as dumb as I look, Hendrik.'

'Of course not, Liz!' I say. 'You could not possibly be!'

* * *

John has collapsed into uncontrollable giggles. I am completely shocked.

'Seriously?' I ask myself, and again. 'Seriously? No comedy in a prestigious lawyer's office, ever?' I thought I was just recycling old jokes. But apparently, jokes are only old for some people, new for the ones who have not heard it before. I suppose this confirms there is not much room in a prestigious lawyer's office for comedy. I keep these thoughts to myself. I feel the urge to defend my innocence. It is irrational and extremely dangerous to satisfy an urge to defend yourself in front of a lawyer.

There is no point in attempting to interrupt John. I will simply have to wait. Just as I was getting concerned and thinking of asking for help, John comes out of the giggles. He dries his eyes with the hanky that normally resides in the breast pocket of his expensive suit. John temporarily relieves me from the urge.

'That poor woman,' he says, 'how you get away with it is beyond me.'

'Seriously, John. You know she is just a character in a novel,' I counter.

'Well, Hendrik, if she is real and she recognises herself, she has every reason to be proud. There is no shame in being smart,' he says. 'You seem to have taken a daring approach with her, and it has worked out.'

I am relieved. I have no idea why because she is just a character in a novel. 'I mean, sure, there is someone or some who inspired the character, I know. But how else to create a character? I cannot see how to create a character without drawing inspiration from real people. It is a tricky one, John. Where do the real people stop, and where do my characters start?' I add.

'And did you really have to write about the nipples?' asks John and very nearly collapses into another round of giggles.

Now I am the one who is amused. Amused and curious. Is there really something about nipples that sends a prestigious lawyer into uncontrollable giggles? It wasn't the recycled joke after all. It is the nipples. Then why did he wait until I finished? Or did he? Perhaps I didn't notice until I finished and paused at the end. I have a teenage urge to say 'Nipples, nipples, nipples' three times. Like a thirteen-year-old boy would after having discovered the magical effect of the mere sight of nipples. But I don't. Instead, I say in my defence, 'I was told that every good novel has some sexual tension, John. This is the best I could muster.'

He does not respond immediately. When he does, he says, 'Honestly! Is that all you can think of to create sexual tension?'

'Is it not enough? I don't know, John. Some people are never sexually satisfied. I suppose some of my readers won't be either.' I am hinting, of course, but John ignores the hint, so I continue, 'I felt it. I looked at Lilly at the time. I was certainly worried that something untoward was going on between Liz and me. That Liz has no shame, you know. And she is single, you know,' I say, realising I am protesting too much. 'Anyway, you will be pleased to know that no one is killed in the novel.'

The eyes tell me that the concern has returned.

'And just like that, you destroy any confidence that Liz is just a figment of your imagination, Hendrik. Seriously, I just cannot pin you down on this, can I?' says John.

'Well, that is my only defence, John. What else can I say? It is written in the beginning of the novel that it is just fiction, that everything is just a coincidence.'

'We have been over that, Hendrik. You cannot put a disclaimer down and then say what you like. Free speech comes with responsibility, you know,' says John. The eyes indicate at the letter on the table.

The letter on the table echoes his concern. The grip comes back with renewed energy.

'The reflection?' I ask to change the subject.

'In this dialogue, we refocus on the battle between the individual and the state, the individual living in reality and the amorphous things we create. The things we create that will make our lives hell. Liz and I had that rather brutal discussion about individual rights, how they are not naturally there. So if they come from anywhere, they come from the amorphous thing—the thing that has made her a sovereign individual and how she is now trying to kill it off.

'She also claims ownership over the body of human knowledge in contradiction with her claim of sovereign individual ownership. All of the rights she wants to claim for herself as a sovereign individual can only come from political negotiations with other sovereign individuals. These rights are therefore political rights, and if they are political rights, then you need a political system to negotiate them. She wasn't incredibly happy with that, but Liz always overcomes her internal resistance to changing her opinions, maybe not on the night but always over time—'

'Hold on, hold on,' says John. Then after making a note, he nods for me to continue. I swear he did that just to annoy me. To annoy him, I don't finish the reflection and move on to the next dialogue.

PART THREE

LEAVING THE CAVE AND INTO THE LIGHT

LUNCH WITH FRANCOIS

It was the duty of philosophy to destroy the illusions which had their origin in misconceptions, whatever darling hopes and valued expectations may be ruined by its explanations.

Immanuel Kant

We are meeting for brunch at the Australian pub again. It should no longer surprise you. But if you are interested, then there is a good reason for this particular pub, which I think would satisfy your curiosity. There is plenty of space and, on a Sunday morning, plenty of free tables. We are limited to eight people per table because of COVID-19 restrictions but also because the tables here seat eight people comfortably. It is entirely coincidental that the table accommodation matches the COVID-19 restrictions. Perhaps there is something about the number 8 and the number of Australians who like to meet up. A natural or culturally comfortable number of people in a conversation. Isn't there also something about the number 8 in Chinese mythology? The number that means infinite prosperity, I think, or is it to make a fortune? I must look that up, but would that mean burning intelligence needlessly?

By now, you should be familiar with the food, not the detail, of course—I have not shared the menu—but with the theme and the standard. The coffee too, but if you have forgotten, it is probably Dimbulah, and you have the option of a large mug, a decent amount of coffee for a decent dialogue. I normally end up having two. Lilly finds it amusing mostly because I get really hyped up by the caffeine overload. I think I get hyped up because it is the only way keeping hold of a dialogue if you are the lucky one to be in control.

There are no rules. Everyone is expected to behave, and most people do, even the newcomers. I recall only one incident where a person was advised not to return. He didn't return, and no one seemed disappointed.

There are newcomers almost every week, and today is no exception. Some people I expect come once, find the conversations of little interest, and vow never to come back. I heard a young woman complain once that the location is too inconvenient. It was a five-minute walk from the nearest train station. In Singapore's climate, that is too much for a young woman of a certain distinction. Exactly what that distinction is, I don't know. Perhaps it is a characteristic of a person without any distinction whatsoever.

I don't remember all the names, and it is also a habit of mine now to not introduce you to everyone. There are typically several distinct conversations around the table, and I am only concerned about the one I am talking in, or one which I think is of interest to you. I will introduce the participants in the dialogues I am sharing with you.

I am apprehensive that you might think participants make it sound like a psychology experiment, and yes, I am concerned about that, but I cannot think of another word. At one time, participants were called subjects until someone pointed at psychologists that the word *subjects* encourage unethical experiments. Experiments such as the Stanford prison experiment, the Milgram experiment, or the Little Albert experiment are but a few that come to mind. Apparently, calling participants subjects invoked a sense of superiority and control, the kind of superiority and control that the sovereign individual might have. It sounds like a psychological flaw pertinent to psychologists.

There is nothing experimental about these meetings. It is just ordinary people talking about a topic of interest. It is not run by me, and I do not do the invitations. I am just another participant, just another ordinary philosopher trying to discuss ordinary problems with other ordinary philosophers.

I was once advised to call participants guests—guests who sit around a table and have a discussion. The idea really appeals to me, and I think I might use it from now on.

I am lucky enough to sit across the table from a newcomer, a young Frenchman called Francois. Francois is the kind of person whom you take an instant liking to. Personable, open, and seemingly transparent. He is also French, which means he probably studied a fair amount of philosophy at school. I heard somewhere that that is the way they do things in France. It explains why French people are happy to discuss politics and share opinions. They are also happy to engage in discussions around political views across the dinner table without causing family fractures or friendship fissures.

Francois has a Napoleonic stature. It sounds like an oxymoron, I know. What I mean by it is something a good friend one said to me about Frenchmen. She admired a particular young gentleman and said he is small but perfectly formed. I can see what she meant by that. Francois looks at you with dark brown eyes, a pleasant and attractive face with a decent haircut. He is small but physically perfect, slim with broad shoulders, and athletic in his movement.

The conversation has been flowing freely for a while now. Someone has mentioned culture. I think it was in a corporate sense. You know, like, 'I like working there because of the corporate culture.' I cannot recall the exact detail to be honest, and I am not going to make it up to satisfy any curiosity you might have in that regard. Suffice to say that I have a great deal of curiosity about culture, and that is where we are heading.

'I am not always sure what people mean by culture,' I say.

It is Francois who answers. 'Oh, I think everyone knows what it means. It is the culture you grow up in. It teaches you values. It is the way of life of a people, the habits, the symbols, the traditions. It is all those things.'

'Well, there must be more to it than that,' I say. 'I am particularly concerned about the use of the word *values*. It implies good, but values can be bad too.'

'Bad values? Culture doesn't have bad values, Hendrik. Surely not,' he says. I am happy to report that other people have conceded the dialogue to me and Francois. They let us get on with it.

'Well, that might be true if you grew up in France, but it is not true everywhere. This is one of the things that bothers me when people talk about culture. Culture does not have enough shape, enough definition for anyone to clearly understand what is being said,' I say, laying the route to the rabbit hole.

'What do you mean more shape, more definition?' asks Francois.

'That culture is actually really hard to define. If you look at a dictionary, it will give you two distinct descriptions of the meaning of culture. One is to do with the collective arts and intellectual achievements of humanity. Let us put that one aside for now. The other description talks about the norms and social behaviours of a people,' I say. 'If you take the second understanding, you can see that there must be clear differences between French culture and, say, Ethiopian culture. Some of it is the same no doubt—'

'Of course, there will be differences,' interrupts Francois. 'That is why people are enormously proud of their culture. That is what makes French people different from everybody else.'

'And you probably have every right to be proud of your culture if you are French. If you consider Nietzsche as a good judge of cultures, then you will have at least one venerated endorsement. But if you are French, you might judge some Ethiopian cultural norms to be completely unacceptable, and I guarantee the Ethiopians will be perplexed by some French cultural habits.'

'You are making it too complicated, Hendrik. It is just common sense,' says Francois.

'Do you mean culture is just common sense, or do you mean it is common sense what culture is?' I ask.

Francois sits back and tilts his head. He maintains eye contact but says nothing immediately. I assume it is one of those occasions when my guest is surprised that I question something that everyone accepts.

'I have never thought about it. I think both,' says Francois.

'Well, what do you mean by common sense?' I ask.

He turns his open palms skywards in a gesture that I think means he is perplexed by it, surprised that I would ask. I wait. No one else offers an explanation. I think it is true for everyone. They all think it is common sense that common sense means common sense. They have never given it a thought.

'Everyone knows what common sense means, Hendrik,' says Francois.

'Perhaps,' I say, 'but it might surprise you when you look at it in more detail. Aristotle was the first one to use the term *common sense*. He used it to talk about what humans have in common with other animals. Our senses that we have in common to interpret the world around us and to respond appropriately. The four *F*s.'

'The four *F*s?' asks Francois.

'Yes, fight, flight, food, or mate,' I say.

He hesitates then laughs. 'Oh, I get it. But that is not what we mean today.'

'No, it is not. Today we might say it means the sound, practical judgement concerning everyday matters or a basic ability to perceive, understand, and judge in a manner that is shared by nearly all people,' I say, realising that I made it sound like a direct quote from a dictionary.

'Yes, our culture, that is what I said,' says Francois, incredibly pleased with himself.

'So our common sense, our culture might have some surprises installed for us, whatever those surprises might be, should be inspected, investigated, and adjusted to get rid of the bad values or common-sense ideas that it contains. So what is common sense for Ethiopians will not be common sense for French people. In fact, there are common-sense ideas in French culture that the Ethiopians might dislike,' I say.

'What about the French culture do Ethiopians not like?' says Francois, sounding a little defensive.

'Oh, I am not Ethiopian, so I can't say. But if I ask you what about the Ethiopian culture you find you have a dislike for, what would you say?' I say, sidestepping the challenge.

'Nothing, I have nothing to say about Ethiopian culture,' says Francois.

'If I tell you Ethiopians widely practise female genital mutilation, what would you say about that?'

'What is female genital mutilation? I have never heard of this female genital mutilation,' says Francois, but it is clear he is preparing himself for being repulsed by the answer. He sits upright and leans forward. A frown forms between his dark brown eyes. It was a stroke of genius to come up with a phrase like that. It certainly creates the desired effect.

'When young Ethiopian women reach puberty, their mothers and aunts cut out their clitorises with a razor blade,' I spell it out directly, crudely.

Francois is genuinely shocked. I think I must have felt that shock when I heard about this practise the first time. I am still shocked if I imagine it in too much detail.

'Why!' Francois almost shouts it out.

'Apparently, it curbs their sexual desires and keep them loyal to their husband,' I say, realising that we are now going for more detail than is required for our discussion.

'Isn't it illegal?' asks Francois.

'No, and until recently, it wasn't even illegal in Britain,' I say. 'In 1985, I think.'

'My god, that is horrible,' says Francois. 'The poor women, what do they do?'

'It is everyday common sense for them, Francois. You might be surprised to hear that they actually look forward to the process with keen anticipation. It is the moment in their lives when they enter adulthood, when they get ready to be married off, to become one of many wives for one man,' I say, hoping I can now restate my question.

'What! They look forward to it?' asks Francois and looks around the table, hoping to find someone to join him in dismissing my explanation as mere speculation, anti-Ethiopian sentiment. I am beginning to regret that I took the dialogue there. I fear I have destroyed a significant innocence in Francois.

'That is the power of culture, Francois. That is what common sense can do. The people inside the culture are not aware of the harmful practices that might be done in its honour,' I say.

'OK, I get it now, what you said earlier. That we must inspect and investigate our culture or our common-sense ideas to remove harmful habits and social norms. I get it now,' Francois says, nodding affirmation in support.

'The problem is, Francois, how do you know which are bad common-sense ideas?' I ask.

'What do you mean?' he asks.

'The young women are completely oblivious to the harm and the denial they will face for the rest of their lives. They look forward to it. They think it is common sense, remember?' I ask.

'Oh yes, they don't see it,' he acknowledges.

'So how can you judge what is good or bad in the French culture. How will you know?' I ask Francois.

There is silence for a while. Then Francois says, 'I have to ask someone that is not in my culture, it seems.'

'Well, that is one way, but another way is to test these common-sense ideas against ethical and moral principles that are universal,' I say. 'If you ask someone else, just remember, they have a culture too and they will be inclined to judge your culture by their cultural norms.'

'What do you mean by that?' asks Francois.

'I mean, if you ask Ethiopians, they might think the French have no common sense because they allow women to express uncontrolled sexual desires and therefore could be disloyal towards their husbands,' I say.

'So I cannot ask an Ethiopian. What if I ask a German?' he asks.

'You will have to judge that the Germans know better than the French when it comes to culture,' I say.

Francois shakes his head. He does not like that option and takes me up on the alternative. 'What ethical and moral principles are not culturally specific?' asks Francois, and I am impressed. It is an important question.

'You may want to look at Kant's deontological ethics,' I say. 'He has devised a test for any moral, that it must be universalizable. In other words, it must be good for everyone, every person. Do you think the Ethiopian practice of female genital mutilation will pass that test?'

'No, absolutely not,' says Francois.

'You may also ask if they are using the woman as a means to an end and not also as an end in herself,' I say. Francois must think about that one.

'Wouldn't that mean educating young Ethiopian women first so that they understand they are being denied or have been denied something that every person should experience, not just the men?' he says, and I detect a little anger in his voice.

'Sure, and then there is the do-no-harm test, which I think is self-explanatory,' I say.

'OK, so I have some work to do,' says Francois.

'Well, before you go,' I say and pause, 'there is more. Culture is an extraordinarily complex concept, a multi headed master. There are cultures within cultures. Cultures that build institutions. Institutions that are culture builders.'

'Now you are just confusing me,' protests Francois.

'Let's look at a corporation. Much have been written about corporate culture. There are people making a great living out of advising the CEOs on building culture. Others help fix toxic work cultures. So it is important to try and understand what culture is and how it comes about. More importantly, what do you need to change to change a culture?' I explain.

'Oh, I see!' exclaims Francois. 'To change a culture, you need to change the habits and norms that underpin it, the common sense.'

'Yes, and how do you change that?' I ask.

Francois begins to answer, then hesitates, then starts to form words. Then he says nothing altogether.

'That is a difficult one, eh,' I say. To help him out, I add, 'Just think of whose behaviour you will need to change.'

'Individual people' is the short answer from Francois.

'Yes, exactly,' I confirm. 'But how does one person change the behaviour of thirty or forty million people or maybe more?'

'Oh god, it looks like an impossible task,' says Francois, falling into a shallow depression.

'Well, it isn't impossible, but it takes real leadership, courage, and persistence. You must really believe that change is necessary, build a coalition, and then grow that coalition,' I say.

'Like building a political movement?' he asks.

'Like building a political movement,' I confirm. 'And be very wary of the warriors.'

'The warriors?' he asks.

'Yes, the culture will send its warriors, its protectors, its bodyguards. Be very wary of them,' I warn him.

'But why? What can they do?' he asks.

'They can kill,' I say.

From somewhere, Francois finds a source of courage, a fountain of bravery, and a mountain of persistence. Napoleon boldness. 'Yes, but it must be done. And someone must do it. Some must take to battle against the master, unseen, shapeless, and deadly as it might be.'

He is being a bit poetic for me, but there you go; that is the French for you.

> There are those who say, there is more bad than good
> in human nature, to which I hold a contrary view, that
> good o'er bad predominates in man, for if it were not
> so, we should not exits. He hath my praise, whoe'er of

gods brought us to live by rule from chaos and from brutishness, first by implanting reason, and next by giving us a tongue to declare our thoughts, so as to know the meaning as what is said . . .

Euripides

Francois turns to another discussion, and I am not offended. Ours have run its natural course. I quietly reflect on the paradox, and I wonder what Nietzsche made of it. People are fundamentally embedded in their cultures. Their culture is the tribe that created them. It is Nietzsche's tribe that created the individual. Then Nietzsche's individual wants to break free from the tribe. Is there something fundamentally wrong with Nietzsche's view? Did Francois have an inclination that he wants to be free from his tribe? Does he now?

It seems that we do not so much want to be free from our tribes or that we want to claim ownership of ourselves. Instead, the main purpose in our lives is to fix the tribe, to correct its bad habits, to become its master rather than being its slave. To polish its common sense to perfection. That is what we should be doing. That is our gift from the gods, if we accept Euripides's advice.

* * *

'If you insulted anybody there, you insulted the French,' says John.

'Is that OK? To insult the French?' I tease.

'One shouldn't go about insulting anybody, Hendrik. Not the French, the Americans, women, men, Gandhi followers, nobody,' John says.

'But what about free speech?' I ask, knowing that it is the most annoying defence.

The eyes make me understand it is the most annoying defence.

'I am just fishing, Hendrik, just speculating as I reflect on the dialogue. There is nothing in there that I think would qualify as libel,'

John says, and he looks a little more relaxed. 'I find it interesting that you seem to be defending culture, Hendrik.'

'I am not the all-or-nothing type, John. Culture is what creates us. Where do I draw the line where culture ends and where I begin? No one knows. Not only that, but culture also created me. If I kill off culture, I will kill off who I am. Remember, I discussed that with Liz.'

'Indeed, you did,' agrees John. 'But you are also conscious of its flaws.'

'Indeed.' It is my turn to agree. 'I am all too aware of cultural flaws. I was born in South Africa to racist Afrikaner parents a year after apartheid itself. I grew up apartheid. I grew up in a family that embraced white supremacy. I also grew up in a religious doctrine. It is only when I watched *Cosmos*, remember Sagan?' John nods. 'It is only when I watched *Cosmos* that I saw a glimmer of light, an exit from this awful Plato's cave that my culture built for me—a Plato's cave that existed entirely in my head. I left South Africa at twenty-four. Escaped the country that year, but it took a few more years before I escaped the culture. If this is what Nietzsche meant, then I overcame the tribe, but only by joining another one. So yes, I know first-hand that cultures are flawed, that they need to be fixed. But I also know that without it, I'd be nothing and that with it I must be its master and not its slave. I must just add that my parents changed too. They became less racist, less supremacist when they got older. They changed with the country, but just like the country not all the way.'

'That is why you worked with Liz, to make her aware of the importance of culture, of society. That, in fact, she wants to kill off the thing that created her,' contemplates John out loud.

'Fancy that I have one more dialogue with Liz. Shall I do it now?' I ask.

'Sure, but can we run through the reflection quickly?' suggests John. I am not sure why he thinks we can do it quickly. I don't.

'In the dialogue with Francois, I shattered his illusion that cultures are all good and valuable to individuals. They are clearly not. Often, they give license to extraordinary bad behaviour and terrible social practices. Cultural practices reflect in our common sense. I am always a little cautious when people plead for common sense or for common sense to prevail. Common sense, in its true meaning, embraces our cultural practices. Sometimes we do not want common sense to prevail. As an example, we discussed female circumcision or how it is more vividly referred to as female genital mutilation.

'There is a lesson here. Always look for the hidden composition fallacy. When we talk about culture, we think about the values and habits that are judged good or perhaps quirky and interesting, but harmless. From that, we conclude that culture is good. In the process of doing so, we hide some of those cultural practices that are clearly harmful to some people.

'We covered only the one cultural practice, but there are more of course. There is a lot of history too, such as the ostracisation of LGBTQs; the submission of women to a lower status in societies, including in France; gender discrimination, which is still incomprehensibly common; the banning of same-sex marriages.

'Many of these cultural practices find their way into the statute books. But many more don't. It is the ones that don't that are the most dangerous ones—the ones that the statute books ignore, turn a blind eye to. Then there are the ones that are protected by claims to religious freedom or individual freedom or freedom of expression or ethnic uniformity and other more evil ideas that are part of the amorphous thing called culture.

'It tells us that we have a duty to each other to constantly evaluate our own cultures and eliminate these practices from them. But there is a difficulty. When you are inside a culture, encased by the amorphous master, you don't see its evils. You need outside help, or you need to judge it against universal ethical principles. Weeding out these harmful cultural practices is dangerous work. Culture will send its warriors, and its warriors can kill. So you need courage, conviction, bravery, and persistence, even boldness, but it does not have to be Napoleonic

'Francois changed his mind. He accepted that his opinion about culture being all good was wrong. Francois was ready and willing to put himself in harm's way to improve his culture. Francois is an example of someone who is the master of his mind. That is what enlightenment looks like.'

The eyes give me the go-ahead. For the first time, they appear to not be ready to judge me. In fact, I see a glimmer of respect, just a glimmer. I dare not get my hopes up. I decide against going direct to the next dialogue with Liz, there is some preparatory work to be done first.

BRUNCH WITH JAMES

> Man's condition is tragic, for he no longer finds fulfilment in life's simple values. For animals, life is all there is; for man, life is a question mark. An irreversible question mark, for man has never found, nor will ever find, any answers. Life not only has no meaning; it can never have one.
>
> *Emil Cioran*

It is a typical Sunday for us. Lilly and I settle down with a group of people as we do for brunch or lunch, but that depends on when you arrive and whether you feel like eating at all. We are back at that popular riverside pub. I told you about it before. I also told you to remember. Here is a bit more information. It is more like a restaurant, but the owner would probably be upset if you call it that. He would prefer gourmet pub, but like I said before, the food would not meet the standards expected for gourmet food, even though it is much better than you would expect from a pub.

It is a large pub with a choice of seating arrangements. There are proper dinner tables with individual comfy chairs. There are tables with bench chairs where you must slide in if you are unlucky enough to sit in the middle or you must get up to let someone in or out if you are unlucky enough to sit at the end. Wherever you sit, you are going to be unlucky. There are high tables where you sit on what is a lot like a bar stool, except it kills your bottom and your back after an hour or so. I often wonder if that is by design, purposefully to limit the length of your stay unless you have anaesthetised your bottom with alcohol.

The other way to anaesthetise your bottom is with exhilarating conversation. We keep coming back to this place, and we sit around the high tables, so you can take it as said that we often have exhilarating conversations. There are newcomers every weekend, so we start with polite introductions.

I go first. I feel it is my duty to welcome newcomers. They, of course, don't know that I am an old hand at this. The newcomer probably thinks I am being a bit forward. 'Hi, I'm Hendrik.'

He stretches out his fist. We are still fist bumping because of the virus. Pushing your fist out that way would probably have been considered an aggressive move before the virus changed greeting protocols. Funny how a pandemic can change culture in unexpected ways. 'Nice to meet you, Hendrik. I'm James. What do you do?'

Now James is being forward. If we followed protocol, he would have introduced himself, then I would have asked him the standard opening question. I think this, but I feel like being polite today, so I say, 'I'm a philosophical practitioner and author. And you?'

There is no point in telling him my real job, the one I earn a living with. It is a conversation killer anyway. And Aristotle didn't get paid for his wisdom either. He had to toil as a stonemason to put bread on the table.

James does not answer my question. Instead, he goes provocative. 'Interesting! So you can answer the difficult question.' The smart-arse response. Smart-arses can be quite irritating because they behave as if they know everything.

I know where this is going, but I ask anyway, 'What question is that?'

James smiles provocatively, one-sided. That might just be a feature of his unfortunate face. It is unfortunate because it is not what you would call attractive. He is young, but his body is in a state of neglect, soft, overweight, and badly dressed. He says, 'The big question, what is the meaning of life? Isn't that what philosophers do?'

I disagree with that, so I tell him, 'I disagree. I don't think so.'

James develops a mildly red sheen on his face, his smart-arse deflated somewhat. He was trying to be smart, but now he looks stupid. I am, of course, not responsible for that. He did stupid all by himself. He glances around the table to see if anyone else is listening. Relieved that no one is paying attention, he comes back. 'What then do philosophical practitioners do?'

I am happy to answer that one. 'They help people with the everyday problems of life.'

James recovers his provocative attitude instantly; the lopsided smile is back. 'OK, you answer the everyday questions. Consider it an everyday question. What is the meaning of life?'

I am impressed with his cheeky mental agility, so I offer an out. 'The first thing we do is to see if the question is something that can be answered philosophically.'

James frowns and shakes his head rapidly from side to side. He is confused now. I do not think he expected the intellectual roller coaster. 'I thought that "What is the meaning of life?" is a fundamentally philosophical question,' he insists.

I told you I disagree with him. Nothing has changed, so I explain, 'Life is a biological condition, James. So you might be better off asking a biologist.' I may as well take him down the rabbit hole.

He follows me down the rabbit hole. 'Oh, come on! Everybody knows what that question means.'

> The fact that an opinion has been widely held is no evidence whatever that it is not utterly absurd; indeed in view of the silliness of the majority of mankind, a widespread belief is more likely to be foolish than sensible.
>
> *Bertrand Russell*

'Well,' I say, 'I dispute the meaning you have, so not everybody agrees with your meaning. Some people might, even most people might. I still disagree, and I am the philosopher.' I try a subtle rebuke to the composition fallacy in his statement.

Of course, he is right. The question is posed poetically and with seriously misleading longing by individuals looking for something beyond their tribes to give them hope, but in the process, they form a new tribe, a tribe lost in a question—a question they cannot answer because it is the wrong question.

James glances around for another seat or another face to engage with. None is available. He has no choice but to follow me deeper into the rabbit hole. 'You are just messing with my head' is all he can offer.

I reply with, 'No, I don't have to. Clearly your head is already messed up. Unless you can persuade me that the word *life* has a different meaning, then the question is still one for biologists to answer. They might say life is about survival, an effective response to the environment, the condition that distinguishes animals and plants from inorganic matter, including the capacity for growth, reproduction, functional activity, and continual change preceding death. And no doubt the answer will be longer than I care to explore.'

James finds courage from somewhere. 'Why?'

I decide to test that courage. 'What do you mean by why? Why is it a biological question, or why don't I care?'

James resolves his own ambiguity. 'Why don't you care?'

I go deeper into the rabbit hole. 'Because I am a philosopher, and my interest in biology is limited. I don't think I care much about the answer.'

'OK, so why is it a biological question?' James asks.

'I thought I explained that already. Life is a biological condition. That is why it is a biological question,' I say. 'I suspect though that you have a different question in mind, so why don't you rephrase the question?'

James relaxes in his chair, well, as much as you can relax on a bar stool. Relief shows in his face; there is an escape from the rabbit hole after all. 'OK, how about this. What is the purpose of life?'

I pretend to reflect on the question. 'Hmm, perhaps still a biological question, but I suspect that an evolutionary biologist will object. If life has a purpose, it would be about surviving long enough to reproduce. But the idea that life has a purpose would really upset evolutionary biologists. Evolution is all about selection, accidental efficient responses to changes in the environment.

'Arbitrary changes in the environment creates conditions in which life survives or perishes. There is nothing purposeful about evolution whatsoever. Thus, you have a dilemma. On the one hand, there is no purpose in evolution and therefore no purpose in life, so biologists will not answer the question, and neither will philosophers because it is not a philosophical question. The question is unanswerable. It is meaningless as a biological question and invalid as a philosophical question. You may want to reconsider your question.'

James has another attempt to make alternative arrangements for his morning. Unfortunately for him, he cannot find another chair or available friendly face. He spends another minute listening to other conversations to see if he can engage. But none is up for offer. I am always surprised at how quickly these conversations take off, even amongst complete strangers. Fascinating. Anyway, James is too deep into the rabbit hole. The only escape lies ahead. 'Are you sure you are not just being a pain in the arse?'

I am not offended, and you shouldn't be either. And don't be offended on my behalf. People sometimes do this when they are cornered, even in a dialogue. Remember what this means for James. He realises he has no good reason to hold on to his beliefs, and he is responding emotionally. His response is mild compared to Robert in the first dialogue and Kristoff, who you met later.

If you are generous, just think how many times he played philosopher with his mates where they pretended to be smart enough to answer 'the big question' but failed, despite many bottles of liquor, beer, and wine and perhaps some other chemical aids to boost mental prowess.

My ploy is to agree with him. 'If I am a pain in the arse, then it is because we often express beliefs without having given due consideration to what is being said. I know that most people will find this process annoying, but how can we possibly try to answer a question when we have not agreed with the meaning of the words that make up that question? I'm only being a pain in the arse because you are asking a stupid question. Therefore, I am only a pain in your arse and avoiding one in mine. Why not have another go at the question.'

It is surprising how the word *stupid* offends people. I am not sure why. We are all stupid at times. Perhaps if we admit that, we will be much smarter. It takes James a while to recover from the offence, but then he tries this one. 'Let me see. How about what is the meaning of my life?'

I tell him bluntly, 'That is the same question as the first one.'

James mutters a swear word under his breath. He tries again. 'What is the *purpose* of my life?' He puts a heavy emphasis on purpose.

His exasperation is palpable. I pause to let it pass. It is a comfortable silence. His exasperation passes. Judging by his changing demeanour, something is happening to James. He is mulling the question, not to find an answer but the sheer clarity the question brings. I sip my coffee. Did I say we ordered coffee? We ordered coffee, and it has arrived in the meantime.

'Actually,' says James, 'if you ask the question like that, it makes a lot more sense.'

> We needed to stop asking about the meaning of life, and instead to think of ourselves as those who were being questioned by life—daily and hourly. It ultimately means taking the responsibility to find the right answer to its problems and to fulfil the tasks which it constantly sets for each individual.
>
> *Viktor Frankl*

'Indeed.' I am a little smug.

James tries to deflate my smugness and asks me, 'So how would you answer the question?'

'You mean, what is the purpose of my life?' We are not quite out of the rabbit hole, not yet. 'Or what is the purpose of your life?'

'What is the purpose of my life,' he insists, but he looks confused. I can see we are heading for the realms of a comedy that will undo the lesson.

I say to James, 'It is not for me to answer. You asked the question of yourself, so you must answer it. It is a great question, and it is a philosophical one. If I must ask you that question, I will do it this way. What is the purpose of your life, James?'

> What makes people despair is that they try to find a universal meaning to the whole of life, and then end up by saying it is absurd, illogical, and empty of meaning. There is not one big, cosmic meaning for all, there is only the meaning we each give to our life, an individual meaning, an individual plot, like an individual novel, a book for each person.
>
> *Anaïs Nin*

James stares at me intently now, but I don't think he sees me. I think for the first time he experienced the force of critical thinking and, more importantly, the force of the critical question: 'What is the purpose of your life?'

I don't expect him to answer, and of course, he cannot. It is not that simple. I offer an alternative. 'If it helps, you may ask it this way, James, "Why am I here?"'

> Those who have a WHY to live can bear with almost any HOW.
>
> *Viktor Frankl*

James has gone into quiet contemplation. The master at work. I find myself looking around for another conversation. None is available.

> Mental consciousness labours under the illusion that there is somewhere to go to, a goal to consciousness. Whereas of course there is no goal. Consciousness is an end in itself. We torture ourselves getting somewhere, and when we get there it is nowhere, for there is nowhere to get to.
>
> *D. H. Lawrence*

I don't think there is one meaning of life for all, but if there is one then it must be to be the master of your mind. That is what we all seek and must seek.

* * *

John says nothing, does nothing. Have I led him down the rabbit hole? Is he contemplating the critical question? I wait.

I wait a little longer. Still nothing.

I break the silence. 'John, that was the end of that dialogue.'

John re-enters the room. I am not sure what to make of the eyes. There is no interrogation, no question for me.

'Sorry, Hendrik,' he says, 'I was just thinking about how I would answer the question. Great quotes though. They really drive the message home.'

I say nothing. I have come to accept the literary advice, or would this be editing, perhaps copy-editing advice? I can never figure out what all these forms of editing means. Perhaps that is obvious to the readers of my novel.

'Well, I don't really have any comments for now on this dialogue, Hendrik. So shall we move on to the next one?'

I am not sure I am ready. Something has happened to John, and I now want to know what. It is important to me as a writer. Either the dialogue was of no interest or it was of significant interest. Perhaps the dialogue reached parts of John that no other dialogue can reach. Is it the character? Did I create a credible character in James? Whichever it is, I want to know.

So I turn into the interrogator. 'No, John. First, tell me what you think of that dialogue.'

'I have to process it some more, Hendrik. I don't really have a comment for now,' he says, avoiding the question.

'You should be able to tell me if I libelled anyone though or if I betrayed confidentiality, disregarded intimacy. You must have seen the mistakes in reasoning,' I insist.

'I did not see any mistakes, Hendrik. To be honest, I thoroughly bought into the dialogue. I was completely captivated by it,' he answers, but he does not commit himself.

'I am not sure what you are saying, John. Are you saying that it made you think about the purpose of your life?'

John hesitates. I am beginning to think he is afraid of giving up the natural authority of a prestigious lawyer by admitting something so intimate as to say the dialogue touched him personally.

He as much as confirms my suspicion. 'I am sure that it meant a lot to James, Hendrik.'

'I think James would agree, but are you not curious about the lesson in the dialogue?' I ask.

'Did you see James again?' he asks.

'He is a character in a novel, John. They come, they serve their purpose, they go. I did not write about him again. If I did, it would have been to help him answer the question. "What is the purpose of my life?" I would not put that in the novel. That would have meant breach of confidentiality,' I explain.

'If he were just a character, Hendrik, you could have written it up as fiction. If you are concerned about confidentiality, he must be real,' says John, and just like that, the prestigious lawyer reclaims authority.

'What about the dialogue, John? I asked some questions about the dialogue,' I ask to avoid that little dance.

'I think the lesson is clear, Hendrik. It is about the question, about making sure you understand the question, that the question is appropriate as a philosophical one. That if it is not a philosophical question, then you must go to a different domain for answering it. It is a process like the one you did with'—John pages back through his legal pad—'the one with Megsum and Amanda. Understand the question, ask which domain it belongs to, and answer it appropriately,' says John.

That is as good an answer as one can give, I think, but I sense he is avoiding the intimacy it provoked in him, his own contemplation of his purpose in life. I also realise it will be inappropriate for me to probe more. No, not just inappropriate, it will be rude, and ordinary philosophers try never to be rude.

'It is such an important question that we should really ask it instead of saying "How are you?" when we greet people, don't you think? It would be more meaningful to say, "Nice to meet you, James. What is the purpose of your life?"' I say.

John nods and smiles but says nothing.

'Just think how much you will learn of a person's character with a question like that,' I say.

John nods again. That's all he does.

'I will finish this with the reflection. The dialogue with James was again about what kind of questions we are asking. The "question the question first" principle. This time, the question is prolific in popular philosophy and has such great importance that few would question the question. So this dialogue is about questioning the question. Get to the bottom of what is being asked. If you ask the right questions, you will come up with the right answer. There isn't anything else in the dialogue.'

John also does not bring up the elephant in the room. The amorphous thing. The myth of the meaning of life. The myth that it is some strange and wonderful thing but also annoyingly illusive. The answer to life is much more pragmatic once you kill the amorphous thing. It is much more real, much more within our grasp as humans.

But we will see it is not any less complicated. That is because we create and sustain many other amorphous beasts. But you can only deal with these if you are the master of your mind.

The eyes look at me, full of goodwill, a new thing for me. I take it on myself to continue to the next dialogue.

DINNER WITH LIZ, V

Is there or is there not some one quality of which all the citizens must be partakers, if there is to be a city [nation] at all? In the answer to this question is contained the only solution of your difficulty; there is no other . . . but justice and temper, in a word virtue.

Plato

We meet for dinner again. I told you this was a regular affair. The table seating is completely mixed up tonight. Perhaps people have finally become tired of their usual companions, and also, of course, they need a break from the people they share a home with. Liz now also shares a home with someone, a woman named Jenny. There are no outbound signals that they are lovers, but the rumours and speculation in the group is rife. I wonder if it is Jenny's arrival that have disturbed the usual pattern of seating preferences. The new arrangements seem to also have gotten rid of the hot seat.

Ray has taken the last seat. No, that is not how it worked. We arrived last. Lilly has taken an interest in Jenny, the newcomer, so the only vacant seat is the one opposite Ray. It instantly turns Ray's seat into the hot seat. You will remember Ray from the dinner after the theatre. He and Liz had that vivid dialogue about deontological and teleological ethics. But Ray is a different character tonight. I cannot pin him down to a decent dialogue. If I must write our conversation up, you will say the dialogue was incompetent, incomplete, and incomprehensible.

Ray is a member of the published authors' tribe, one who has found the outside approval of a revered publisher. Revered by the revered. He has published three books. It gives him a certain authority within the writers group. He is the inhouse critic that provides outside approval to the other members. That outside approval manifests itself in a builder of fragile courage and conviction with the new writers, but equally it manifests itself as the deadly assassin of that same fragile courage and conviction. If you are sinical like me, you might ask how else would he sustain his revered position?

Frankly, I do not see how Lilly can find enough to talk to him about that will take up an entire evening. Yet Ray and Liz also had that vivid dialogue the other night. Do you think it is me? Do you think I have that effect on some people?

Ray is in trouble tonight. The snake knows it has come face to face with his nemesis. The small vacant blue eyes track mine. He leans back and flares his chest in a defiant final fuck you pose, resigned to receive the deadly grip from the lethal talons of the swooping Snake Eagle.

Lucky for him Liz distracts the Snake Master and comes to his rescue. The snake slides off to the left to search for safety in the washroom.

'I have been meaning to talk to you, Hendrik,' says Liz. I thought she meant ominously, but then her face expresses curious excitement instead. I say curious excitement because Liz appears to be in a mood to exchange ideas, to discover something new, a dialogue without provoking confrontation. I suspect she will find out that I am the wrong conversation partner for pleasant chitter-chatter.

I top up our wine in anticipation of a long evening. 'How are you, Liz? I see you have a companion.'

Liz makes no attempt to let me into the secrets of the companionship, and I end up with nothing to add to the gossip. Perhaps she revels in everyone guessing and the gossip. She knows she maintains a certain availability heuristic by being secretive. That means the same as everyone is talking about her. 'I have been thinking some more about sovereign individuals. Actually, my Philosophy of Life group won't give up on it. Libertarianism, that is.'

You may be curious why I don't respond to the title. That is, if you recall the dialogue with James. What is there to discuss in this group that you cannot get from your first biology lesson? You should know now that I am compelled to let a lot of things go, things without merit. No point in burning intelligence on a senseless, silly subject. This is one of them.

'I am not surprised,' I say. The group is founded on the notion of promoting libertarianism. The idea has been killed off or severely wounded, and they are desperately trying to resuscitate it. The tribe must resuscitate the idea to resuscitate the tribe. Otherwise, the tribe will lose its raison d'être. I join the attempts to resuscitate. Why not? There is another rabbit hole to go down, I am sure. 'I think there is an important question there, Liz. Where do you draw the line between the individual and the collective?'

She looks at me. I think she is still processing my first response. The 'I am not surprised' one. Upon reflection, I can see how that is interpreted as a negative perception of the group. Clearly that is not where she wants to go. I think I can now see disappointment on her face. She tries anyway. 'I was thinking that we want to dismiss society, not for the sake of the individual but because it imposes a hierarchy. It establishes an order for decision-making.'

I want to address the abuse of 'we' in her opening sentence. It implies that I am one of the 'we'. I am not. She meant libertarians. I am very much in favour of society. It is humanity's greatest achievement. No, it is more than that. It is the only important one. It has its flaws. But that we can work on. I do not say any of this as I am curious about the direction she proposes. 'I am curious about the direction you propose,' I say instead.

Liz smiles. It looks like the good mood has returned. Is this because of Jenny? Or does she have something else up her sleeve? She has something else up her sleeve. 'Great. I think we are not objecting so much about the state as we are objecting to institutionalised hierarchy.'

'I am not sure what you mean by hierarchy,' I say.

'It has all to do with the principle of being the supreme decision maker, the principle of sovereignty. The sovereign individual is the supreme decision maker over what they do in their lives,' she explains.

I agree. 'If you want to claim your sovereignty, that is the thing you claim: to be the supreme decision maker over your life.'

My agreement raises her level of excitement. She says as much. 'Great, we agree. That is why libertarians disagree with large governments and things like welfare taxes designed to help other people.'

'Last time, I thought we agreed that the sovereign individual is probably, mostly a product of society. It is produced by society,' I remind her.

'Yes, it appears that way,' she agrees.

'Then what has changed? Are you saying that we should also get rid of hierarchy in society instead?' I ask.

'Yes,' says Liz, 'everyone should be allowed to be the supreme decision maker over their lives.'

'Sorry, Liz,' I challenge, 'are you suggesting that even babies, the sick, the poor, and people suffering some other misfortune should also be the supreme decision makers over their lives?'

'Well, come on. You are being belligerent. You know what I mean. Once a person is a fully functional adult, that person becomes the supreme decision maker in his or her life,' she says. I get a little satisfaction from Liz's willingness to challenge my belligerence. It means our relationship is on a trusted footing.

'Can you think of any circumstance where this idea will result in a tragedy for the supreme decision maker, the sovereign individual?' I ask.

'I assume you can, Hendrik, so why don't you?' says Liz. She is a bit tetchy now. I told you about me being the wrong person for normal chitter-chatter.

'OK, let's try this one,' I say, offering her an analogy. 'You, a sovereign individual, are driving home one night. You lose control of the car. Let's say it is not your fault. It is freezing, and you have just hit a bit of black ice. The car rolls over several times, and you suffer serious injuries which, if not treated immediately, will kill you. You are also unconscious. Thanks to a lucky coincidence, another motorist happens on the accident and calls the emergency services. The emergency medical services arrive on the scene. They can save you, but they must make decisions on your behalf. You are unconscious. They respect your sovereignty and your supremacy over your decisions. They are forced to watch you pass away. Sadly, of course.'

'Oh, Hendrik, how nice of you, feeling sad at my demise,' she says warmly. I think she means it. 'There are clearly times and instances when one surrenders that supremacy over decision-making.'

'So you are saying that at times and under some circumstances, people automatically surrender their sovereign rights?' I ask.

'Yes, I just said that. I agree,' says Liz. The tetchiness has replaced the warmth.

'Can you list all of those circumstances?' I ask.

'Oh god, that would be impossible,' she says.

'Well, maybe and maybe not. I can think of two. When you are not educated enough to be a sovereign individual and also when you are medically incapacitated are clearly two circumstances, even if the circumstances are broadly defined as they are here. I don't think one can deny it,' I say.

'Sure, I can accept that. It is conceptual enough for us not to get distracted by conventional facts,' she says. I swear I nearly fell of my chair. Her demonstration of philosophical sophistication leaves me speechless for a moment.

After that moment passes, I offer her some more examples. 'What about poverty, hunger, and isolation? Other misfortunes not necessarily associated with stupid decisions?'

'What do you mean stupid decisions?' she asks.

'I am sure as a libertarian, you want people to be able to make their own decision. More than that. They must make their own decision, and they must suffer the natural consequences of those decisions,' I explain.

'What do you mean suffer the natural consequences?' she asks. Frankly, I thought that would be self-explanatory.

I start, 'Most decisions are teleological therefore—'

'Teleological?' she interrupts.

'You make a decision and hope for a beneficial future outcome. That future outcome is the natural consequence of the decision, the beneficial outcome and the other, perhaps unforeseen, not so beneficial outcome,' I explain.

'Oh, like you must take responsibility for your decisions and the natural consequences,' she rephrases.

'Yes, sure. Let's go with that.'

'Yes, sovereign individuals must deal with the natural consequences of their decisions, good and bad.' She grins, clearly pleased with the idea.

'Not so quick. I think there is more to say about natural consequences,' I say, dampening her enthusiasm.

'Like what?' she asks with somewhat dampened enthusiasm.

'We can start with a view of the natural consequences of life. That is to say, to be alive has natural consequences. We talked about it before. When we are born, we are wet, cold, hungry, and lonely. Action is needed immediately to deal with the natural consequences of being alive—'

'Sure, we have been over this ground before,' she says. A dampened spirit has turned into an impatient spirit.

'Sure, I am sorry, but I am trying to get to a type of natural consequences where one must make decisions to avert disaster. So one must make decisions to get dry, warm, fed, and find company. Those actions will require persistent action by the sovereign individuals throughout their lives. If they don't maintain the desired state, entropy will set in, and they revert to the natural state,' I say.

'OK, I see where you are going with this. We must have primacy over decisions that deal with the natural state and the natural consequences of that state,' she says.

'Yes, but we need to learn how,' I say.

'Hence, education and development,' says Liz, picking up on the point.

'Then there are other natural consequences of decisions we make about life, such as careers, employment, skills development, or entrepreneurship, whether we get married, have children, where we want to live, and so on. We must obviously have the primacy over decision-making when it comes to those things,' I say.

'Agreed, definitely.' Liz nods vigorously.

'What about the consequence of events over which the individual had no control?' I ask.

'When those events happen, the sovereign individual must make decisions to address the consequences of the event,' she says and frowns a little.

'Like when you had your accident,' I say.

Liz shifts around, agitated. 'OK, I concede. Sometimes shit happens, and we need help.'

'Also, there are consequences such as disease, sickness, incapacity, poverty—all kinds of things where the sovereign individual has no resources or means to make decisions and might need a helping hand,' I say.

'I see where you are going,' she says.

'What about the natural consequences of decisions other people have made?' I ask.

'Hmm, give me an example,' she says.

'Let's say the global demand for a particular mineral disappears. Actually, let's consider a circumstance where a mine has to close because some international competitor has discovered a deposit of substantial volume that can be mined and distributed around the world at significantly less cost. The workers in our mine lose their jobs because the mine is forced to close. Do we just leave those people to their lot?' I ask.

'Well, they can find other work, can't they?' protests Liz.

'That is not what I mean. I mean that the sovereignty of those individuals has been stripped from them. They are at the mercy of the decisions made by other sovereign individuals who probably don't even know they exist,' I say.

'So what are you actually saying?' asks Liz, clearly frustrated, but resisting the rabbit hole.

I decide to come to the point. 'When we, and I include myself and people in general, talk about certain rights or certain undeniable axioms, we often make the mistake that we think about them as all-or-nothing rights. In other words, sovereign individuals are either the primary decision makers over every aspect of their lives or they are not primary decision makers at all. Reality is, you are the primary decision maker in your life under some circumstances or on some aspects. But whether you like it or not, you are not the primary decision maker all the time over everything.'

Can you spot the composition fallacy in the definition of the sovereign individual rights? The assumption is to find a solution to give the sovereign individual supremacy over all decisions. The mistake is that if the sovereign individual is the primacy decision maker for some aspects, then that primacy extends to everything.

Liz looks at me with considerable curiosity. The dampened spirit has dried up, and the spark of curiosity has returned. 'So you are saying if we take the approach that we are sometimes the primary decision makers in our lives, then we can find a way to hold on to our sovereign individuality and simultaneously be a member of a society and citizen of a country.'

'Well, that is a very concise and elegant way to put it,' I say. 'Yes, if we move away from thinking about the individual and the collective as a dichotomy, then we might dissolve the false dilemma. If we think about it more like a dimension where we can slide control from full primacy to no primacy, then we have a system that works for all circumstances.'

'Where do you think we should give up primacy?' she asks.

'Difficult question. There are probably several obvious places. Some aspects of healthcare, some aspects of education, but I think the most obvious ones are risks we share equally with our fellow citizens, like the police, the military, and the many other risks that life naturally offers.'

'That is it?' she asks.

'Think of the state, Liz,' I say. I have no intention to do all the work for her. 'Think of how the state regulates the incredible uncertainties in your life. We discussed a few here. You cannot build a healthcare response system at the point where you need to respond to the natural consequence of an event. It must be built in advance so that it is ready to respond. So like the healthcare system, the state prepares for future events such as pandemics, weather disturbances, flooding, hurricanes, and other possible events that will disrupt the peace in your country of sovereign individuals. These things are not going to be provided under negotiation between sovereign individuals. Who will take the risk of building a system for pandemic response when it only happens once in a lifetime or maybe once in several lifetimes? These preparations are incompatible with the short-term thinking of individuals acting in their self-interest.'

'OK, I get that. So whether we like it or not, there will always be some hierarchy at work in our lives. Sometimes we are on top, and sometimes someone else is on top,' she says and winks. I have no idea what to make of the wink, so I pretend to ignore it. But I look briefly at Lilly to see if she noticed. She didn't.

I agree with Liz. 'Of course, there is then the question, who determines or how do we determine the hierarchy?' I ask.

Liz looks deflated. 'And what is the answer?' she asks.

'It depends,' I say. True to my belligerent nature, I deliberately drag her agony out.

Liz is not stupid. She won't let me. 'That is what I asked, isn't it?'

'Studies have shown that hormones are intricately involved in determining hierarchies,' I say.

'You mean studies on animals?' she asks. I can see my statement have produced the perfect conditions for a lightning fast strike.

'Yes, but are we not just animals?' I ask. 'Jordy argues that we are, that we display the same serotonin responses as lobsters, and through those responses, we establish hierarchies.' On that night, I might have mentioned Jordy's full name.

'Who the hell is Jordy?' she asks. A different colour has entered her face. She is suddenly alert, upright and the golden eyes track.

'He is a psychologist who has written books on the subject. He provides counselling for men to reclaim their dominant position at home. Apparently, he has helped thousands,' I fill her in. I must come clean that I am taking a great deal of pleasure in being the provocateur.

The snake is provoked. The tension is coiled, the strike is about to happen. 'Oh my god. What a fucking idiot!' Liz strikes. A momentary silence descends on the table. 'Not Hendrik,' cries Liz at everyone. 'This Jordy idiot.'

I am relieved. Frankly, I thought I am going to be permanently excluded this time.

'What does he say, this fucking idiot?' asks Liz. I am not sure what about fucking makes you a special kind of idiot, more idiot than any normal idiot. I suspect she has in her repertoire another word in mind but is too angry to use it.

To be honest, I am getting a little worried now. Her reaction was just on the edge of a physical confrontation. Thank goodness Jordy isn't here. I should try to direct the threat away from myself, but I cannot resist. 'He also claims women are naturally agreeable whereas men are naturally confrontational. That is why men negotiate better salaries and higher positions than women. He claims there is no discrimination whatsoever.' I told you I am a provocateur. I am secretly enjoying stoking this rage against an unseen enemy.

'Filthy arsehole!' shouts Liz. The silence now descends over a wider area in the restaurant. 'He should try that bullshit with me!' says Liz as she takes up the deadly threat pose. 'I will have his nuts for breakfast!' I do not think the threat is real. I cannot imagine her eating nuts for breakfast.

I decide to channel her anger somewhat. 'Do you think a system for negotiations that favours disagreeability over agreeability is discriminatory, especially if it is true that women are more agreeable than men?' I ask.

'You are fucking right it is. Probably designed by men so that they can have dick-swinging contests over who is the boss and who gets the biggest paycheck. If it is not testosterone, it is serotonin. Why can they not just use their fucking brains,' she says, still loud but not shouting any more.

The language draws attention and causes a kerfuffle in a wider audience. Jenny wanders over and massages her shoulders. Liz calms down almost immediately. There must be some truth in the gossip. It is the first time that there is a public display of affection between them. 'Surely there must be a better way for us to do this, Hendrik,' pleads Liz.

'You mean, organise hierarchies and negotiate salaries?' I ask.

'Yes,' she says, her voice down to its normal level. She sists back and the deadly threat pose has gone. The conversation in the wider space and around the table picks up again.

'Well, it seems that Jordy is arguing for things from the way they are. That is to say, if he is right about how hierarchies are determined by serotonin. There are many examples of hierarchies in the animal kingdom where males are clearly subordinate. In particular, from animal species with which we share a much more recent lineage than lobsters. So I am not convinced. Also, anthropologists will disagree with him. Male dominance in humans is a relatively recent development. It just goes to show how weak arguments by analogy can be. All you have to do is find one example where it isn't true, and boom, there goes your theory. These examples alone hint that there is a different way to do this,' I explain.

'Damn right there is a different way,' says Liz.

'Indeed. Jordy is proposing that we return to the caveman approach to organising society. We can do better than that. Humans do not do things simply because they are biologically or evolutionary tuned to do them. In fact, Plato, in his allegory of Phaedrus's chariot, demonstrated that humans have a noble side that can temper the animal side. That we have a rather unique ability to temper our passions. The one thing you have claimed in one of our earlier discussions is that we reason. That means we can reason about building a different system, a system that minimises hierarchies and eliminates gender-based dominance. In other words, we can reason about how things ought to be.'

'Exactly,' says Liz.

'That is what you are trying to do with libertarianism. But a serious question mark is left hanging over libertarianism. If we abandon social structures including the state, are we not submitting ourselves to the caveman approach to organising society? To find a better way to organise society we must accept the necessity of social institutions.

'You are not accepting the status quo, Liz. You disagree with some of what you see. And you are trying to reason for something better. Keep up the good work, but make sure that you fix some of the glaring holes in the libertarian ideology. Is there not sufficient reason here for you to make this the purpose of your life?' I say, thinking that it is enough for one night. In anticipation of taking a long break, I top up my wine to the brim.

'The "Why am I here?" question?' asks Liz. Then she says, 'If I stop thinking about being pinned on the horns of a dilemma, I can solve some of the problems of libertarianism. Although I must tell you, Hendrik, it looks like I am getting much the same system of government as I already have. Maybe I should be less critical of it and work towards a better distribution of the primacy over decision-making.'

'Indeed. There is one more thing about libertarianism and hierarchy that's troublesome,' I say

'Oh yes, go on then what is it,' says Liz. She is very alert again. Her eyes tracking.

'Remember last time we talked about the naivety, that there is an assumption that all sovereign individuals have a basic decency,' I say.

'I do and so? Asks Liz.

'There is also an assumption that in a libertarian system where people basically negotiate all transactions that all sovereign individuals start negotiating from a position of equality,' I say.

'I see that, and that cannot be true of course,' adds Liz.

'Not only is it not true, but those with the advantage will inevitably take a higher position in the hierarchy,' I say.

'Yes, of course. So hierarchy is unavoidable, even in a libertarian society,' she concludes,

'Not only unavoidable, but also unregulated, and that is a threat to any society. There is a considerable risk that the problems of naivety and romanticism will be abused by some people, where the natural consequences of their decision are catastrophic for other people even when it is good for the decision maker. It lays the foundation for American disaster capitalism like the opioid pain killer crisis, the financial crisis, industrial farming and the environmental crisis, and others. The system of restitution after the event is often too late for the victims,' I say.

'You know I think I am going right off the idea of libertarianism. It sounds quite romantic, all that freedom and personal authority. But it will lead to a broken society, wont it. This all-or-nothing approach to primacy over decisions is a false dilemma, isn't it?'

That is the second time tonight that Liz has caused a significant drop in my blood pressure. The second time that she has used a reasonably sophisticated philosophical reference. Two in fact. I am impressed and tell her so.

'You see, Hendrik,' says Liz, smiling, 'you will make a philosopher out of me eventually.'

'You already are, Liz,' I say. 'I don't deserve any credit for that.'

* * *

I look at the eyes. They look back at me. All the goodwill has left them. They look disappointed.

'And just like that, you shatter any view that I might have had that you can be a nice person, Hendrik,' says John, anticipating that it is the end of the dialogue. He anticipated correctly.

I, on the other hand, am confused. I thought this was a very decent outcome for a dialogue. 'I was genuinely nice towards Liz. I told her she is a philosopher,' I say. Frankly speaking, I am a bit surprised he did not pick up on that.

John looks up at the ceiling. I wonder if he is sending up a silent prayer. I don't do prayer. Prayer is good for god's CV, not for mine. It gives god bragging rights, none for me. I get nothing. The Rastafarian monotheistic god can boast to the other thirty-three million Hindu gods that he receives the most prayers, sometimes some people pray three times a day to him. He can boast about the economies of scale gained from consolidation. No god gets my prayer, no god deserves my prayer.

But right now, I swear I feel like joining John. I am exhausted. Worryingly, I regain a little faith every time I am exhausted. I drink some coffee. It is a bit cold, but thankfully, it kills the little faith. *Oh, hello old friend, now fuck off.*

John has finished his apparent prayer. 'To Jordy, Hendrik, and don't tell me it was Liz, that it wasn't you,' he says, and I sulk a little. I have come to like that little dance. *Oh hello old friend.*

'You assume that Jordy is real, don't you?' I ask.

'Well, is he real?' he asks.

'Yes,' I answer. John throws his legal pad down on the table, gets up, and walks over to his pristine rosewood desk and back again.

'Then you have insulted a real person, Hendrik. Don't you think that is a bit audacious of you?' asks John.

'Me and about half a million women, John. I've said nothing that other people haven't said already. Notwithstanding the fact that I and many others have pointed out the sheer stupidity of his reasoning,' I say.

'Where, where did they say that?' asks John, no, challenges John.

'It is all over the Internet, Twitter, blog posts, everywhere,' I answer.

John sits down again and picks up the legal pad, ready to make notes. 'Any noteworthy persons?' asks John, seeing an opening to a possible defence.

'Several really. Opinion pieces in reputable newspapers,' I say.

'What do you mean reputable newspapers?' asks John, clearly excited that I may have an escape.

'The *NYT*, the *Washington Post*, papers like that,' I say.

'And you can find this by doing a simple search on the Internet?' asks John just to be sure.

'Yes.' That is all I have to say. Frankly, I have made my point a while ago. I have some more cold coffee.

I don't wait for a prompt from John. I just start with the reflection. 'In this dialogue, I am pleasantly surprised when Liz seeks me out later in the evening. Her proposition is that libertarian sovereign individuals are objecting to hierarchies and, specifically, hierarchies that structures decision-making, relegating personal decision-making lower than social decision-making.

'We discussed whether hierarchies are naturally there, and she nearly loses it when I reference Jordy and his claim that men are naturally or hormonally more inclined to dominate, more so than women, and that we share this with lobsters. Of course, Jordy is very selective in his claims that we have inherited this through the evolutionary tree of life. If you want to do that, you should really go to more immediate species families, not one that you share a common ancestry with going back billions of years in evolutionary history. If you do that, you could also claim you share behaviour characteristics with a single-celled bacterium. But then many other people have pointed this out, but stupid single-celled men believe in his rubbish so much that they have made him an extremely wealthy man. If Jordy is brave enough, he might ask Liz about her serotonin levels when men try to dominate her.

'Liz is showing real wisdom outside of this discussion: a mastery of her own mind. Don't misread the apparent loss of temper as a weakness. She was in full control of her mind there. Despite her vigorous objection to the idiocy of Jordy, she clearly accepts that a social world without hierarchy will not work. Moreover, she discovers that we are, in fact, pursuing a solution to a false dilemma, the individual versus the collective. It is false because we commit the composition fallacy when we think about the primacy over decision-making as an all-or-nothing demand. We can dissolve the false dilemma by considering some aspects of life where the individual has primacy over decisions and some aspects where the community has primacy over decisions. That primacy divides neatly between suffering the natural consequences of your decisions or suffering the natural consequences of things outside of the individual's control.'

John finishes his notes and looks up. Some goodwill seems to shine from the eyes again. I take it as my cue to move to the next dialogue.

COFFEE WITH LILLY

What I advise you to do is, not to be unhappy before the crisis comes. Some things torment us more than they ought; some torment us before they ought; and some torment us when they ought not to torment us at all. We are in the habit of exaggerating, or imagining, or anticipating, sorrow.

Seneca

Lilly has asked to meet for a coffee. Just that, no explanation. But an explanation is not required. We know each other through our business activities. So it is not that unusual to meet for a coffee. She has proposed this place. It is conveniently close to the doors that leads into the tower where 'the business' resides. Her business, that is. To be clear, the one she works for, not the one she owns. The entrance to the coffee shop is right next door to the revolving door and security gates through which she goes to work. Work is where she narrows her mindset to become part of 'the business'. That machine that limits human creativity, to box its employees into predictable policies, practises, and standards. The place where management frameworks are imposed on otherwise talented individuals who are required to perform repeatable tasks in a repetitive manner, measuring predictable data points to impose a certain minimum standard of performance, which translates into a profit for the shareholders. The same place where a few leaders have a monopoly over talent and centralised control. Liz would point out a monopoly of the primacy over decisions. How bizarre that a capitalist institution has embraced a communist idea.

Lilly proposed we meet in the coffee shop. I am repeating it here because it means that this is not a business meeting. If it were a business meeting, we would have gone through the revolving door and security gates to install us into the framework. We are here because she anticipates a more open discussion, to explore a solution to a more intimate problem she has.

The place where we are meeting is ambiguous. It is both a coffee shop and an office space. A temporary workspace for hire. The office space is separated by a security gate where you enter into the framework. We are staying on the open-minded side. You can stay here provided you buy a coffee and perhaps something to eat. If you go through the gates, you have to pay for both, for being installed into the framework and for any coffee and perhaps for something to eat that you want to take with you. You can, of course, charge that to the shareholders provided you can justify it and follow the framework's policies, practices, and standards for expenses.

I arrive first and take up place in the queue to the barista, but only after I leave the book I am reading on a free table for two towards the back where it is quieter. I nervously look towards the door to see when she arrives. I see her now. Her perfectly proportioned body is exemplified by the summer dress, a perfectly proportioned female shape that is a balance between hips and shoulder, a thin middle accentuated by firm breasts. It is the way she moves that will grab your attention first.

I can best describe it like this. She moves like a Latin dance, not a particular Latin dance but all Latin dances. It completely confounds you. She moves like a composition fallacy of Latin dances. That is all I can say. And then there are her legs, long, slim, perfectly tanned legs. Lilly's long legs kick up the skirt of her short summer dress as she dances through the double doors of the coffee shop. Mesmerising.

Lilly sees me in the queue and dances straight past those behind me. Nobody minds.

She kisses me lightly on the cheek.

This is new.

It sends my heart racing.

She knows.

Lilly knows exactly what she is doing.

We say hello, queue to buy coffee, get to the front of the queue, buy our coffee, get our coffee, and settle down at the table I reserved with the book. I am not going to tell you more about the 'Hello' and 'How are you?' protocols. Take it as said. In typical Lilly directness, she gets to the question immediately.

'How do you deal with uncertainty?' she asks.

'Oh, what do you mean by uncertainty?' I ask. You probably think this is an annoying habit of mine, but you should know by now that I always want to make sure we agree on the meaning of words.

'My brother is going through a health scare. He has been diagnosed with cancer,' she says. I now see the deep worry lines on her face.

> When we are no longer able to change a situation, we are challenged to change ourselves.
>
> *Viktor Frankl*

'I am really sorry to hear that,' I say, and I mean it. 'I can see you are very troubled by that, but before I ask you to tell me more, can we go back to my question?'

'What question?' she asks.

'When I asked what you mean by uncertainty. I understand you are uncertain about what the future holds for your brother and your family. But what is uncertainty?'

Lilly needs a few minutes to process the question. I give her a few minutes. Why not? I have plenty of minutes to give since I stopped entering the framework. I also have an infinite supply of minutes to give Lilly. I look at her face. She has one of those rare faces that assembles its parts into a perfect symmetry, a perfectly beautiful symmetry in an oval face, framed by a tidy bob that accentuates her firm jawline. If you look at the parts, you might say they are too big, too small, eyes too far apart, but look at the whole, and it blows you away. There is an unmistakable sadness about that beautiful face today.

I sample the coffee. It is good coffee, well, reasonably good, for an independent coffee shop attached to a workspace for frameworks.

Lilly has given thought now and is ready to answer. But first, she samples her coffee and nods in agreement with me when I suggest it is good coffee.

'I believe it means that things don't always work out, and we anticipate that it won't. When we anticipate that things might not work out as we planned or expected or maybe even desire, then we feel uncertainty,' she says. You must admit that that is a good explanation. Makes me feel a little redundant, but that is what I have come to expect from Lilly.

'That is a really good explanation,' I say to Lilly. 'I am curious though. Why do you say unexpected, that it is when we anticipate the unexpected that we feel uncertain?'

'Oh, I don't know. Life appears to be working out well enough, and then shit happens. I suppose that is what I mean,' is her attempt at an answer.

'Is it perhaps because we are seduced by an illusion of certainty that generally life works out? That all the plans we are taught to make from the time we enter school to when we enter "the business" will work out? Plan for success,' I say, doing air quotes around 'the business,' like that. It has become a habit, and it is a bad one. It has come up before, so you shouldn't be surprised. Sometimes it provokes a whole new discussion. Sometimes the new discussion is a welcome relief on the boring one we were having at the time. Not this time though. Lilly has asked an excellent question, and I am glad she ignores the air quotes.

'I suppose you are right,' she says, 'but is it really an illusion?'

'Well, what in our lives create that illusion, and if that thing disappears, will our illusion be shattered?' I ask.

'I am not sure where you are going with this. Help me out,' she says with just a hint of frustration. She is not the kind of person who willingly enters the rabbit hole.

'We live in an illusion of certainty maintained by our society or, more specifically, firstly by our family, then community, then society, then the government, and finally, the world order,' I say. 'Without this certainty, this superbly regulated environment will collapse into chaos.'

'Oh, I see. I can agree with that, but why do you call it an illusion?' she asks.

'Because chaos is always there. The apocalypse is happening. It is just not evenly distributed. All you need to do is look elsewhere, other countries in Africa, the Middle East, the USA under Trump presidency, the pandemic. These are but a few examples of the apocalypse. It is only through hard work, diligence, awareness, and constant application of effort that we keep the apocalypse at bay,' I explain.

'That is a frightening thought, Hendrik. That does not make me feel any better,' Lilly says, no, pleads. The worry lines have deepened.

'I am telling you this because I want you to know that uncertainty is always there. The world is significantly more volatile, uncertain, complex, and ambiguous than we experience within our illusion,' I say.

'But why don't we see it that way?' she asks, hoping for hope.

'Because a lot of people in a lot of institutions in governments and businesses are working hard to make sure we live in a stable world where our predictions and plans for the most part come through,' I tell her.

'And you think it is all an illusion,' she tells me. It may sound like a question, but it is more of an accusation.

'I call it an illusion because we pretend not to be aware of it all the time. We have become wonderfully comfortable in our routines and expectations that things always seem to work out. We go to the shops, and we are spoiled for choice for food. We do not see the worrying supply chain management teams that are sourcing, packaging, shipping, and storing food so that we have a constant and reliable supply,' I explain. 'But not everything can be controlled this way.'

'Like my brother's cancer,' she says.

'Yes, like your brother's cancer. Some things we can control, and some things we cannot,' I say.

Tears well up in Lilly's eyes, and tiny dimples form on her chin. 'What can I do about it though?' she asks softly. There is no quiver in her voice. Her self-control is immense, and my respect for her reach new heights. Under the same circumstances, I would have sobbed like a five-year-old. I have an urge to divert the dialogue to let her talk more. But I also know where we are going with this, and where we are going will give her more comfort than any sympathy I can express.

'Some problems we cannot solve. Some problems we can. For the ones we cannot solve, we hand them over to an expert. Completely. Totally. We give them full responsibility to solve the problem. Also, to worry about it,' I say.

'Like his doctor, his oncologist?' she asks.

'Like his doctor or oncologist,' I answer.

'And what do we do?' Lilly asks. I imagine she is seeing a little hope now.

'We carry on with our lives, Lilly. We continue to do the things we need to do to control the other uncertainties in our lives. This one, your brother's cancer, you hand that over to the specialists. Tell him, tell your brother. It is the experts' problem. Ask them what you must do to help them be successful. Do that,' I tell her.

'What do you mean ask them?' she asks me.

'You should ask them what you can do. Your brother will need to support their efforts. Eat healthily, stay isolated as much as he can, particularly if he goes through chemo- or radiotherapy. There are lots of things you can do to help the specialists. But ask them. Don't ask me,' I explain.

'You know what, I am going to do that. I am going to tell my family that we must help my brother support his specialists. That is the best chance he will have, the best chance he can give the specialists to be successful.' Lilly looks decidedly less troubled.

'It is still going to be hard, Lilly. But now you have something concrete and positive to do to help you deal with this uncertainty. You are preparing. Once you are prepared, dealing with the problem will be a lot less troubling, and so will the uncertainty,' I say.

'Thanks, Hendrik. It gives me a whole new way to look at the future,' she says.

> Never let the future disturb you. You will meet it, if you have to, with the same weapons of reason which today arm you against the present.
>
> *Marcus Aurelius*

'Do you want to talk some more about preparing for uncertainty?' I ask.

'There is more? Sure, but let me get you a fresh coffee.' Lilly gets fresh coffees.

I try the new coffee, but it is a bit too hot. So I make a start while it cools down. 'To prepare as best as you can, always consider the future as three arrows of time.'

'What do you mean three arrows of time?' she asks, genuinely interested.

'The first arrow of time represents the things that are going to happen because of what you have already done and what you have already committed to,' I say.

'Like I have committed to go to work in "the business". I can expect my salary to be paid with reasonable certainty,' she says and smiles at me when she does the air quotes round 'the business'. I smile too as I now know it did not go unnoticed.

'Yes, indeed. The second arrow of time is the things that you are hoping will work out and that you are planning for or working towards long-term,' I say.

'Like working towards a promotion, taking on more responsibility in "the business"'—she does it again—'but I cannot be sure of the promotion until it arrives.'

'Very good, Lilly,' I say, and I mean it. I have to suppress a little laugh as she is clearly teasing me about the air quotes. 'The third arrow of time is the shit that is coming your way. You don't know what it is, you don't know when, and you don't know how, but it can happen.'

Lilly ponders this for a while. 'Like the pandemic! It is like a pandemic, isn't it? You know it could happen, but you don't know when!' she exclaims, clearly pleased with herself.

'Indeed, like the pandemic,' I confirm for her.

'What do you do about the third arrow of time?' Lilly asks.

'You prepare. That is all you can do,' I answer.

'But if you don't know what is going to happen, then how can you prepare?' she asks.

'There is a way. Think of possibilities. Things that can possibly happen,' I say. 'Take the pandemic as an example. Some countries dealt with it expertly, and some failed miserably. The ones who have dealt with it expertly were prepared. They considered it as a possibility. They had protocols in place, healthcare facilities, doctors, financial reserves to soften the economic fallout. Countries that were prepared and were willing to manage expectations dealt with the pandemic very effectively,' I say.

'That is true,' says Lilly. 'It all makes sense. You carry on living life along arrow 1 and arrow 2 and prepare for arrow 3.'

'One more thing,' I say, 'when you prepare for possibilities, you must ignore probabilities. Probability is the mathematical chance of something happening. The mathematical chance of a pandemic was less than one-tenth of a per cent. Some countries thought they can manage on a risk-appetite basis. In other words, they can take a risk of it not happening. What are the chances, eh? So you do not consider the probability, only that it is possible.'

'But how can you prepare for arrow 3 events if you don't know what is going to happen?' she asks again.

'You can do something called scenario planning. Scenario planning is what you do when you ask what-if questions,' I say.

'Like what if my brother gets cancer?' she suggests.

'That is right. What if the house burns down? What if the house gets flooded? What if "the business" goes belly up? Then you plan to deal with those. You will be surprised when you see how the preparations for all of those scenarios are the same or remarkably similar,' I explain.

'I can imagine they would be. It is all about having enough reserves and resources to ride out the storm, isn't it?' she says.

'One more thing,' I say, 'let's think back about the illusion of an ordered world. There are some possible future events that we cannot prepare for on our own. For those, we collaborate with family, communities, and as citizens of the state.'

'I see that now,' says Lilly. 'To be honest, I never thought about it that way. I always thought the state is overbearing and intrusive.'

I nod. 'The state is just other people Lilly. Other people holding the apocalypse at bay.' There isn't much more I can say.

'Will you tell me one more thing, Hendrik?' asks Lilly mischievously.

I nod again, cautious this time.

'Why are you doing air quotes every time you mention "the business", like that?' she asks. When she smiles mischievously like this, her dimples are more pronounced and perfectly frame her full mouth.

I laugh. 'You do not want to go there, Lilly. It is a whole different rabbit hole.'

> Don't hope that events will turn out the way you want, welcome events in whichever way they happen: this is the path to peace.
>
> *Epictetus*

Lilly leans forward, places her long, elegant hand on mine, and gently squeezes. She says, 'Promise you will take me down that rabbit hole soon.' I promise. How can I not promise those green eyes?

* * *

John is preoccupied with his legal pad. He looks up urgently, startled, like a new mother who suddenly remembers she has a baby somewhere and she can't quite remember where she left it.

'My god, Hendrik. You were a thoroughly nice person in that dialogue!'

I protest unnecessarily, 'I am always a nice person, John!'

'I mean, not a single insult, not to her, not to any country or group or ethnic group or men or women—'

'I get it, John,' I interrupt him. No point in letting him get too much joy from it.

'If you were that nice to everybody in your novel, we won't be here,' says John.

I know that, of course. So why agree with the obvious? Instead, I say, 'If everybody was as nice as Lilly, we won't be here, John. I have to deal with some real arseholes at times.'

'Just when I gather together a meagre amount of hope, you go and spoil it, Hendrik,' says John.

'What do you mean?' I ask.

'Think back at what you have just said. You so much as admitted that your characters are real people, did you not?' interrogates John.

'It is just a figure of speech, John,' I try innocently. Yes, yes, I know, innocent doesn't work. Secretly I am really pleased that John finds my characters real enough to think they have bodies. They may or may not have bodies. I am not going to reveal any of that. In my self-defence, of course.

'I am going to let it go for now, Hendrik. We are going to have to get clarity on this matter later. We must, before Jennifer Rawlings does, if she does not already,' says John. 'What is next?'

'The reflection,' I say. 'In the final dialogue with Lilly, we come full circle on the amorphous thing called the state. The state provides us with such a regulated environment that we live in an illusionary world. We think and experience life as a predictable, plannable process. But that is an illusion. The state has become invisible. We don't see the armies or the armies of people working to provide us with water on tap and energy that flows reliably, a police force keeping the peace, borders protected by our military. We don't see the scores of people working hard to ensure we have a reliable and resilient supply chain of food, fuel, and other commodities we need for living. Isn't it ironic that this illusion encourages libertarians to think they can destroy the state, that they don't need it?

'Lilly and I discussed this and also the three arrows of time. That for the third arrow of time, we prepare for uncertain events. Uncertainty is not like probability. Probabilities, we can measure. Probabilities only have merit when we have identified an underlying causal connection with competition that gives us a reasonable, predictable result. Possibilities are different. We can prepare for uncertainties all our lives and never have to call on those resources we put aside to deal with those events. Lilly draws enormous comfort from reasoning, comfort that she desperately needs in a difficult personal and intimate situation. She is a delight. She moves in the light.'

John nods, which, of course, is my cue to move to the next dialogue. But that was the last one. I tell John it was the last one.

THE VERDICT

If you are ever tempted to look for outside approval, realise that you have compromised your integrity. If you need a witness, be your own.

Epictetus

John appears relieved. He asks to confirm, 'Is that it, last dialogue?'

'Yes' is all I need to say. 'Yes' is all I say.

'I am having difficulty drawing a line where the novel ends and where our conversations begin, Hendrik. If I manage even vaguely, then the novel seems incomplete,' says John.

'That is because it is, John. We blurred that line when we blended together the reflections on the dialogues with our discussion. Moreover, we have yet to discuss the conclusion,' I explain.

'Of course, the conclusion,' says John.

I am beginning to sense that John is getting tired, running out of fuel. There is only so much energy in a rye bread and pastrami sandwich.

I am also tired, and I am also hungry. By some miracle, the young man enters the room. He has a tray with fresh coffees and what could be a classic afternoon tea, except it is not. The cakes, pastries, and biscuits have been adjusted to go with coffee instead, sweeter, more indulgent, and there is no tea. And just like that, he vanishes. I am still pondering this magic when John interrupts.

'Shall we take a short break? When we get back, we can discuss the conclusion.'

We take a short break. The detail is of no relevance, but when we restart, we are refreshed and physically comfortable.

'Right,' says John, 'the conclusion.'

'May I remind you of the introduction?' I ask, and he nods.

'In the conclusion, I tie things back to the themes, main topics, and areas of interest I foreshadowed in the introduction. You mentioned earlier that there is a certain pattern in the novel, a revealing of amorphous structures that come into focus,' I begin.

John nods agreement. I detect a little self-congratulation in the eyes but let them keep it. Even prestigious lawyers need outside approval every now and again.

'And also, that there is this ongoing battle between the individual and the tribe. In reading tribe, consider culture, state, "the business". I must stop doing that, I know, and other crazy, amorphous structures we build, as if we don't have enough to content with. In the first half of the novel, we find ourselves in intellectual dead ends and dark alleys. There is opportunity to learn, but characters in the dialogues are largely too close-minded, too trapped in their tribes or caves to escape. I would say there are potentially two exceptions. Peter seems to grasp the folly of what he is doing, but he takes no escape offered to him. He resorts to tribe almost immediately. Liz is an exception, but there, the lesson was for me: do not lecture. As we learn later, she is the one who transforms the most. Thomas takes us to the pivotal point. This is where we take a firm and unforgiving stance against conspiracies, that is, conspiracies of characters. I have no doubt that people conspire too, but they get caught. Characters are amorphous things. They cannot get caught.

'In this first section, we learn about raw composition fallacies and how dangerous they are. Incidentally, I hear Trump wants to punish China for the alleged lab leak of the virus. Let me just add that there is no proof of this whatsoever. Nevertheless, he wants to punish the whole of China for the negligent act, if true, of perhaps one person. When Asian people are attacked, we see the converse of the composition fallacy, the divisional fallacy. This is when thick skulls believe Trump and then take revenge on individual Chinese diaspora living in the USA. Similar things have happened in the UK. I think a Singaporean was attacked in London. For God's sake—'

'You are digressing, Hendrik. You have already made this point, so stick to the conclusion,' John says.

'We also learn about the equivocation fallacy in the dialogues with Kristoff and Edwin. This is a tricky one to identify, and it is perhaps less dangerous than the composition fallacy. The English language invites this fallacy as it entertains different meanings for the same words. Always make sure you know which meaning you use and use it consistently. You may want to look up *entertain* to see what I mean.

'We have come to the top of the arc in my novel, or is it the bottom of the arc? I never know which way round the arc curves. Things promise to turn around. There are glimmers of light and hope.

'We are now heading to enlightenment. Enlightenment is not about knowing everything. It is about being curious about everything, about what you can know that you don't know. Enlightenment is about changing what you know when facts and logic flows against your opinion. Most importantly, enlightenment is about being discerning about your own beliefs. It is about learning and applying the skills to discriminate true facts from false facts, to be able to distinguish valid and sound theories from conspiracies.

'In the dialogue with Francois, we learn more about hidden composition fallacies. Hidden because we use collective nouns and labels. We assume that all parts of the whole, the label is the same, but it is not. Remember the laws in the discussion with Martin or the decisions of the sovereign individual in the dialogue with Liz, to give a few examples. So always look for hidden assumptions. Philosophers call these enthymemes. So be careful of your enthymemes.

'Finally, there is the matter of Nietzsche's battle where the individual is wrestling with the tribe for self-ownership. In the first chapter, we see individuals who are not even trying to engage in this battle. They are not even aware that there is one. They are also not even aware if they are being held captive by the tribe. Bukowski would probably say they have swallowed the tribe.

'Robert is in a tribe with an intolerable internal contradiction. A tribe that is founded based on individual freedom. How can you be simultaneously free and in a tribe; a tribe of free individuals? It suggests the individuals have won the battle for self-ownership, but they are simultaneously owned by a tribe. It is more likely the tribe has won a battle against another tribe.

'Megsum and Amanda is being held captive by that tribe called The Business. They limit their mental faculties to those dictated by this tribe. The Business as a legal person has more freedom than a natural person. More freedom to cause harm to people and society, more freedom to damage the environment, more freedom to lie and deceive. And the curious thing is that this freedom is sanctioned by society, particularly the tribe founded on individual freedom.

'Peter is an interesting case. Peter will pay attention to the folly of the two tribes: Trumpism and The Business. But Peter cannot break free. The moment he steps away with his newfound understanding the pull of the tribe gets too strong. He succumbs to his irrational loyalty to these tribes.

'There isn't much to say about James's tribe. If there is one it exists around a failure of thinking. A myth about the question "What is the meaning of life? To call this a tribe will be a step too far. James's dialogue was a supporting act, and so was the one with Liz. Both these dialogues centre around the question and whether we are careful enough to question the question first.

'Kristoff is a complete slave to tribes. He is not a master of his own mind. He follows the tribes, accepts ideas too readily and once he believes he will not change his mind. He is a tribal warrior. He comes out fighting. The only thing that stops him from getting violent is a meagre sense of public decency. Sufficient though to prevent tragic consequences. Will he ever change?

'Ricardo's dialogue is another supporting act. But here, the sense of a tribe is stronger than with James. The tribe is centred on the myth that a claim to the right to an opinion is a decent defence of the opinion. This myth must be addressed with intellectual force. As must be the myth that the truth is relative, the second dialogue with Kristoff. The idea that there is such a thing as my truths is an offense to intelligence.

'Edwin belongs to a tribe that has swallowed religion, that thinks they can dismiss a formidable and elegantly argued theory by paying partial attention to its detail. This tribe is not only cognitively lazy, but they are also wilfully stupid. They must be dealt with unceremoniously and with forthright dismissal. There is truly little to gain from engaging in detailed dialogue. There is no reward waiting at the end.

'To close the first chapter, we meet with Thomas. Thomas demonstrates the uncanny ability of people to produce mythical and secretive tribes out of nothing. They submit their minds to an illusionary master. These tribes are the most mysterious, have truly little definition. The tragedy is that we burn a great deal of intellectual capital on these tribes. I continue to build on the idea of being a master of your own mind.

'In the second chapter, we meet individuals who can distinguish themselves from the tribe with a little help. They are prepared to call it out. These individuals offer a glimmer of hope.

'Rosemary discovered the secret tribal dance she constructed with her sister. The little protocol they have for disrupting their lives, their relationship, and those of her entire family. It also has the potential to restrict her plans for progress through life.

'Liz is perhaps the only character where we see a transformation to a more open-minded person. Liz is also the only one engaged in an active group that discusses philosophical ideas. They are not perfect, but philosophy rarely is. Philosophy is a work in progress.

'Martin and Victoria display a willingness to engage in a respectful conversation, a willingness to change their opinions. Martin might not do it outwardly and with fanfare, but he does. It would be a small step to go from "I have to think about that" to "That has changed my opinion".

'All of the characters in the second chapter are prepared to challenge their tribes somewhat.

'In the final chapter, we meet Francois and Lilly. We also see Liz develop into a fully open-minded person, even though her spirit is undimmed. There is nothing wrong with being a spirited philosopher. Liz's battle with the state is also symbolic of Nietzsche's battle between the individual and the tribe, the battle for self-ownership. But we see that self-ownership does not require the destruction of the tribe. In this chapter, we also see that tribes, or some tribes, are not only necessary but also vital for our survival and personal well-being. These are the tribes worth investing intellectual capital in. The question is not to do battle with the tribes, but to master them. Let's be discriminating where we spend that intellectual capital.

'I finish with a final flourish of wisdom. Realise this now. You cannot lose your tribes. To do so is to lose parts of yourself. You cannot do battle with your tribes. To do so is to do battle with parts of yourself. You cannot defeat your tribes. To do so is to defeat parts of yourself. You cannot search for your tribes. You already have them. That is because your tribes live also in your mind.

'The only thing you can hope for is to become the master of your own mind. To be the master of your own mind is to be the master of your tribes. But you must also master the twitching, the automatic responses to parts of you being poked. It will twitch. When it does, welcome the twitch as if it is an old friend and then tell it to fuck off. That is the true supreme decision maker: the true sovereign individual. Smarter, wiser, and resilient against stupidity. A Snake Master.

I go silent. John makes notes, or so it seems.

'I see,' says John. Then he says something that tells me he doesn't see. 'It doesn't seem to work chronologically.'

What? No comment on the final flourish? Really! I can only hope it has more of an impact in the novel. The middle child twitches. *Oh, hello old friend. Now fuck off.*

'What do you mean? I ask.

'Well, it appears there are background facts that don't make sense,' he says.

'Like what? I ask.

'Like the giving up of smoking and drinking. You appear to have done that in the first half of the book. In the downward arc, I think you called it,' he says.

'Yes, that is true, but I told the dialogues in a logical arc, not a chronological arc. Chronologically, it won't show the transformation,' I explain.

'Of course, you said that when we started,' says John, satisfied with my explanation.

John goes back to making notes.

I look at him, trying to make sense of what he is thinking. He is deep in thought, but what would be the point in interrupting him?

After a while, the urge to get his attention overwhelms me. The urge becomes the point in interrupting him.

'What do we do?' I ask.

John sits back in his dominant chair. 'Nothing,' he says. 'From what you told me, it looks like she'—he interrupts himself, picks up the letter, and reads her name—'Jennifer Rawlings, is on a legal fishing expedition. She is vague enough in her letter to provoke a response, which she hopes will give her case more impetus. We will respond because that is protocol but without giving her anything.'

There is a pause, then John says, 'There is the glaring omission though.'

The grip in the pit of my stomach takes hold again. 'What glaring omission?' I ask.

'In the disclaimer. Let me read what you told me.' John reads from his notes, 'All characters and events, even those based on real people, are entirely fictional, and any resemblance to people and events are purely coincidental, even when they are meaningful.'

He looks up. I shake my head slightly. I don't get it.

'If it is written that way, it is missing a clause. The clause that says "any resemblance to real people or facts are unintentional",' he says.

I stare straight ahead. I am trying to get my head around the natural consequences of this omission.

'I suppose I can always claim the characters were just expressions of my character John, expressions of sub characters of my character. That I am a quadrophonic schizophrenic. They are the parts of me that twitch? Desperate to find expression before it is too late,' I say and smile.

'Be serious Hendrik. Was that done intentionally? Did you deliberately intend for people to find meaning in the coincidences?' he asks.

The grip in the pit of my stomach is intense. I am unable to come up with a response.

John must have sensed that. He says, 'Think about it, Mr Logic Master. You have not specifically identified people by their names, have you?' I feel the grip weaken.

'Not deliberately,' I say innocently. It had the same effect as with Father, but you know that already. John rolls his head back and says nothing; he doesn't have to. I know this game, so I explain, 'Well, I used quite general names, like Reg and Brent and Thomas and so on, so if it is the same name as the actual person, it is purely coincidence.'

'Really?' asks John.

'Of course.' I smile mischievously, too mischievously.

'But no surnames?' he asks to confirm.

I shrug. John is busy on his legal pad and didn't notice. He must have sensed my answer. Concern washes over his face.

'Only partial histories of the persons, people often identify themselves with their histories . . .,' I hesitate.

'What do you mean by histories?' he asks.

'Their past, how I came to know them, big events in their lives, you know,' I say.

'Was that part of the plan?'

'Yes, it was intentional, but for a different reason that you might think.'

'What reason could that be?' asks John sceptically.

'Artistic license or perhaps literary structure,' I say. 'I wanted to keep the characters quite flat. They serve a limited purpose, except for Liz perhaps. She is a bit more rounded.'

'So you are saying it was an intentional decision on your part to keep the dialogues pure,' says John.

I am not sure at all about his phrasing, but there is no point going down that rabbit hole. 'There are other ways in which I round out the characters,' I say. 'Like Kristoff's mercurial personality, Peter's wandering wonderings, and Rosemary's irresponsible responses. But I am not sure that is enough to identify anybody.'

'I think we saw plenty of that,' says John.

'Thanks, John. Another way in which I round out the characters is in revealing their tribes, their interpersonal and cultural characteristics, their personal battles with tribes, or personal ignorance of their tribes. That forms a substantial part of the dialogues and reflections,' I say.

'I think that is enough, Hendrik. I get the picture,' says John, keen to move on.

'But I show as little of the characters as I can get away with,' I say, regardless of his keenness to move on. 'Otherwise, it would have made it too easy to identify the real persons.'

John looks up. He does that every time I mention real person. The grip intensifies again.

'So you also give no details of any of the locations, no place names or dates?' he asks.

'No,' I confirm. His concern dissipates slightly and simultaneously releases the grip a little.

'So the only way they can prove that you identified them is by proving that they were the person in the dialogue,' he states.

'Yes, they also express their characters by expressing their opinions of the world,' I agree with his statement.

'In which case, the stupid ones have to prove they are stupid,' he says.

'I see,' I say, curious about where this is going now.

'And if they succeed in demonstrating they are stupid, how can there be grounds for libel?' he asks triumphantly.

'Hah' is all I can come up with, which, of course, is not a great word for an ordinary philosopher to use.

John goes on to state the defence, 'And if the smart ones prove their identity by proving they are smart, then how can there be grounds for libel?'

'Hah' is all I can come up with again. I am worried now that I might start to use this newly acquired word as a matter of habit.

I sit in silence for a while. John has a self-satisfactory smug grin on his face. 'Fancy a lawyer teaching a philosopher logic,' he says as if to himself.

I decide to give him this one. I accept there will be more. 'So are there any unfriendly facts that you can identify?' I ask.

John's response intensifies the grip in the pit of my stomach. 'Yes, but only from our discussion. I don't think Jennifer Rawlings will be able to.

'Are you saying we just hide the truth? I ask.

'Yes, but leave the hiding of the truth to me', says John and smiles. 'Attorney-client privilege, remember. But don't relax just yet. You have insulted a lot of groups of people, religions, Americans, French, English. Do I need to go on?'

'Amorphous things, John, amorphous things. They have no bodies. They cannot sue or be sued,' I say.

John disagrees. 'Oh, they can, Hendrik. What did you say to Francois? Be careful. They will send their warriors.'

The grip tightens considerably. Is it the hiding of the truth that tightens the grip?

John reads his notes. He looks up. 'Just to be clear, your wife'—he looks down—'Lilly . . .' He looks up sharply, makes the connection, and then continues, 'She had nothing to do with the novel, no editing, no proofreading, nothing.'

I hesitate. The grip intensifies. The eyes pick it up. 'Look, Lilly has not read the novel or any manuscript of it, and that means she did no editing or proofreading, but for me to claim she had nothing to do with it would be a lie. She inspired me. Without her, I would probably never have written the novel. She told me about story arcs, about plot development, about starting in the middle, and character development. She also had told me about leaving no loose ends. Without her, I would not have known any of that.

'We were also perfect complimentary opposites. She was a perfectionist. She was all about meticulous planning and precise execution. In contrast, I am an adventurer. Adventures are messy. They have no precise end goal. Adventures sometimes lead to dead ends. You have to abandon those and retrace your steps to some reasonable prior place where you can set off in a different direction. Sometimes you have to abandon the adventure completely. Sometimes you discover new things, new ideas. You cannot plan to discover new things. That would undermine the meaning of discovering. Also, you never quite know when the adventure is done. If she had been involved in my novel, it would have been perfect.'

'If she had been involved in your novel, you might not have been in this pickle,' says John. I thought he is joking, but the eyes tell me otherwise.

Then he asks. "Was? Hendrik, did you just say Lilly was?

'Yes, the big C took her brother first, then her'.

Tears well up in the brown eyes. John's voice is thick.

'So you are—'

'—alone'. I finish for him.

The eyes soften with regret.

John needs a few moments to compose himself. Only a few moments though. Prestigious lawyers have seen it all.

'As much as I trust you, I will have to study the dialogues for myself,' he says. 'What is the novel called?'

Shit, I think to myself, *I have to pay a prestigious, expensive lawyer to read my novel.* Father's words come back to me: *Hendrik, what the fuck have you done now?*

Here I am, both hero and villain. Writing the novel wrestled me away from the formal approach to crafting philosophical essays. The dialogues only vaguely form a coherent argument where logically connected premises support a conclusion. But the novel was only partially successful. Partial because the novel still has an introduction and a conclusion. What kind of novel has an introduction and conclusion?

It is also only partially successful as fiction too. The arc of this story is fragmented and incomplete, if there was an arc at all. It makes no sense chronologically. There is no tidy plot and satisfactory ending. How true to life would a perfect arc be? It is an illusion that we live our lives in a linear progression of time, with a past, present, and future. Instead, we live our lives in a landscape of events, a landscape of memories that come and go and linger. Our imperfect memories let us conveniently forget some and inconveniently never forget some. Let us conveniently remember some and inconveniently never remember some. You poke at one memory, and other memories twitch.

The characters are unceremoniously introduced. We need them only for their opinions—their opinions born out of stupidity or intellect. Their characters don't develop beyond fragments of their back stories. But is an opinion of the world not also an expression of one's character? They are stripped of their only worth, their opinions, and then they are unceremoniously discarded—half-formed characters, flat, of no further use to the story's broken arc.

But who can draw a fully formed character in a novel? What does a fully formed character look like? A character without secrets and hidden depths? Who claims to be able to draw the full landscape of a character with clearly defined form and shape, no longer an amorphous thing? Such a character does not exist in the real world. Characters are half-formed things in the real world too.

We do not know what happens to the characters in this novel. We do not know if they live happily ever after. We never find out if their character changes, if they go through some profound transformation and become better at reasoning, more engaged in pursuing the truth. We do not find out in the novel.

And Lilly? In one sense her transformation is complete. Complete because it will go no further. In another it is incomplete. What secrets and hidden depths had she yet to share with the world? She was still building the courage and the conviction; the "fuck you" defiant bloody mindedness required for success. Her confounding playful movement stopped. The composition fallacy of Latin dances knocked down in a sharp short sentence, "You have three months."

Isn't it strange? Despite all our attempts to define what an individual is, we trip over all kinds of amorphous things, a landscape of Venn diagrams of overlapping opinions, cultures, family values, parental personalities, crazy ideologies, conspiracy theories, political views, and disruptive events in the formative years—character configurations that are impossible to unpick. You poke at one end, and the whole thing twitches. When you remove one part, the whole dies. If you take the whole somewhere, all the parts go as well. Yet the illusion persists—the illusion of the sovereign individual, the fully functional adult.

Start in the middle, some say. All good storytelling starts in the middle. Start at the end, others say. If I started at the end, would I then have to end at the beginning?

The eyes track me. They draw me back into the room. One eyebrow raises to remind me I owe John an answer. The red glow appears on my neck and rushes up to cover my face. I blush. I have forgotten the question. I must look stupid. Knowing already that it is not going to work, I try innocence. I ask, 'What is an ordinary philosopher to do, John?'

'Ordinary philosopher?' asks John incredulously. Now both eyebrows are raised. He answers his own question, 'You are not an ordinary philosopher, Hendrik. Hapless maybe, no, on second thought, definitely not hapless. Shameless perhaps, brazen, bold, daring, audacious, adventurous, or unspeakable, but not ordinary.' John repeats his question, 'What is the novel called, Hendrik?'

I can only smile. *'The Snake Master and, The Outrageous Philosopher.'*

The eyes laugh.

I see it all perfectly; there are two possible situations—one can either do this or that. My honest opinion and my friendly advice is this: do it or do not do it—you will regret both. Laugh at the world's follies, you will regret it, weep over them, you will also regret that; laugh at the world's follies or weep over them, you will regret both. This, gentlemen, is the sum and substance of all philosophy.

Søren Kierkegaard